One Door Closes

Jennifer Bacia

About the Author

JENNIFER BACIA writes romantic suspense and promises her readers a story that is impossible to put down. Her first novel was bought for a record-breaking advance and was an international best-seller. Jennifer's novels have been translated into German, Polish, Swedish and Greek.

Jennifer is the author of 8 novels, two works of non-fiction and dozens of short stories.

Visit her website jenniferbacia.net for information about her best-selling works which include *A Very Public Scandal*, *Whisper Her Name*, *Never Forget Me*, *Indecent Ambition*, *Everything to Lose*, *Best Kept Secrets* and *One Door Closes*.

Jennifer's last name is pronounced 'batcher'.

With love for brave, beautiful Michelle, and Rylee.

Chapter 1

'NOW LET ME TELL YOU about *him*...' Above the hubbub of conversation and laughter, Marnie Ingram spoke close to her friend's pearl-studded ear, discreetly pointing out a well-known retired politician.

Lee Kingsford listened half-disbelieving, as Marnie filled her in on the subterranean affairs of the city social set. It always amazed her how much Marnie seemed to know. How could you spend all day on a building site and still tune in to the glitterati grapevine?

'Ever thought of being a gossip columnist instead of a property developer?' she asked.

'Listen,' Marnie retorted, 'given what I'm facing these days, it might be a viable option, believe me. At least I'd be the one throwing the crap.' The language was earthy but the accent was breathy, modulated.

Lee was surprised by the sharpness of her friend's response. It had always taken a lot to rattle Marnie.

'Want to tell me about it?'

'Not really. You didn't do a three hour drive from that wilderness you call home to listen to my problems, darling.'

But as light as she had kept her tone, Marnie couldn't put her dilemma totally out of mind. The situation was growing more convoluted by the day and the costs were mounting. She knew she was going to have to solve it somehow — and soon.

With an effort, she brushed off her mood. Tonight she had to keep it cool, play her role as the amiable hostess, make sure everyone was having a good time. Including her old friend. Placing a hand on Lee's arm, she said, 'Come on, let me introduce you around. If I've got to listen to all the bullshit here, you can too.'

Lee followed nervously in Marnie's wake. She felt awkward around people like these, the movers and shakers, the rich and powerful, people whose names she read in the newspapers and whose faces she saw on her TV screen. The women in particular intimidated her, made her feel frumpy and self-conscious in her cheap department-store dress.

She would never have admitted to anyone how these functions of Marnie's made her feel. Not only inferior, but envious too. Earlier in the evening, she had spied a well-known actress in the crowd, a glamorous-looking woman in her late thirties. Lee had felt an envy so fierce it made her almost physically ill. And intertwined with that emotion was another that was inevitably coupled with it — a deep burning anger that welled up inside her, so palpable it almost choked her. If things had gone as she'd planned, her future would have been so different. Instead, she'd ended up with the sort of life she had always sworn she would never ever settle for.

'Jack ... Christine ...' With an arm around Lee's waist, Marnie drew her into a circle of well-dressed men and women. 'This is a dear friend of mine, Lee Kingsford. We go way back. I told her she'd find out every secret in Sydney by coming along tonight.'

'You're not from Sydney then?' As Marnie moved away, a very slim brunette, wearing more gold jewelry than Lee had ever seen on one person, asked the question.

'No ...' Lee shrank inwardly. God, why did that have to be the first question? They were all looking at her, politely waiting for her answer.

'I'm from Newcastle.'

Lee saw the lack of interest instantly shutter their eyes as the group resumed their conversation.

For the umpteenth time she wondered bitterly why she came to these affairs. Was she so desperate that even being a spectator to the life she'd missed was better than nothing at all?

Tina had worked the room as best she could. Marnie's fund raisers weren't that useful as a source of business. Most of the women here tonight were relying on the fact that their marriages would last the distance to assure their financial security. But there had been a few who had learned by the lessons of their friends and they were the ones who had accepted Tina's business card. Not that she'd been obtrusive about it, not at one of Marnie's dos. But business was business.

She glanced at her watch and decided it was time to slip away. When you worked the hours she did, late nights were best kept to a minimum.

She scanned the room looking for Marnie to say goodbye but without success. Still, that didn't matter. They'd chatted a while and caught up. Funny, even though they didn't see each other that often, it took very little effort to fall back into the same easy relationship they'd had as girls. And she felt the same with Lee.

It was more than twenty-five years since the three of them had shared the beachside house at Bondi, and despite their busy lives, they'd always kept in contact. Which was probably why she'd picked up on Lee's mood tonight. She had seen her expression as one of the guests, a well-known actress, had posed for a roving social photographer. It was clear to Tina that her old friend was still living with regrets.

Outside, the night air was cool and she slipped gratefully into the leather-seated comfort of her silver BMW, one of the symbols of her success. The way Tina saw things, she had worked damned hard and deserved her rewards. The luxury vehicle, her designer wardrobe, the house at Cremorne Point were all tangible evidence that she had fulfilled her dreams.

When she'd first arrived in this city, she had promised herself she would own a home on the harbor by the time she was thirty. When it finally came to the crunch, she had seen the sense of plowing her money back into her fledgling business and her goal had been deferred a few more years. But eventually she had kept that vow to herself. First with an apartment, now with her beautifully renovated North Shore home.

Not bad, she occasionally congratulated herself, for a migrant kid from a working-class Brisbane suburb. A kid whose own mother had told her often enough to forget her crazy dreams. There had never been any support from home. How could there be, from a father who gambled away every spare cent and a mother who lacked both language and any other saleable skill?

George Christo had emigrated from Greece not long after the war. He'd met his Maltese-born wife in the crowded migrant camp on the outskirts of Brisbane and got her pregnant soon after. Following a hasty marriage, Maya Christo had found herself solely dependent on a husband who showed little inclination for hard work. As soon as her baby daughter was old enough to be looked after, Maya had become the primary breadwinner. Ill-paying, arduous factory work had been the only possibility and as her daughter grew up, Maya had taught her to expect absolutely nothing in life. People like them, she warned repeatedly, weren't ever going to get more, so what was the point of wishing for something that would always be out of reach?

It was an attitude Tina had accepted without question until the turning point that had come when she was eleven years old. From then on, she had begun to realize that her own life had the potential to be very different from that of her parents.

Now in her early forties, she could clearly call herself a success. She had wanted it all and made damned sure she'd got it. Yet, in the long run, the financial success she had promised herself hadn't been enough, and only in recent years had she come to realize that. Money hadn't filled the emptiness she felt inside, the sense of something missing. It had taken the relationship with Dean to prove that.

Now, as she headed for home, she realized she was going to lose the battle she'd been fighting subconsciously ever since turning the key in the ignition. It wasn't the first time, and it wouldn't be the last, that she'd given in to her impulse.

Twenty minutes later she drove past the turn-off to her home and continued towards Mosman.

The impressive two-story house was in one of the suburb's most expensive streets. Sometimes, if it was late enough, she would park in the shadow of the trees and, in the evening silence, imagine the life that went on behind those intricate wrought-iron gates. A life where Dean belonged to someone else.

Tonight, she didn't stop. As she drove slowly past, there were no lights visible behind the high brick wall. Perhaps the two of them were out or had gone early to bed. She felt herself grow tense as her imagination went into overdrive. This was crazy. She was crazy. Why was she torturing herself like this?

Turning back towards Military Road, she told herself again that it was time to come to a decision, to take control of her life as she had always managed to in every other way.

Weakness was an emotion she had always despised.

Her own home was in a cul de sac with views of the harbor through the trees. She had bought the place six years ago. Then, it had been a gloomy, red- brick bungalow with small, depressing rooms and an overgrown garden. Not that that meant she had got it cheap, not in a location like this. At the beginning, she'd had a huge mortgage but over time, the ever-booming Sydney real estate market had almost tripled her investment.

Working with an architect, she had turned the simple bungalow into a beautiful, elegant home. Floor to ceiling windows made the most of her views, a top floor was added with a master bedroom, ensuite and study, and in a piece of intricate engineering, a swimming pool had been cut into the rock face overlooking the view. Given the cost involved, there were times when Tina wondered if the latter had really been a good idea. Despite all her good intentions, twelve-hour working days left her little time for exercise. All she seemed to do was pay the pool guy's maintenance bills.

Her home was on a battle-axe block, narrow to the road and fanning out and falling away towards the rear. With the garage at street level, a dozen or so steps led through expensive landscaping towards the house.

As soon as she opened the front door, she knew something was wrong. The dusty white footprints stood out clearly all the way down the hall carpet and her heart seemed to drain in shock and anger.

It had happened again.

Marnie hadn't got to bed until well past one, but that didn't stop her alarm going off at the usual time of six the following morning.

As she dragged herself out of the warm sheets and into a stinging shower, she felt like death. There'd been a time in her life when she could manage on four hours' sleep for days at a time. But not any more. These days, if she missed her usual six or seven hours, she felt every bit her forty-three years. Another one of the joys of getting older, she thought wryly, as she stepped out of the shower and wrapped herself in a thick towel.

Peering into the mirror, she knew that only make-up would save her today. Her routine had barely changed in years. Darkly lined eyes, coral-colored lipstick, a sweep of blusher and she was ready. When she was younger, her dark good looks had often drawn comparisons to Elizabeth Taylor in her prime, but at least with age she'd added none of Ms Taylor's pounds nor sought the help of a scalpel. Well, not yet, she reminded herself. Lines were beginning to form around her eyes and the corners of her mouth, but so far, she figured, she was hanging in. But there still days when it was hard to face the fact that her time on center stage had passed. She tried to console herself with the knowledge that she had traded the power of her youthful looks for a different sort of power. One that lay in the strength of her personality and an unshakeable belief in her own abilities. And that, she told herself, was more important than the ephemeral advantages of beauty.

Yet the memory of the teasing conversation she'd had with one of last night's hunky waiters brought a smile to her lips. How old had the guy been? Late twenties? Early thirties? It still gave her a kick to know she could tickle their balls now and then, and certainly, if the opportunity presented itself, she wasn't about to say no.

Then, as she pulled on her usual work-a-day uniform of black pants, shirt and sweater, her thoughts grew more sober. Sex wasn't exactly the biggest priority in her life at the moment. She was saving her energies for her major ongoing battle with the bureaucrats in the local council. The injunction had been placed on her inner west site four months ago and they were finding every possible obstacle to prevent her from going ahead with her plans. Their objections were based on the fact that at one stage the site had been a dumping ground for battery waste and the resultant contamination therefore made it unsuitable for any further excavation.

But it was a specious argument, Marnie knew. She was absolutely certain the council were being paid off. It was Rod Sawyer who was behind it, without a doubt. The rival developer had missed out on the site himself but, still determined to get it, was pulling out every trick in the damned book. When her problems first began, she'd done some investigating herself and eventually discovered that her competitor had been slowly buying up the blocks of old units contiguous to the property now in dispute. The problem was that she'd come along to stuff up his plans, pipping him at the post to the extra land he'd earmarked for his own. She was certain that as soon as she was out of the picture, the council, suitably rewarded, would manage to find a ready loophole for Sawyer to go ahead with his plans.

Marnie frowned as she made herself a quick coffee. The lawyers were involved now and that meant things were going to get expensive as well as nasty. But she couldn't afford to let herself be bullied either by Sawyer or the council. They were trying it on because, first and foremost, she was female and the boys thought she was going to yield to a little pressure. Well, they could think again. She was determined to get the matter solved and construction under way as soon as possible. Hopefully, by bringing her own legal eagles into the picture, she'd prove to them all she wasn't going to roll over as easily as they imagined.

In the meantime, she had her latest project to finish and release to the market. With her future plans stalled for the time being, a quick cash injection was even more essential, and given a bit of luck, the townhouses should be completed in about four weeks. She'd put together the parcel of land almost three years ago. Then, there had been little happening that far south of the harbor, but only last month the property pundits had referred to the growing interest in the area. With two other sites in the Sutherland shire already pinned down, Marnie had the smug satisfaction of knowing she'd picked up some of the best land available. Seeking out locations before the market pushed up prices had always been one of her strengths. But it also meant that with her money tied up a fair way ahead, it was imperative the current situation be resolved as soon as possible. The banks wouldn't keep lending if she couldn't keep her cash flow happening.

Releasing her mobile from its charger, she slung it into the capacious leather shoulder bag that carried all her essentials. Minutes later she had cleaned her teeth and was out the door.

From her room on the twelfth floor, Lee could see the glittering waters of Rushcutters Bay and hear the steady thrum of early morning traffic along New South Head Road.

It had been a last-minute decision to spend the night in a hotel.

Tina had done her best to talk her out of the long drive back to Newcastle so late in the evening. 'You know you can stay at my place. It's certainly no trouble, Lee. Just leave when you want to in the morning.'

'Yes, I know, and thanks for the offer, but it won't take me that long at this time of night. Certainly better than getting stuck in tomorrow morning's peak hour.'

She'd felt guilty about the lie but how could she really explain? That because of everything that had happened at home she wanted, somehow, to pay them all back. That for once she was going to forget about the cost and indulge herself in a night alone in an up-market hotel. Tina wasn't married, she didn't have kids, so how could she be expected to understand Lee's bitterness. It wasn't bad enough that Brad had ended her own dreams, now he was helping to end the dreams she'd held for her daughter too.

Tight-lipped with anger she repacked her small overnight bag. She would never forgive him. Never. So what if he hit the roof when he got the credit card bill for the room? Stuff him! Stuff the lot of them. She'd sacrificed everything for all of them and where had it got her? They didn't care. Maybe, she thought defiantly, she should start doing things to please herself a hell of a lot more.

It was only just eight and there was no point in rushing off. The traffic would be impossible for an hour or so yet and anyway, breakfast was included in the price of the room.

The elevator was full of men in business suits as she made her way down to the mezzanine level where breakfast was being served.

'There isn't a spare table. Do you mind sharing?' The hostess was a frazzled-looking woman who had pinned her name badge on upside down.

'No problem.'

Lee followed the woman to a table where a middle-aged man was eating alone. He wore a business shirt and tie and his jacket hung on the back of his chair.

Sure, he was happy to share, he answered in response to the hostess's query, and half rose as Lee took the seat opposite.

'Malcolm Field,' he introduced himself. 'And I can't remember the last time I got so lucky over breakfast.'

'Oh — thank you.' Lee was taken aback by the unexpected compliment.

'A business lady?' he asked as he broke open his muffin.

'Uh... yes.'

The lie slipped out before she could stop it. She amazed herself. Why hadn't she told the truth? Because she didn't want to admit to being a wife and mother and very little else? Now that her job with Anita was finished, she really couldn't count the couple of afternoons a week she put in at the dance school.

Excusing herself, she got to her feet and made for the buffet but as soon as she returned with her plate of cereal and fruit, her breakfast companion persisted with his queries. 'What sort of business are you in?'

'Lingerie, actually.' This time she was telling the truth. For a couple of years, until Anita's move to Sydney, she had worked part-time at a lingerie boutique in Newcastle's Garden City mall.

'Lingerie ...' He gave her a grin. 'Now why couldn't you and I swap jobs? You could be the wine rep and I could help fit the corsetry.' His eyes appraised her over the top of his coffee cup. 'Still, with a figure like yours, I can see why you got the job.'

It was then Lee realized he was flirting with her. Her cheeks warmed. My God, how long had it been since any man had looked at her like that? She couldn't remember. It was silly, light-hearted talk but it made her feel wonderful.

'Oh, come on,' she teased back. 'It's my brain they hired me for.'

'Looks *and* brains! You've won me.' He smiled at her again as he put his empty cup down in its saucer. 'You know, that's what I like about older women — they're usually smart and feminine with it. Not like these kids who'd slay a bloke for paying them a compliment.'

By the time she was ready for her bacon and eggs, Malcolm Field had finished his meal and said goodbye. But not before leaving his business card on the table. 'Just in case you ever run short of a Chardonnay,' he'd said with a smile.

Lee slipped the card into her handbag and on the long drive home, found herself smiling every time she replayed their brief conversation. She wondered what it would feel like to be single and free again and living in Sydney.

She'd barely had time to find out the first time round.

'Do you still want to stick to the same dates for the Melbourne seminar?'

For a moment, Tina barely took in her PA's question. The whole morning had been a shambles. First the police, then the insurance assessors and finally the cleaners. She had left them to it, unable to spend another moment in her home until everything was scrubbed and vacuumed and mopped — and she could try to pretend that the disaster had never happened.

But it had. For the second time in less than three months.

According to the insurance rep, this was the way some of them operated; they waited until the first lot of stuff was replaced and brand new, and then came back for another go.

'So you mean I'm a sitting target for them to hit again?' Tina's cheeks had flushed with anger. 'The place is already like Fort Knox. And who the hell takes any notice of alarms these days? They're always going off.'

The man had looked at her with pursed lips, as if he thought that by daring to have a skylight she'd deliberately made it easy for the useless low-lifes who had trashed her house and stolen her property.

Last night, when she'd seen the flour and coffee, the orange juice and honey thrown over her walls and carpets, she'd been numb with shock. At least the first time they hadn't done that.

As she'd moved from room to room, Tina had felt suffused with a terrible rage. Every single thing she owned she had paid for herself; no one had ever given her anything. And now some useless, envious morons had done their best to take it all away from her.

As her shock and anger had worn off, they'd given way to a terrible sense of vulnerability — and that wasn't an emotion she was used to dealing with. With tears filling her eyes, she'd known better than to expect the understaffed police to come at that time of night. It wasn't life-threatening, they'd say. But these animals, whoever they were, had impacted on her life in a different way, had shown her that no matter how hard she'd worked, no matter how many sacrifices she'd made, she wasn't entitled to either her possessions or a sense of security.

Despite the late hour, she'd longed to put a call through to Dean, to tell him what had happened and wait for him to come and wrap her in his arms. But even as the idea had entered her mind, she had known it was impossible. There was no way you could expect your married lover to leave his devoted wife at a dinner party somewhere or slip out of the marital bed and come to comfort his distressed mistress.

It wasn't fair... Her response, she noted in the rational part of her mind, was as plaintive and absurd as a child's. But it was how she felt. Even when she really needed Dean, the same barriers were there.

Too fearful to spend the rest of the night in the house, she had grabbed a few clean clothes and toiletries and gone to the nearest hotel.

Barely able to sleep, first thing the next morning she had tried Dean's mobile even before she rang the police. To her dismay and agitation, it was turned off and she was forced to leave a message: please ring her urgently.

It was eleven-thirty by the time she finally got to her North Sydney office, having dealt with the police statement and insurer's forms in all their painstaking detail. On the way, she had tried Dean again, and now it was past midday and still she'd had no response.

Linda, her PA, was looking at her from across the desk, waiting for an answer. Tina had to ask her to repeat the question.

'Melbourne ... yes, yes,' she replied, making an effort to concentrate. 'Early October, before they're all distracted by the Cup.'

It was eleven years since Tina had established Wealth for Women. It had been the city's first investment advisory firm aimed specifically at the female market. The company had evolved from her passion to alert women to the need to take responsibility for their own financial future. Her clientele included not only the growing ranks of divorcees, but also those women who were choosing to remain single. It brought Tina immense satisfaction to help others achieve the sort of security she had always craved for herself.

Through WFW, her aim was to demystify the formerly male-dominated world of investment and finance. Her well-trained teams of advisers ran seminars in all the east coast capitals and had recently branched out into a number of major regional centers. It meant long working days and little time for a personal life but a full-on relationship had never been a major priority for Tina. Over the years there had been affairs, more usually with married men, and she had sometimes found herself wondering about that. Did it make her feel safer to know a man had a wife and family and was therefore less likely to make demands on her time and her emotions? Or was it something to do with her overriding need to be in control, to avoid ever becoming as vulnerable, as open to exploitation, as her mother had been?

In the long run the reasons hadn't really mattered. What did matter was never letting anyone get too close or under her skin.

But then she had met Dean and everything changed. Why, she asked herself as her PA left her office, had she eventually let her defenses down?

Being brutally honest, she wondered if age had had something to do with it. She was in her mid-forties; did that imply some sort of growing desperation? Was she now more open to a commitment, aware that her chances were running out?

When she had first met Dean three years ago, the affair that followed had seemed, initially, like all the others. She had expected it to burn itself out in a couple of months. But with Dean Ashley things had been different. The longer they had known each other, the more they had found in common, and the closer they'd become.

Eventually, the intensity of her feelings had begun to alarm her. In that first year there had been a couple of occasions when she had tried to pull back from the relationship but each time Dean had refused to accept the finality of her decision.

'But I don't want to do this to myself,' she'd protested. 'I went into this without any expectations and now that's changing. I don't want to live like this.'

'Tina, darling.' They were having after-work drinks together in some nondescript bar where no one they knew was likely to spot them. 'You know I can't leave my children, or at least not now, I've told you that. But what we have together is too good to simply walk away from. You feel that too, I know you do. Why should we give up on something that adds so much more to both our lives?'

And, despising her weakness, Tina had allowed herself to be convinced, had let the love affair continue. She had taken what pleasure it gave her and tried to stop thinking about the future.

But it was at times like this, when she longed for Dean's comfort and support, that she was brought face to face with the painful fact of her self-deception. How could she go on like this? How long was she prepared to wait on the sidelines and take whatever leftover time and energies he had to offer her? As much as she could love anyone, she loved Dean. They'd been introduced at a function held by her accounting firm. Dean was a client too, the principal of a leading architectural group. When he'd discovered what she did for a living, he'd seemed impressed.

'The world's a different place these days,' he'd said. 'I think every woman needs to accept the responsibility of looking after herself. I'll certainly be encouraging my own daughters in that direction.'

Of course he was married, she'd assumed that. The nice ones always were in Tina's experience; only the rejects and basket cases were single and available.

They'd stayed chatting for quite a while, the conversation becoming more relaxed. She'd always been a sucker for a man who could make her laugh and Dean Ashley had a keen sense of humor. Still, when she'd gone to move on, he'd surprised her by asking for her number.

'Perhaps you might care to have lunch with me one day,' he suggested.

Tina hesitated. Suddenly the whole equation between them had been subtly altered — and she was old and cynical enough to know that it was never a mere meal on a man's future agenda.

'In broad daylight, you mean?' There was a teasing in her tone that hadn't been there previously.

But her underlying message was clear: I know you're married. Don't think you're doing me any favors. I know exactly where you're coming from.

He gave her a smile. 'Oh, don't get me wrong. I think you're the sort of lady who'd look great by candlelight too. But lunch is much more respectable, isn't it?'

Their cards were on the table. All she had to do was decide to weaken or not.

They met at a buzzy place at Cockle Bay. Far too exposed to give any rise to rumour. When he stood up to welcome her, she noted again how attractive he was with his salt and pepper hair and strong- boned, tanned face. A sailor's tan, as it turned out. Every Saturday possible, he told her, he could be found on the harbor; sailing was his passion. And of course it was easier to talk about safe subjects like that than anything more personal and revealing.

It was two weeks later that they ended up in bed together. 'Inevitable,' he had whispered as he took her in his arms. 'I wanted you from the moment I met you.'

Their lovemaking was pleasurable, but she was too cautious, and too wise to the guile of men, to let her emotions connect too deeply. It was Dean who did the chasing and she told herself she'd enjoy the game while it lasted.

As time went on, he spoke of his wife, Kathy, and his two daughters, Belinda, twelve, and Elizabeth, two years older. 'There's nothing intrinsically wrong with my marriage,' he'd said with simple directness.

'We don't hate each other, there's no real source of conflict. Essentially, we've just grown into two very different people.'

The children, it seemed, were all they had in common. His wife was a good mother but had no interest in his business beyond the fact that it gave her the lifestyle she had always aspired to.

'I didn't see it at the time, but beyond landing an appropriate husband, Kathy had no other ambitions, nothing she felt passionate about. To be totally truthful, I find myself with very little to say to someone who has few interests other than shopping, tennis or lunching with her girlfriends.'

Still, Tina understood quite clearly that he had no intention of ever ending his marriage. 'My father left when I was eleven and my sister two years younger. I'll never forget how devastated I was when it happened. There's no way I could ever do that to my own kids. No way.'

And to begin with, that had suited Tina fine.

It was mid-afternoon before he finally returned her call, full of apologies.

'Sorry, my love. Stuck in two damned meetings back to back, and then lunch with some important clients. You sounded upset, is there..?'

Relieved to hear from him at last, Tina quickly told him what had happened. 'I can't believe it,' she ended, 'twice in less than three months. What the hell else am I expected to do? Turn the place into a fortress?'

She wasn't expecting any solutions or gratuitous advice; all she'd really wanted was a release of tension by sharing her bad news with the one human being she knew really cared for her. And she wasn't disappointed. Dean soothed her in the way she had longed for, his caring and concern immediately making her feel calmer.

He understood her so well. Like no one else ever had. Professionally, she never allowed herself to show any weakness, and somehow that seemed to translate to her social situation as well. The image of strength and independence she projected was one she encouraged — and, most of the time, it was how she felt. But there was another side to her as well, one that she had allowed only Dean to see and, even then, never in its totality. She was too cautious for that, too conditioned. Or so she had thought. More and more frequently, she was seized with panic at the realization that the relationship was undermining the foundations she had built for herself, the foundations she had used to survive alone for so long. A neediness, she recognized — and despised — was now far too close to the surface in her relationship with Dean.

'Listen,' he spoke softly. 'I have to see you, darling, I need to know you're okay.' He was silent for a moment and she knew he was running through the difficulties. 'It's the worst possible night. Kathy's parents are in town and we're taking them to dinner.' He paused again and then asserted, 'But it won't be too late a night and I'll manage it somehow, I promise. I don't quite know how, but I'll get there.'

'Please come, Dean, whatever the time.' Despite all her resolutions, she was incapable of hiding the pleading in her tone.

Chapter 2

HE LOCKED HIS APARTMENT DOOR and walked down the hallway to the elevators, his expensive runners almost noiseless on the tiled floor.

When the doors slid apart, he stepped in and nodded at the only other occupant — a young woman in a black suit wearing ridiculously high heels. As they continued smoothly downwards, he sensed her giving him the once-over but avoided eye contact. It was the anonymity of the Pyrmont apartment building that had attracted him; he had no desire for any communication with his neighbors. It was safer that way.

At the ground floor, the young woman stepped out and as she moved past him he took in the exaggerated length of her slim legs and the tightness of the skirt across her buttocks before the doors closed again. There was no mistaking the quick reaction in his groin.

It was the same sensation he'd felt the other evening. That was the first time he'd got really close to his latest object of interest. The turn of phrase lifted the corners of his lips in a half smile. Well, what else could he call her? His prey? His victim? Perhaps.

In that crowded function room, full of the raucous laughter and braying voices of the so-called social elite, he had circled her as closely as he dared, aware as always of the current that ran through him at watching someone who was so totally oblivious to his presence, his interest, his knowledge. It was a thrill that never ebbed. Yet, at the same time, he never lost his objective edge; he prided himself on his thoroughness.

Now, as he stepped into the basement parking lot, he smiled at the thought of the task that lay ahead.

'You've seen the landscaping schedule, Keith. There can't be any delays. This lot have to be finished and unloaded asap and I don't have to tell you why.'

Marnie was on the site of her almost completed project: a dozen cleverly designed townhouses, five already sold off the plan and another two sales pending.

Keith Ridge, her project manager, nodded his assurance. He was a wiry, fair-haired man who had worked with Marnie for six years. 'No worries, it'll happen.'

After a string of unreliable idiots whose incompetencies had driven her crazy, Marnie had finally found in Keith someone she could trust. He had a quiet, unassuming manner, yet never had any trouble keeping the various sub-contractors under control, and he understood the vital importance of bringing in a project on schedule and within budget. As far as she could remember, Marnie had never seen him rattled. Even on those occasions when she was stressing out, Keith kept his cool. They were a perfect team.

Now she glanced at the time. 'Shit! I've got a meeting in town at three. I'm out of here.' She brushed a hand over her dusty pants. 'Too bloody bad,' she shrugged, 'the legal boys are just going to have to take me like this. See you in the morning.'

Keith Ridge watched his boss stride off across the rutted ground, a tall, slim figure, the dark, glossy hair hanging straight and thick to her shoulders. In all their years together, he'd never quite got used to the peppery language delivered in that beautifully modulated voice. Somewhere along the line he'd heard that she came from a well-connected Melbourne family, but there were no airs and graces to the woman he knew. Marnie Ingram was upfront, direct, a tough operator, but always fair. She stood head and shoulders above most of the male wheelers and dealers he'd ever had to work for.

Marnie slid behind the wheel of her SUV and turned the key in the ignition. As she bounced over the site to the road, she found herself doing her usual mental calculations. It was going to be touch and go, but if the last of the stock here sold quickly, it would tide her over just long enough to get the next project started, even if that didn't immediately mean the problem site in the inner west. Not, she thought grimly, that she was giving up. That was the point of this afternoon's meeting with her lawyers. To discuss alternative strategies now that the council had played its next hand.

Why, she asked herself, as she headed back into the city, was life so full of shit sometimes?

It was an hour and a half later before she finally emerged from the city offices of Crosby and Cornelli and, as she approached her parking spot, she swore under her breath at the sight of the ticket stuck under her windscreen wiper. Snatching it off, she threw it on the passenger seat beside her. That was all she needed. Four hundred dollars an hour for the boys in suits and a parking fine to top it off.

Still in a bad mood, she headed for Alexandria; not the best time of day to make the trip, but when else was she going to find a spare hour or so in her crazy schedule? She'd been promising the girls she'd call in for almost three months now; it was good for morale and a way of keeping herself in touch.

The house she was looking for was in a quiet side street and this time she parked defiantly in the driveway. Before she had closed the SUV door behind her, she was met by a smiling young woman dressed in flowing velvet pants and a baggy jacket.

'Marnie! Great to see you! We've been hoping you'd make it.'

Shaking off her own worries, Marnie returned the smile. 'Hi, Clare. Better late than never, as they say. Is Judy here?'

'Inside, talking to a new arrival.' The woman was leading the way up the stone steps of the shabby-looking bungalow. 'I'll tell her you're here. Want a cuppa?'

'Yeah. But let her finish. I can wait.'

It wasn't quite true, but Marnie knew there were other things in life that were important too. Like offering a woman safe haven from a violent and dangerous situation. At the start, Marnie had bought and equipped the first halfway house herself, but since then had managed to raise the money for half a dozen more through her various fund-raising events. Some might see it as a sop to her capitalist conscience, but whatever, it was fulfilling a real need and made her feel she was doing something worthwhile given her own advantages.

She followed Clare into the old-fashioned kitchen where four women of different ages sat around a chipped pine table. One held a gurgling baby on her knee while another displayed the fading evidence of a black eye. As Marnie pulled up a chair, Clare made the introductions and switched on the kettle.

'Marnie's the lady who started the first of the houses,' Clare announced proudly. 'Back ages ago, wasn't it, Marnie?'

Marnie nodded. 'Almost fifteen years. My mother left me some money, my grandmother too. A little too much to spend on tiaras and caviar.'

One of the women giggled nervously, another smiled shyly, but neither made any reply. Marnie had seen the same passivity often enough before. The timidity and lack of confidence with a stranger, the lack of self-worth and fear of ridicule that made them hesitant to reply even to such a light-hearted remark. These were women who had endured abusive relationships with men, who had been told so often how worthless and useless they were that they'd come to believe it. Only when driven almost to the edge had they been lucky enough to find their way to the refuge, usually through the intervention of supportive doctors or community workers. Even then, most of them still lived in mortal fear that their hiding place would be discovered and they'd be confronted by a vengeful, angry man, furious that his power had been usurped.

Some of the women, despite all the help that was offered, ended up returning to the situation that was familiar to them. But Marnie had also seen others grow stronger in the safety of their new environment as they learned the skills they needed to cope on their own.

Her own circumstances had been so different. Money, in particular, had made her independent of any man and that was the way she liked it. While it was a more fashionable attitude these days she supposed, marriage, or a committed relationship, had never been on her agenda. A long time ago, she had discovered the danger of trying to define herself by a man's approval. It had been a hard lesson, but one she had learned well.

As she accepted the cup of coffee from Clare, Marnie remembered the only man who had hurt her. She had refused to let him defeat her, but the scars he'd left had only made her all the more determined to never depend on any man again.

'Hi, Judy, how's it going?'

The social worker, looking tired and drained, shook her head wearily as Marnie sat down beside her in the small, cluttered office.

'Did you see the woman who just left?'

Marnie nodded. She'd said hello as she'd passed the haggard-looking young woman who had turned her face away in an unsuccessful attempt to hide her tears.

'Tell me.'

'Fran Morris, thirty-one, one kid, recovering from two cracked ribs and a ruptured spleen. She left once before, but he found her at a friend's house, told her that next time she tried to leave he'd kill her. The poor woman's terrified. She only found the guts to run this time because he put a knife to her daughter's throat.'

'Where did she live?'

The social worker named a suburb on the other side of town. 'We've told her she's got nothing to worry about, but really, how can we be sure? Some of these bastards never give up. They know we exist; it's only a matter of tracking down the address.'

That was the problem, Marnie knew. On one hand, they needed to publicize their facilities; on the other, it helped make it easier for the women who sought safety to be traced.

They discussed that and a number of other issues before she finally stood up to go.

'Thanks for coming, Marnie.' Judy walked her to the door. 'It always helps.'

'Me too,' she said with a smile. And she meant it. Calling into one or another of the houses inevitably put her own problems in perspective.

It was after seven by the time she got home. Her apartment was on the tenth floor, overlooking the green oasis of Centennial Park. She never could have coped living in a free-standing house, her life was too frantic to deal with gardens and maintenance. Yet, for someone who worked with architects and designers on a regular basis, she was well aware that her own living quarters were less than complete. Sure, the rooms were large and filled with light, but books were stacked in shaky piles along one wall still awaiting their custom-made bookcase, and the dramatically painted walls were almost free of decoration.

The place had three bedrooms. She used one as an office, but the papers and files, the samples of fabrics or tiles or paint charts, inevitably spilled into the living area. Her once-a-week cleaning woman had strict instructions not to move any paperwork and Marnie sometimes thought the woman must have the easiest job in town.

In the kitchen, the light was flashing on the old-fashioned answering machine. It was a feeble attempt to keep her personal and work life separate. There were three messages, two from friends, then the third:

'Hi, it's Josh Ambrose. D'you remember you gave me your card the other night? Said to call if I was looking for ...' the pause was deliberate ... 'some extra work. I thought you might have had something in mind.'

She gave a slow smile as she listened to the return mobile number. It was the young barman from the fund raiser. She remembered the good looks and appealing body. Now there could be a very pleasant diversion indeed.

There was, after all, a distinct difference between having sex with a man and letting him push your emotional buttons.

Lee was still intent on making them suffer. Every evening, when they all sat around the dinner table, she spoke only in monosyllables. To begin with, Brad had tried to get a conversation going, but what the hell, why should she make it easy for him? He'd ruined everything; he was the one who'd encouraged Julie to defy her.

As she cut into her steak, she threw a glance across the table. Her eighteen-year-old daughter was tall and beautifully proportioned with expressive hazel eyes and a blonde ponytail that hung halfway down her back. It made Lee's heart ache to know what the girl was throwing away. She thought of the sacrifices she'd made over the years, the time and money and dedication, the driving and the waiting around, the concerts and eisteddfods, the singing and dancing and drama classes. In the end, it had all been for nothing.

She hadn't been able to believe it when Julie had finally told her. It was three weeks ago, while they were washing up together after dinner, that she'd made her shocking announcement.

'I know you're going to be mad, Mum, but I have to tell you now.' Julie's words had come out in a nervous rush. 'I don't want to audition for NIDA. My marks were good enough and I've decided I'm going to take up the university offer. To study human movement. I've given it a lot of thought and I reckon it'll be better for me in the long term.'

Lee, her gloved hands in the water, felt as if she'd been turned to stone.

'But — you can't be serious, Julie.' Stunned, she turned to stare in disbelief at her daughter. 'This is what we always planned, what we always had in mind. You've known that since you were a little girl.'

'Well,' the teenager's nervousness was obvious, 'I've changed, Mum. I'm sorry, I've done better at school than I thought I would and that's given me more options. I've decided I really want to go to uni —'

'Uni!' Lee spat out the word, her cheeks flaming as she ripped off the gloves. 'For what? To do this...' she struggled to remember what Julie had just told her '... this human movement course.' She didn't even know what that meant. 'You mean you're going to waste all the years you've spent getting to this level, throw away your talent to bury yourself in some moldy library —'

'Please, Mum!' Julie had anticipated her mother would be upset, but the intensity of her anger was more than she'd bargained for. 'I don't want to fight about it. I mean, really ... to tell you the truth, I haven't enjoyed it all for a while now. It's not what I want to do any longer; it's not the sort of life I want. It was just difficult to tell you how I felt. And I wanted to see what my marks —'

'You *can't* do this to me, Julie.' Lee cut across her, her voice harsh and shaky. 'Not after all the sacrifices I've made. You can get there, I know you can. It's easier now than when I started. Aussie actors, singers, dancers — they're in demand. You've had every chance; you can't let me down like this.'

'But that's just it, Mum!' Julie too was getting upset. 'For a long time now, it's felt like I'm doing it more for you than for myself. Sometimes I think you want me to make up for what you missed out on.'

Immediately, the girl regretted those last emotional words when she saw the expression on her mother's face. Lee felt as if she'd been struck.

And Brad hadn't done anything to back her up. Oh, the way he put it, of course, was that their daughter was old enough to make her own decision. But his betrayal had shocked Lee. He hadn't taken her side, hadn't tried to understand, or to convince Julie that she was making the biggest mistake of her life.

Infuriated, Lee had confronted him, insisting he had to support her. She'd argued with him for days, but when he still refused to try to help her change Julie's mind, she'd returned inevitably to the running sore inside her that had never healed.

'You wrecked it for me, Brad, and now you're going to do the same for her, is that it?' Her anger was white hot.

Normally one to avoid emotional confrontations, her husband felt his temper rising. 'You never let it drop, do you, Lee? You've always been an expert at making me feel bad about what happened. Only it takes two to tango, you know. You can't lay the blame entirely at my door.'

But to Lee it was, and always would be, Brad's fault. She would never forgive him. And now he was helping to kill the dreams she held for Julie, too.

In the aftermath of her daughter's announcement, Lee felt increasingly restless. The two afternoons a week she taught in the local dance school weren't enough to fill her days and, somehow, they only served as a painful reminder of what Julie was throwing away. Perhaps she should give them up, just forget about it all.

She wished she still had her other part-time job. But her former employer's husband had been offered a promotion to Sydney and Anita Haywood now had a boutique somewhere in the busy Chatswood area.

As she cleaned up after breakfast, Lee continued to brood on her problems. She supposed she should start looking for something else to keep her busy but employment opportunities in Newcastle were limited. Bar work or waiting on tables in some lousy coffee shop certainly weren't options. She had enjoyed selling the pretty and sexy underwear, and had got on very well with Anita. In the end, there had been little she hadn't known about running the business and that had given her a sense of real achievement and satisfaction.

To begin with, Brad hadn't wanted her to work. Maybe it was a macho thing. But she'd got to the stage where the kids didn't really need her as much and she'd had time on her hands. The few hours she put in at the dance school Brad had never really thought of as proper work and he hadn't been too pleased when she'd wanted to find something more. In the end though, he'd come round about her working at Anita's and certainly he'd had no objection to the extra money — nor to the lingerie she occasionally bought herself with the discounts Anita offered. Not, Lee thought grimly, that there had been anything sexual between them these last few weeks. Ever since their confrontation over Julie, she'd hardly been in the mood.

The familiar anger welled up inside her as she carried the washing out to the line. How could she have ended up like this? A nobody housewife in a humdrum suburb. It was everything she had always wanted to escape. That evening in Sydney had only served to bring home again how different her life had turned out from her dreams. Marnie's functions always left her unsettled. Each time she promised herself, not again. But the temptation to breathe in that heady scent of wealth and power and exclusiveness, if only for one night, was always too great — even when she knew she would have to pay the price of an envy so sharp it was almost a physical pain.

It had tormented her all that following morning when she had driven her seven year old Mazda back to the boredom of her marriage and the city she had once been so determined to escape. How could she help comparing her own life to the lives of the women she had seen that night? Some, no doubt, were kept by men, but others, like Marnie and Tina, had made it on their own. Just as she'd planned to. When they'd shared the house at Bondi, they'd all had their dreams, yet Tina and Marnie's success had only served to emphasize Lee's own failure. At eighteen, she'd had ambition, talent, energy and the full quota of determination to break into the showbiz career she had always dreamed of. But Brad had robbed her of that. And now he was going to rob Julie as well.

By the weekend, she had begun to thaw. For one thing, it was the Sunday they visited her parents.

Her mother liked to see them all regularly, and the family get-togethers were held once a month.

Lee didn't find the occasions particularly enjoyable. She'd never felt as if she fitted in with the rest of her family. Even as a child, she'd had little in common with her two sisters, had always been the odd one out. While her whole focus had been to escape the limitations of her home town and establish a career as a performer, her sisters' only ambition had been to get married as soon as possible. They'd teased her when she went off to her tap or ballet or singing lessons, but then she was equally scornful of the time they wasted painting their nails, dyeing their hair or sewing the latest fashions in order to trap unwary males. It was clear to Lee that no one in her family understood how driven she felt by her ambition. When her mother began to grumble about the cost of her 'obsession', Lee made time in her already busy schedule for a couple of part-time jobs and took up the burden of payment herself.

If it disappointed her not to have any of them in the audience when she appeared on stage or won prizes in a competition, she never let it show. One day, in the not too distant future, she knew she would prove to all of them that her efforts and dedication had been worth it.

She had just turned sixteen when she met Brad. Good-looking in a wiry sort of way, he was cheerful and quick-witted and could always make her laugh.

An apprentice panel beater, he was the brother of one of her school friends and they'd felt at ease with each other from the start. Most importantly of all though, Brad took seriously her ambition and commitment to her dream. Lee liked him a lot, and even more so when he began to come and watch her when she appeared in some local production or competition.

'You were great, Lee, really great.' The awe in his eyes, the pride in his voice as he drove her home afterwards made her heart sing. But she knew she couldn't let herself fall more deeply for Brad. He represented everything she was running away from, and she was never going to let him, or anyone else, stand in the way of her goals.

Or so she had thought.

They were the last to arrive that Sunday. Julie was playing in a netball final and couldn't make it but Troy and Danny were with them. The boys didn't mind; they enjoyed the company of their cousins and usually disappeared inside the house to play pool on the second-hand table Lee and her sisters had bought their father for his sixtieth birthday.

'More like a present for all of you lot,' her sister, Maureen, had joked as her husband and the other males grinned and commandeered the cues.

Now, as she followed Brad down the side of the house to the back garden, Lee did her best to mask her feelings. It seemed as if she needed to do that more and more often these days. After all, whom could she really talk to about her resentment and frustration? It hadn't been possible to bring up the subject with either Marnie or Tina the other evening and, anyway, their lives were in a totally different orbit from her own these days. How could she expect them to be interested in her problems? It was different from the time in the house at Bondi, when they'd shared so much.

Only to Anita had she sometimes unburdened herself when the shop was quiet. But with even that outlet closed to her now, Lee had no one to express her anger and disappointment to over Julie.

Certainly she wasn't about to find any solace in her family.

As always, everyone was sitting on the white plastic chairs set out on the concrete strip by the back steps. A couple of towels hung limply on the Hills Hoist, and nearby the barbecue was smoking in readiness.

'Hi, Lee! Hi, Brad!' The greetings rang out as Lee kissed her mother and handed her the bowl of potato salad, her usual offering to the lunch.

'Got a new perm, love. D'you like it?' Her mother patted a hand to her metal-grey hair which sprang back like steel wool from her stubby fingers.

'Looks great, Mum.'

Lee smiled at her father, whom she couldn't remember kissing any of them, ever. 'How are you, Dad?'

She got a grunt and a raised stubby in reply. Her father had retired six years ago and had the lost look of a man who was no longer sure of his role. His narrow face was deeply lined and seamed with shadows, as if, Lee thought, the dirt of the mines had never really washed away. It was the only work he had ever done, just as it had been for his father and grandfather. He still couldn't understand why they'd had to shut the place down. Economic rationalism was only a term he'd heard on the television news.

'You lost weight, Lee? You look like you need a good feed.'

The comment came from her middle sister, Joy, who could have lost at least fifteen kilos herself as far as Lee was concerned.

'Shane likes a bit more meat, don't you, love?' Joy eyeballed her husband, daring him to disagree. 'Wants a woman with all the right curves.'

'Yeah, well, you're right then, Joy, you've got more curves than the Pacific Highway.' There were guffaws all round and Maureen ducked as her sister threw a peanut at her.

With a tight smile, Lee accepted a glass of cask wine while Brad was handed a beer by one of his brothers-in-law who began to talk to him about the local football team.

As she took a seat, she felt overwhelmed by suffocating panic. How was she going to endure the rest of her life like this?

She'd been just seventeen when she won a spot on the hottest music show on TV. *Countdown* was the program everyone watched, and to appear on that was a dream come true. Bursting with excitement, Lee had taken the train to Sydney, her outfits carefully packed in the brand new hold-all she'd bought for the occasion.

Brad had tried to insist on driving her, but she hadn't wanted him to take time off work.

'Come and pick me up instead,' she'd suggested. To be totally truthful, she was looking forward to the time alone on the train to get herself in the right frame of mind for her performance. This would be her first experience of television and she was determined to make the best impression possible. Who knew what offers might develop from here?

She'd booked herself into a cheap hotel at Elizabeth Bay. The television channel wasn't picking up the tab, but she'd have paid double the price to get the opportunity she was being offered.

Not long after lunch, a taxi was sent to fetch her in time for rehearsals. The moment she walked through the glass entry doors into the TV station's foyer, Lee knew she had found the only world she wanted to live in.

Large smiling photographs of the stars adorned the silver foiled walls and behind the curved reception desk sat two of the most beautiful and elegant young women she had ever seen.

Trying her best not to feel intimidated, she gave her name and the blonde with the long straight fringe and black-rimmed eyes checked it off on her list.

'Take a seat,' she said crisply, 'someone'll be along in a minute.'

Lee sank into the long low sofa, her hold-all on the floor beside her. There was a television set placed high up in the corner of the room and she watched it, her excitement growing at the thought that this very evening it would be her face, her voice, on that tiny screen.

About five minutes later, a cheerful freckle-faced girl in a short skirt appeared carrying a clipboard.

'Hi!' she smiled at Lee, 'I'm Donna Myer, the production assistant. They're almost ready for you so we'd better get you changed and into make-up.'

Leading the way, she pushed open a pair of heavy doors and took Lee into a labyrinth of endless corridors and stairways.

'You can change in here.' The assistant opened a door to reveal a small room with a row of lockers. 'Leave the rest of your stuff, it'll be okay. And up there,' she pointed to an open doorway a bit further along, 'you'll find make-up. They're waiting for you. Okay?'

Lee nodded. 'Yes. Thanks.' Her breath was quickening.

With a smile, the girl patted her shoulder. 'Don't worry, you'll be fine.'

As soon as she'd changed into her stage outfit — a softly clinging dress that showed just a hint of cleavage — Lee made her way down the hall as directed.

The make-up room was exactly as she'd imagined it. Mirrors edged in bright bulbs, a clutter of boxes and bottles containing all sorts of make-up, boxes of tissues, hair rollers and wigs on stands.

'Hi, hop up.' Another friendly young woman threw a protective cloak over her dress as Lee took a seat in the spinning chair. In a similar chair beside her, a girl about her own age was also having make-up applied.

'You a dancer or singer?' the girl asked while her face was being dusted with powder.

'Well, both actually,' Lee replied, then explained how she'd had to win three local competitions in a row to land a singing spot on the show. 'What about you?'

'I'm a regular. There're eight of us in the dance troupe.'

At that moment, Lee couldn't think of anything she'd want more in the world than to be a regular on television.

And in the end she had got her chance. Sort of.

Her exhilaration following that first appearance had stayed with her for days. On the way back to Newcastle with Brad, he'd told her over and over again how great she'd been. He'd watched the program at home with her parents, her sisters and most of their relatives and neighbors.

'You should've heard them, Lee. They were beside themselves. Couldn't believe it was you or how great you were. Your mother said she didn't really think you could sing as good as that. Thought you might be miming or something.' He threw her a quick sideways glance, a note of pride entering his voice. 'But believe me, I put them straight.'

Lee smiled, but made no reply. She wasn't surprised by her mother's reaction. None of them had ever bothered to come and listen to her, so how could they have any idea? She saw for herself though, when she got home, what an impact her appearance had made. The fact that she had appeared on television had suddenly made a huge difference to them all.

So when she told them a month later that she was moving to Sydney as soon as she could find a suitable job, there were no objections.

Funny, Lee mused to herself afterwards, that she'd been thinking about that particular time of her life just when the phone rang. It was Anita Haywood, her old boss, and the proposal she had to offer came as a total surprise.

'You ran that place like clockwork, Lee. Totally reliable. D'you know how difficult it is to find people like you today? These kids are here one week and gone the next, a total waste of time trying to train them. That's why I'm hoping I'll be able to convince you. I know it's a big ask, but it's an emergency and there's just no one else I can turn to.'

As she'd taken in Anita's proposal, Lee had felt a stir of excitement begin to grow inside her. Why not? Why not help a friend in need? Of course, she'd have to run it past Brad, but a part-time arrangement for a few weeks surely couldn't be a problem. After all, it was really no different from what she'd been doing for Anita all along. Except that it'd be in Sydney.

She promised to give Anita an answer as soon as possible.

That evening, she waited until they were getting ready for bed to bring up the subject. If Brad had no objections, then she'd call Anita first thing the next morning.

'Postnatal what?' He spoke over his shoulder from where he was cleaning his teeth in the bathroom.

'Postnatal depression.' Lee slipped off her dressing gown and hung it on a hook behind the bedroom door. 'Seems her daughter's got it quite badly, even neglecting the baby. Anita's worried and wants to spend a couple of days a week with her. All she wants is someone to keep the business ticking over in the meantime, someone she can trust.'

'Well ... it's a hell of a long commute to do twice a week; cost more in petrol or train tickets that you'd probably earn.' Brad walked over to the bed wearing only a pair of boxer shorts. At forty-four, thanks to regular exercise, his body was still trim and muscular.

'I wouldn't have to commute,' Lee countered. 'Anita's sister has a serviced apartment in the city. I could use that she said.' She was surprised how difficult it was to keep the excitement out of her voice. Suddenly it had become more than just helping out a friend. She knew she really wanted to do this for *herself.*

'How long did you say?' He slipped in beside her.

'Probably a month all up. Just till her daughter can cope a bit better. I really want to do this, Brad,' she put in quickly. 'Not just to help a friend in need, but also as a distraction.' Her voice grew cooler. 'I don't need to tell you why.'

In the silence, she switched off the bedside light and they lay side by side, their bodies not touching. Lee could hear her husband's breathing.

'Well,' he said at last, 'I've got no objection, if you really want to do it. The kids and I'll probably manage, if it's not for that long.'

Carefully, Lee let out a long breath of relief. Now she would have something to look forward to, a chance to spend some time in Sydney by herself. The thought made her incredibly buoyant.

At the same time, she was able to sense her husband's unspoken anticipation. This evening was the friendliest they'd been since everything had blown up about Julie.

'Thanks,' she said. 'I'll ring Anita tomorrow. She'll be relieved.'

A couple of minutes later, Brad moved closer and this time she didn't turn away as she had on so many recent occasions. Yet during the lovemaking that followed, her mind was somewhere else, and afterwards, as her husband's breathing grew deep and rhythmic, Lee lay wide awake, her mind abuzz with plans and lists and excitement.

Chapter 3

THEY'D HAD TIME TO MAKE love, but already Tina was aware of Dean's surreptitious glances at the bedside clock.

Why did it always have to be like this, she wondered as she lay with her head against his chest. Both of them aware of the pressures of time, never able to really relax and enjoy the aftermath of their lovemaking, always in fear of arousing Kathy's suspicions. Could she really keep hoping that things were going to change?

'Have you heard anything more from the police?' Dean broke into her thoughts.

'No, and I don't expect to. Just another couple of druggies getting off scot-free. It makes my blood boil.'

'Can you really be sure of that?'

Tina propped herself up on an elbow and looked down at him. His hair was tousled and she could see the beginning of a beard shadow on his chin.

'What are you getting at?'

'I'm worried, darling, and I'm trying to look at this from all angles. It occurred to me there might be some connection to your work with these break-ins.'

'Investment advice?' Tina stared at him in surprise. 'What's that got to do with break-ins?'

'Well, the fact is, it's happened twice now. I don't want to upset you, but I can't help wondering if there might be some disgruntled husband or partner involved here.'

Tina frowned as she caught the gist of what he was saying. 'You're kidding... You mean some guy with a grudge because his partner's got her finances in order enough to wave him goodbye?'

'That's exactly what I was thinking.'

She lay back on the pillow. 'Well, I mean I'm sure it's happened, women getting it together so they can leave. Enough of them have made it very clear that's exactly what they're planning to do. But no,' she was adamant, 'I can't really believe there'd be a comeback like this. Not against me, not personally.'

He turned towards her and ran a fingertip gently down her cheek. 'Well, you're probably right, darling. I hope so. Forget I even mentioned it. I worry about you that's all.'

'I know — and I love you for it.' Tina smiled and kissed him on the forehead. 'Actually, if it'll make you feel better, I'm considering renting out the flat over the garage; thought it might be good to have someone else around the place. I was telling a friend what happened and it was her suggestion. She even has someone in mind so I said I'd think about it.'

It was Marnie who'd put the idea in her head. There was a builder, she said, from somewhere up the central coast. She'd just put him on the payroll. He seemed respectable enough and was looking for a place to live. She would check him out and give Tina the details.

'It's worth considering, I guess.' Dean pushed back the sheet and she recognized the getting-ready- to-leave signal. 'Male or female?'

'I thought I'd feel safer with a man around the place.'

'Well, just make sure you get some background on him first.'

'Marnie's seeing to that.'

And if there was anyone, Tina thought with a half smile, who knew how to check out the opposite sex, it was Marnie Ingram.

Dean was dressing to leave. Wrapped in her bathrobe, Tina stood with her hands cupped around a mug of lemon tea and watched him button up the shirt his wife had probably chosen, and step into the trousers she no doubt took to the dry cleaners. How could he do it, she wondered, continue to live with someone for whom he had long ago ceased to feel any love or passion. How do you play-act through every day, keep the whole farce going? And when, if ever, do you finally confront the truth?

Nor was she blind to the fact that she was doing much the same thing. Except that her game of pretend meant hiding how much she really wanted Dean, concealing the depth of the pain she felt when he walked away from her back to his other life. And it was a game that was getting harder to play all the time.

At the front door, he turned to kiss her one last time. "That was wonderful. I know what I'll be dreaming of the rest of the night.'

She smiled, but her lips felt tight as she tried to shut out the image of his marital bed, of Kathy beside him, secure in her ownership and her future.

'And I'll let you know ASAP if I can arrange something for your birthday,' he added.

Her forty-fourth. She hated the thought.

'Getting away together would be wonderful,' she said.

'Leave it to me. I'll do my absolute best.'

He kissed her again and she watched as he climbed the steps to street level, the garden lights illuminating his way.

Finally, when she heard him start his car, she closed the door and turned back into the house which had suddenly grown colder and more lonely.

The trouble was, Tina often thought, that she'd never had any goals for the personal side of her life. Her ambitions had been centered only on her career.

For so many years that had been her focus to the exclusion of all else.

She'd been eleven years old when she met the woman who'd shown her she didn't have to accept the same limitations her mother had accepted in life.

Dorothy Lane was sixty-seven, a retired schoolteacher and spinster. She lived in a large, rambling home in Laurel Avenue, one of the loveliest riverside streets in Brisbane's leafy western suburbs. The house, a classic Queenslander with wide shady verandahs and lace-work railings, was where Dorothy and her two brothers had grown up. But with one brother dead and the other, a bachelor, living in Canada, it was Dorothy who had inherited the place on the death of her parents.

The house was far too large for her alone, she knew that, but she couldn't bear to part with it. There were separate maids' quarters underneath and, in her years as a teacher, Dorothy had often played host to a variety of exchange students. She enjoyed being around young people, got real satisfaction from stimulating their curiosity and introducing them to the joys of learning about the world they lived in.

Retirement didn't suit her. She was scornful of pastimes like bridge or golf that occupied so many of her contemporaries. To Dorothy, such pursuits were a waste of time. When she'd first left full-time teaching she'd travelled widely and on her return to Australia, had immersed herself in volunteer work, mainly involving children.

Then a fall and an injury to her knee had more or less curtailed any strenuous activities. She began to tutor children at home and, at the same time, looked around for someone to take on the weekly cleaning tasks. The house had become too much for her.

Maya Christo came into Dorothy's employ through the recommendation of friends whose homes she had worked in for a while. Very honest, very reliable, they had assured her. The retired schoolteacher found her new cleaning woman reserved and monosyllabic, but her work was thorough and that was the important thing.

While Dorothy was busy with her students in the big book-filled room she called her study, Maya quietly went about her tasks. When she was finished, she took the money Dorothy always left under the sugar bowl in the kitchen and let herself out without disturbing her employer.

The communication between the two was so insignificant that it came as a surprise one day when Maya knocked on Dorothy's study door with a nervous request.

The older woman was alone, reading, and it took her a few moments to make sense of her cleaner's mumbled words.

'Your daughter? Is that what you mean? You want her to come with you here next week?'

Maya nodded and in her broken English tried her best to explain about the painters that were coming to paint all the housing commission homes in the street beginning the next week. It was the school holidays and, with simple directness, she made clear to Dorothy that she was afraid to leave her young daughter at home with so many strange men around.

At last Dorothy understood.

'Of course, Maya, of course you must bring her. She and I can have a nice chat while you do your work.'

And that had been the start of it.

By getting to know Dorothy Lane, Tina had entered a world she hadn't known existed. Their relationship began with those two Fridays when she had accompanied her mother to work, and continued for a long time afterwards.

Even at the beginning she hadn't been nervous of the older woman. There was something very comfortable about Dorothy Lane's company. She was gentle and patient, interesting and fun, but, most of all, she was inspirational. It was a word Tina hadn't heard of when she first made Dorothy's acquaintance. All she knew was that none of her own teachers were anything like this elderly woman who was never critical or bossy, never laughed at or brushed aside the questions that rattled around in Tina's head.

It was Dorothy who really opened her eyes to the magic world of books. 'A book can give you the answer to absolutely anything, Tina. You can go anywhere in the world, meet famous people, even travel beyond the stars. A book is another world you can carry with you everywhere.'

When Tina began to spend her Saturdays at the house on the river with the retired teacher, her mother didn't like it.

'The old lady, she grow tired of you,' she protested, 'and then what happen with my job?'

Maya was always nervous about work. With George Christo spending most of his time either at the racetrack or playing cards, she was left alone to bear the financial burdens.

In the end, it was Dorothy herself who reassured Maya that her daughter was more than welcome in her home. She enjoyed the girl's company, she said, they had fun and learned a lot together.

That was exactly how Tina saw it too. Nothing ever tempted her away from her Saturdays with Miss Lane. She loved it when they read sad poems together or stories from Shakespeare or listened to crackly recordings of famous singers and orchestras.

'Pop music is fine, Tina,' Dorothy would say, 'But it's important to learn to appreciate all sorts of music.'

Tina wasn't the least bit shy of asking exactly why it was important to know so much about so many things. Then Dorothy Lane would explain that it simply made you better able to enjoy and understand the world and the other people you shared it with, that it gave you confidence in yourself and an awareness of so much that was interesting and challenging. She often made the point too that acquiring knowledge wasn't just about passing exams, that learning was something that should keep happening all your life.

She had once pointed to the stack of books in a shaky pile beside her comfy old armchair. 'See these? I'm trying to read them all at once. There's so much I don't know and I haven't that much time left to find things out.'

Tina was glad she had started early so she'd have plenty of time to read everything she wanted. Right from the beginning, Dorothy had let her choose anything that interested her from the bookshelves that lined so many of the walls in her house.

But the first time she took a book home, her mother had looked askance. 'Why you have that? That belong Miss Lane.'

Even when Tina explained that she had the old lady's permission, her mother was still not happy. She didn't want Tina wasting her time with books. There were chores to do in the house and she needed her daughter to help. It was how a woman learned to take care of a husband and family.

When Tina grudgingly put her book aside to do as she was asked, she couldn't help wondering why her mother had to do so much to 'take care' of her father. Didn't a man have his chores too? It didn't seem right that her mother worked at home and had to earn the money as well. It was as if, she thought, her mother was her father's ... slave.

And it was then Tina made a silent vow to herself: that if marriage meant having to be a man's servant, then she was never going to get married.

She had gone out with men of course, but never allowed any relationship to grow serious. Her focus was always on achieving the security she craved. When other girls her age were marrying, having baby showers, ferrying children to school, Tina was working, saving hard and concentrating on a different sort of future.

In the back of her mind there had probably been the thought that 'one day', when she had achieved her ambitions, reached the goals she'd set herself, she would find someone with whom she could share her life. But, even then, it would be on her terms. She would be the one calling the shots.

Now, looking back, she could only wonder at her naivety. What had made her think that suddenly, just because she was good and ready, there'd be the perfect partner waiting for her? It amazed her too that such a realization had taken so long to dawn.

To start with, financial success and material rewards had been enough. She had reveled in the growing profile and profitability of WFW, the sure knowledge that her business was filling an ever-increasing need in the marketplace. And after a decade working for other major financial institutions, it also gave her great satisfaction to acknowledge the ethical base of her earning capacity. Profit without greed was a guideline that had served the company well.

In those busy formative years of her business when she'd barely had time for anything not related to work, a committed relationship was the last thing on Tina's mind. There had been lovers, short affairs, but no one capable of distracting her from the success and security she craved.

Only later, when she finally had the breathing space to take stock, did she realize the limitations she had subconsciously placed on herself. As time passed, she tried to tell herself that it didn't really matter, that she had grown used to the single life, enjoyed it. The advantages were many.

She could live exactly as she liked, never answerable to anyone else's demands. She didn't have to justify herself or apologize for the hours she worked or the takeaway meals. Had no need to consult anyone else about how she placed her furniture or what car to buy.

But increasingly, scratching away beneath the surface of her supposed contentment, was the thought of what she had missed out on. Some nights when her restlessness was greater than usual, the freedom and independence of her single life didn't seem adequate compensation for the company and comfort of a soul mate. Someone to curl up to in bed, to plan holidays with, to share the ups and downs of everyday life.

As she sat in the solitary splendor of her living room with its expensive furnishings and carefully selected paintings and *objets d'art*, she would find herself wishing she had been less rigid in her focus, had worked at extending herself beyond the boundaries of a career and financial security. After all, it seemed as if plenty of women managed more or less successfully to combine work, marriage and family.

But then, she reminded herself in an attempt at consolation, maybe their backgrounds had been different from her own, their childhoods far more stable and secure. Perhaps they hadn't lost a father before they were fourteen, hadn't seen their mother slaving as factory fodder or on her knees, sweating, as she cleaned other people's floors. So much in Tina's childhood had made her feel different, ostracized and inadequate; she'd had so much to prove.

Part of the problem too had lain in the conflicting emotions she felt towards her mother. When she was old enough, she had clearly recognized the difficulties Maya Christo had faced in trying to adjust to a new country, to a husband who had always been a burden more than a support, to grinding poverty and early widowhood. Yet, despite all that, there had been times when, with the hyper-consciousness of youth, Tina had been ashamed of her mother's poor English, her lack of education and social graces, had despised her meekness and timidity in the face of any sort of authority.

Later, that shame had been redirected towards herself — that she had ever felt that way about a woman who had had so few chances in life. In later years, as her income grew, Tina had tried to make up for her mother's hardships. But the gifts, the holidays, the treats, had only embarrassed Maya Christo. She was uncomfortable in the world in which her daughter moved, was clearly more confused than proud of all Tina had achieved. It was as if she barely recognized the woman in the expensive tailored suits, the diamond studs, with the perfect manicures, as her own flesh and blood.

She had died a few months into her sixtieth year. Only Tina's friends had been present at the funeral. Always an outsider in her adopted country, Maya Christo had made no connections of her own. Yet despite her friends' support that day, Tina had faced a clarifying moment of truth as she watched her mother's coffin slide out of sight behind the parted curtains and into the fire that would consume her. The last link was gone. She was truly alone in a way she had never felt before. The realization distressed her more than she could have imagined. It was then, more than at any other time in her life, she had longed for the comfort of a partner, a husband, to mouth the clichéd words, to stroke her hair, to let her cry and talk and remember.

Had it been that state of mind which had made it easier, two months later, to begin the affair with Dean Ashley?

She was on her way to work the following morning when her phone rang and she heard Marnie's voice.

'Won't keep you, darling. It's just about that guy, Mark Galloway, remember? The builder. I'll give you the info and you make up your own mind if he sounds okay.'

'That was quick.'

'You know me…okay, he's divorced, no surprise, two kids who live with the ex on the central coast. Needed more work than he was getting around there. I've put him on for about three months, but after that, it depends what's happening work-wise back up the coast. So he doesn't want to tie himself down with a lease. Sounds respectable enough. At least you could try it, see if you can handle someone around the place.' Marnie chuckled. 'Better the burglars than a nosy bore you might have trouble getting rid of.'

'Thanks, Marnie. I really appreciate it.'

'I'll text you his number.'

'Thanks a million. I'll let you know what happens.'

'No prob — and good luck.'

It was almost midnight. Marnie had said goodbye to Josh Ambrose half an hour before. No matter how great a time they'd had in bed, she had no desire to have a lover spend the night. She was neurotically protective of her own space, found it difficult to sleep if not alone in her own bed. Nor did she wish to face the usually awkward intimacies of the morning after.

Now, as she straightened the twisted sheets, her body glowed with sexual satiety. This was the third night in a week that the young waiter had spent in her bed. He was young and attractive and she enjoyed his energy and inventiveness even if her own sense of abandon was more tempered these days. For one thing, she was becoming conscious of the changes in her body; the slackening of her breasts, the softening of her backside, the faint rippling of the skin on her thighs. No matter how youthful she might feel in mind and spirit, the signs of ageing were unmistakable and they sapped her confidence — at least, she thought wryly, as far as younger lovers were concerned. Her clichéd tactics now included soft lighting and diaphanous lingerie and she hated the feeling of not being totally at ease with her nakedness.

But she had another reason for feeling uneasy in Josh Ambrose's company. He'd told her he was trying to break into the music industry, was taking any job he could find in the meantime to make ends meet. It was tough, he said, but he was determined not to give up.

Marnie had every reason to admire his ambition, but it was the flip side of his determination which had aroused her suspicions. She realized now that the signs had begun to emerge the first evening they had spent together. They were insidious to begin with: his unstinting admiration of her apartment, its size, its location, its outlook; the questions about her background, her work and achievements. On the surface, his interest had seemed harmless enough, even flattering, she supposed. But then there was the way he'd helped himself a little too freely to her range of booze, the way he made mention of the difficulty he'd had in finding an affordable apartment, the quick joking reference to his hefty credit card bills. It was only later, when she added everything together, that she'd found herself on alert.

Much as it might have been a blow to her ego to acknowledge her suspicions, she wasn't about to become easy pickings for some young guy on the make. If Mr Cute Waiter thought he'd found himself a meal ticket, he was going to have to think again. The sex might have been hot but she hadn't got so desperate that she needed to pay for her fun — and wasn't likely to. As she switched off the bedside lamp, Marnie promised that the next time her ambitious young lover called, she'd make it clear the affair was exactly that. A fling, something to take the edge off her sexual appetite, to keep her juices flowing until the next time.

Not that she'd state it in quite those terms. But Josh Ambrose would get the message. She'd put that little show pony in his place — just as she had the others before him.

And it would bring her the same primal sense of satisfaction.

The call woke her out of a deep sleep. Heart racing, she fumbled for her phone.

'Who the hell is it?' Her throat was dry and raspy as she tried to focus on the bedside clock. Shit ... three-thirty in the morning.

'Sorry to wake you, Ms Ingram. It's your security service. There's been a bit of a problem on the site.'

Immediately, Marnie was wide awake, taking in what the man at the other end of the line was telling her.

'I'll be there as soon as possible,' she snapped.

She was out of the apartment and behind the wheel of the SUV in just as much time as it took her to throw on some clothes and grab her phone and shoulder bag. As she sped along the deserted streets of Sydney towards the almost completed development, her face was grim. This was no coincidence; she didn't believe that for a moment. This wasn't some rampage by local vandals. She knew exactly who was behind what had happened. Every damned window smashed. With the building boom at the moment it was going to take weeks to get them all replaced. As full realization dawned, her anger turned to gut-wrenching fear. This delay was going to bring her closer to the brink than she'd ever been before.

With the help of her own headlights and the security guy's torch, she'd managed to survey most of the damage. The site was still fenced and padlocked, but that was merely a deterrent as was the regular night time patrol.

Marnie couldn't hide her shock. 'I can't believe it! The bastards have smashed the architraves as well.'

'Must have happened between my 1 a.m. visit and when I came back a couple of hours later. They've climbed the fence and just run amok.' The burly, balding guard looked at her nervously. 'I can show you my patrol sheet, Ms Ingram. Everything's documented.'

Marnie was barely listening. She was working out how many arms she could twist among her suppliers to get the damage mended as fast as possible. And how many chippies she could spare from the start of her next project. Silently, she cursed Rod Sawyer and his dirty games.

It was too late to drive home. By the time she got there it'd be almost time to turn around and come back again. She sat in the SUV until dawn broke and then found an early opening cafe where she bought herself a cup of coffee. It was instant and weak, but hot enough, and she drove with it back to the site. While she sipped from the disposable cup and waited for Keith to arrive, she tried to put some order into her worried thoughts. Somehow she was going to have to find the manpower to rectify the damage here and still get a start on her next project. The slabs were due to be poured next week and that meant the juggling act of loan repayments and cash flow had just got a hell of a lot more serious.

But, she told herself grimly, there was no way Rod Sawyer was going to win.

No way.

Marnie had always thought herself too pragmatic to believe in myths and old wives' tales. But by that evening she had begun to wonder about the old adage of disaster coming in threes.

She'd had a draining day dealing with the ramifications of the early morning rampage. By the time she got home, it was after seven and she'd been on her feet almost sixteen hours. Exhausted, she decided that a warm bath might help to ease her tension.

While it was running, she poured herself a decent shot of gin. A search of the fridge revealed only half a bottle of flat tonic and no lemon, but that didn't matter. The way she felt right now, she could drink the stuff straight.

Her landline rang just as she was about to take her first mouthful.

She swore under her breath. What now? She wasn't in the mood for a social call and she sure as hell didn't want to be told about any more problems. Testily, she picked up the receiver.

'Marnie Ingram.'

'Marnie, it's Anthony Corkdale.'

As soon as she heard the measured tones of her father's long-time lawyer, she knew that something was wrong. Anthony Corkdale wasn't likely to call at this time of night for any trivial reason.

Succinctly, he told her the bad news.

'It happened late this afternoon. A stroke, more serious this time. Elaine found him in the garden. They've got him in intensive care at the Freemasons'.

Elaine Drake was the carer who had lived with Charles Ingram for the last four years. Following a minor stroke, her father had grown more forgetful and vague, and it was Anthony Corkdale who had suggested to Marnie that his client and friend was beginning to need more assistance than a housekeeper alone could provide. Of course Charles Ingram had protested strongly. Like any man who had once been physically strong and mentally acute, the suggestion of any decline was anathema to him. In the end, it was only Anthony's gentle persuasion that had convinced his friend to agree to employing an experienced carer. At the time,

Marnie remembered thinking that her father had been more acquiescent to his friend's advice than to his daughter's. But then, when had he ever paid much heed to her?

Now, as she digested what the solicitor was telling her, she knew that the news couldn't have come at a worse time.

'I've a lot on my plate just at the moment, Anthony. I'll explain when I see you, but of course I'll get down. Only it won't be until tomorrow afternoon. That's the best I can do.'

'I'm sure that's all your father would ask of you, Marnie.'

She wondered if she was imagining a hint of reproach in the solicitor's tone. But then, she had always suspected that Anthony Corkdale shared his friend's attitude to his only child.

They hung up, and immediately she organized to book her flight.

As she selected her date and times from the internet site, she began to analyze her feelings about the news. Of course she was upset, but there was another emotion too that she couldn't quite ignore.

Guilt.

Yet, surely, she told herself, she wasn't the one with any reason to feel guilty.

Chapter 4

MARNIE WAS ONLY FIVE YEARS old when she decided that her father hated her.

Before then she had probably never had a chance to notice his real feelings. It was her mother who was the center of her life and with whom she spent all her time. Her father was someone who left the house every morning in his pinstriped suit and snowy white shirt. Marnie would watch as he came into the morning room and bent down to kiss her mother goodbye. Veronica Ingram would smile the lovely smile Marnie still recalled, and for a moment she would feel jealous that her mother could give someone else, even her father, the same smile she gave to her. Sometimes she thought it might have helped if her father had given her a kiss as well. That way she would have felt as if she were part of the feeling she sensed between her parents.

But that never happened. A nod, a reminder to be a good girl for her mother, and Charles Ingram left for the office in the long dark car that Lewis drove for him.

For the rest of the day, Marnie had the delight of having her mother all to herself. Together they would listen to music, do puzzles, draw and paint. Marnie knew that the 'sickness' prevented her mother from doing anything too active. It was something to do with her mother's bones and she knew too that it could sometimes hurt a lot. But it hardly ever stopped them having fun together.

'You're my little princess, Marnie, darling.' Her mother would kiss and cuddle her as they sat on the sofa together reading a story. 'I waited a long time to have you and that makes you extra special.'

The house they lived in made Marnie feel like a princess too. It looked like the pictures you sometimes saw in fairy stories. Set behind thick hedges, it had high pitched slate roofs, leaded windowpanes and ivy-covered walls. Outside, surrounded by springy green lawns and colorful flowerbeds, there was a swimming pool and a tennis court. If it was a fine day, her mother would come and watch while Marnie was taught to swim and then she'd try extra hard to show Mummy how clever she was.

The house was run by Ruby and Lewis. Ruby cleaned and cooked, while Lewis drove the car and did all the odd jobs that Marnie figured her father didn't have time to do himself. There was also a gardener whom Lewis often helped.

'You're very lucky to live in a house like this,' Ruby sometimes told her. 'Only very rich people can afford to live in Toorak.'

'Is it because Daddy works hard?' Marnie asked.

'Well, yes, there's certainly that. But he also inherited a lot of money from his father. Your grandfather started the stockbroking firm that your daddy runs now.'

Ruby was polishing the silver coffeepot while she answered Marnie's questions. Veronica Ingram was upstairs taking her afternoon nap. It was getting harder for Ruby to help her climb the stairs and there were plans afoot to put in a small elevator. The arthritis was only going to get worse as time went on.

It was a real shame, Ruby thought. Mrs Ingram was such a lovely lady and it was clear that the two of them were very close. She'd seen the look on Mr Ingram's face sometimes when she was helping his wife into the shoes that were specially made for her, the extra soft leather accommodating toes that were slowly becoming clawed. Ruby knew it was hitting him hard. And, of course, Mrs Ingram did her best to cover up much of the pain. Ruby guessed it had a lot to do with the fact that she didn't want her husband to know that it was getting more difficult for her to care for the child.

To the housekeeper, it was as clear as the nose on her face that Charles Ingram hadn't wanted his daughter. Ruby had been with the couple long enough to see that. It was Mrs Ingram who had been hell bent in that direction, despite her ill health.

'Charles worries about me, Ruby, but I know with your help I'll be able to manage.' Veronica Ingram had been glowing with excitement when she broke the news of her pregnancy and it was obvious to Ruby how much her employer wanted this baby. But at twenty-seven, she was pushing it a bit in the housekeeper's opinion; not to mention Mr Ingram being a good ten years older than that. But then things didn't always happen just when you wanted them to, she supposed.

After the child was born and time went on, Veronica Ingram's condition began to deteriorate markedly despite the drugs she was prescribed. Her fingers started to curl inwards and there were some days when she couldn't get out of bed.

Marnie could clearly remember the day she had returned home after a trip to the beach with Ruby to find her mother missing.

'She's had to go to the hospital, my love.' It was Ruby who tried to explain. 'Just for a little while, so the doctors can try their best to make her better.'

'Can I visit her?' Marnie was distressed. She and her mother had never been parted from each other before.

'You'll have to ask your daddy that.'

But Charles Ingram brushed aside his daughter's anxious questions. He was sick with worry about his wife and certain that the stresses of childbirth had accelerated her decline. It had got so that even the sight of the child irritated him. Why had he allowed Veronica to talk him into agreeing to the pregnancy? They had been quite happy and content by themselves. If she'd only listened to him, he was sure her health wouldn't have deteriorated as it had.

Marnie remembered how lost and frightened she had been without her mother. The house now seemed so quiet and empty and she rarely saw her father. In the evening, she ate her dinner with Ruby in the kitchen while her father dined later alone in the large wood-paneled dining room.

When Ruby tucked her into bed, Marnie would ask tremulously if Daddy was angry with her.

'I'm sure he's not, my love. It's just that he's worried about your Mummy. Not,' the housekeeper added quickly, 'that she's not going to be home soon and much better.'

But as each day passed without her mother's return, and without any effort at comfort from a father who seemed to have forgotten all about her, Marnie grew more certain about what was happening.

Her mother wasn't ever coming home.

And somehow she sensed, her father blamed her for her mother's illness. That's why he didn't want anything to do with her.

He must surely hate her.

It was a thought that stayed with her even after her mother eventually returned from the hospital.

Marnie was shocked when she saw her. Her face was very swollen and, in place of the cane she'd been using, she now sat in a wheelchair.

With a cry of delight, Marnie had run forward to greet her. She'd been so looking forward to this moment. All she wanted was to give Mummy the biggest hug in the world. But to her shocked surprise, her father had swung out an arm and roughly stopped her in her tracks.

'No! You can't do that! If you touch her, you'll hurt her.'

The harshness of his tone brought tears to Marnie's eyes. How could he think she would hurt Mummy? All she'd wanted to do was hug her.

It was Veronica Ingram who in a weary, quiet voice, did her best to explain the situation to her tearful daughter.

'I'm sorry, my darling, Mummy's too sore to be touched too hard. We can hug each other but we've got to be very gentle.'

Marnie had imagined that when her mother came home from hospital, everything would be the same as it was before. She and Mummy would spend time together, having fun, just as they always had. But the reality was very different.

Now her mother spent a lot more time in bed or, when she was up, preferred to sit quietly in a chair with the television murmuring softly in the background. Sometimes they would read a story together, but her mother seemed too tired to do even that for very long. If her father was around, it wasn't long before Marnie was ushered away and sternly admonished not to exhaust her mother any longer.

Some weekends they still made the trip to the house by the sea. Marnie loved being at Portsea. She loved the village, the pier and the old sandstone houses. Their own home stood on a cliff top and had wonderful views of the ocean. Kneeling on the window seat in her bedroom, she would watch the cruise ships sailing in and out of Port Phillip bay while at night the lights of Melbourne were visible in the distance.

But where once she and her mother had explored the beach looking for interesting shells, building sandcastles with moats and paddling in the warm shallows, now things were just as restricted as they were in town. The only difference was that her father was with them all the time and that made Marnie feel even more excluded.

When lunch was served on the wide sheltered terrace she would do her best to tell them about her adventures that morning with Ruby: about the pippies she'd dug up, or the piece of driftwood she'd found that might just have come from some old pirate ship. Her mother would smile and agree that yes, maybe once there had been pirates around Portsea; but her father never paid much attention. Too often he would interrupt her stories, dampening her excitement and telling her to eat her lunch before it got cold. Then afterwards, he would disappear into the library with her mother, shutting the door so that Marnie was left outside.

She hadn't thought things could get any worse, but the year she turned seven, they did. It was Daddy who took her aside and told her about her new school. Somehow, she realized that he was trying to make it sound exciting, more grown-up, to be away from home. But Marnie was happy going to St Catherine's where Ruby walked her every morning, unless it was raining when Lewis would take her in the car.

'But I don't want to go away, Daddy.' Her eyes were bright with tears and her heart fluttered nervously. She couldn't remember ever talking back to her father.

Charles Ingram looked at her, his face stern. 'I didn't ask if you wanted to go, Marnie. I'm telling you that this will be best for your mother. It doesn't do her any good to have a noisy, demanding child around the house. You know how sick she is; don't you care what happens to her?'

A heavy sense of guilt settled on her. Of course she cared about Mummy. Wasn't she as quiet as could be? Didn't she remember to keep her cuddles gentle? Didn't she run and get everything Mummy couldn't get for herself?

But maybe that wasn't enough. At least, not enough to please Daddy. It had begun to seem as if nothing she did was going to be able to achieve that.

As time went on, that realization was reinforced by her father's continuing distance and criticism. Despite all her efforts, nothing she did ever elicited his praise or interest. In the school holidays, Marnie often felt as if they were in competition for her mother's limited energy. Whenever she tried to spend time with Mummy, he was there, warning her that she mustn't tire her mother out, mustn't be 'so demanding'. In time, Marnie felt excluded from both their lives. Nor was she able to talk to her mother about her feelings. It would only upset her, she knew, and make both of them feel guilty.

As she moved into her teenage years, a different Marnie began to emerge. She was no longer someone forever trying to be the 'good' child, the compliant and easily manipulated daughter. As her behavior deteriorated, her schoolwork also suffered and gave her father even more reason for criticism. She could still recall clearly one afternoon during the Christmas holidays at Portsea. A number of neighbors had been invited in for drinks and Marnie, now sixteen, was helping Ruby to pass around the canapés.

'So how did you go in your exams, Marnie?' The wife of a banker friend of her father's asked the dutiful question.

Her results had been abysmal. Before Marnie could conjure up some evasive reply, her father's voice cut coldly through the chatter.

'I'm afraid Marnie is quite hopeless academically. But at least, as a girl, I suppose we can marry her off.'

Marnie felt her face blaze. In the moment of silence that followed her father's remark, everyone seemed to be staring at her and she felt dizzy with embarrassment. Yet at the same time, something hardened inside her. Later, she realized, it had been a sort of turning point. A catalyst for the woman she would eventually become. A woman who would never have any need to please a man, who would cherish her freedom and never again let a man manipulate her emotions.

As soon as school finished, she found herself bundled off to Europe with her mother's best friend and her daughter, Charlotte. Marnie saw no need to protest. It was something she wanted to do and there was nothing for her at home.

The eight months she spent in London and Europe were the most exciting of her life. They had rented a flat in Knightsbridge and while she and Charlotte were supposed to spend three days a week at a sort of finishing college that offered cordon bleu cookery, art appreciation and French conversation along with the more traditional secretarial skills, they still managed to escape the eye of Charlotte's mother often enough. In fact, Mrs Dunne was easily distracted by her shopping trips to Harrods and lunches with her own friends, so the two young women in her care were able to enjoy to the full what London offered.

They soon hunted out the most interesting of pubs and clubs where they took to smoking colored cheroots and were never short of male attention. Soon, they were receiving invitations to the polo and Ascot, to Cowes and to weekend house parties at lavish country estates.

Marnie relished her popularity with young Englishmen. To her, they seemed a lot more interesting than the boys she had met back in Australia. With the arrogant forthrightness of youth, she knew she had been blessed with good looks. Compared to the pale insipidness of English girls, she had the exotic attraction of a hothouse bloom with her honey-colored skin, her waist-length curtain of dark, glossy hair and large, teasing hazel eyes.

She quickly learned the tactic of erotic suggestion, saw that she was capable of raising a young man's pulse to the stage where control of the situation lay in her hands alone. It was a revelation that gave her a potent recognition of her own power.

Whether she realized it or not at the time, it was the flip side of how she had been made to feel by her father.

On her return, she tried, for her mother's sake, to avoid confrontations at home. While she'd been away, Veronica Ingram's arthritis had reached the stage where her legs were now encased in calipers. She was still unsteady on them and Marnie, concerned and upset by this evidence of greater deterioration, spent time helping her mother to adjust. For once, her father did not protest.

But a month after her return to Melbourne, a full- time nurse was employed to assist with her mother's care.

'Your father thought it was best, darling. Neither of us want to stifle you. You're young, you've got your own life to lead. You shouldn't have to spend your time looking after me.'

Marnie was torn between love and pity for her mother and the selfish demands of her own interests. One of the boys she'd gone out with a few times before she'd left for England was Ben Wilton, son of a well-known Melbourne businessman. He was very keen on her, she knew, and before long was pressing for an engagement. No doubt, she thought with dry humor, it was the only way he felt he was ever going to get her into bed.

But she hadn't been saving herself for Ben or any other bloke back home. In England, she'd lost her virginity with a sexy young Spaniard she'd met one day in Hyde Park. A student at the London School of Economics, he was living in a small apartment with three other young men. After a party, they'd gone back to his place and Marnie had had her first sexual experience in Carlos's cramped single bed. It was a revelation.

She found that she enjoyed sex and had no inhibitions about making that obvious to any young man who took her fancy. What made everything easier was the fact that she never allowed herself to develop any emotional attachment to her lovers. If anything, she found this made them more interested, and when Marnie herself called off the relationship, it was inevitably the young men who sulked or suffered.

Yet somehow that seemed absolutely the way it should be.

Her father however, was beginning to make it very clear that he expected her to settle down and get married now that she was home. Ben Wilton's name was raised, among others but Marnie refused to discuss the subject.

'I'm not interested in marriage yet,' she would reply, adding the 'yet' only to placate her father. She had no intention of giving up her freedom for the shackles of marriage. Not now, not ever.

But that didn't stop her parents from returning to the subject. For her mother also seemed to feel that an engagement was the best option for her restless daughter. To Marnie, it felt like a week didn't go past when she wasn't being introduced to some worthy young man her parents deemed suitable.

By that time she'd been back in Australia for almost three months and knew she was going to have to find somewhere of her own to live if she wanted to escape the pressures being exerted on her. The allowance she received from her father wasn't enough to ensure her autonomy so she looked around for a job and eventually found herself a position in a prestigious interior design firm. At the beginning, it was secretarial duties she was hired for, but she had picked up enough of her mother's good taste and eye for fine things to ensure that before very long her talents were recognized and encouraged. Not that she took her work too seriously. There was far too much fun to be had now that she was sharing a flat with friends and free of her father's control.

Then, not long after Marnie's twentieth birthday, something terrible happened at the Portsea house. Her mother, stumbling on unsteady legs, fell onto the hard stone terrace and suffered a fatal blow to the head.

Veronica Ingram was dead for almost six hours before her daughter was told of the tragedy.

It was for that, above all else, that Marnie had never forgiven her father.

It was these thoughts and memories that now occupied her mind on the afternoon flight to Melbourne. She'd inherited a good deal of money from her mother's estate and not long afterwards had moved to Sydney. It had been a way of escaping from expectation and criticism, — and responsibility too, she supposed.

Over the years since then, she and her father had had minimal contact. There had been the dutiful visits for his sixtieth, seventieth and eightieth birthdays, celebrations planned for him by his sister and friends in which Marnie had played an insignificant role. On both occasions, she had not even been invited to spend a night in the family home. That favor had been reserved for others, not the daughter who had always been so incidental to Charles Ingram's life. Had that hurt her? At the time it must have. But she had kept her emotions to herself.

Marnie had learned that particular lesson in its sharpest form when her father had finally given her the news of her mother's death. In her shock and sorrow, she had reacted spontaneously, moving to enclose him in an embrace and expecting, at least in these circumstances, some form of comfort in return. But Charles Ingram's reaction had frozen her in her tracks.

His repugnance clear, he had turned sharply away, shunning his daughter's touch.

'I've lost her and it's all because of you.' His voice trembled with intensity. 'She'd never have got as bad if there'd only been the two of us. It was you who exhausted her. She did nothing but worry about you — and now you've killed her.'

Marnie felt as if a hand had closed around her throat, restricting her breathing. The shock of his naked emotion left her speechless. Was that what he'd always thought? Did his hatred of her run so deep?

And from then on, she had known she owed him nothing.

Nothing at all.

She caught a taxi from the airport to the Freemasons' Hospital at Malvern. Anthony Corkdale was waiting for her in the foyer. He stood up to greet her, a smallish, impeccably dressed man in his late sixties.

'They've stabilized him. Now it's just a matter of waiting to see what damage has been sustained.' He spoke in the dry, emotionless tones of his profession as he led the way to Charles Ingram's private room.

Marnie had last seen her father on his eightieth birthday almost a year before. He'd been slower and a lot more forgetful, but had still looked robust enough with the presence and forceful personality she remembered. Now she was shocked by the changes. His hair had turned completely white and the flesh seemed to hang off his shrunken frame. His mouth was pulled into a tight knot and his cheekbones protruded sharply through ash-white, translucent skin. For the first time, he looked like a very old man close to death.

She moved to the bed and could hear the rasp of his breathing. For a moment she hesitated, then reached out and touched one of his dry, withered hands that lay on top of the tight covers.

As she felt his cool flesh, Marnie found it difficult to pin down her emotions. Pity jostled with sorrow and with guilt. But why should she feel guilty? Because she hadn't kept in touch? Hadn't maintained a dutiful link in spite of her father's obvious animosity?

Surely that had been impossible and of no benefit to either of them.

But if she managed to rationalize her guilt, she couldn't do the same with her sense of overwhelming regret for all that she felt she had missed with this pathetic old man who lay struggling for life.

Chapter 5

IT WAS A HOT SUNDAY morning. Lee planned to leave for Sydney after breakfast; that way she'd have the rest of the day to go over things with Anita before taking sole charge of the shop on Monday and Tuesday. After this first week, she'd be going down mid-week and working on the busier days of Thursday and Friday, before returning home on Friday evenings.

Full of anticipation at the prospect of the change to her routine, she'd made sure everything was organized at home. No point in giving Brad and the boys anything to grumble about. Her eldest son, Troy, had recently moved into a flat with a couple of his mates but that didn't stop him coming home for dinner at least four nights of the week and bringing his dirty laundry.

Maybe she'd done too much for them all, she thought as she zipped up her small suitcase. Made herself a slave, and now they all expected it. Even Julie. Of course, she reminded herself tightly, the reason she'd never asked her daughter to help out at home was so she could concentrate on the things that really mattered. After all, anyone could be a household drudge, and she'd wanted a hell of a lot more for Julie. But what had she got in the end? A slap in the face, Julie's total and devastating refusal to take advantage of the opportunities Lee had worked so hard to give her. It was something she still found hard to believe and even harder to accept.

But she didn't want to think about that any longer. From now on, she'd decided, she was going to be just as selfish as the rest of them. Do what *she* wanted for a change and let them see how they'd manage without her.

Her packing finished, she checked her appearance in the mirror. Usually she let her fair curly hair dry naturally, but today she had blow-dried it into a smarter, sleek bob. Her make-up was discreet and the gold clip-on earrings made her feel dressier. Satisfied she was looking the part she put her head out of the bedroom door and called out, 'Can you carry this down for me, Brad?'

'He's busy, Mum, cleaning the car for you. I'll get it.'

Danny, sixteen and still at school, bounded heavily up the stairs. He'd shot up taller than Brad in the last three months. Lee only hoped the two large casseroles and the cold chicken for this evening would be enough for them all. For the first time, she felt a stirring of doubt about leaving. How were they going to manage? They'd never had to cope without her before.

Then she pushed away her anxiety. They'd just have to get by, wouldn't they? Maybe they'd all appreciate her more in the future.

'This it?' Her freckle-faced son lifted the suitcase off the bed.

'And the small hold-all.'

She'd worried about what clothes to take. Sydney was different from Newcastle. She wanted to make sure she looked smart in the shop, not like some hick who didn't know any better. In the end, she'd probably packed more than she really needed. Perhaps she'd buy herself a couple of things while she was there; it'd be good to have time to look around the shops. Usually when she had reason to go to Sydney, she tried to get out of the place before the roads became clogged with after-work traffic.

Following Danny outside, she found Brad giving a final wipe to the Mazda's windscreen. He was stripped to the waist, wearing a pair of baggy work shorts that were patched with sweat.

'That's better, isn't it?'

He was looking at her, waiting for her approval, and somehow that got under her skin. Why did men always need lavish thanks for every little thing they did for you? She hadn't noticed any of them singing her praises every night after dinner. Still, she couldn't deny it had been good of him to think of cleaning the car for her.

'Looks great. Thanks a lot. Not,' she added 'that I'm going to be competing with all those Mercs and BMWs.'

'I'm going to get a Beamer when I'm working, aren't I, Dad?' Danny was putting her luggage in the boot. 'Remember you said you'd help me do up one of the 323s.'

Brad grinned as he wrung out the chamois. 'First things first, mate. Work on the job bit, and then we'll take the next step.'

'Well, I'd better get going.' Lee cut across the father-son exchange. 'I don't want to have to rush.'

'Take care then, love. Give us a call when you've got a moment, and we'll see you Tuesday evening right?'

Lee opened the door. The car was hot inside; if it had been left in the garage it would have been cooler. She could have lived with it dirty. 'Yeah, around eight-thirty, I guess. Make sure you take the casserole out in the morning to defrost. I've left all the instructions on the fridge door.' Apart from when she was having the kids, it was the first time in all their married life she'd be spending more than a night away from her husband. No wonder he looked a little anxious.

'Give us a kiss then, just a small one. I won't get you dirty.'

As he leaned towards her and kissed her lightly on the lips, it was all Lee could do not to flinch away from his sweaty face. Her reaction shamed her a little but she couldn't help it. She could even taste the salt on his lips.

Her son, in contrast, stayed way out of kissing range. 'See ya, Mum.'

If Lee knew Danny, he was probably glad she'd be out of the way for a couple of days. No one to nag at him about a thing. And it probably wouldn't occur to Brad to check whether he'd done his homework or not.

'You be sensible, Danny, it's only a couple of days.' Her voice held a note of warning.

The boy grinned. 'Trust me, Mum. I'll make sure Dad toes the line.'

Ignoring her son's attempt at humor, she slipped behind the wheel and turned the key in the ignition. Earlier that morning, she'd said a cool goodbye to Julie as she left for her usual Sunday stint at the local supermarket. And, Lee thought sourly, with the fortune she'd have to find for those school fees, she was going to need all the money she could get.

A moment later, she was heading down the quiet suburban street on her way to Sydney.

The drive gave her time to be alone with her thoughts. She was surprised at how excited she felt. After all, it was only a couple of days a week for a month or so. But the prospect of spending some time by herself in Sydney really appealed. Maybe, she thought with a hint of bitterness, it would help to make up for lost time. All those years ago, she'd just been getting to know the city when everything had gone wrong. Sydney had been like a magnet to her when she was young. Irresistible, exciting, fascinating. The place where she was going to make her dreams come true.

At the beginning it had seemed as if things really were going to happen like that. She'd found board with a family at Bondi and landed herself a part- time job in a nearby cafe. The owners were Italians, loud, happy and willing to be flexible when she needed to rearrange her working hours to attend auditions.

In those days, she felt her main chance lay in cabarets and big show venues. There were usually dozens of girls trying for each position on offer but Lee was determined. It took her a few weeks of trying but, in the end, she eventually landed a singing/dancing role in a major revue that performed twice nightly. Fortunately, the Cocozzas allowed her to start work later in the morning which meant she was able to keep her job in the cafe too.

She remembered that time of her life as exhausting but exhilarating. Her contract was for three months. After that, if she were lucky, she'd be invited to perform in the next show too. Back then life had seemed perfect. She loved the glamour, the camaraderie with her fellow performers, the sheer delight of performing — and she felt sure it was just the start.

Every couple of weekends Brad drove down for the Saturday night and she knew he was blown away by seeing her on stage.

'You were brilliant, Lee, absolutely the best! You stood out head and shoulders from all the rest of them. I couldn't take my eyes off you.'

His reaction made her laugh with delight. When he took her out after the show, she could have listened to his words of praise for hours.

Usually, they went off by themselves. She sensed that he wasn't comfortable around her new friends. Brad had always been a bit shy, but she thought he might be jealous too, even though she did her best to reassure him. Yet she felt guilty about doing that. Not because it wasn't true that she wasn't interested in anyone else, but because she felt as if she were leading Brad himself to the wrong conclusion. At this stage in her life, she didn't want to be any man's exclusive property. There was too much she wanted to do and she didn't want to feel tied down in any way. As fond as she was of him, Lee wished she could make that clear to Brad. He still thought of her as his girlfriend, she knew; had hinted now and then about marriage when he finished his apprenticeship. But such talk irritated her. What did he think she was going to do — work on her career for a couple more years and then give it all up when he'd saved enough for a cheap ring and the deposit on a house? Just the thought of a future like that made her shudder. She'd promised herself she was never going to end up living like her sisters, driving the kids to school, playing pokies at the club and having Sunday lunch with her parents. They'd all laughed at her when she'd told them what she wanted to do with her life. But they weren't laughing now.

Still, she hadn't been able to completely finish things with Brad. She had to admit, it was nice to have someone who flattered her as much, who was so intensely interested in her and everything she was doing. As well, no matter how much she tried to deny it to herself, there were times when she felt lonely in Sydney, when it was good to have Brad to ring up and speak to whenever she felt like it.

Lee knew that she was the one in control of the relationship. In every way. They would kiss passionately, explore each other's bodies, and Brad might get hot and excited, but it was always up to Lee how far they went. Even in Sydney, when they wanted to kiss and cuddle, it still had to be in Brad's car. She never would have dreamed of asking him into the room where she boarded. Sure, it would have been lovely to lie on her bed together, but what if the family heard them? She'd die of embarrassment. So he always drove back to Newcastle in the very small hours of Sunday morning.

She felt safe with Brad, unlike some of the guys who would join her and the other girls in various coffee clubs and supper places after their performance. Many of them were much older, worldly men and occasionally they'd place an exploratory hand on her leg under the table or try to kiss her when the night ended. Some of the girls teased her about her reticence, about 'saving herself for her little boyfriend from home' and Lee did her best to laugh off their comments. She wasn't going to admit it but, apart from Brad, she'd had no experience with men and these older would-be suitors made her nervous.

Now, as she headed down the expressway to her fill-in job in the city, Lee remembered how it was one of these older men who'd been the catalyst for all that had changed in her life.

Peter Holding was his name. He'd slipped her his card one evening at the usual post-show gathering. He was a producer, he told her, on one of television's leading cabaret shows. 'We're auditioning next week. A permanent position with the Channel's dance troupe. I think you'd be great, Lee.' His hand had squeezed her thigh, but she was too distracted by what he was telling her to object too strongly. A permanent position on TV! That would be fantastic exposure. And the producer himself was inviting her to audition. She listened, eyes shining, as Peter Holding gave her the details.

She knew she'd do anything to get a job like that.

Flushed with excitement, she had turned up the following week at the appointed time. In the cavernous studio, girls in costume milled around in the dimness, waiting to be called onto the floor under the bright arc lights.

When it was Lee's turn, she followed the same routine: looked into the camera and gave her details, handed her music to the accompanist and sang one verse of a popular song and then performed a short dance routine. She'd given it her best; now she had to wait for the call that would tell her if she'd been successful.

It came thirty-six hours later. The telephone message was sitting on her bed when she returned from that evening's performance. Heart racing, Lee read the words again and again, trying to convince herself they were true. Yes! She'd done it! They wanted her in two weeks' time. She thought she was going to jump out of her skin with excitement.

The next morning she was up earlier than usual to ring home and tell them all her wonderful news.

'TV, love ... well, well. That's pretty special, isn't it?' It made Lee feel good to hear the note of pride in her mother's voice. It had been a long time coming. 'I guess we've got a real star in the family now.'

'This is just the start, Mum, you wait. I told you, didn't I? I told you I was going to do it.'

Brad was at work, so she left it to her mother to pass on the good news. 'Tell him I'll try to ring him tonight.' At times like this, she really wanted to share her joy with him.

An hour or so later, she was getting ready to leave the house when she received her second wonderful surprise.

As she took delivery of the bouquet of sweet- smelling roses, Lee could hardly believe they were for her. But the card had her name on it. They couldn't possibly be from Brad, she thought, perplexed. He'd never have got the news and arranged them so quickly.

She had to sit down on the bed when she saw the name on the short message of congratulations. My God…Peter Holding.

I knew you could do it. Congratulations. I'll see you when you start rehearsals.

This was amazing; the producer of the show had taken the trouble to send her flowers! She couldn't believe it. Her mind was full of questions. What did it mean? Did he do this for all the new girls? Or was it just her? She could barely remember what he looked like. Thirtyish, she thought, with fashionably long hair. But it was his confidence and charm she recalled more clearly. It thrilled her that she was going to work with someone like that.

From then on, everything seemed to happen at once. She gave her notice on the revue and the very same day was told she'd have to vacate her rented room. Her landlady's sister was coming back from Queensland and needed a place to stay. For Lee, it couldn't have been worse timing.

As soon as the paper was delivered the following Saturday, she began to search through the columns of share accommodation. The house at Bondi was one of those she ringed. She knew the area now and she liked the sound of the place. It was the second house she looked at and her reaction was instant. She knew this was where she wanted to live.

Built of local sandstone, the place was set high on a hill above the ocean. Some of the paintwork was peeling, the kitchen and bathroom were dated, but that was more than made up for by the spaciousness of the rooms with their high pressed- metal ceilings and working fireplaces. Best of all was the shady verandah with its rusting ironwork railings and views of the water through the gnarled old jacaranda in the overrun back garden. It was there Lee sat having coffee with Marnie as they both sussed out if they were compatible enough to share.

Lee thought she had never seen such a gorgeous creature. Marnie Ingram's skin glowed like burnished copper, her cascade of blue-black hair fell almost to her waist and her short denim skirt showed off perfect legs. This was the sort of girl, Lee recognized, who would drive boys crazy.

There were two spare bedrooms and, determined to land one of them, she explained about her two jobs, assured Marnie she could afford the rent and that she was neat and clean and quiet.

She remembered how Marnie had laughed out loud at the last bit.

'Well, I'm not — tidy and quiet, I mean. I love music, I'm going to throw a party every excuse I get, and I'll probably forget to wipe down the shower and throw out the garbage. So how does that grab you? Can you stand all of that?'

Slowly, Lee's lips had spread in a grin. 'Thank God,' she said. 'I thought you were just gorgeous but you're human too!'

It was the first time she had ever complimented another woman so openly. Maybe that's how you knew you were going to be friends.

Moving into the house at Wattle Street made Lee feel truly independent. Now she was really in charge of her own life. She got on well with both Marnie and the other girl who joined them the same week she moved in. Tina, from Queensland, had been staying in the YWCA before answering Marnie's ad.

The surprising thing was how different they all were: Marnie so outgoing and casual, Tina self- contained and quite private, and herself so often impetuous and excitable. Yet they all managed to get on. Maybe it was their differences that made them compatible.

They quickly got to know each other. Tina had started work in a bank although she didn't like it much. While she made it clear that saving money was her primary goal, she was typically circumspect about her larger ambitions.

'I'm aiming to start my own business as soon as possible. I've got something in mind but I'm not going to talk about it just yet. Not till I've thought the whole thing through.'

'Jesus, I could never work in a place like that,' Marnie grimaced, referring to Tina's job at the bank. 'Who needs some smart-ass boss hovering over you all the time, telling you what to do?' It was Saturday morning and she was pouring them all a coffee as they sat on the patio. It wasn't the instant stuff Lee was used to; Marnie made it in a special pot and it was strong and tasted delicious.

Of course, Lee told herself, money made Marnie independent. And it seemed like she'd already worked out what she was going to do with her mother's inheritance.

'I'm not leaving it up to some boring old stockbroker to make the decisions for me.'

'But isn't your father...?' It was Lee who asked the question. Marnie had told them a little about her background.

Marnie grinned. 'Yes, a boring, conservative stockbroker. And it's driving him crazy that I'm cashing in some of the stocks and won't listen to his advice. But there isn't a damn thing he can do about it.'

'So what *are* you planning to do with the money?'

Lee recalled how interested Tina, with her own secret schemes, had been.

'Property,' Marnie answered as she set the coffee pot down on the wicker table with a flourish. 'I've decided that I'm going to buy up and renovate old houses. I'll be making money for myself and not be dependent on my father's advice or input in any way.'

The undercurrent in her voice had been Lee's first hint that there might be something amiss in Marnie's relationship with her father.

'So, really we're all the same.' Lee grinned as she lifted her coffee mug in salute. 'Three fiercely ambitious women for whom, it seems, marriage will be a long time coming.'

'If ever.' Marnie raised a cynical eyebrow.

Tina touched her mug to Lee's. 'I'll drink to that. No housewives here. The guys can wait until we're good and ready. And we'll be worth waiting for.'

Well, it hadn't quite worked out that way, had it, Lee thought now, as she concentrated on the road. And who could she blame for that?

There wasn't a simple answer. The dice had rolled from many directions. But Brad was the only one at whom she could still direct her anger and frustration.

She remembered how he'd been beside himself when he saw the house for the first time. 'This is great!' He was clearly impressed. And the fact that she now had a room of her own

and was answerable to no one was clearly a huge bonus as far as he was concerned. He'd shut her bedroom door behind them and slipped his arms around her, pulling her close. 'Now I won't have to drive home every Saturday night, love. We can spend the whole night together at last.'

Looking into his shining, expectant eyes, Lee realized that the situation between them had the potential to seriously change. She knew then that she was going to have to find a way to tell him it was over.

For the next couple of weekends until she started her new job, she managed to make excuses to keep Brad from coming to visit. He wasn't easy to convince but, short of insisting, there was nothing much he could do about it.

'I've got so much to do before I start the new job,' she'd pleaded. 'Please understand. I... I'll see you as soon as I can.' It was a lie and she hated having to tell it.

Marnie teased her about Brad's phone calls as she was the one who usually took the messages.

'He's serious, Lee, I can always tell. I'll bet he just wants to get a ring on your finger as quickly as possible.'

'He knows how important my work is to me,' Lee asserted defensively. 'He knows I'm not going to let anything get in my way.' But she realized she was going to have to confront Brad with the reality of the situation as soon as possible.

Her first rehearsal went well. The other girls in the troupe were welcoming enough although there were a couple who were more stand-offish than the rest. The competitive instinct in her profession was something Lee had grown used to over the years and she didn't let it worry her.

What mattered more was pleasing Peter Holding. He had been there at that first rehearsal and she'd felt his keen appraisal. Later, as she was heading off the floor, he'd complimented her on her efforts.

'You're fitting in well with the others, Lee. Same fluid style. Just stay nice and relaxed and you'll have nothing to worry about.'

She'd felt herself blush at the compliment. Peter Holding was really going out of his way to boost her along. She was flattered by his attention — and even more so when, the next day, he asked if she'd like to have a drink with him sometime. 'I like to help the new girls feel at home,' he'd said with a warm smile.

'Well, thanks, that'd be great. It's really nice of you.' Lee meant it. Imagine a busy producer taking the time for her.

'I'll let you know,' he said as he walked off.

He rang her two days before her first appearance on air. They met in the cocktail lounge of a city hotel. It was dimly lit and romantic and Lee couldn't help noticing how people turned to look at them as they walked in. It made her feel special to be seen with this older, sophisticated man.

She'd been a bit nervous about what they'd talk about, but the conversation was easy. Peter asked her a lot about herself and seemed genuinely interested in her replies. It was only when he inquired if she had a boyfriend that she'd hesitated.

'Uh — well, yes, there was someone. But that's over now.'

She'd felt the producer's hand pat her knee, a quick, friendly gesture.

'That's good. You're too pretty to tie yourself down at your age. And also far too talented to give it all away for a wedding ring.'

Lee's eyes shone at the compliments.

After that, she knew she could no longer procrastinate. Perhaps the comparison with Peter Holding hadn't helped, but the break-up had been on the cards before that. What was the point in prolonging things, making Brad believe there was a future when there wasn't?

Taking the coward's way out, she tried to tell him as gently as possible, that as much as she really liked him, she didn't want to continue the relationship, that she was 'too young to get seriously involved' with anyone. Her career had to come first and she'd always done her best to make that clear.

Brad's reaction was as Lee had expected. He rang her a dozen times in the next few days, begging her not to do this to him, to them; telling her that she was all he had ever wanted, that he'd do anything to make her happy. Yes, she had her career, but surely she wanted to marry one day, have children? He'd move to Sydney if that's what it took. And he'd wait. Wait for however long she wanted, but, please, don't tell him it was over.

Eventually, in the face of her continuing refusal to change her mind, Brad drove down to see her and Lee was forced to repeat her decision face to face, her resolve so firm that eventually he had to accept that she wasn't going to back down.

'I'll wait for you, Lee.' His face was stained with tears and the sight really upset her. But she'd tried to make him understand before this, had tried not to lead him on, had always sidestepped his talk of a future together.

'I love you,' he told her emotionally. 'Totally and utterly. There'll never be anyone else. I don't care how long it takes, I'll wait for you.'

The sight of his misery made Lee feel guilty and cruel. But everything was just starting for her; she didn't want anything or anyone holding her back. Brad had been good to her, but he only reminded her of all she was running away from. She should never have let it last as long as it had. She knew Sydney much better now, had the company of Marnie and Tina and had made other friends as well.

The cruel truth was that she didn't need Brad as she once had. She'd outgrown him. His ambitions were so limited, his experience of life so narrow. The longer she'd been away from home, the more stifled she'd begun to feel in his company.

But in the end, she thought now as she approached the outskirts of the city, Brad had won.

Anita had given her directions to the apartment at Willoughby which belonged to her sister. She and her husband used it, Anita explained, when they came down from their country property. It would be Lee's alone for the time she had agreed to help with the shop.

The place was on the second floor; nothing pretentious, but clean and quiet enough. There was a single garage for her car as well.

Anita helped carry up her bags. She was a biggish woman, always impeccably groomed and made-up. She opened a couple of the windows and showed Lee how everything worked in the place.

'There's fresh milk, margarine and bread in the fridge and I bought you some orange juice as well. You'll find coffee and sugar in the cupboard.'

'Thanks, that'll do fine for breakfast.'

'And there's a deli on the next corner plus a takeaway place as well. Do you eat Thai?'

'Sure.' Brad didn't like spicy food. He was the original steak and mashed potato man. Lee had only eaten Thai a couple of times before but she'd quite liked it.

'It's so good of you to do this for me, Lee. I really appreciate it. Did Brad mind?'

'Not at all. He knows how much I miss my job.' No need to enlarge on Brad's initial reluctance. She'd got here, that was all that mattered. She'd be helping a friend and would have the rare treat of time alone.

'Tell me,' she asked as Anita put on the kettle before they headed for the shop, 'how's your daughter coping now?'

The other woman's expression became serious. 'It's a real worry. She hasn't bonded with the baby at all. Her doctor's quite relieved I'm taking the time to be with her. Postnatal depression isn't something you take lightly these days.'

As Anita talked, Lee remembered how she'd struggled with her feelings about her own first child.

But for very different reasons.

Afterwards, they drove the short distance to Chatswood. The shop was called Veronique and located in the mall. A young cheerful girl was handling the Sunday trade alone and Anita introduced them. Her name was Tracey.

'She's actually very good,' Anita explained when she and Lee were out of earshot and Tracey was busy with a customer. 'But she's a uni student and can only do weekends and Thursday nights.'

They spent a couple of hours going over the stock, the computer, the banking arrangements and basic paperwork. As far as Lee was concerned, it was all quite straightforward. Things were run very much as they had been in the Newcastle shop. She felt confident she could handle it all.

'Just call my mobile if there's anything more you need to ask,' Anita said when she dropped her off later at the apartment.

'I will, but I can't see there'll be any major problems.'

Anita had invited her to have dinner that evening with her husband and herself at their home at St Ives, but Lee had made her polite excuses. She was tired after the long drive, she said. She'd take a shower and get to bed early so she'd be fresh for the next morning.

As she turned the key in the front door of her temporary living quarters she felt an incredible sense of freedom. She couldn't remember when she'd last felt like this. No dinners to cook for anyone, no last-minute ironing of school or work shirts, no lunches to prepare, no arguments over homework or television programs.

It was bliss, she decided, as she walked through to the compact kitchen with the chicken dinner she'd bought on the way back from the mall. Absolute bliss.

She took a shower and, wrapped in her dressing gown, ate some of the chicken while she watched '60 Minutes'. It felt weird to be eating alone, but a nice kind of weird. I could get quite used to this, she thought happily, as she wrapped up the rest of her meal and stored it in the small refrigerator. In fact, it felt wonderful to think she had another month of this to look forward to.

In the small white-tiled bathroom, she cleaned her teeth and emptied her wet pack of the things she'd need the next morning. Finally she set her alarm and slipped into bed with a novel she'd brought with her. At home, she never had enough time to read, and Brad wasn't keen on her having the light on while he was trying to sleep.

Half an hour later, she turned down a corner of the page and put the book down on the bedside table. Only then, as she lay in the darkness, did she begin to feel the first stirrings of guilt. Were Brad and the kids managing all right? Had she left them enough to eat? Had Danny been able to make himself some lunch for the next day? With an effort, she forced her uncomfortable thoughts away. They were all grown-up enough to look after themselves, she reassured herself. It wouldn't do them any harm to have to manage on their own for a while.

As she took in the faint rumble of city traffic, Lee realized that apart from her recent night in the hotel at Rushcutters Bay, this was the first time in years that she'd slept totally alone anywhere, without anyone else in the house. It felt strange, but the thought didn't trouble her. She felt quite safe.

With a sigh, she closed her eyes.

Chapter 6

HE'D BEEN SITTING IN THE dark for almost half an hour, his car parked in the shadow of some nearby trees. Patience was a virtue he had in abundance, and with the car radio tuned low to his favorite station he had no problem in passing the time. It was twenty minutes later when he saw headlights turn the corner and move towards him. The vehicle turned into the driveway he was watching and he knew it was her.

Alone again.

Tina had managed to get away from the office earlier than usual. Two days ago she'd rung the number Marnie had given her and talked to the guy who was looking for somewhere to live. Although she'd been hesitant about meeting him on home ground before she'd checked him out, he'd sounded okay and she decided she'd have to trust Marnie's judgment.

He was already waiting, standing on the footpath as she drove up to the house. His white Holden ute, the tray packed with his work tools, was parked by the kerb. Tina gave him a wave of acknowledgment as she maneuvered her BMW into the garage.

He sauntered towards her with a smile as she emerged from behind the wheel.

'Hi…Mark Galloway. Hope I'm not too early.'

'Not at all. Just the usual traffic hassles, I'm afraid.' She shook the proffered hand. It wasn't soft and smooth-skinned like the male hands she was used to. 'Tina Christo. Pleased to meet you.'

He smiled again, white teeth in a tanned, rather weather-beaten face. He was in his forties, she guessed, neatly dressed in jeans and a short-sleeved shirt that revealed the physique of a man used to physical labor.

'Yeah, they warned me about Sydney. I gave myself plenty of time.'

'Where are you living now?' Tina hitched her briefcase under her arm.

'Staying with a mate and his family at Coogee. But I need to find a place of my own asap.'

'Come on in then and I'll show you what I've got. If it appeals, we can discuss things further.'

'Sure.'

She led the way through the door at the rear of the garage. To the left was an external staircase which gave access to the compact flat above.

'I lived here myself for a while when I was renovating.' She spoke over her shoulder as he followed behind her. 'I got my cleaner to give it a bit of a dust and tidy up the other day so I hope it's still okay.'

She found the key on her ring and opened the door. The room stretched the length of the garage. At one end was a tiny kitchen area with a two-ring cook top, a bar fridge and a sink; the other end was partitioned off to provide privacy for sleeping.

"The furniture's not too flash,' Tina said, 'it was just stuff I had in my old apartment.' There was a caramel-colored sofa, a cane easy chair and a dark timber coffee table.

'Looks okay to me.' Mark Galloway walked over and peered behind the wall of the bedroom area. He saw a single bed and a small chest of drawers. Empty hangers hung on a metal rack that stood against one wall.

'There's a shower and toilet through that door to the left,' Tina said. 'Not big, but adequate.'

She watched as he swung the door open and checked that out too.

'Fine, just fine.' He nodded, taking everything in as he walked back to her.

'How long do you think you might want the place?'

'How long is it available? If it works out, I'd be just as happy here, I reckon, as in something bigger.'

'Well, why don't we have a coffee and discuss the details?'

Tina trusted her intuition; it had rarely let her down. Mark Galloway didn't seem the sort of man who would be a problem to have living on her property.

Half an hour later they'd worked out the details of rent and conditions and Tina was handing her new tenant the key. He was to move in on the weekend. They agreed they'd give it a try for three months and extend it from there if both were satisfied with the arrangement.

Tina felt reassured that it was going to work out okay. Mark would be here most evenings keeping an eye on the place, as well as every second weekend. The other weekends he drove back up the coast to visit his children. He had three, he'd told her, two boys and a girl.

'I miss them,' he'd said simply. 'Divorce is hard on kids too.'

It was their only personal exchange during the entire conversation. Tina had volunteered only the basics about her work, her usual schedule.

After all, she wasn't looking for a buddy. What she needed was a sense of security.

He waited until he was leaving to lob a ball from left field.

'There's just one more thing I have to ask you,' he said. 'I hope it won't change your mind.'

She felt a stab of irritation as she waited for him to elaborate. If there was something that might prove a problem, why couldn't he have brought it up before they'd gone through the whole rigmarole?

'Perhaps,' he added, 'it'll be easier to explain if you don't mind walking out to my truck.'

Tina frowned. What the hell was this about? But Mark Galloway volunteered nothing more as they walked up the steep path to the front gate.

Out on the street, he pointed in through his half- open passenger window. 'That's Digger. He's totally house-trained. We're a team and I would really hate to break us up.'

Tina looked in at the dog that sat panting on the seat. It was some sort of shepherd-cross, she figured, and the last thing she needed around her expensive landscaping.

She turned to the man beside her. 'Does he live up to his name?'

Mark Galloway chuckled. 'No, sorry. You'll still have to bury your own bones.'

Tina was a little taken aback. She hadn't expected the warped sense of humor.

'Well...'

'If I may say another word in his favor: he's a top watchdog.'

She had mentioned the two break-ins to him. In the circumstances, she decided that perhaps having a dog around would be a bonus as far as security was concerned.

'Okay I guess, if the dog's as good as you say he is.'

'Thanks. I really do appreciate that.'

She looked at him, surprised at the relief she could see in his face. Next minute she got an inkling of where her new tenant was coming from. All sign of humor gone, he said flatly, 'There are just so many break-ups you can handle at once.'

A little warning bell rang inside her. Oh no, a bitter, depressed divorcee. What had she landed herself with?

Then she shrugged inwardly. What did it matter? They would hardly ever see one another.

By the time she arrived home with her groceries late on Saturday morning, the ute was parked inside the garage. She hadn't minded sharing the space. It would save the guy having to pack and unpack his gear every night.

As she dragged her plastic bags out of the car, she could hear her new tenant's footsteps overhead. It would be only polite, she supposed, to call out a welcome.

But by the time she got outside, her bags in each hand, Mark Galloway was already coming down the steps with Digger right on his heels.

'Hi.' She smiled up at him, squinting in the sunshine despite her sunglasses. 'Everything okay?'

'Great. I bought some spare sheets and a couple of extra towels.'

She was about to say he could have borrowed some from her when she remembered that it was important to keep this arrangement formal. The last thing she wanted was to get too friendly and feel as if she were losing her privacy .

'Can I give you a hand with those?' He was beside her, reaching out for the grocery bags. The dog was sniffing the cuffs of her trousers and she could see its pale hairs rubbing off onto the dark fabric.

'Oh, no, thanks. I can manage. I'm used to it.'

'Come on, they look heavy. You wouldn't want to slip on that path.' As he spoke he was easing them from her hands. It seemed churlish to argue further.

'Well, okay ... Thanks.'

He told the dog to sit and stay which to Tina's surprise it did.

'He's good.'

'I told you. House-trained. Like me.'

She led the way down the path to the house, hoping he wasn't going to expect her to offer him a coffee or something. There was paperwork waiting for her in the study, and Dean was coming to dinner later on. It was one of the rare occasions when Kathy and the kids were spending the weekend with her parents at their holiday place at Pearl Beach. Tina wanted to cook something special. She enjoyed being creative in the kitchen when she had the time.

But Mark made it clear he wasn't going to impose. 'There,' he said, lifting the plastic bags onto the granite kitchen bench. 'I'll leave you to it. You've probably got as much to do as I have.'

'Always — and thanks again,' she added as he turned to go.

'No problem. Give me a yell if I can give you a hand with anything. I certainly don't mind.'

While she packed her shopping away, she found herself trying to remember the last time there'd been anyone around to carry in her groceries.

Not in living memory.

She was expecting Dean about seven. Everything was ready to go in the kitchen and she had time for the rare indulgence of a leisurely bath.

Daylight saving meant it was still light outside and as she relaxed in the warm water she enjoyed the view from her bathroom window. She was excited about tonight. There weren't many Saturday evenings that she and Dean were able to spend together. She hadn't asked what excuse he'd given his wife for remaining home this particular weekend. There were a few subjects they avoided and his marriage was one of them.

Tina supposed she was hoping that the day would come when he'd tell her that he'd changed his mind. That he couldn't live like this any longer. That he wanted to be with her all the time. It sometimes felt as if she were continually trying to resist raising the topic that was always hovering in the forefront of her mind. But she knew what a disaster that would be. It had to be Dean's decision to leave, without any coercion from her.

She had to fight too against feeling guilty about their relationship. That hadn't really been a problem for her before but that was probably because those other affairs had been fleeting and of much less importance. With Dean it was different. She was well aware that she was putting another woman's marriage at risk. But then, she told herself, Dean wouldn't be with her if that marriage were totally fulfilling. Yet it seemed it wasn't quite bad enough for him to leave either. And his commitment to his children was another stumbling block.

In her more neurotic moments, she couldn't help wondering if the kids were only an excuse. If, in reality, he was enjoying both the security of his marriage and the pleasures of a secret affair. If that were the case, then she knew she had no hope of a future with him. She'd either have to accept being the mistress indefinitely or somehow find the courage to get out.

And why, she brooded, would she do that? In the hope that she was still young enough to meet someone else? In Sydney? Where every single woman she knew bewailed the fact that it was impossible to find a decent man.

Professional guys had it made, she thought. Why would they bother looking at anyone over thirty, never mind forty, when there were all those twenty-somethings eager to avoid the fate of their depressed and lonely older sisters? And if the marriage didn't work out, there was yet another batch of twenty-somethings in the wings for whom the power, wealth and sophistication of the greying male was an irresistible lure.

Well, she told herself as she stepped out of the cooling water, dwelling on all that wasn't going to help her feel any better. One day at a time, wasn't that what they said? And, in the meantime, she'd make the most of things.

She toweled herself dry, giving her body a critical glance in the mirror. Not too bad for a woman in her mid-forties. At least she was slim. There had been a time in her childhood when that wasn't the case. Existing on her mother's inadequate wage had meant a diet aimed at filling her up above all else and, as she'd grown larger, she'd become the butt of her schoolmates' teasing.

It was a situation that had only become worse when, under the tutelage of Miss Lorne, she'd won a scholarship to a respected private girls' school.

'Fat greasy wog! Fat greasy wog!' The cruelty of those schoolgirl taunts had shattered her. She remembered only too clearly the exaggerated way her pretty long-limbed class mates had pinched their noses when she'd opened the lunch of fetta, olives and salami her mother had packed.

'Phew! What a stinking mess! Tina Christo eats pig swill.' They'd chant that final sentence over and over again.

Crushed and humiliated, she had felt cast adrift amid a sea of heartless, privileged, Anglo-Saxon snobs.

Nor could she bring herself to tell Miss Lorne what was happening to her. It had been with Dorothy Lorne's help and encouragement that she'd applied for the scholarship to the school from which the older woman herself had retired. Tina knew how proud her mentor was of her achievement. How, then, could she reveal the nightmare that she faced on a daily basis?

Her only way of fighting back, she decided, was to outshine them all academically. Not that her success had served to lessen her torture, but by the time she ended up dux of the school, it hadn't mattered any longer. Her moment of triumph came at that final speech night when she crossed the stage and accepted her prize from the smiling headmistress. By then she'd managed to diet herself two dress sizes smaller, so that no matter what any of them threw at her, they couldn't deny Tina her overwhelming sense of satisfaction and victory.

Her mother hadn't attended that night — and Tina had been shamefacedly relieved. She could imagine the looks on her tormentors' faces when they compared Maya Christo, in her worn, outdated dress with her thickset figure and blushing shyness, to their own elegant, confident mothers. The thought was too much to bear.

But Miss Lorne had been there, honored with a seat in the front row, her applause the loudest when Tina, wearing the white dress Dorothy herself had bought her, walked onto the dais to accept her prize.

Yet the retired teacher had been bitterly disappointed when Tina made it clear that she had decided not to go to university.

'But you've worked so hard, my dear. Why in the world would you throw away this opportunity?'

Nothing she said could change her protégé's mind. Tina had found a new strength in her success. She was determined that she wasn't going to waste the next four years of her life with more study. Filled with a growing impatience, she wanted a more concrete reward than academic achievement could provide. It was an underlying, and perhaps unacknowledged, sense of inferiority that propelled her. She wanted the material success that she felt certain gave her peer group and tormentors their unconscious confidence and self-belief. In time though, she did come to recognize the value of formal qualifications but whatever study Tina undertook was in after work hours. Nothing was allowed to get in the way of her upward trajectory.

And now, she thought, as she dressed for the evening ahead, she had it all. Financial security, professional respect, and the knowledge that she had thrown off the shackles of her background.

The only thing missing was a man with whom she could spend her life.

The front bell rang at ten past seven. When Tina released the gate, she could hear a dog barking through the intercom.

Oh, Jesus! She'd forgotten about that.

By the time she hurried up the path, Dean was standing inside the gate with Mark Galloway beside him, holding the dog by the collar.

Hell, she really didn't need this... Catching her breath, she began to apologize. 'Dean, I'm sorry, I forgot —'

'I'm the one who needs to apologize.' It was Mark who interrupted her. 'But now they've met each other, it won't be a problem again.' Digger was sitting at his heel, tongue lolling, with no sign of aggression.

'Look it's fine, no problem,' Dean put in. 'I just wasn't expecting him, that's all.'

'I'm sorry,' Tina apologized again, 'I completely forgot to tell you.'

'Anyway, it won't happen again, I promise you,' Mark said. 'I'll keep him inside whenever you're expecting someone.'

'Thanks, would you?' Tina knew she sounded abrupt but she still felt flustered. There'd been no need for the two men to cross paths. Now, somehow, she felt as if her privacy had been intruded upon.

'Good night.' Mark turned to go. 'Nice to meet you,' he added to Dean.

'Yeah, same here.'

'Well, as long as you feel comfortable about him. On first impressions, he seemed fine to me.'

Dean was pouring their wine from the bottle he'd brought with him while Tina filled him in on what she knew about her new tenant.

He handed her a glass. 'I should have realized there was someone there when I saw the lights on above the garage.'

'Still, you couldn't have guessed about the dog.'

'You're right.' He laughed. 'Gave me a helluva fright. But it won't hurt to have that sort of security around the place.'

She settled herself beside him on the cushioned day bed. 'Well, that's what I thought, but now I'm beginning to wonder.'

'Don't worry about it. At least I'll know you're safe with the hound of the Baskervilles on guard duty.'

To Tina, it was the most perfect of nights. They ate by candlelight and caught up on each other's news. When the wine was finished, they moved through to the bedroom and made love with the abandon and hunger she'd grown used to. Despite the intensity, her orgasmic joy, there was always a part of her that was left unsatisfied. The part that needed to feel that their abandonment encompassed the full emotional range, that she was completely loved to the exclusion of anyone else.

Instead, she was always careful to restrain herself, to make sure she concealed the real depth of that need in order not to alarm the man who could hold her in his arms only when his schedule as a husband and father allowed.

Afterwards, she lay amongst the rumpled sheets and watched him get dressed. He had no idea, she knew, that for her, his actions held as much intimacy as that which had gone before. Yet, at the same time, she was assailed by a familiar sadness. Even on this occasion, he didn't dare stay with her the entire night. It would mean risking too many lies — to the running partner he met with on most Sunday mornings or the neighbors who might catch sight of his early return.

He smiled at her as he buttoned his shirt cuffs. 'I think you can count on your birthday gift.'

Her heart leapt. She'd avoided asking the question for fear of disappointment. 'You mean you can get away?' She sat up in the bed, her breasts revealed, still tender from his experienced assault.

He nodded, putting his foot on the carved wooden chest at the end of her bed to tie his shoelace. 'I think it'll be okay. I'll confirm with you by Tuesday at the latest.'

Again, no explanations, no details. But what did it matter, she asked herself. As long as he could pull it off. She could count on one hand the number of times they'd managed a weekend together. Now, with her birthday a fortnight away, there seemed a real chance that he was going to give her the best gift of all.

'That's wonderful.' But she didn't dare let herself get too excited. Not until it was definite.

He was ready to leave. Tina swung out of bed, wrapped herself in a pale blue gown and walked with him to the front door.

'I guess I'd better say goodbye here.'

She'd forgotten about the dog and the man who now lived over her garage.

'He said he'd keep it inside. You should be safe this time.'

'I'm not worried.' He slipped his arms around her and gently pulled her close.

'It was wonderful, my love. You were wonderful.'

At times like this, she found herself flinching inwardly at the clichéd response. As if he were playing the part of an adulterous husband in a soap opera. Only this soap opera was her life.

Chapter 7

JUDY LARKIN, THE SOCIAL WORKER, rang while Marnie was on her way to the new site at Blakehurst. The slabs had been poured a week ago and the frames were ready to start.

'Sorry to worry you, Marnie. We had a slight problem here last night and I was hoping it'd be possible you could spare a guy to do some repairs.'

'Shoot, what happened?' Marnie spoke through the green apple she was crunching. She hadn't had time for breakfast.

'You remember that woman, Fran Morris? She'd just come in the last time you were here.'

Marnie had a vague recollection of the tearful young woman she'd passed on the way into Judy's office. '

'What about her?'

She listened as Judy quickly explained how Fran Morris's husband had somehow managed to track her down.

'He went berserk. Smashed a few windows and then lost it even further when he realized there were bars as well. Must've been drunk or drugged not to have seen them to begin with. Finally he drove his car through the front fence and onto the patio. Fran was terrified. Everyone was. We rang the cops, but of course they took for ever. He only pissed off when he saw he wasn't going to be able to get at her. So, for everyone's sake, I'm going to have to move her. There isn't a bed available anywhere else for a couple of nights so I thought I'd lift some petty cash and put her and the daughter in a motel somewhere. Not that she's keen on the idea. Too scared shitless he's going to find her and really make a mess of her.'

'When did you reckon there'd be a bed free, somewhere?'

'Two days. Karen's got one coming up.' Judy was referring to another halfway house on the other side of the city.

Marnie frowned. 'I don't like the thought of leaving them alone in a motel somewhere.'

'Neither does she, but what else can I do?'

'How old's the child?'

'Nine.'

'I'm just wondering if I could put them up at my place for that time. It's been done before.'

'Has it?' The social worker's tone was innocent.

Marnie chuckled. 'Cut the crap, Judy. I know your game plan exactly.'

'Only in an emergency,' the other woman answered gently. 'And I'll think of you in my prayers.'

'Sure, sure. Look, get them out of there safely and think of somewhere I can pick them up. I'll meet them around five, okay?'

"Thanks a million, Marnie. And the repairs ...?'

'I'll work that miracle, too.'

The rest of her day was frantic. Keith was handling things on the new site but there was still plenty they had to discuss. It was after midday before she got away.

On the way back to the city, she called in at home and changed from her work clothes into something a little more up-market. A couple of months ago, a journalist from the *Sydney Morning Herald* had requested an interview for a Property special. They were interested, he said, in doing a profile on a successful female developer in what was still, predominantly, a man's world.

With everything that had been happening in her life recently, Marnie had been on the point of cancelling through sheer lack of time if nothing else. But when she finally paused to give the idea some thought, she changed her mind. A profile in the *Herald* might be just what she needed at this point in her negotiations with the local council. It would show them she was a force to be reckoned with, give her a bit of leverage. Maybe she could even get in a dig or two about her problem if she picked her words carefully.

She was due to meet the journalist in the foyer of the Intercontinental Hotel. A photo would be needed too they'd told her, and with that in mind, she pulled on a black pantsuit she'd bought a couple of years ago in New York. It fitted her like a glove; who cared if black was in, or out, this season? An off-white silk shirt, slim heels and a gold necklace completed the effect. In the bathroom mirror, she raised an appraising eyebrow at her reflection. She'd show that bastard Sawyer and his council cronies and lap dogs. If they thought they were dealing with Shirley bloody Temple they had another think coming, didn't they?

The journo, Sean Allen, was young enough to be her son. Close-cropped fair hair, casually dressed, fashionably insouciant manner. God, Marnie thought, save me from these 'hip' kids.

The accompanying photographer got his part of the action out of the way first. He took a dozen or so quick shots, uttering no more than the necessary instructions. When he left, drinks were brought and Sean Allen placed his small tape recorder on the table between them.

Marnie had no objection. At least, hopefully, it meant she'd be accurately quoted.

'Let's get rolling then, shall we?' Clearly, he was not about to waste any time in small talk. Flipping open a small notebook, he shot her a question.

'So, tell me, how long have you been in the industry?'

Matching his clipped style, Marnie replied, 'I renovated my first house in my twenties. Made money, and thought to myself, how easy's this? Did a few more renos and eventually began to buy sites to develop as multi-projects about twelve years ago.'

'As a woman, what do you feel you bring to a project that might be different from a male developer?'

'A lot. I think my strength as a woman is to understand what people really need, to be comfortable in a home. In other words, I don't allow practicality to be subordinate to form. I've seen too many major developments where the principal concern is the overall look of the place rather than how it will actually work for the human beings living there. People can't really enjoy living in something that is primarily a work of art.'

They explored that point for a while as well as Marnie's past and current projects. When the young journalist asked if she found the business tough as a female in the field, she got her chance to make a subtle reference to the problems on the inner west site.

'I think the whole issue of the decision-making process by councils should be open to scrutiny. In my own case, I'm sure there are opposing interests involved.'

Sean Allen expressed doubt on what they could print in that regard. He made a show of scribbling a note in his flip pad, but Marnie felt sure he'd sidestep the issue in his article. The threat of legal complications had made everyone gutless.

'Okay, we're just about through, I guess. But I wanted to ask about the halfway houses.'

Marnie realized he'd done his homework.

'That goes way back,' she explained. 'I'd only been in Sydney a few months, was sharing a house near the beach with a couple of girls. It was a big place with a separate room and bathroom underneath. One night we were having a party, when someone asked if we'd help out a friend who'd been bashed by her husband and needed a place to stay for a while.'

Marnie took a sip of her drink, remembering how it had all started. 'Back then, I had no idea such things happened. I was shocked, to tell you the truth. But I soon discovered it was a problem that existed at all levels of society. Later, I guess it became a pet project of mine. When I was buying up places to renovate, I'd let three or four women stay in them until I was ready to pull them down. Now there are permanent safe houses, funded by donation and run with the help of a very small staff. I oversee the fund-raising committee.'

Sean Allen, king of cool, tried not to look impressed. The woman was a dynamo.

'Yeah, well, I guess that brings me to my last question. What the hell do you do to chill out?'

Marnie laughed. 'Are you kidding? My idea of relaxation is to get to the hairdresser once a month. And even then I hate sitting still. But,' she added, 'I do try to get to Bali every year. I've got a house at Ubud. In the mountains. That's my retreat. Although,' she grinned, 'I do have a small sideline importing custom-made furnishing — looks good in my display units too.'

Pointedly, she gave a glance at her watch. She'd have to ring Judy and see where to pick up that woman and child.

Sean Allen switched off his tape recorder. He'd got all he needed. He could do something with this. With a bit of luck, it might even get him a cover.

Fran Morris was sitting in the social worker's car at the service station in Randwick Road, waiting to be picked up.

As she and her daughter transferred to the SUV, Marnie could see the woman's nervousness.

'Everything okay?' she asked as she took the small, shabby suitcase from Judy's hand.

'Yeah, we were careful. I'm sure we weren't followed. I haven't heard from the cops, but maybe they've put the shits up him. They came and did a report on the damage.'

'Well, we all know we can count on the boys in blue, don't we?'

The social worker ignored the cynicism. 'Karen's promised us a bed by the day after tomorrow. I'll call you.' She nodded towards the SUV. 'D'you think you'll need me to drop in on these two any time? While you're not there, I mean.'

'I'll see how they go.'

'Okay, well... Thanks again, Marnie.'

Fran Morris was monosyllabic in reply to Marnie's attempts at conversation. In the back seat, her nine- year-old daughter said nothing as they made their way through the peak-hour traffic.

It wasn't until Marnie opened the door of her apartment that the little girl finally spoke.

'Do you live here alone?'

She stood on the threshold, staring up at Marnie with serious blue eyes too big for her pinched, anxious face.

'Yes.'

'I mean, really alone. Without any ... man?'

Marnie suddenly understood. Crouching down, she took the two small hands in her own. The child's name was Shelley. 'There's no one here but me, darling. And now just you and Mum too. We'll all be quite safe, I promise.'

What had this child seen, she wondered. How deep were the scars from the frightening world she'd grown up in? Marnie remembered her own childhood and thought about the many different ways there were to damage children.

'Now,' she said, as she stood up and ushered them both inside, 'what about a warm bath and then we can make dinner together?'

It wasn't until her daughter was asleep on the sofa in Marnie's office that Fran Morris finally began to speak, hesitantly and nervously, about the nightmare of her marriage. It was a story Marnie had heard many times before. A too-young marriage founded on a woman's economic need and the fantasy of love, that had blinded her to the reality of the man she had chosen as her 'protector' and mate. For Fran, as for so many others, the bashings had started even before the pregnancy had gone full term.

'But I didn't know where to go, or what to do. And, you know, I still loved him then, I really did.' The thin young woman spoke in the defeated, apologetic tones of the natural victim. 'And I thought it'd get better when we had Shelley to bond us.'

How many times had she heard that, Marnie thought. Didn't these women ever look around them and see what was happening in the real world? Hadn't they seen the examples of their friends?

But, she reminded herself, so many of them had never been taught to envisage options or value their own individuality. There were some who, even when they'd found their way to the transitory safety of a halfway house, made excuses for the men who had broken their ribs or blackened their eyes. As in Fran Morris's case, it was only when their children's lives were also threatened that some of them finally found the resolution to leave for good.

Marnie could see that it was doing her unexpected house guest good to talk. For Fran Morris, the next step would involve finding a job, a permanent place to live and fighting for her legal rights in relation to the bully she'd escaped from. This was where Judy and her colleagues worked hand in hand with government departments. It was a difficult process, and a slow one but the sense of achievement for everyone concerned when they could help a woman turn her life around was the best of rewards.

The next morning, she left her two house guests happily eating breakfast together in the sunny kitchen. Marnie had never seen either of them in her life before, but she had to trust them in her home. Anyway, she thought, as she took the elevator to the car park, what did she have that was so precious? Her lips curved in silent amusement. Maybe only her design schedules for the stalled project.

She was almost at the site when her mobile rang. It was Anthony Corkdale in Melbourne. At the sound of his voice, she felt herself tense. She'd been in touch with him regularly, checking on her father's progress. There must be something wrong.

'Marnie, I wanted you to know straightaway — there have been some positive signs since we last spoke. Charles is responding to stimuli and they are fairly sure he's going to pull through. To what degree they're not sure of course, but what it means is that they'll want to move him as soon as possible.'

'Move him?' Marnie didn't understand.

'I mean to a nursing home somewhere. You know how it is with hospital beds these days: all the money in the world won't keep you there if there are other options. Just where that move will be, is a decision I think you must have the major say in.'

Marnie frowned. 'So there's no chance he'll be able to go home?'

'Not according to his doctors. Of course, as I say, they're not sure just how much of a recovery to expect but, whatever happens, they're of the firm opinion that he'll certainly need more specialized care and a more protected environment.'

'I see.' Marnie was thinking through the implications as she kept her eyes on the road. 'That means I'll have to do something about the house too then?'

'That's right. I was going to bring that up with you. And I've put together a list of possible nursing homes for your consideration. When do you see yourself free to come down again?'

Free? She was never free ...

'Let me check my diary and get back to you, Anthony.'

She switched off her phone. Jesus ... how much more was she going to get on her plate at once?

For the rest of the journey, Marnie was forced to confront her conflicting emotions. She knew she should feel glad about her father's chance of recovery, but, if she were brutally honest, it made little difference. How could she feel for a man with whom she had had so little connection for most of her existence? If anything, her overriding emotion was of resentment at the demands now being made on her already busy life. After all, how many times had her father ever put himself out for her?

It didn't escape her notice that the voice she heard in her head sounded like that of a wounded child.

Lee felt her irritation grow from the moment she walked in the door. The television was blaring in the family room with no one watching it and the kitchen benches were littered with the crusts and leftovers of someone's sandwich lunch.

She switched off the TV and walked over to call sharply up the stairs. 'Anybody here?'

A damp towel hung over the banister rail, and with a frown she snatched it off and threw it across the hall into the laundry. For God's sake, couldn't any of them have tidied up when they knew she was due home?

Danny appeared at the door of his room, phone stuck to his ear. He gave his mother a distracted wave and disappeared again.

Where the hell was Brad? Irritated, Lee went to look for him in the back garden.

She found him next door, still in his work clothes, peering into the engine of their neighbor's vehicle.

'Oh, hi, love.' He gave her a wave over the fence. 'Won't be a minute. How was it?'

'Great,' she answered coolly and walked back into the house. It would have been nice to get a kiss, to find someone interested in sitting down and hearing about how she'd managed.

She was in the kitchen, cleaning up the mess in order to start preparing dinner when Brad finally walked in.

He planted a kiss on her cheek and didn't seem to notice her coolness. 'So how'd it go? Any problems?'

She felt like saying that the only problem had been coming back to her messy home and ungrateful family. But, she reminded herself grudgingly, it was the first time she'd ever left them to cope alone.

'No. Anita was pleased. Everything went fine.'

'How was the flat? Did you hate it too much being on your own?'

Lee kept her eyes on the bench she was wiping clean. Hate it? How would he react, she wondered, if she told him the truth? That in actual fact she'd really loved the time by herself.

'It was okay.'

What really got to her, she decided, was that Brad thought — they probably all thought — that she couldn't exist without them. It never occurred to them that maybe she could actually enjoy her own company. That the four of them didn't have to be the only focus in her life.

'Well,' Brad turned on the tap to wash his hands, 'only three more weeks to go, then things'll be back to normal.'

Something felt like it was about to explode in Lee's chest.

Julie had rung to say she was having dinner at Joel's place. They'd been together almost eight months; Joel, a couple of years older, worked in a suburban real estate office and was studying surveying at night. A pleasant, good-looking boy, he had recently moved into his own flat and that was worrying enough as far as Lee was concerned. She was hoping the relationship would break up when Julie started university next month. She had bigger aspirations for her daughter than the 'boy next door'. But then, she thought tartly, perhaps that would end up being a pipe dream too.

The two of them turned up just as Lee was getting ready to go to bed.

'Hi, Mum.' Julie kissed her mother warily on the cheek. She wasn't sure if things were still going to be awkward between them. 'How'd it go? What's the shop like?'

'Busy. But I coped fine. What have you two been up to?'

It was Joel who answered. 'Buying Julie's uni books. Got a lot second-hand.'

Julie looked as if she wished he hadn't mentioned anything about her starting university. Picking up the electric kettle, she changed the subject. 'We're just going to have a coffee before Joel goes.'

Lee had known Brad would want to have sex that night. After it was over, she couldn't help thinking that it felt as if he were trying to mark his own ground again, reclaim ownership, remind her that her single life was only temporary.

Then again, she thought dryly, that was probably assuming a bit too much introspection on Brad's behalf. His lust was no doubt as simple and straightforward as always: once or twice a week. Her orgasm first — even if she didn't feel like it, she had to crank one up so his ego didn't suffer — then the silent surrender of his own release. He never uttered a word or a moan, even though once, long ago, she'd plucked up the courage to tell him that it would excite her if he was more vocal. He'd made a few awkward attempts, before silence had ruled again, and she'd never revisited the subject.

But at least, she thought now as she lay with her head against his chest, he did like to cuddle afterwards. According to what she heard from her girlfriends, that was hardly the norm. And he was, all in all, a considerate lover. They'd never really had a problem there. It was just that sometimes she felt they could push the boundaries a little more.

'I missed you, love. Seemed strange not to have you here when I got home.'

She should have been able to say that she'd missed him too. But, in all honesty, she couldn't. The words seemed glued somewhere deep in her throat. She knew it was because they would have been a lie.

Yet she didn't want to hurt him. She patted his cheek instead. And thought how she couldn't wait to get back to Sydney.

The apartment was sparsely furnished: a sleek, black leather sofa he'd waited to pick up in the June sales, a simple glass dining table with four chrome and leather chairs.

The man's tastes were expensive and he would rather do without than settle for crap. He had always been ambitious, filled with a self-confidence that made him certain of his future. One day, the rented apartment would be exchanged for a place of his own with the obligatory water views, the second-hand BMW replaced with the latest model. Whatever it took.

He grinned now as he took in his appearance in the bathroom mirror. Smart suit. Designer tie. Fashionable haircut.

Looking the part took you a long way in his line of work.

This time, Lee was in charge of the shop from Wednesday to Friday She left home very early Wednesday morning and arrived back late Friday night. On Thursday evening, when Veronique was open late, Tracey, the young university student, came in to help and Lee was able to take a short break. Not that she minded the hours. It was no real chore to work in such a pretty, feminine environment. She enjoyed helping her customers find what they were looking for, or coaxing them into matching bits and pieces they might never have chosen for themselves.

Nor were women her only customers. The men who ventured into Veronique fell, as usual, into two main categories: those who were quite at ease amongst the frills and lace of intimate female attire and those who couldn't quite conceal their discomfort. Some were married, some had girlfriends, some brought pictures from men's magazines to indicate what they were looking for. It always amused Lee that, while many of her women customers put comfort and practicality first when buying lingerie, men invariably went for the raunchier option. Garter belts were a favorite, as well as bustiers and G-strings, even though there were few of her male customers who had much idea of their partner's size. Lee had to fight to keep a straight face when they actually brought grapefruits and rock melons into their reckoning! In the end, she would always steer them towards a smaller size when they weren't sure, opting for flattery as the better option in the circumstances.

'Don't worry,' she would assure them, 'the garments can always be exchanged.'

Logically, the men who were most certain about their partner's size were the married ones. Compared to the shop in Newcastle, Lee couldn't believe how much money some of them were prepared to spend on gifts for their wives. That morning, for instance, a well-heeled customer had bought two of their most expensive La Perla bra and brief sets as well as a beautiful silk nightdress.

Later, when Anita rang, Lee mentioned the impressive sale. 'I couldn't believe it!'

'That sounds like Mike Tolman. One of my best customers. Did you see the name on the card?'

'Yes, that was it, I think. Attractive, dark-haired, very well dressed?'

'That's him. He's a regular. Comes in about once a month or so.'

'Well,' Lee replied, 'lucky wife is all I can say.'

Anita rang every day to check that all was well. Lee was happy to report that things were running smoothly. She knew her employer had enough to handle coping with her daughter.

'How's Terri managing?' she inquired now.

'Not well.' She could hear the tension in Anita's voice. 'Nothing seems able to snap her out of it. If she isn't crying, she's back in bed, sleeping till all hours. Totally ignoring the baby. The doctor told me it'll take a while, but I'm really at my wits' end.'

'Well, don't worry about anything here. I can manage.' Lee hesitated and then added, 'You know, if you need me for longer, I'm sure I could manage it.'

'Thanks, darling. That's a wonderful offer. Let's just hope I don't have to take you up on it.'

Lee thought about Anita's predicament as she was closing up the shop that evening. While not wishing her employer's trauma to continue, she would certainly love an excuse to keep spending the three days a week in Sydney. Brad would kick up a fuss, of course, but she'd find some way of handling that. He certainly didn't have a problem with the money she was bringing home.

Tonight, though it was late closing, and she'd arranged to meet with Tina and Marnie for a meal at North Sydney, a spot fairly central for them all. A pity, she thought, as she crawled the streets searching for a parking spot, that she only had two nights in Sydney and one of them was late-night closing. It'd be great to catch up with her friends more often, as well as have time to explore what the city had to offer. She wondered how Brad would take it if she told him she was going to spend an occasional Friday night away as well.

Not too bloody well — of that she was certain. As she finally found a spot and eased her car into the kerb, Lee felt a familiar irritation. Why did she have to feel like a prisoner? What harm would it do just to spend an extra night catching up with her old friends? Brad had his outlets —

indoor cricket, coaching the Under 12s football team on Saturday afternoons, fishing. She didn't tell him what he could and couldn't do. Why should it be any different for her? It wasn't as if she were doing anything to jeopardize her marriage.

The restaurant was noisy and busy. It took her a moment to see Tina waving at her from a corner table. Marnie was there too.

'Hi!' Lee smiled widely as she bent to kiss her friends. 'Am I late?'

'No, just in time,' Marnie replied. 'Hope you're hungry. The laksa here is legendary.'

Lee pulled in her chair. 'I've never —'

'Try it, you'll love it,' Marnie interrupted her.

'So tell us about the job,' Tina said as the waitress poured water into Lee's glass. 'Are you enjoying it?'

'Loving it. And just loving being in Sydney. It's brilliant.'

'Very different from when we were kids,' Tina said.

'Yes,' Marnie put in, 'bigger, dirtier, noisier — but it still beats Melbourne hands down.'

'Have you been down south recently?' Tina asked, suddenly remembering that maybe it wasn't a good idea to remind Lee of that time all those years ago.

As Marnie filled them in on what was happening with her father, none of them noticed the well- dressed man who had slipped onto a seat at the bar. Concealed by the crowd around him, his eyes were fixed on the three women.

It was just a matter of time, he told himself. He knew exactly how to deal with the problem. All he had to do was convince the other party involved.

As far as Tina was concerned, she barely knew her lodger was there. He left for work before she did and, by the time she got home, his ute was in the garage and he was out of the way upstairs.

Occasionally, on the weekend, their paths crossed. She'd be driving out of the garage just as he came home, newspaper under his arm, Digger on a lead. They'd wave, exchange a few polite words and that would be it. Every second Friday, he'd leave his rent check in her mailbox, so she really couldn't say that he interfered with her privacy.

At the same time, it gave her a feeling of security to see the light on above the garage when she came home late. Just knowing there was someone else close by helped to ease her fears about another break-in. The dog was an excellent deterrent, too. It knew the sound of her car now and never reacted, no matter how late she arrived home. Yet it still barked from inside the flat when anyone else, including Dean, came to the gate.

'It's really working fine,' she'd told Marnie the night they'd all met for dinner. 'If he wants to stay on after the three months, I won't have any objection.'

'Well, I've got plenty to keep him busy for a while,' Marnie replied. 'He's a good tradesman. Not to mention a hunk,' she added, giving Tina a teasing look. 'Or hadn't you noticed?'

Tina rolled her eyes. 'Get serious, Marnie.'

The following Saturday morning, Tina had a reason to talk with Mark Galloway. She was making her way up the back steps to the flat, but before she could knock on the door, it opened.

'Digger told me!' Mark smiled at her surprised expression. 'Low growl number four, someone approaching. Low growl number three is when I've forgotten to feed him by 6 p.m. There's a subtle difference.'

'Oh.' Somehow, he always seemed to flat-foot her with his left of field remarks.

'Look, I'm sorry to disturb you,' she began.

'Would you like to come in?' He stood back from the open door.

'Oh, no. Thanks, really.' There was no way she was about to break the no-socializing rule. 'It's just that I thought I should mention I'll be away next weekend. I'm leaving Friday morning and won't be back till Sunday night. Will you be around?'

'Sure. It's not my weekend to see the kids.'

'Well, that'll work out fine then. Someone will be here. Thanks a lot.'

She turned to go and then, remembering, stopped to add, 'I won't be taking my car.'

'Okay.'

There was no curiosity and she was thankful for that. She wasn't about to offer any explanations.

She had taken a step back down the stairs, when he said, 'Can I ask you something?'

Tina stopped and turned to him. 'Sure.'

'It's about the pool service. The guy was just leaving when I got home the other day. Don't know what it's costing you, but I'd be happy to do it. For nothing, I mean. I've got plenty of time in the afternoons.'

'Oh.' She was quickly running through the ramifications of the offer. Was she being backed into a corner? Did it mean he wanted her to offer to let him use the pool too? It hadn't occurred to her. But then was that really such a big deal? She barely had time to use the damn thing herself.

'Well ... if you really don't mind. That'd be nice of you. Just let me know what I need to get in the way of supplies, salt or whatever.'

'I'll pick them up if you like, and drop the bill in with my rent.'

'Actually, that was something else I can probably bring up with you now.'

She saw his expression change. Maybe he thought she was going to ask him to leave.

She hurried to reassure him. 'If you're happy to stay on for another three months, that's fine with me. I think it's working okay.'

He smiled then. His white teeth were perfect, she noticed. 'That's great. It's working for me too.'

As the week progressed, her excitement grew at the thought of spending two whole days and nights with Dean. They were driving to a resort in the Hunter Valley wine district. Dean would pick her up at home around 4 p.m. and hopefully they'd beat the worst of the Friday night snarl heading out of the city. She could hardly wait.

On the Thursday, she had been invited to be the guest speaker at a fund-raising luncheon for the Children's Hospital. It was the sort of request she often received from various organizations and was usually happy to comply. Not only did it help to raise money for good causes, but it was also an excellent way of attracting business.

The luncheon was being held at the Sheraton on the Park and, as Tina entered the function room, she could see it was well attended. The chatter from groups of expensively dressed women, drinks in hands, filled the air.

'Looks like you're popular, Tina.' The hotel PR was all smiles at the excellent turn out. 'Let me get you a drink and introduce you to a few people.'

Tina accepted an orange juice from a passing waiter as the PR led her to a nearby group.

'Ladies, I'd like to introduce our guest speaker, Tina Christo.' She turned to Tina. 'This is our hospital committee. They're the ones who do the hard work of thinking up ways to pull money out of people's pockets.'

The four women were introduced in turn and Tina had just begun to make some polite remark when she was interrupted by a voice behind her.

'Oh, am I too late? I really wanted to meet this clever lady.'

One of the group laughed and said, 'Kathy's on the committee too, but she's always late to everything.'

An attractive, fair-haired woman in a grey silk suit and pearls held out her hand to Tina and smiled. 'Don't take any notice of them. I'm Kathy Ashley. So glad to meet you. Thank you for doing this for us today.'

Tina felt the blood drain from her face. She came close to losing her grip on her glass.

It was Dean's wife.

She had seen her a couple of times from a distance when she'd been parked outside the house. And there had once been a photo in some social spread. She couldn't believe this was happening.

'My — my pleasure.' She was still feeling the shock.

At that moment, to her enormous relief, the PR interrupted. 'It's past time,' she said, pointing to her watch. 'I think we should get everyone sitting down, don't you?'

She turned to the guest speaker. 'You're at the same table as the committee, of course, Tina.'

Tina felt as if she were going to be sick.

It was the worst two hours she could ever remember. She had to sit across the table from the wife of her lover and try to make normal conversation, then gather herself sufficiently to make her usually dynamic presentation.

What made it more difficult, if that were possible, was the fact that Kathy Ashley was such a nice person. Not that Tina had ever tried to imagine what she was like; her way of dealing with the situation had been to make every effort not to think of Dean's wife at all. And suddenly there she was, sitting so close to her, listening to her talk about her daughters, about the renovations to her home, even the fact that she was visiting her parents at their holiday house this weekend.

'My poor husband can't make it of course,' Kathy Ashley said as she broke open her bread roll. 'He's one of those driven types, I'm afraid. There's always some conference somewhere that he really can't get out of. But,' she raised a shoulder in a shrug of resignation, 'I guess I've learned to live with it. He's happy, so I guess I've got to be too. It's the girls I really feel for. They adore their father and see so little of him.'

Tina knew that in the normal course of events, her next question to this warm, intelligent woman should be to inquire what her husband did for a living. But she couldn't; she just couldn't. Her fingers curled tightly around her fork. She cut up and moved the food around her plate barely able to swallow more than a mouthful. How could she be sitting here opposite the wife of the lover with whom she was intending to spend the weekend? How could such an unbearable situation have happened? All she wanted was to give her talk and run out of the place as quickly as possible.

The afternoon finally ended and she made her escape, but she was too shaken to think of going back to the office. The situation had unnerved her. Kathy Ashley had been such a likeable woman. Not only attractive, but clever and gently amusing. In some crazy, warped way Tina felt bad about Dean's deception.

But why focus only on Dean? As if she herself were some naïve innocent party. It was all too horrible to think about. Her anticipation of the weekend was completely spoilt now. How could she enjoy herself in her lover's arms with the image of his wife to haunt her? Her stomach churned with confused emotion.

But of one thing she was certain: she wasn't going to mention this unexpected meeting to Dean.

'You're a bit quiet, darling.'

It was Friday afternoon and they were in Dean's Audi, heading up the highway out of Sydney.

'Am I? Just thinking about work, I suppose.' She'd have to make an effort. She couldn't let what had happened spoil the whole weekend.

He took a hand off the wheel and patted her knee. 'Work's off the agenda for the next two days, okay?' he chided with a smile.

Tina forced a brightness she didn't feel. 'You're absolutely right. We're going to make this a weekend to remember.'

She had no idea how true her words would be.

The resort was comprised of one- and two-bedroom villas set amongst rolling parkland. 'Golf for those who want it,' Dean joked, as they settled in, 'wine and women for the rest of us.'

'In what order?' Tina teased. She was feeling a little better. Perhaps it had something to do with having left Sydney behind.

In reply, Dean moved up behind her and slowly drew down the zip of her dress. 'I'm greedy,' he whispered into her neck. 'What about a wonderful chardonnay drunk on that enormous bed?'

Tina shivered as he slipped her dress to the floor.

For once, they had the luxury of time. But even with protracted foreplay, Tina found it difficult to become aroused. Like most women, her mind and sexual response were finely intertwined and, try as she might to rid herself of the thought of Dean's wife, she wasn't entirely successful. As a result, her ability to respond to Dean's caresses was directly affected.

By now they understood each other's bodies so well, and she could tell he was aware of her difficulty. In the same way, she could sense his anxiety. Like most good lovers, she knew he would blame himself for her lack of normal response. She didn't want that to happen. Nor could she tell him the reason for her difficulty. In the end, she did something she'd never had to resort to before. She faked an orgasm.

Afterwards, they took a shower and had dinner delivered to their villa — a matter of discretion as well as convenience. With an effort, Tina managed to act as if everything were all right. But she was uncomfortable, and frustrated physically — and feeling even worse about the pretense.

Still, better that, she told herself, than having to tell her lover the truth.

The next morning, Dean headed off for a swim in the resort pool and afterwards they ate breakfast together on the patio. It was a glorious day and the only sounds were bird calls and the occasional whack of a golf ball.

'So what's on the agenda?' she asked, as she poured them both another cup of coffee.

'What say we try the vineyard tour? They can arrange transport at the front desk. We'd be back by mid afternoon.'

'Sounds fine to me. I'd be happy to have a look around.'

Neither of them broached the subject, but they were both aware of the threat, no matter how remote, of bumping into someone who knew Dean. It was a constant fear wherever they went and Tina hated the need to be always on the alert. If Dean were free, they could go wherever they wanted, be totally open about the way they felt for each other. But as time went on, she was starting to believe less and less that that dream would ever come true. Maybe this was all her life was ever going to be with him, she thought — rare, snatched moments in out- of-the-way places until...

Until what? He got sick of her? She couldn't bear it any longer?

As she went to clean her teeth and gather up her things, she told herself that she wasn't going to let such thoughts intrude on this weekend. But that was the ongoing problem, she recognized. She always ended up doing her best to avoid confronting the issue head-on, and certainly she dodged it openly with Dean.

Which meant that nothing changed and she was left with her inner doubts and growing despair.

They arrived back at the villa just before four.

'Amazing what a little sip here and there can do to you.' Dean grinned as he slipped the keycard into the lock. He'd enjoyed tasting the various wines and had bought a couple of boxes of reds which he would leave at Tina's.

'Good thing one of us knows her limits,' she joked. She'd never had much capacity for alcohol, but had enjoyed the afternoon visiting the various wineries, some of them well-known names, others the boutique outlets.

'I think I'll take a shower,' she added, heading for the bathroom — then stopped in her tracks when she saw the expression on Dean's face. He had picked up his mobile and was listening to his messages.

As soon as he'd finished, he dialed again, clearly agitated when his call was not answered.

'Kathy, it's me. It's ...' he checked his watch, 'ten past four. I'll leave straightaway and see you at the hospital.'

Tina felt her belly tighten. 'What is it?'

He answered quickly, his distraction obvious. 'Belinda's had an accident at netball. She's been taken to North Shore Hospital.'

'Is it serious?' But Tina knew her weekend was over.

'Something about an accident on the concrete steps as she came off the court. Kathy's message was a bit garbled. I think she's too upset to get things straight. Wants me to come straight to the hospital. She's probably had to turn her phone off in the emergency room.'

He moved closer and put his hands on Tina's arms. 'I'm sorry, darling. I've got to get back. You understand, don't you? There's no way I could stay and enjoy myself when I'm not sure what's happening with my little girl.'

Tina stared back into his anxious face.

'I'll drive,' she said simply.

She was home just after seven-thirty. Dean had carried in her suitcase and the two cartons of wine then headed directly to the hospital.

They hadn't spoken much on the trip back. She could tell he was lost in his worried thoughts and her sense of exclusion was total. There was no role for her in this family drama; just as she now knew there would never be a legitimate role for her in his life. All this emergency had done was highlight what she already knew and had done her best to ignore: that the man she loved had a whole other existence which didn't include her and never would. She would never have the hold on him that his wife and children had. He would never leave them, no matter how much she continued to hope he would.

During the quiet intensity of that car journey together, she had bluntly imagined her life over the next ten or fifteen years. Always on the outside. Existing on the crumbs of his time and whatever emotion he had left over when the other women in his life had been satisfied.

She had seen the person Kathy Ashley was and for that reason alone Tina could no longer fool herself. Dean was far from enduring a penance, a hell on earth. He had told her himself that there was no real source of conflict in his marriage. And, if there was nothing so terrible about his life, why should he ever feel any pressure to leave?

Her only option now was to extricate herself from the situation as quickly and with as much dignity as possible. But this moment of crisis was hardly the right time. Rather, her agony would be prolonged as she endured the days until they were able to meet again.

In the front hall, he had kissed her a quick goodbye. 'I'll let you know. I'll call you when I can.' She could tell by his voice and expression that he was already somewhere else.

As she shut the door behind him, she faced the bald truth that she felt little emotion about his child's accident beyond her concern for Dean himself. The child wasn't hers. Why should it affect her more than any other accident she skimmed over in the paper and felt a momentary sympathy about?

Utterly drained, she carried her small case upstairs. Lifting it onto the bed, she automatically began to unpack. It was something to do instead of wallowing in her misery.

But when she came to the sexy lingerie she'd packed with such excited expectation, the tension of the last few hours hit home. Dropping onto the bed, she covered her face with her hands and began to weep. It wasn't fair. It just wasn't fair. Why should other women be happy and not her? Why was the one man she loved not free to love her back?

A moment later a sudden noise distracted her from her distress. What was that? She sat up, rigid and alert, alarm leaping inside her.

Heart racing, she moved quickly and quietly to the top of the stairs. She could clearly hear something outside. At once she thought of Mark. He said he'd be here. Why hadn't he heard anything? And what about the dog?

The next moment a voice called out. 'Is that you, Tina? Are you home?'

Relief pumped through her as she recognized Mark's voice. She hurried down the stairs. Of course, he must have seen the lights and had the same fears as herself.

'Yes, it's me!' she called out as she snapped on the hall light and made her way to the front door. She could see his shadow through the side glass panel.

The key was in the lock and she opened the door, still weak with relief. Mark was standing on the doorstep, the dog by his side.

'I'm sorry,' he apologized. 'I didn't realize you were back. I went out to get some takeaway and when I drove in, I saw the lights on.'

'It's my fault. I just completely forgot. I...'

'Is everything okay?' He was looking at her with concern and she realized there was perhaps enough light for him to see the evidence of her distress on her face.

With an effort, she forced a lightness into her tone. 'Yes, fine, really. Something ... just came up and we — I — had to come back. No real problem.'

For a moment he said nothing, merely stared back at her. His gaze made her uncomfortable. For God's sake, she thought, why didn't he just go?

Finally, he nodded. 'Well, if you're sure you're okay, I won't disturb you any longer. Good night.'

'Good night. And thanks.'

Chapter 8

'IT'S ME, DAD, MARNIE.'

Charles Ingram's faded blue eyes slowly moved to focus on the woman sitting by his bed. His mouth spread in a vague smile and his fingers tightened weakly around Marnie's own.

'You see, there is some response now.' Anthony Corkdale bent and spoke quietly near Marnie's ear. 'We have to think positive.'

On the surface, the stroke appeared to have left no evidence beyond a minimal droop to the right side of her father's mouth. But to Marnie, there were other less obvious but more poignant changes.

It was as if the enormous gusto and energy of the man had been sucked out. He lay under the too- tight sheets like a felled giant. A curious, old- fashioned expression, she thought, but the one that sprang most quickly to her mind. All her life, her father had had immense presence, a commanding persona. She hardly recognized him as this feeble figure tucked into a hospital bed.

During all the time he had lain still and unresponsive, her reaction had been overtly rational and pragmatic. He might die from the stroke or he might recover, but if he recovered, she had expected him to be the person she remembered. Now she saw that her father was never going to be that person again.

The shock she felt was sharp and unexpected. This vague and frail man who lay in front of her was a stranger. The father she had known was gone. For the first time, she acknowledged that somewhere deep inside her she had held onto a vague hope of some measure of reconciliation. Only now did she realize that the part of her that was still that needy child had been waiting for a miracle, a time when her father would reach out to her and try to explain the reasons why he had treated her like he did.

The warmth of tears filled her eyes. At the heart of the grief she felt now, lay the realization that there was no longer any chance of that miracle happening.

Afterwards, Anthony dropped her off at the house. Her plan was to spend the weekend sorting through her parents' possessions. A challenging task, but one she couldn't delegate to anyone else. Then on Sunday afternoon, she would have to make time to visit the two aged-care facilities that the solicitor had narrowed down from the list prepared for Charles Ingram.

'It's not quite a matter of autonomous choice,' Anthony Corkdale had explained as they drove away from the hospital. 'Your father's level of care has been assessed by a government aged-care team. It was up to them to indicate which places they considered most appropriate.'

Marnie said nothing, absorbing what she was being told. It was a whole new world; one she had never given any thought to before. It had never occurred to her that her strong, resilient and fiercely independent father would ever end up so diminished and in need of such all-encompassing care. She still found it hard to believe that he would never return to the home he had lived in for more than forty years. How much would he understand of that as time went on? Would enough of his faculties be left intact that he would blame her for removing him from all that was familiar?

The questions played on her mind as she tackled the draining task of trying to decide what to keep and what to throw away from the family home. Should she keep the rosewood grandfather clock that had been a wedding present from her grandparents? What should she do with the dozens of photo albums, her mother's favorite LPs, her father's business records, the paintings, books and other keepsakes collected over a lifetime?

The furniture was simple, she figured: she'd get a dealer in to give her a price for the antiques and better pieces, and the Salvos could have the rest. But she felt an emotional tug at the thought of parting with her parents' carved cedar bed and the faded wingback chair her mother had sat and cuddled her in while they read together.

Trying to keep anything much for herself was not an option. Modern accommodation made little allowance for storing the mementoes of the past. And what would be the point anyway? She had no children of her own to pass them on to. There were no future generations to take any interest in the residue of lives that had preceded and given rise to their own.

She was more affected by her task than she could have imagined. Perhaps because everything had happened so quickly. One moment she was totally involved in living her own life with barely any contact with her past, the next she was forced to delve into its minutiae with all the emotionally charged reverberations that entailed.

Yet she still chose to spend that Saturday night in the room she had slept in as a child. The same frieze ran around the ceiling line, the same small desk was tucked under the window, her set of Arthur Mees encyclopedias and other childhood books still sat on the painted wooden bookshelves. It was like sleeping in a tomb, she thought, as if she were one of those Egyptians who had been buried with her possessions.

Surrounded by the relics of her girlhood, Marnie found herself thinking more deeply than ever before about where life had brought her. She'd had no interest in marriage or having a family. However much that had to do with her upbringing, only a psychiatrist would be able to tell. But she had fled the 'ordinary', the rigid conservatism that her parents had personified. Freedom had been her catch cry; keeping her options open her only rule.

And where, in the end, had it brought her, she asked herself now as she lay in the narrow bed. Was she happy? Truly happy? Was her work — and freedom — enough? Until perhaps this very weekend, she might have said so. Or at least pretended. Now, faced with the shock of her father's decline, she realized that she too had received a wake-up call.

The years had flown since she had grown up in this house. And as she got older, they seemed to pass faster still. What did she really want to do with the time she had left? Where, and how, could she find the sense of contentment she would only now admit to missing?

She didn't yet know the answers, but at least she'd realized she was running out of time to look for them.

The first nursing home — "aged-care facility" Anthony Corkdale had corrected her pedantically — was at Balwyn.

Marnie's first sight of the residents' living area left her speechless. Frail men and women with lolling heads, vacant stares, dribbling mouths sat around the walls like hand puppets waiting for someone to animate them. A carer, a plump uniformed woman in her forties, pushed a wheelchair past them. She talked to the old man in her charge as if he were a half- witted child. To Marnie, the line from Shakespeare seemed suddenly so apt: *Old fools are babes again.*

As they were shown around the sleeping accommodation by the too-cheerful woman from the administration office, Marnie caught the faint stench of urine, or something worse. She could barely conceal her horror. And this was meant to be one of the better places! She couldn't let her father live like this. She just couldn't.

She said as much to Anthony as they made their way to the next place at South Yarra.

'But what is the alternative, my dear?'

She recognized a new sympathy in his tone. Perhaps it had been just as great a shock for him. And a foreshadowing of his own, not so distant, future.

'I could find him a flat somewhere, get a woman to live in.' She was thinking wildly, appalled by what she had seen.

'But the accommodation needs to pose no risk,' the solicitor gently pointed out. 'When a person is losing his faculties, as poor Charles is, they have no idea of danger. Knives have to be hidden, showers made safe, cupboards locked. It's a huge responsibility for one woman alone.'

"Then I'll get two of them/ Marnie retorted. 'Two could manage. I'm sure he could afford it.'

'We're talking twenty-four hours a day, seven days a week,' Anthony cautioned quietly. 'And who knows how long Charles may live. Any carers will need holidays, breaks, time away. In the end, the price becomes prohibitively expensive. And as well as that, good people, committed people, are hard to find I imagine, and they don't stay for ever.'

Marnie looked out at the streets of Melbourne, too upset to formulate a reply. She wasn't used to feeling powerless, to facing a problem she wasn't readily able to solve.

In an awkward gesture of comfort, the man beside her patted her arm. 'I understand how you're feeling, my dear, but we have to be practical too. Let's see what the next place is like. We can do the necessary paperwork at both and see where a bed comes up first.'

St Helen's was at South Yarra and, as far as Marnie was concerned, there was little to choose between the two. Each was a holding yard for those whose lives were almost at an end. It's an industry, she thought. A terrible processing of the no-longer- useful. The pity of it all made her want to cry.

It took her until Monday afternoon to do all she had to at the house. She would leave it to Anthony to find a reliable agent.

When he dropped her at the airport, she gave him a' spontaneous kiss on the cheek as she said goodbye.

'Thanks so much. I don't think I could have managed these last two days without your help.'

He looked flustered, then to her surprise he reached out and gripped her hand in both of his. 'You know, my dear, Charles always spoke of you with pride. He was very impressed with your success.'

For Marnie, it was probably the greatest shock of the whole weekend.

As she locked up on Friday evening, Lee waved at the two women who ran the shoe shop next door. Anita had introduced them the first day and they were always friendly.

'Good week?' they asked as they pulled their own doors closed.

'Not too bad at all. Anita's pleased.'

She was aware that the two of them were speaking quietly together and the next moment, the brunette, Lyn, called out, 'Want to have a drink with us? We always have a couple on Fridays.'

Lee hesitated. Her suitcase was already in the car, she was all set to drive home. But the thought of a quick drink with these two lively younger women appealed. She wouldn't be that much later home. She could always tell Brad the traffic was awful.

Immediately, she felt herself bristle. Why the hell did she have to make excuses to Brad? If she wanted to have a drink after work, she damned well would. Yet she couldn't help feeling a prickle of guilt. They'd be waiting for her. Dinner would be late. She knew she really should be getting home.

She smiled and said, 'Sure. Sounds great.'

The place was the sort of blond wood and stainless steel establishment she'd seen in magazines. It was already busy with the Friday evening crowd. As she pushed her way to the bar behind Lyn and Casey, Lee felt a surge of excitement. This was great. It felt like being at a party, the sort of party she hadn't been to in years. Men in suits and laughing, well-dressed women circled the room, moving from group to group as they sipped their drinks. It was a long way, she couldn't help thinking, from peeling potatoes in the sink at home.

The atmosphere made her feel carefree and happy. Most of the crowd were in their twenties and thirties, but there were others, men and women, closer to her own age. Times had changed, she reminded herself. People got divorced, or didn't marry at all. Most venues would have to cater for a range of age groups.

She bought a drink and, standing beside her new companions, surveyed the room. The buzz of conversation, the press of bodies, the ease with which people talked to each other was exciting.

'We always come here on Friday nights.' Lyn had to speak close to Lee's ear to make herself heard. 'We know a lot of the guys. Usually we end up at dinner together. Or,' she gave a giggle, 'somewhere else.'

Did she mean bed, Lee wondered, a little taken aback. Even with the threat of STDs, did women still sleep around with anyone who took their fancy? Certainly, there were any number of attractive men here but she couldn't imagine jumping into bed with a stranger. For her, there had only ever been Brad. The excitement had long gone — what could you expect after almost a quarter of a century of marriage? — but at least he was safe. And she was absolutely certain he had never been, and never would be, unfaithful. The thought made her smile. It would never occur to him.

She sat on her one drink for half an hour and then told the two women she'd have to go.

'So soon?'

'It's quite a long drive home.'

'Yeah.' It was Lyn who replied. 'I couldn't stand to live in Newcastle.' She grinned at Casey. 'We couldn't afford a taxi that far home, could we, Case?'

As she headed up the highway, Lee kept thinking about how much she'd enjoyed herself. For that very short time, having a drink with the two young women had made her remember how it felt to be young and free.

But, her eyes suddenly darkened, she was neither. She was a forty-something wife and mother heading home to boring Newcastle.

It was the weekend Julie was moving into Women's College at Sydney University. Joel was driving her down. Preparing lunch for Brad and the boys, Lee watched from the kitchen window as the two of them packed Joel's car with Julie's belongings.

She still couldn't believe this was happening. There had been a ray of hope inside her that maybe, at the last minute, Julie might reconsider and realize what she was throwing away. But no, she thought bitterly, she was going ahead with this craziness and it didn't matter for a second what it was doing to *her*.

A few moments later, as she was washing the lettuce for the hamburgers, Julie came into the kitchen.

'I'm off now, Mum. Just wanted to say goodbye.'

Lee didn't turn around from the sink. 'Goodbye then.' Her voice was flat and cold.

'Mum ...' Julie broke off. She didn't know how to handle this. Why couldn't her mother be happy for her? Why couldn't she just accept that this is what she wanted to do with her life?

'Maybe we can get together next week. It'll be your last in Sydney, won't it? I could meet you after work, we could have a bite or something.'

'I don't really think that'll be possible, Julie. I'll have to get back to your father and Danny.' Even without looking, Lee could sense her daughter's hurt and confusion. But that was okay. She felt exactly the same way.

'Mum, I wish you wouldn't be like this when I'm about to go. I — I want you to be happy for me.'

Lee turned around then, tight-faced and unable to contain her emotions. 'That's exactly what I did want, Julie. To be happy for you. But how can I be, with what you're doing now? I know, even if you don't, what you're walking away from. And the chance will never come again.'

Her daughter looked back at her, pain reflected in her hazel eyes. She said quietly, 'This is what I want to do, and I'm going to do it whether you support me or not.'

Turning on her heel, she walked away.

A moment later, Lee watched through the window again as Brad hugged his daughter goodbye and Danny high-fived her through the passenger window.

Nothing else in her life, she thought, had hurt her quite as much as this moment.

'Have you had a chance to catch up with Julie, love?'

Brad had surprised her by calling her at work, 'just to see how things were going'. But it hadn't taken him long to get to the real point of the call.

'No, and I don't think it's going to be possible.'

He took a moment to reply. 'I think you should, you know, seeing as you're both in town. Don't worry if you're a bit later Friday. Danny and me can manage.'

Why could men make endless sacrifices for their daughters, Lee wondered with a spark of anger, when they couldn't bother to for their wives? Last Friday night, he'd had his nose out of joint because she'd come in later than usual. This week, it was okay because it was Julie he was worried about.

'Don't be too hard on her, love. I know it's not what you wanted for her, but she's the one who's got to be happy about it.'

Lee felt her cheeks redden with annoyance. God, she was sick of being told how happy Julie had to be.

'Brad, I've got to go. I've got a customer.'

Next time, she thought as she hung up, she'd make it clear that, unless it was an emergency, he wasn't to call the shop.

It was Tuesday morning and she was hanging out the washing when she heard the phone ring.

It was Anita and she sounded frantic.

'Lee, oh, thank God you're home. Listen darling, something terrible's happened here. They've admitted Terri to hospital. She's beyond coping, totally beyond it. Which means I've got the baby full-time until God knows when. I know you mentioned you might be able to stay on for me, but this'll mean five days a week — at least until I can organize a reliable sitter.' She stopped and caught her breath. 'Is there any way you can do it for me, Lee? I'll make it worth your while, you know that. I can't let my daughter down, but I can't afford to neglect the business either.'

Lee felt her heart leap. Five days a week in Sydney.

No matter what sort of stink Brad kicked up, she was going to do it. Absolutely going to.

Dean called her at the office first thing Monday morning to tell her what had happened with his daughter.

'A dislocated shoulder. A bit painful, but thank God that's all it was.' He lowered his voice. 'I'm sorry again, darling, about the weekend. But I couldn't take the chance. You'll forgive me, won't you?'

'There's nothing to forgive, Dean.'

'I'll make it up to you. I promise.'

Tina's stomach tightened. She had to be strong. She'd made up her mind. But it wasn't something she wanted to bring up over the telephone.

'Any idea when we can get together?' She was aware of the strain in her voice. Dean didn't seem to notice.

'What about Thursday evening? Are you free then?'

She checked her desk diary. 'Looks all right. What time?'

'Let's try for sevenish.'

For the next three days she was on edge. Work, as usual, kept her busy, but the thought of what she was about to do was never far from her mind.

There were times when she could feel her resolve weakening. Then she would force herself to remember all the arguments for sticking to her decision. Yet none of them made it any easier to imagine a future without the man she loved.

There was really no one she could confide in, not even Marnie or Lee. That had never been her style: she had always tackled her problems alone. It was an attitude bred, no doubt, from her childhood days as an outsider. Experience had taught her to internalize, keep her emotions to herself, avoid the temptation of self-revelation. To let down her guard was to make herself vulnerable, and she had learned the dangers and humiliations of that.

But there were occasions when she had come close to forgetting those lessons with Dean. Times when she had longed to open her heart, to make him privy to her overwhelming need for him. Yet somehow she had always managed to curb her runaway emotions, had adhered to the boundaries that were set for her by her lover and his life.

And so, for that reason, she determined, she wasn't going to lose control now. Not right at the end.

He kissed her hello and threw his jacket onto the nearest chair.

'Just a drink, darling.'

It was his way of telling her there would be no time to make love. And for the first time since she'd known him, Tina was grateful about that. This was going to be hard enough without having to sidestep that added complication.

'Hard day?' He took the glass of wine from her hand and sank back onto the sofa, legs crossed.

Tina shrugged and took a seat opposite. 'The usual. Too much to do in too little time, but business is very good.'

'That market can only grow. It's only logical in this day and age that women take care of their own financial futures.'

Tina wondered if he recognized any irony in his words. Kathy, as far as she knew, hadn't worked a day in her life. She'd been looked after every step of the way. How did it feel to have a man pay for your hairdresser, your new season's wardrobe, your gynecologist and tennis lessons, she wondered. It was beyond her imagination.

She took a deep breath. There was a tremor in her fingers as she placed her glass on the table by her elbow. She hadn't intended to broach the subject so quickly, but now that he was here, she found herself with no patience for small talk.

'A woman has to look after her emotional future too,' she said. There was a quiver in her voice.

He must have got a sense then of some undercurrent in her words. 'Meaning?' He cocked an eyebrow at her and put down his glass.

'I mean that I think this relationship has run its course, Dean.' There was a moment's silence as she saw her words take effect.

Frowning in consternation, he sat up and leaned towards her.

'What are you trying to tell me, Tina? That it's over? Just like that? After all this time. Why, for God's sake?'

'It's a dead end for me, Dean, that's why.' She fought to keep her voice calm. 'I love you, you know that. You've given me so much, but not what I need the most. You'll never leave Kathy and the kids. I saw that with great clarity last weekend. There really isn't any place for me in your life.'

'Oh, Tina, come on! Don't hold that against me. I had to go to my daughter. But it doesn't take anything away from you, from us.'

How, she wondered, could she make him understand how she had felt last Saturday? All her life she had fought for acceptance. To prove she was worthy. She needed a man who could enhance those feelings for her, not undermine them. With Dean, she would always be second best. Not good enough to leave his wife for. How could that ever make her happy?

But to try to explain that now would only further undermine her self-esteem.

'You were upfront with me at the start, Dean. You told me you were never going to leave. It's taken me all this time to finally accept that. Now I've come to the conclusion that I don't want to be your affair on the side any longer. My happiness is important too. If you care for me as much as you say you do, you'll understand that and accept it.'

He stared back at her for a long moment. 'I still love you, Tina. More than I can make you believe perhaps.' His voice was gentle. 'But if that's your decision, then I have to accept it.'

When he was gone, she sat rigid and dry-eyed, staring at the place where he had sat. It struck her that she had ended the most important relationship in her. life with the same cool proficiency with which she conducted her business meetings. It had been the only way she could manage to cope.

Now her self-composure began to crack.

Rising from her chair, she moved restlessly through the house, trying to grasp the reality of her actions. It was over. She had lost the battle she could never really admit to fighting. And now everything would be different.

Her shoulders began to shake with deep, silent sobs.

With an angry gesture, Marnie threw aside the latest correspondence from the council. This time they were trying to tell her they wouldn't accept *her* analyst's survey of the contamination at the inner west site. Instead, they were insisting on a 'more substantial' analysis of the ground from 'proven experts'.

It was stonewalling, she knew. An attempt to keep her tied up with expensive legal costs in the hope that the escalating expenses would eventually push her into surrender. Then, of course, as soon as the site became his, Rod Sawyer's 'proven experts' would miraculously identify that the lead contamination was 'minimal' and could be 'easily rectified'.

Simmering with anger, she tried to bring her attention back to her paperwork. Her life was so frantic she'd fallen behind in the chore these last couple of weeks. Now she frowned and tried to make sense of bank statements, tax invoices and sales contracts.

There were only two of the townhouses left to move. Hopefully, with the recent cut in interest rates, she'd get rid of them by the end of the month. At least now she could concentrate her efforts on the Blakehurst development. That was more than enough while she still had the other issue to deal with too. The older she got, she realized, the harder it seemed to juggle all the balls at once.

The real estate section from that morning's *Herald* made her feel a little better. They'd put her picture on the cover — not a bad start. Inside, under the less than inspiring caption, *The Feminine Touch: A Woman Developer Makes Her Mark*, Sean Allen's piece had been allocated a whole page. All in all, Marnie was pleased with the feature. Not too many misquotes thanks to the tape recorder, and even a very carefully worded line about the intransigence of some local councils. It might give her a little more clout or, more likely, she thought cynically, encourage her lawyers to increase their fees.

An hour later, she stretched her sore back and pushed herself to her feet. It was after 8 p.m. and she hadn't eaten yet. From somewhere in the depths of the fridge she pulled out a stand-by: one of those tasteless supermarket lasagnas. It'd have to do.

She ate in front of the TV, washing the meal down with a glass of red. What she needed was a break, a week away. Things at the new site were almost at the stage where she could leave most of the overseeing to Keith.

Yes, she decided as she carried her dirty plate to the kitchen, tomorrow morning she'd ring and check out the flights. The house in Bali was always be the perfect antidote to the stress of her life in Sydney.

Marnie cursed under her breath as she scrolled through the airline's website. How could so many people manage to plan their lives six months in advance? In the mad hope she might be able to find a seat she even rang the airline, her irritation growing as she punched buttons and listened to music and messages that only served to waste more of her precious time. In the end, a real human being had answered and was forced to deal with yet another angry would-be customer.

How much did they pay these people to be the butt of so much abuse, she wondered, as the 'customer service operator' at the other end of the line checked the availability of flights to Denpasar.

But it was a waste of effort and time. She'd have to wait another three weeks before there was a flight that suited.

Anthony Corkdale had managed to pull a few strings and, despite the waiting list, her father had been admitted ten days ago to St Helen's, the place they'd visited at South Yarra.

'At least it's a bit closer for when you visit.' Anthony had rung Marnie with the news after she'd sent back all the necessary paperwork.

Visit? Marnie frowned. Who said she was going to visit? Just because her father was losing his mind didn't mean to say they were going to miraculously get closer. Perhaps the man at the other end of the line sensed her reaction.

'I know you're busy, my dear, but it would help so much, I'm sure. The more poor Charles can be reminded of the past, the longer he might be able to hang on to what remain of his faculties.'

Marnie felt herself stiffen with cold resentment. And what am I supposed to remind him of, she asked herself. All the times he ignored me? The way he criticized me in front of other people? The times he kept me away from my mother?

'What about his friends?' she asked, aware she sounded sharp and ungracious. 'Can't they help?'

She heard Anthony Corkdale's soft sigh. 'At your father's age, there aren't that many friends left. Those who are still alive can be past driving, or else they're in much the same state as Charles themselves.' The solicitor sounded depressed, as if contemplating his own not-so-distant decrepitude. 'All in all,' he went on, 'there are only the two of us, my dear. Charles and I always got on well. We were more than solicitor and client for a good many years. I feel it's the least I can do for him.'

The subtle admonishment was not lost on her and she resented the pressure.

'I'll have to see what I can do, Anthony.'

She left it like that.

At least some things were going right. The new project was coming along faster than she had expected and, so far, there hadn't been any major hold-ups. If she could just keep it on track and off-load the last of the townhouses, she'd be able to keep the bank happy enough until the inner west situation was finally resolved. Everything in life was about timing, she told herself as she left the site that afternoon.

On the way home, her phone rang and it was Judy.

'Hi, how're things?'

'Not too bad. Could do with another half a dozen beds, but that's par for the course. Oh, and I must say, I loved the article. From what I hear, it brought in a few quite nice donations.'

'Why else would I play cover girl at my age?'

They talked for a few more minutes and then Judy mentioned Fran Morris. 'She's taken out an AVO.'

'Great — whatever good that'll do.'

Judy was used to Marnie's cynicism. 'At least it means she's getting it together,' she said. 'Not being the victim any longer.'

'I'm glad.'

'She's in a place of her own and landed a job too. Housekeeper in a motel.'

Marnie was always pleased to hear of their successes. 'Good on her.'

'She wanted me to ask if she could come and thank you personally.'

'I hope you told her there was no need.'

'You and I know that, but I think it's important to her. Part of the process of acknowledging that she is getting on her feet. She was very touched that you took her and Shelley into your home.'

'Look, tell her I'm very glad it's working out for her, but I'm flat to the boards as always.'

'What about a weekend?' Judy persisted.

Judy was the quintessential 'fixer', Marnie thought. Everyone had to be made happy, all psychological ends tied up.

'Actually, I'm off to Melbourne this weekend.'

Where the hell had that come from, she wondered in surprise.

As she turned off her phone, it occurred to her that perhaps Judy wasn't the only one with psychological ends to tie up.

This time she told Anthony not to worry about picking her up at the airport. She would get a taxi. 'I'll see you afterwards,' she said. There were still some documents to sign regarding the house and other matters relating to her father's affairs.

When she arrived at St Helen's, the young woman at the front desk called for a staff member to direct her to her father's room. As Marnie walked down the long, wide corridors she glanced into the open doorways. Most of the aged residents — predominantly women, she noted — were sitting watching T.V. A few were reading, a couple knitting, and some had a visitor or two. It's like a boarding school for the aged, she thought with a shudder as they passed a small sitting area where four women sat playing bridge, the cards held in knobbly, age-potted hands. But at least they seemed to be enjoying themselves.

'He's in here,' her guide said, pushing a security pad by a set of doors that closed off the hallway.

'But why...?'

The woman saw Marnie's baffled expression.

'Security. So they don't wander off. Some of them do, you know.'

Marnie felt her stomach turn over. Security? How could they be doing this to her father? Keeping him under lock and key as if he were some dangerous criminal. Surely it wasn't necessary?

The woman left her outside her father's room. The door was partly ajar; with a soft tap, Marnie pushed it open.

Charles Ingram was dressed and sitting on the edge of his bed staring out of the window. He didn't appear to have heard Marnie's entrance.

'Dad ...' The word always seemed so awkward on her lips. 'It's me.'

As she walked towards him, he turned his head. His blank expression slowly gave way to a smile and he put out a hand.

As she gripped it in her own, Marnie felt a catch in her throat. It occurred to her that, for the first time in his life, her father seemed to need her.

She was with him almost two hours. Following Anthony's suggestion, she talked a lot about the past. About his work, her mother, their homes at Toorak and Portsea. Nearly all the conversation was initiated by herself.

Some things he responded to; others caused him to look bewildered. 'I don't remember that,' was his constant reply. When she tested whether he could recall something they had just been talking about, she noticed he had no recollection. It was as if the topic had been mentioned for the first time.

Later, they took a stroll in the garden attached to the special-care unit. A few other residents were sitting outside, some with visitors. These were mostly middle-aged women; probably daughters like herself, Marnie thought. She couldn't help wondering how long some of them had had to cope with all this. And that mightn't be the whole picture. What if they also had difficult teenagers at home, unsupportive husbands or demanding jobs? It amazed her how strong women were expected to be.

Only one of the visitors that Saturday morning was a man. He was serious-looking, greying, casually dressed in jeans and a yellow pullover. A son doing his duty by his father, Marnie guessed. No doubt he'd prefer to be on the golf course. He looked the type.

Just after twelve, lunch was served in the dining room. In the sunny area, four round tables were each set with four places, and some of the elderly residents were already seated and waiting when Marnie entered with her father. Perhaps meals were the only interesting thing about their day.

A staff member pointed out her father's place. 'Pull up an extra chair if you like,' she invited Marnie. 'There's plenty if you want to stay.'

Marnie politely refused while recoiling inwardly at the thought. It was bad enough to leave her once proud father in this kindergarten for the aged. Already, she could see the tension on his face at being forced to sit with this group of strangers.

'I'll come again soon, Dad.' She bent down beside his chair and spoke softly near his ear.

The look he gave her brought tears to her eyes as she made her way to the exit. There was nothing intrinsically wrong with the place. It was clean, and the staff seemed caring and competent, but still it was horrible, just horrible. She never would have dreamed that a man like her father would end up this way.

At the door, she realized she didn't know the code to get out.

'I'll get it.'

The voice came from behind her. It was the man she had seen in the garden.

'Your first visit?' He punched the four-digit code into the keypad.

Marnie nodded, trying to blink away her tears. 'Yes.'

'It's awful, I know. My father's been here almost six months and it still affects me.'

Marnie felt her throat tighten. Oh hell, surely she wasn't going to cry in front of this stranger.

He pushed the door open and stood back for her to go first.

As it fell shut behind them, he said, 'I'm Steven Royce, by the way.'

Marnie wished he would just go away. She wasn't in the mood to be polite. She was barely holding it together.

'Marnie Ingram.'

He fell into step beside her as they made their way back to the main entrance.

'At least you can be assured that the place is well run. There are plenty that aren't, let me tell you.'

They were near the front desk. Marnie slowed her pace. 'Will you excuse me? I have to speak to them here.'

With a sense of relief, she turned away.

She caught a taxi to Anthony Corkdale's home, not far away. His wife, Anne, a small, articulate woman, had prepared lunch for the three of them.

'This is good of you, Anne. I really didn't expect it.'

It was warm enough to sit on the terrace and the Corkdales' two dachshunds waited patiently at their feet for scraps.

'My pleasure. I know they don't feed you anything edible on planes these days.'

Afterwards, Marnie went into Anthony's book-filled study to attend to the outstanding paperwork.

There, with just the two of them, she finally allowed herself to reveal her emotional reaction to her visit. 'I'm shattered by it, Anthony. I can't tell you how much.'

From the other side of his antique desk, the solicitor looked at her with sympathy. 'It was very sudden, my dear. First the stroke and then the aftermath. None of us expected it. But I'm sure it made him happy to have you there.'

'He barely communicates. And he has so little memory — unless I remind him of things.'

She could tell by the way he looked at her that her father's friend knew exactly what she was getting at.

Charles Ingram had forgotten that he had once so disliked his only child.

Chapter 9

BRAD WAS STILL PULLING FACES about it, but there was nothing he could do. Until Anita was free to return to the shop, she was depending on Lee to keep things ticking over.

'Well, how long's this going to last?' Brad sounded petulant as Lee served up dinner on Saturday night. 'When you said you were taking this on, I didn't expect it to end up a full-time caper.'

'Neither did I, love.' Lee was keeping things sweet. 'But it won't be much longer, I'm sure. And look at the money. The way I'm going, we can probably get away for a week somewhere when this is over.'

She saw that had some effect. 'Think about it,' she added, pushing her advantage, 'maybe we could even afford one of those islands up north. They've got some great deals occasionally.'

Brad snorted. 'A new carport'd be more like it. Danny'll need somewhere when he gets his car.'

'Well, whatever. I don't mind.'

It was true. She didn't care what they did with the money as long as she could keep the job in Sydney going as long as possible. Sometimes she found herself fantasizing about not telling Brad when Anita did come back. But she knew that was crazy. No, she'd just make the most of the time she had.

'How's the lamb?' she asked.

'Great, Mum.' Danny spoke through a mouthful of food. Her elder son Troy and his girlfriend, Jasmine, who had also dropped in for dinner were equally appreciative.

Lee looked pleased. She'd made sure they couldn't complain about not being fed well, even when she wasn't there. If that meant she spent most of the weekend cooking things to freeze, it was a small price to pay for the freedom of running her own life for the other five days of the week.

During her time away, she found it easy to pretend she was a single woman enjoying the buzz of city life. When she'd known she was going to be spending more time in the flat, she'd taken a few things from home to give it a more personal touch — her own towels, her coffee mug, her pillows for the bed. Occasionally, on the way home from work, she'd buy some flowers and even just the act of arranging them in a vase to suit herself brought her a rare pleasure.

There were other pleasures too. At night, she could cook whatever she felt like eating, or not cook at all if she preferred. There were plenty of takeaway food places to save her the trouble. And after dinner, there were few household chores to burden her. She could simply relax and watch exactly what she wanted on TV or read a book or a magazine.

In actual fact, she was flying high on the sense of independence this unexpected experience was offering her. Yet she was careful to hide her exuberance from Brad. In front of him, she made it seem as if she were pushing herself to do a favor for a friend, a favor that she didn't relish at all. She knew it wouldn't help for Brad to think she was actually enjoying herself.

In the city the following week, she tried to tee up another dinner with Marnie and Tina, but they were both busy. For a moment, it crossed her mind to eat out somewhere on her own, but she wasn't quite game enough for that. She'd feel far too obvious, a woman on her own in a restaurant. The same way she'd feel in a bar if she wanted a drink and some company. It was different for men, she thought with more than a hint of envy. They could go anywhere without a worry. No one gave a man on his own a second look.

On Thursday evening, Tracey came in at six o'clock as usual and Lee was able to have her meal break. She'd taken to going to a coffee shop in the complex. The food was quite good and it was the sort of place where she didn't feel uncomfortable alone. On Thursday evenings it was quite busy, yet she usually managed to snare a table outside on the mall. While she ate, she enjoyed watching the passing parade.

That evening, she was just finishing her meal when a man, brushing past her to secure a nearby table, bumped against her chair, dropping his tray and plate of food with a crash.

Lee cried out in shock as some of the hot potato and gravy fell into her lap.

'I'm so sorry! Oh, God, please, let me help you.' The man was on his knees beside her, doing his best to scrape the mess off her skirt with a paper napkin.

'No, really, it's okay.' Lee pushed her chair back and did her best to hide her irritation. How could people be so clumsy? If he didn't stop what he was doing, he was going to make the stain even worse. 'I've got to get back to work. I'll go to the ladies and clean myself up.'

'I am just so sorry. I can't apologize enough. You must let me at least pay for the dry cleaning.'

She raised her head to see a man of medium height with thick fair hair, dressed in a white business shirt and dark tie.

'No, no, it'll come off, don't worry about it.'

'But I feel terrible. You must let me pay to have it cleaned.'

All Lee wanted was to get out of there. She was due back at the shop and couldn't afford to waste any time if she was going to clean herself up as well.

She moved away, leaving him to scrape up the rest of the mess.

It was the following Monday afternoon; she had just finished checking the day's takings and was getting ready to close.

'Hi. I hope you won't chase me out of here.'

Surprised, Lee looked up to see a man approaching the counter. She frowned. There was something familiar about him, but she couldn't quite place ...

'Last Thursday night.' He offered an explanation in response to her expression. 'I was the idiot who dropped his dinner on you.'

'Oh...yes.' She recognized him now.

'I said I wanted to pay for your dry cleaning and I meant it. The girls at the coffee lounge told me where you worked. I hope you don't mind.'

Lee didn't. In fact, she was touched by the gesture. It was very sweet of him to have gone to the bother. She'd forgotten about the incident entirely.

She told him as much and added: 'I didn't even need to go to the cleaners. Hand washing got the mark out.'

'Are you sure? You're not just telling me that?' He was looking at her with a smile and Lee couldn't help noticing how nice that smile was.

'Cross my heart.' She smiled back. 'But thanks for the offer. It was nice of you.'

'My name's Graham, by the way. Graham Park. I work just up the road. The insurance company.'

'Nice to meet you, Graham.' She answered with automatic politeness. 'I'm Lee. Lee Kingsford. I'm managing this place for a friend.'

'If you're closing, can I buy you a coffee or something? Just to try and say sorry again.'

Lee smiled but shook her head. 'Thanks, but there's really no need. And anyway,' she lied, 'I'm meeting some friends after work.'

There was no way, whatever the excuse, she was going to let herself be picked up by a strange man. No matter how nice his smile.

By that weekend, she was feeling bad about not having made any contact with Julie. After all, they couldn't keep avoiding each other and she knew too that Brad was upset that she hadn't been in touch. It wouldn't help any of them to let the problem keep simmering.

The following Monday evening, after cooking herself a cheese omelet, she rang her daughter's mobile.

'Oh, Mum ... Hi.' Lee could hear the surprise in Julie's voice. But there was a note of relief too. 'How are you?'

'I'm fine. What about you? Where are you?' She could hear a lot of noise in the background.

'I've got a part-time job in a restaurant just off George Street. I'm on my way there now.'

Lee came straight to the point. 'I think we should get together, Julie. Clear the air. How are you placed the rest of the week? The evenings, I mean.'

'Oh, God, that's a problem. I work two nights and the other two nights I've got classes. There were timetable clashes. I couldn't fit them in during the day. I really only have Friday and Saturday off.'

'Sounds frantic. Are you sure you're not taking on too much?'

'It's okay, I'm managing.'

Lee made a snap decision. 'Then why don't we catch up Friday? I'll stay down the extra night. Dad won't mind when he understands. Tell me where you'd like to meet.'

They teed up a time and a place, and Lee rang off.

She felt better after that. It was a huge disappointment what Julie had done to her, but maybe the situation wasn't entirely hopeless. What if Julie was already discovering that the academic life wasn't for her? All those years of boring study and the huge sum to pay back at the end of it. Lee herself had done waitressing when she first came to Sydney but that wasn't on top of a day spent at lectures or writing assignments. Maybe Julie was realizing how difficult it was going to be. If she was having second thoughts, there might still be the chance of encouraging her to try for next year's NIDA intake.

When she rang Brad to tell him about her change of plan, there was a moment of silence on the line. She could tell he was disgruntled, but in the circumstances he wasn't going to make a fuss.

'I guess we'll see you Saturday morning then,' he responded finally.

They met in a cheap and cheerful trattoria in Glebe Point Road. The first thing that struck Lee when her daughter walked in was the weight she'd lost. Not a lot, but enough to be noticeable.

She frowned. Julie had never been overweight, so what was the problem? Wasn't she eating properly? Surely she wasn't stupid enough to be dieting.

'Hi, Mum.' Julie leaned down and gave her a tentative kiss on the cheek. 'How are you?'

'I'm fine. But I'm just looking at you — you've lost weight. Aren't they feeding you enough at that place?' Surely the food at Women's College couldn't be that bad.

Her daughter slid onto the hard wooden seat opposite. 'I guess I'm on the run a bit. Nothing to worry about.'

There was an awkward silence, neither of them knowing what to talk about next.

'So, how's uni? Is it what you were hoping it would be?'

Julie shrugged. 'I guess. It takes a little while to find your feet. The place is huge. And there are so many kids, it's unreal.'

A young waiter appeared and handed them dog-eared menus. 'Why don't we order,' Lee suggested, 'then we can talk without being interrupted.'

All in all, the evening had not gone too badly. As if by tacit agreement, neither had said much more about the subject of university. Instead, they'd talked about Lee's work in the shop, about the incredible prices in Sydney and other safe topics.

'The place is a bit overpowering,' Julie said as she nibbled at a plate of nachos, 'but I like it.'

'What about Joel? Does he get down to see you much?' Lee thought she might as well try to judge how that was panning out.

'It's hard. He's working every Saturday. Usually he drives down Saturday evening and stays with a mate at Chippendale. We have Saturday evening together but then he has to get back by Sunday lunchtime if he's got open houses.'

So there might be a chance of that burning itself out, Lee surmised hopefully.

'How are Dad and Danny coping on their own?' Julie asked.

'Better than I would have thought. It's done them good to have to manage by themselves. Men can do it if they really have to.' She made a joke of it, 'Even men like Dad and your brother. Oh, I shouldn't say that I know,' she caught herself. 'Sometimes I feel terribly guilty at leaving them by themselves but it's not for that long and I really couldn't let Anita down with all she's facing at the moment.'

By the time the evening was over, the tension between the two of them had eased. They stood outside on the sidewalk, waiting for the friends who were picking Julie up to catch a late movie. When the car drew into the kerb, Lee gave her daughter a kiss on the cheek.

'I'm still not happy about what you're doing, Julie, and I can't pretend to be. But you've made your choice and you're the one who has to live with it. If you need me, I'm just a phone call away, whether I'm still in Sydney or at home, okay? I really mean that.'

Julie looked back at her. For a moment, Lee thought she was going to tell her something. Then she nodded and gave her mother a quick hug.

"Thanks, Mum. It's been great. I hope we can do it again while you're here.'

'I think we should.'

Once the football started on TV, Lee thought, Brad would hardly notice if she was there or not on Friday night. Then, as she quickly walked to where she'd parked her car, she admonished herself for her cynicism.

Driving back to the apartment, she realized that, while they might have done something to clear the air, it was still obvious Julie wasn't about to change her mind about university. Nor about Joel.

It was so frustrating to have to stand back and see a kid with all that potential waste her youth on the wrong career and on a relationship that was going to take her exactly nowhere. But what could she do about it? Perhaps if they spent a bit more time together she might be able to exert some influence without seeming to be pushing too hard.

Even though it was late, the streets were busy. It still gave her a buzz to drive over the bridge. The city seemed to throb with unlimited possibilities.

She dreaded the idea of going back to Newcastle and all that meant. Those tedious Sundays with her parents and sisters, nights at the club or at Rotary dinners with Brad, squabbling with Danny. Her mouth tensed at the thought of it. Sydney was where she wanted to be; in a place where things *happened*. Where she could eat in interesting restaurants every night of the week if she wanted to, listen to live music in bars, meet people who could talk about more than the footie and the price of spare parts.

I should never have married Brad.

She let the thought linger in her mind instead of pushing it away.

But she had, because it had been her only option.

She'd loved her job on television. Being a permanent member of the dance troupe on *Variety Live* meant hard work devising new routines for each week's show, but Lee thrived on it. The pace was hectic but exciting, and she knew she was doing well because Peter Holding made a point of telling her.

'I'm going to claim you as my personal discovery, sweetheart. You make me proud.'

His compliments made her glow. He had singled her out. She still remembered that night they'd shared in the cocktail bar, how grown-up it had made her feel to have a man like Peter so clearly interested in her and her career.

As time passed, she found herself wishing he would ask her out again. She even began to hang back after the program ended in the hope that he might suggest dinner or a drink. Finally, she got her wish. There was a note left for her in the make-up room, inviting her to dinner the following Saturday evening. Excited as she was, she knew better than to speak about it to any of the other girls. It could make things awkward, lead to jealousy maybe, and she didn't want that.

She spent the whole of Saturday getting ready. First the hairdresser and a manicure, then she went shopping and spent more than she should have on a dress and matching shoes.

At six, she took a bath, so as not to wet her hair-do, and by quarter to seven she was dressed, made-up and waiting nervously for the bell to ring.

It was the best evening she could have imagined. First they had eaten at Beppi's, where it was clear Peter was a regular. When she was handed the huge menu by a smiling Italian waiter, Lee was bewildered by the choice. There were dishes listed she had never heard of. What was gnocchi? Or vitello al limone?

Sensing her confusion, Peter leaned across the table and said gently, 'Shall I order for both of us, sweetheart?'

Lee smiled and nodded in relief.

For the first time, too, she drank French champagne, and it went straight to her head. But she loved the sensation. It made her feel relaxed and more confident.

At the end of a wonderful evening, Peter said goodbye at the front door of the Wattle Street house.

'Now you get a good night's sleep.' He smiled as he tipped her face up to his, an index finger under her chin. 'I'd hate to think I was responsible for any bags under those beautiful eyes.'

"Thanks, Peter. I had a great time, really terrific.' She wondered if he could pick the slight slur in her voice. Her limbs felt heavy and she couldn't stop smiling.

He gave her a chaste kiss on the cheek.

'And we'll do it again, princess.'

He was as good as his word. Over the next month or so, he took her to dinner on two more occasions; they even went dancing at the Cross afterwards. Peter danced well and she knew she was showing off on the floor, but she loved the admiring looks she saw on other men's faces. It made her feel good about herself and acutely aware of her femininity.

On every date, Peter was the perfect gentleman. At the end of the night, he would drop her at her door with never anything more than a quick kiss. He respects me, she thought. He's not going to push me into doing anything I don't want to.

Just as it had been with Brad, she was the one in control.

She'd been with *Variety* almost four months. Occasionally, she still went home on weekends and somehow Brad would always find out when that happened. Perhaps one of her sisters' boyfriends let him know.

When he rang 'just to say hello' she didn't want to hurt his feelings by refusing to speak to him. After all, they'd been very close once and, if Brad could accept the limits, there was probably no reason why they couldn't still be friends.

'I watch you every week, Lee. You're the best on that show by a mile.'

His too obvious approval irritated her, but she didn't let him see that.

'Thanks, that's lovely of you to say so. I love the job. But I still see it as a stepping stone, getting my face known. What I'm really aiming for is a singing role.'

Lee had given a lot of thought to her next move. She knew Peter had great faith in her and felt sure she could convince him to let her enlarge her role on the program.

She'd been hoping he would ask her out again so she could sound him out about her proposal, but when she hadn't heard from him a fortnight later, she decided to take the initiative. Dropping a note to his secretary, she asked if they could meet to discuss an idea she had. She was pleased when, later that day, he popped his head around the dressing room door. 'I'm free this Thursday afternoon,' he said. 'See you in my office around six.'

One of the other dancers was in the room at the time. She arched a dark, perfectly plucked eyebrow at Lee.

'Careful there, sweetie. He's a real smoothie, you know. Hardly the type for an innocent little country maiden.'

Lee felt her cheeks flame with indignation. Was that what the others thought of her? How dare they. For a moment, she was tempted to reveal how many dates she'd already had with Peter Holding. How capable she was of looking after herself. Instead, she said curtly, 'It's a business matter, Marilyn. That's all.'

Peter was running late. It was almost six thirty by the time he arrived. His secretary had left for the day and he invited Lee into his office.

'Like a drink? Gin and tonic?'

'Thanks.' Lee had never tasted one before, but she wasn't going to admit that.

He opened the bar fridge and filled two glasses with ice, Gilbys and tonic water.

'Let's sit over here, it's more comfortable. I've had a helluva day.'

She followed him to the long navy blue sofa and sat down beside him.

He touched his glass to hers and took a swallow of drink.

'Ah ... that's better. So, my princess, what's the problem?'

'No problem. Just something I wanted to bring up with you.'

'Shoot. Tell all.'

Lee had rehearsed her words carefully and now she broached the subject of becoming a solo singer on the show.

'Well, well.' He looked at her with some amusement. 'Ambitious little lady, aren't you?'

'I... yes, I guess I am.' She didn't think she had to apologize for that. ' I love dancing, but that's not going to get me where I want to go in the long run. Acting and singing are my first loves.'

'So you're after me to give you a break, are you?' He was smiling at her. Finishing his drink in one long swallow, he put his glass down on the table in front of them.

Lee smiled back. 'I was hoping.'

'And do you think you should be doing something for me in return?'

There was a note in his voice she hadn't heard before.

'I...' She wasn't sure what he meant.

In one deliberate movement he took the glass from her hand and placed it beside his own. The next moment she froze in shock as he pulled her close and she felt his hand sliding up her thigh. Her skirt was fashionably short and his hands were on her bare flesh.

'Peter!' She tried to push him away, to pull free from his hold.

'Come on, princess. I've been very patient. All I'm saying is, if you want a favor then I want one too.'

Her eyes widened in alarm as she got the gist of his message and this time she pushed him away more forcefully. 'No, I didn't mean —'

Ignoring her struggles, he pulled her further down on the sofa until his body almost covered her own. To her horror, she could feel the hardness between his legs. And she remembered the warning she had received about Peter Holding. The warning she had ignored.

'No, Peter, please! I'm ...' But she couldn't bring herself to say the word, virgin. 'I've never done this ... I've never had ... sex before.'

She was resisting him now with all her strength, but her words only seemed to inflame his ardor. His mouth covered hers, his lips hard and demanding, his tongue probing for entry.

Lee couldn't believe what was happening. This was the same man who had taken her out for dinner and dancing, who'd treated her like a lady, who had made her feel so special. Now, while he used his weight to pin her down, she felt him ripping her pants off and then his knee was between her legs, forcing them apart.

'Come on, come on ... You'll love it, I promise.' His face was flushed and his breathing rapid as he used one hand to fiddle with his own trousers.

It was her chance. Somehow, she managed to yank up her knee and thrust it hard into his groin. She heard his gasp of pain and, as his grip weakened, used the precious moment to wriggle free.

But as she struggled to her feet, his hand shot out and his open palm connected with her face.

'You bitch! You dirty red-neck bitch!'

Tears of shock and pain running down her face, Lee grabbed her bag and ran from the room.

When she let herself into the house, both Marnie and Tina were in the kitchen.

'Hi!' It was Tina who called out. 'We've just made some spaghetti. D'you want some?'

Food was the last thing on Lee's mind. But she needed to talk, to tell them exactly what had happened to her.

When she walked into the kitchen, they could tell at once that something was wrong.

'What's up?' Marnie put down her cutlery with a frown. 'You look terrible.'

Lee felt her throat tighten. She shook her head and her eyes filled with tears.

'Lee ... sit down.' Tina was on her feet, one hand on Lee's arm, the other pulling out a chair.

Lee dropped into the seat and covered her face with her hands.

'Darling ...' Marnie moved to kneel beside her as Tina's arm encircled her shoulder. 'Tell us. What's wrong? What the hell's happened?'

Stumbling and tearful, she told them what she'd been confronted with in Peter Holding's office.

Half an hour later, drink in hand, she was feeling a little better.

'Listen, sweetheart, that's men.' Marnie had refused to let her take the incident too seriously. 'They're all the same, no matter how they might pretend otherwise. Sex is all they want. If you're like me and want it just as much, you beat them at their own game. You stay in control and never let them use you.'

'But I trusted him,' Lee said plaintively. 'I thought he was just being nice.'

Marnie gave a humorless laugh and shook her head. 'Number one: never trust them. Number two: they're never 'just being nice.''

'Well, Brad was,' Lee protested. 'He never pushed me to go further than I wanted to.'

'Oh, come on, darling,' Marnie responded. 'Boys like Brad are different from the sort of bloke you're telling us about. Look at the job this creep's in — he's used to preying on naive, young birds. He probably thought you were panting for it. That's usually the way they justify themselves.'

'What am I going to do now? I'll feel so embarrassed seeing him again.'

'Act as if nothing ever happened,' Marnie advised emphatically. 'And stay out of his way as much as possible. You've got nothing to be embarrassed about; he was the one who got the kick in the balls.'

Tina hadn't said much then but later, when Lee was in bed, she knocked on the door and asked if she could come in.

'Sure.' Lee was sitting propped up against the pillows, a cup of milky coffee in her hands.

'I just wanted to make sure you were okay.' Tina sat on the edge of the bed.

'I guess so. Like Marnie said, I'm going to try to forget it ever happened.'

'I know it won't be easy, but things could have been worse. I guess Marnie can be a little more blasé because she's got a different outlook where men are concerned. Don't get me wrong,' she added quickly, 'I'm not putting her down, but I suppose most of us are looking for something a bit deeper than just sex. And sometimes we make mistakes. It's a matter of being more careful and discriminating until the right man comes along.'

Lee could hardly hide her surprise. She'd never known Tina to be so forthcoming. Just for a moment, she had let down the barrier of that self-contained exterior to comfort a friend. Lee was touched.

She reached out and squeezed Tina's hand. 'Thanks, Tina. Thanks for trying to make it easier.'

As she fell asleep, she thought how fortunate she was to have two such caring, if very different, friends.

And that might have been where it ended, if not for what happened a week later.

Friday afternoon, when she picked up her pay check, there was a note folded in the envelope as well. As she read it, Lee felt the blood drain from her face. It couldn't be true. It just couldn't be.

There was no one at home when she arrived back at the house. Tina worked at a second job on weekend nights and Lee remembered that Marnie had said something about going away for the weekend with a boyfriend. That meant she was alone in the house with her terrible news.

She was sitting at the kitchen table, reading the typed note for the umpteenth time, when the ringing of the phone made her jump.

She forced herself to answer it. 'Hello.'

'Lee. It's me.' She recognized Brad's voice. 'I'm just ringing to see how you are. Wondering when you're going to be home again.'

Her mind was still taken up with her own dilemma. 'I really don't know, Brad.' It was the first time he'd rung her in Sydney since their break-up. Vaguely, she wondered why.

'I guess I should tell you why I'm calling.' She could hear the sadness in his tone. 'I... I went for a walk on Caves Beach this afternoon after work. It made me remember how we loved going there together. And ... I suppose I was really missing you. I just wanted to hear the sound of your voice.'

Suddenly, it was too much for her. A sob caught in her throat.

'Lee ... what's wrong?'

She took a shuddering breath. 'Nothing.'

'Yes, there is. I know there is. Please, you can tell me. We could always talk about anything.'

If was the kindness and concern in his voice that made her lose her fragile control.

'Listen,' he said, his voice firm now, 'I'm coming straight to Sydney. Whatever's wrong, I'll help you. You know I will. Just wait for me.'

She felt too choked to reply.

'Will you? Will you please be there?'

'Yes,' she managed through her sobs.

Chapter 10

SHE COULDN'T BELIEVE THE COMFORT she felt when he held her in his arms. He listened without interrupting as she told him everything that had happened with Peter Holding.

'And now this,' she said tearfully, pointing at the short, curt note dismissing her from her job on *Variety Live*. 'It isn't fair! I didn't do anything wrong. He's doing this because I wouldn't ... because I made it clear I wasn't going to sleep with him.'

Brad's face was tight with suppressed anger, but he kept his voice calm. 'You're right, it's his way of getting even. The bloke's as weak as —' He bit off his words. 'But there are other jobs, Lee. You're smart, talented. I know you'll find something as good, if not better in the long run.'

She pulled another tissue from the box on the coffee table. 'But that was my biggest break. How long am I going to have to wait before something that good comes along again?' She blew her nose.

Brad did his best to make her think positively. 'I'm sure there's still a lot going on at the Cross. There's always shows or revues or cabarets. It's just a matter of watching the paper and going for auditions.'

He made it sound so easy, Lee thought, but she knew it wasn't really like that. Now she'd have to find an ordinary job again, hope she could get time off, and join the queues of other girls in competition for the few really good positions.

'I guess so.'

'I know so,' he said firmly.

They were sitting close together on the sofa. Brad's arm was around her and, worn out by her emotions, she was enjoying its comfort.

'Listen, why don't you go and freshen up and I'll take you out for a bite somewhere. It'll do you good.'

Lee glanced at her watch. It was almost quarter to ten. 'It's late. I don't know if we'll find anything open now.'

'Well, that won't be a problem at the Cross.' Brad quite liked the idea of visiting Kings Cross by night. He'd only been there a few times before, when he'd gone to see Lee on stage.

'It'll make it very late for you getting back.'

He looked at her, but saw no indication that she was considering letting him spend the night. If she had, he'd have thought up some excuse for work the next morning.

'Let me worry about that,' he replied.

Lee ran a hand through her hair. She felt a wreck. The thought of getting dressed and made-up to go out at this time of night held no appeal.

'To tell you the truth, I think I'd really rather stay home. I can make us something here. What d'you think?'

She did look tired. 'Whatever you like,' he replied.

They ended up eating toasted cheese sandwiches and tinned tomato soup. As far as Brad was concerned, all that mattered was being together. It was just so good to be with her again; he even managed to make her laugh a couple of times.

As they ate and talked, Lee could feel her familiar sense of ease in Brad's company. They knew each other so well, and, as he'd said, could discuss almost anything. Peter Holding might have been worldly and sophisticated, but she'd never felt as relaxed with him as she did with Brad.

As that old closeness came back to her, she had to admit to feelings of confusion as well. It would be so easy to go back to how things had been, but did she really want that? Wouldn't it just bring up all the old conflicts again about how she was going to fulfill her goals and ambitions? Much as he might think he could make a life in Sydney with her, Brad's future was in Newcastle. When his father retired, he would be able to take over a ready-made business. Sydney could never offer him the same possibilities.

But she cared for him, she thought. She really did. No one had ever been as good to her as Brad. It didn't make anything easy.

She still hadn't clarified her feelings by the time he said goodbye.

'Do you think we could see each other again next weekend?'

They were standing at the front door. He held her hands as he looked down at her and asked the question.

Lee could see the trepidation in his face while he waited for her reply. This boy adored her, she realized. He would never let her down. Right at that moment, nothing else seemed to matter as much.

She made her split-second decision. 'Yes, Brad,' she said softly. 'I think we should.' And lifting her lips to his, she kissed him a warm goodnight.

From that evening on, the relationship was re-established and Lee found herself happier than she might have expected. Whatever problems it might cause in the future, at this point she needed Brad in her life.

Things were working out on other fronts too. Remembering the Cocozzas' words when she had left the job at their Bondi cafe, she rang and briefly explained that she was looking for work again.

'Of course, Lee, *bella!* You very good worker.' Angelo Cocozza's voice boomed down the line. 'Come tomorrow and we see how we fit you in.'

As she hung up, she suddenly felt confident that her setback would soon be overcome and everything would work out fine after all.

Over the next few weeks, Brad made it to Sydney as often as possible. By now both their families knew that the relationship was on again. When Lee had gone home for her mother's birthday, she'd hated being the butt of her sisters' teasing.

'So, nothing wrong with a nice local boy, after all, eh?' Joy had smirked.

'At least you've put the poor bloke out of his misery,' Maureen put in. 'When are you picking the ring?'

'I'm not bloody getting married,' Lee had insisted fiercely. 'We're seeing each other again, that's all!'

She hadn't missed the glance her sisters had exchanged. 'Yeah, yeah. Sure.'

On those Saturdays when he didn't have to work, Brad stayed the whole weekend with her in Sydney.

Lee was a little self-conscious that first Saturday morning when he followed her into the kitchen where Marnie and Tina were making breakfast. But she soon got over that. After all, there were many occasions when one of Marnie's boyfriends might be there too.

The difference was that she wasn't sleeping with Brad. They might get pretty steamed up in bed, but they always stopped short of going all the way. Yet, as time passed, she was aware of a growing physical urge as well as a curiosity about what it would be like to let Brad make love to her. She could tell too that he was finding it more and more difficult to draw back from the edge.

After all, she convinced herself, they weren't kids any longer and were in a strong, committed relationship. As long as they took precautions, why shouldn't they take the next step? She sensed that Brad, not wishing to jeopardize things, was leaving the initiative to her.

One night when they lay in each other's arms after another passionate session, Lee broached the subject.

'I want to, Brad. I'm ready,' she whispered close to his ear in the darkness.

She heard his quick intake of breath, felt the leap in his excitement.

'Are you quite sure, love?' He stroked her hair. 'I wouldn't ever want to do anything to hurt you.'

'I know you wouldn't. I've thought about it a lot. I'd like us to be the first for each other.'

The very next week, she had gone to a doctor and requested a prescription for the pill. The way the male doctor looked at her made her feel nervous — and dirty, somehow. She sensed he'd have preferred to deliver a lecture on sexual morality rather than sign his name to a prescription for contraception. But he gave her what she asked for.

Afterwards, at the pharmacy, she felt as if all eyes were upon her as she signed her script and accepted the package that would give her her sexual freedom. That night, when she swallowed the small orange tablet with a sip of water, she felt as if she were taking another step from her girlhood towards becoming a woman.

When Brad arrived two evenings later, he was as full of anticipation as she was. 'Oh, God, Lee, I can't wait. I really can't. I've dreamed of this for so long.'

The sound of his excitement increased her own. With a soft giggle, she put a finger to the tip of his nose. 'Well, you're going to have to cool it until next weekend, buster. I have to take at least four of these things, preferably seven, before I'm guaranteed safe.'

But the next night, lying naked in his arms, all logic and restraint disappeared.

'It'll be okay, Lee.' His heart was pounding against her, his breath hot and ragged in her ear. 'Trust me, darling ... Trust me ...'

Over the next few weeks, Lee's life seemed busier than ever. She was working as many hours as possible in the cafe, attending every audition she thought worthwhile, and spending every weekend with Brad. On two occasions, she made it to the final possible draw for roles in major shows. But each time someone else got the part, and she had to work hard at not feeling too dispirited by her defeat. It wasn't easy. The competition was fierce and the audition process so relentless, it was difficult not to get despondent.

But Brad helped keep her spirits up and she was grateful for his support. Their relationship had developed a deeper connection now that they were sleeping together, yet always in the back of her mind was the nagging worry that she was leading him on. For, even if the very worst happened and nothing worked out with her career, she had no intention of burying herself in the suburbs of Newcastle for the rest of her life. She had tried to make that clear to him but wondered if he'd really accepted what she was saying. She hated the thought of hurting him all over again.

It was a subject she brought up with the others and Marnie made it abundantly clear that she thought there would be troubles ahead.

'There are thousands of guys out there,' she told Lee. 'I think you're crazy to tie yourself down. The longer you let him hang around, the more he's going to expect it to lead to the obvious. And, sweetie, I don't think you're going to be happy spending the rest of your life vacuuming the three-bedroom brick veneer.'

Her words were flippant but Lee knew they resonated with truth — a truth she found frightening. In the same way, Tina's comments, while more measured than Marnie's, held the same note of warning.

'You know, Lee, even if Brad managed to live with you in Sydney, you have to ask yourself if the relationship will last. Is he really the man you want to spend your life with?'

Her friends' words gave her lots to ponder, but still Lee put off making a decision. On one level, she knew she should end the relationship straightaway. Her goals and ambitions were just so much larger than Brad's; she wanted so much more out of life and needed the sort of man who would help her to grow, not stifle her. Yet, with everything she was facing at the moment, Brad was her backstop, her support. Someone she could trust and depend on. Inevitably, she kept pushing the conflict to the back of her mind. It would resolve itself some way, she convinced herself, when the time was right.

Pale-faced and feeling sick, Lee sat at the kitchen table and broke her news.

'Are you sure?' It was Tina who asked the question.

Lee nodded, her hands twisting in her lap. 'Yes. I rang the doctor this afternoon.'

'You twit!' Marnie looked at her in disbelief. 'I thought you were on the pill!'

'I am ... It's just ... We didn't wait long enough the doctor said.' Lee's voice revealed her panic. 'I told Brad we had to wait a week!'

'And he was all for that, of course,' retorted Marnie. She shook her head in exasperation. 'Je-sus. Well, you're going to have to do something, aren't you.' It was a statement, not a question.

'What do you mean?' Lee looked at her with wide, frightened eyes.

'What do you think I mean? An abortion, of course.'

'But... I couldn't do that. I just couldn't.'

'Why not?' Marnie asked. 'You're only about ten weeks gone, right? It's the only possible option. You don't want to marry the bloke, do you?'

Lee shook her head. She was still trying to come to terms with the shock. Now she understood why she'd been feeling so tired, so unwell. She'd thought it had to do with working hard, with facing the relentless knockbacks at auditions. But this afternoon, she'd had to face the terrible reality — a reality she was certain would ruin everything.

'So what's the alternative?' Marnie went on .more gently. 'Have the child and give it away? There's a year out of your life anyway, isn't it?'

'Yes, but maybe I can ...' Lee gave a gulping sob. She couldn't hold back the tears. 'Oh, I don't know. I just don't know what to do.'

She covered her face with her hands.

Lee waited in the small ante room, her teeth chattering, but not from cold. Marnie had driven her to the unpretentious terrace house in one of the winding, hilly side streets that ran off Oxford Street but she hadn't been allowed to come in.

'They told me to call in a couple of hours,' Marnie said, as she hugged her friend in the doorway. 'I won't be far away.'

Lee had been welcomed by a middle-aged woman who took her details then disappeared through another door. She was left to wait alone on a hard-backed chair in the dimly lit room. A faded Persian rug covered the floor and a vase of plastic flowers stood on a small polished table beside a pile of tattered magazines. She wondered how anyone could possibly read while they waited for what was to come.

It was Marnie who had tracked down this place, Marnie who had offered to lend her the money. 'I'm not talking you into anything,' she'd cautioned, 'only giving you another option if you want it.'

It had taken Lee three agonizing days to make up her mind. Tina had been sympathetic, but made it clear that the resolution ultimately rested with Lee alone. 'It's probably the most difficult decision you'll ever have to make,' she'd said with quiet understanding, 'but it has to be your own. Only you know what you can live with.'

While she had never been particularly religious, Lee found herself wrestling with the terrible thought that abortion was as good as murder.

But then she would think of the options.

In the end, she had managed to convince herself it was the only way out. The "baby" wasn't human yet; it was only a small group of cells inside her. As long as she held on to that thought, she would manage to go through with it.

A moment later, the same woman poked her head around the door. 'Doctor's been held up a little. As soon as he's finished with this patient, I'll let you know.'

Lee felt her stomach turn to liquid. Amazingly, she hadn't given a thought to the idea that the doctor might be operating on someone else before herself. Somehow, she'd imagined that she'd be the only patient — as if such operations were far from routine. Now, she realized to her horror, she was just part of a gruesome assembly line where women lined up to have their unborn babies torn from their insides. As the graphic image filled her mind, she felt the nausea rise in her throat. Oh, God, no ... she couldn't go through with this. She just couldn't.

She didn't go home until three hours later. When she finally turned up, she found Marnie waiting for her, clearly worried and upset.

'What happened? Where were you? When I called, they told me you'd gone.'

Lee stood in the middle of the room, her face pale and drawn. She'd spent the hours walking the streets, her thoughts wild, her emotions churning. Finally, she'd caught a bus home.

'I couldn't do it,' she said. 'I just couldn't.'

As the tears rolled down her cheeks, she felt Marnie's arms go around her in comfort.

Her dream was disappearing with every day that passed. Everything she had hoped to achieve was slipping further and further out of reach. Even after she carried this baby to term and gave it up for adoption, nothing would be the same. She'd be a year older. There would surely be some toll on her figure. Other younger girls would be her rivals.

She knew she had to tell Brad; she couldn't put it off much longer. The following weekend, she broke her news during a late evening walk along Bondi Beach.

She kept her eyes on his face as she told him she was pregnant and how it had happened. It was hard to keep the bitterness out of her voice.

For a long moment he didn't say anything, but she saw the struggle he went through to keep his expression neutral. With a flash of insight, she realized that he was happy. Actually happy at what had happened!

'Oh, God, Lee ... what can I say? I'm so sorry. But you know how I feel about you. This doesn't have to change —'

Coldly, she interrupted him. 'I'm having it adopted. I've already decided that. There's no way I'm keeping it.'

His expression changed. 'But you can't! I mean ... you know I'll marry you... Of course I will. It's all I've ever wanted.'

'What about what I want, Brad?' Her tone was sharp and angry. 'Don't you understand? I don't want to get married.'

'But... this is our baby. Yours and mine. We can't just give it away.'

'And what about my career?' she asked bitterly. 'Am I just supposed to forget about that? Is that meant to go down the tube too?'

He gripped her by the upper arms, looked beseechingly into her eyes.

'It doesn't have to mean that, love. After you have the baby, everything can go on like before. We'll manage. You can go to auditions, establish your career just as you planned. A baby doesn't have to change everything. But this child is ours, love. Yours and mine. We can't give it away.'

In her heart, Lee knew she felt the same.

The marriage was arranged quickly. No one ever commented to her face about how quickly; they were all just happy that she was going to marry Brad. It wasn't anything her mother said, but Lee got the impression that the family were relieved she'd got the stars out of her eyes and was going to settle down to a "normal" life. She knew that, as far as they were concerned, she had always set her sights too high. Lee saw no point in telling them that she hadn't abandoned her dreams.

Brad was a great father; he adored his little daughter and he stuck to his promise that Lee could try to re-establish her career. By dieting furiously and pushing a sleeping Julie in her sister's second- hand pram around the streets, Lee managed to get her figure back quite quickly.

But having the baby changed everything. When Julie was a year old, Lee made a few attempts to revive her dream of a career, but it didn't take her long to see the futility of that. Going for an audition meant leaving the baby with her mother or Brad's, driving to Sydney, often running late, looking at the rows of fresh-faced young rivals and knowing she had missed her chance and that it would never come again.

The three of them had finally found another date to have dinner together.

'It sometimes strikes me,' said Tina, as the waiter flapped open the napkin and spread it on her lap, 'that I have a lovely home yet I hardly ever entertain. I just never seem to find the time to get to the supermarket, buy the stuff I have to cook, set the table, flush out the good wine glasses and all the rest of the performance if you're going to do things properly.'

'Don't worry about it,' Marnie smiled. 'I'm the same. A table for three's the answer. Let someone else do the cooking.'

'I'll drink to that.' Lee raised her glass.

Marnie swallowed a mouthful of wine. 'So what's new?' she asked.

Lee shrugged. 'I'm talking to my daughter again. Decided it's her life, she can blow it if she likes.' Aware of how harsh she sounded, she made an effort to soften her tone. 'No, really, there was no point in letting it come between us. I just have to accept that she's made a decision she's happy with.'

Marnie nodded. 'Well, at her age, I guess that's all you can do.' She looked across the table at Tina. 'What about the lodger? How's that going?'

'Fine. No problems. We hardly ever see each other. He offered to clean the pool and we say hi, that's about it.'

'Okay, so what about the important stuff — like your love life?'

Tina hesitated. She had never offered any real details about her affair with Dean. 'I've broken up with Dean,' she said finally.

'How's he taken it?' Lee was quick to ask the question.

Tina shook her head. 'Doesn't matter. It's over. I was wasting my time. Too bad it took me so damn long to face it.' She raised her glass to her lips, hoping to indicate that the subject was closed.

'Well, let me tell you my news,' Marnie announced. Her gaze moved between Tina and Marnie. She was playing for optimum dramatic effect. 'I've decided I'm going to have a daughter.'

The others stared at her, speechless.

Marnie gave a short laugh of delight, enjoying the impact she'd made.

'Yeah, well, joke! But let me tell you, the only ones who give a stuff about you when you're past it, are women — nieces, sisters-in-law, friends and daughters.'

Then, more soberly, she told them about the home in Melbourne, of her horror at what her father had been reduced to.

'It's awful. The place is full of these poor creatures who don't even know their own names or what day of the week it is. I can't believe it's happened to my own father. I really can't. For all the hell he's given me over the years, I can't bear to see him like that.' Her tone grew gentler. 'In some ways, I can't help thinking that my mother died too young and my father will die too old. Does that make any sense?'

'I think I know what you mean,' Tina said quietly.

'Well, what I want to know is, who the hell is going to look after me when I reach that stage?' Marnie's tone was joking again. 'D'you think it's too late for me to produce the sort of kid who'll visit me three times a week and smuggle me in a bottle of vodka now and then?'

Lee smiled. 'Well, you might have left it just a little late.'

'Oh, *please*, science is there to help. Though I'm just not sure what I'd be looking for in a father: the body of Brad Pitt or the compassion of a Florence Nightingale? What d'you think is more essential when you're eighty not out?'

As she joined in the laughter, Lee couldn't decide whether to break the mood and tell them she was thinking of leaving Brad.

They parted outside on the sidewalk, kissing cheeks, promising not to leave it too long until next time. In the darkness, none of them noticed the man who sat at the wheel of the car parked nearby.

Yet he was ready. And when they drove out of the parking lot, he followed the one he'd been waiting for. Experience had taught him it was far too soon to abandon his prey.

Chapter 11

IT WAS FRIDAY AFTERNOON AND Tina was flying home from Brisbane where Wealth for Women had run a series of seminars aimed at introducing women to share-market investing. The seminars had been run in three different locations over three days and Tina had been one of the speakers. Only now, as she relaxed into her business class seat, did she realize how tired she felt. The pace had been unflagging, she'd been surrounded by staff or prospective clients almost every waking minute and she was glad to be going home. Or sort of glad. Since the split with Dean, home meant being totally alone.

There was so much she missed, she realized. His calls during her working day and occasionally in the evening, those unexpected times when he was able to steal an hour or so to be with her, his wit and sense of humor, his support and encouragement, their passion for each other in bed.

The sense of loss was so great that she couldn't help wondering if she'd done the right thing. It was at those times she was tempted to pick up the phone, to hear his voice again, to tell him she'd been crazy and, if he'd only come back she'd accept everything on his terms and never ask for more.

Deep as that longing was, she knew better than to give in to the temptation. There was no point in rehashing the old arguments to herself. In a nutshell, she knew that, as far as her future was concerned, it was a no-win situation. She had to stay strong and keep herself too busy to have time to think about him.

Work was a savior of course, but it was a pity when that was all you had in life. Now there was no one and nothing to break her relentless routine. No one to relax with. No one to laugh with, see a movie with, to share dinner and a bottle of wine. The weekends were the worst. Not that she had seen Dean often then, but at least there had been the knowledge that he was in her life and that they'd get together somehow, somewhere, in the following week.

Now there wasn't even that to look forward to any more.

On Friday nights, she stayed in the office as late as possible, or occasionally went out for a drink with some of her staff. But she knew she wasn't good company. Her thoughts were too taken up with herself, the continual pondering on whether she'd cut off her nose to spite her face. But the only way to keep going was to push that doubt away. She had done the right thing, she assured herself. She had set herself free from the agony of useless hope — even the barely admitted hope that he might have got in touch and begged her to resume the affair.

'Oh ... I'm sorry. I'll come back later.'

Mark Galloway stopped in his tracks. He had come around the side of the house carrying the pool-cleaning equipment and found Tina in the pool. The dog was by his side.

Tina was equally surprised. It was Saturday morning and she had felt like some exercise. God knows, she rarely had time for a swim or anything else.

'That's okay. I've just about had enough.' She pushed back her wet hair and gave a self- deprecating laugh. 'I'm not fit enough for much more, let me tell you.'

'I normally clean every second Thursday afternoon,' he offered in explanation, 'but something came up this week.'

Tina side-stroked to the pool steps. 'Don't worry about it. You're saving me a small fortune and it's looking great.' She squinted up at him in the dazzling sunshine. 'Why don't you have a swim yourself? Maybe I never really made it clear, but I hope you realized that was the deal.'

'Thanks, I probably will sometime.'

A little self-consciously, she hauled herself out of the water and reached for the towel she'd draped over an outdoor chair. Quickly wiping her face, she tucked the towel around her waist. 'I'll leave you to it then, okay?' She gave him a smile and turned towards the house.

From the bedroom window, as she changed into pants and a shirt, she could see Mark going about his task. Strangely enough, his presence gave her a sense of comfort. In the state she was in at the moment it just felt good to have someone there. It made her feel less alone, less sorry for herself. Away from work, her life seemed lacking in normal human contact. A lot of that, she saw now, was due to her relationship with Dean. She had forsaken friends and ordinary social life to ensure she was always on call for those times when he might be able to get away. Rare as those occasions were, she had considered the possibility more important than maintaining her own personal life. Now she was paying the price.

What would she do to fill her day, she wondered. The newspapers for an hour or so, then the afternoon could be taken up with paperwork she'd brought home from the office. It scared her to think that, apart from those few words with Mark Galloway, she probably wouldn't speak to another soul for the rest of the day.

She'd already had breakfast but felt like another cup of tea. Downstairs, she walked into the kitchen and came to a dead stop. A pool of water was spreading over her expensively tiled floor. What the hell — where had that come from? As she watched, the water ran onto the timber kickboard below her kitchen cabinets. Something had sprung a leak. It had to be coming from under the kitchen sink. Quickly, she threw open the doors but there was no sign of water there. So where in the world ...? Then she realized that water was seeping out of the lower edge of the dishwasher door. Tina swore out loud. What the hell did you do to stop that? If she opened the door, even more might gush out.

The mains, she thought. She'd have to turn the water off. But where ...? She thought it was up on the footpath somewhere, but she wasn't sure. And she didn't have time to make a mistake.

Then .she remembered Mark. Surely he'd know! She could see him from the kitchen window, still working on the pool.

Letting the screen door slam behind her, she ran outside. 'Mark! Please! There's water everywhere. I don't know where it turns off. It's flooding the kitchen.'

He caught on at once, dropped the long-handled broom he was using and hurried towards her.

'It's coming from the dishwasher,' she explained quickly as they entered the house. 'Water's seeping out of the door.'

'Might be a burst pipe. It turns off under the sink. Let me see.'

In the kitchen, the pool of water had spread even wider.

'Oh my God, it's worse.'

'Hang on. Let me have a look.' Stepping through the puddle, he threw open the cupboards below the sink and, reaching inside, turned off the tap on the back wall. Then, carefully, he eased the dishwasher out of its storage space.

'I'm sure a hose has come loose.'

That was exactly what had happened. While Mark fixed the problem, Tina found some old towels to soak up the mess on the floor.

'Let me give you a hand,' he said as she dropped the sodden towels into a bucket. 'I'll take them outside and squeeze them.'

'No, really, I don't want to trouble you —'

'Come on, they're heavy now.' He was taking the bucket from her hand as he spoke.

Fifteen minutes later, order was restored and the towels were in the washing machine.

'Well,' Tina sighed, looking around, 'all I can say is, thank goodness it wasn't a work morning. Can you imagine what I'd have come home to?'

'I've fixed that properly. You won't have the problem again.' He started to move towards the door. 'Guess I'll just finish outside.'

'Look, the least I can do is offer you a coffee or something. Would you like one? I was about to make myself a cup of tea.'

He looked back at her and for a moment she thought he was going to refuse. 'Yeah, well... a cup of tea'd be nice. I'm almost finished. Give me a couple of minutes.'

Tina put everything on a tray and they sat on the back terrace.

'Sorry, I don't even have a biscuit in the place to offer you.'

'Don't worry about it,' he replied. 'Tea's fine.'

'The last thing I want to do at the end of my working day is spend a moment longer in the supermarket than I have to,' Tina said as she spooned sugar into her cup. 'I buy the basics and get out.'

'You work long hours. I sometimes hear you come in.'

Tina held her mug in two hands. 'Yeah, well, when you own your own business that's what it's like.'

'I'm not quite sure what it is you do. Something in finance, isn't it?'

She briefly explained and they chatted for a short while longer until the pot of tea was empty. About work, Sydney; nothing personal on either side.

Then, as he pushed his chair back to leave, Mark asked a question. 'Look, I've got a favor to ask you. It's my younger son's birthday next Sunday. My ex is coming to Sydney for the weekend but she wants to go out Saturday night. I'm wondering if you'd mind very much if the kids stayed with me. Just for the night. Next day I'm taking them to the zoo and out to Manly, show them around the city a bit. They won't be hanging around.'

The request caught Tina unawares. She hadn't expected to be putting up a bunch of kids as well.

'They're very well behaved. I promise you they'd be no problem.' He was doing his best to reassure her. 'Two of them can sleep on the sofa bed and I'll stick a mattress on the floor for the other one.'

She could hardly refuse.

The following Saturday night, she was determined not to sit at home staring at the walls. She asked a friend whose husband was away on business to go out to dinner. They had agreed to meet at seven thirty in a well-reviewed restaurant and Tina had just opened the garage door when Mark's vehicle turned into the driveway.

'Perfect timing,' he called out with a smile as he pulled in beside her BMW, the three children crammed into the seat alongside him.

Tina waited until they had all emerged. It would only be polite to say a proper hello.

'These are my three,' Mark said, as the children slid out and came around to join him. 'David's ten, Angie's eight and Christopher will be six tomorrow. Say hello to ...' he slurred something between a "miss" and a "miz" '... Christo.'

'Hello.' The two eldest children greeted her, the boy quite confidently, the girl more tentatively.

'So you're the birthday boy.' Tina directed her comment at the youngest who had said nothing. He nodded, eyes cast shyly down.

'Where are you all going tomorrow?' She included the others in the question.

'The zoo,' David answered. 'Dad's taking us to see all the animals and then —'

Not to be outdone, the little girl cut across him. 'Then we're going on the ferry to Manly.' Her hair was fairer than her father's and hung in two thin plaits to her shoulders.

'Sounds lovely. You have a good day then.' Duty done, Tina smiled, opened her car door and slid behind the wheel.

As she reversed, she saw Mark take his daughter's hand and lead them all towards the flat. Thank goodness she'd put nothing she really cared about in there.

The next morning, Sunday, she was up early as usual. She'd enjoyed her evening. The restaurant had lived up to its reviews and Liz was always good company. But she couldn't help thinking that maybe that was all she could expect in her life from now on — the company of a handful of women friends. Well, if that was it, she'd just have to accept and appreciate it.

As she made her way downstairs, the tall windows by the staircase gave her a view outside and she saw Mark and the children leaving the flat. They were neatly dressed, not making any noise, and the little girl,

Angie, was again holding her father's hand. Nice children, she thought. Well behaved. Despite what had happened between them, the parents had clearly done the groundwork.

The day was like every other Sunday. She attended to a few chores, finished reading the papers, and then forced herself into her study. It was lovely weather again, but what was the point of walking in a park or on a beach alone? The sight of all those couples and families would only depress her.

Sometime later in the afternoon, the phone rang just as she was thinking of giving up on the paperwork.

'Tina, it's Mark.' He was on his mobile and she could hear the noise of traffic in the background. 'I'm sorry to disturb you and I hate to put you on the spot like this, but I've just had a call from my ex. She's decided she wants to spend another night in Sydney and has asked me to hang on to the kids.' Tina could hear the edge to his voice. 'She'll pick them up early Monday morning, she says. And I guess I need to know if having them spend another night will be too much of an ask of you.'

Her thoughts still with her work, Tina was caught off guard. 'I... well, no, I guess that's okay.'

'I know it wasn't part of the deal, and I'm sorry to have to ask, but I promise you they won't cause any trouble.'

'No, no, I'm sure. They seem like good kids.'

'They are. Despite their mother's flakiness.' His voice was grim. 'I reminded her they've got school on Monday, but this sort of irresponsible behavior is about par for the course with her.'

'Listen,' Tina said impulsively, 'why don't you bring them for a swim. And what about dinner? There's only that tiny kitchenette in the flat.' The words were out of her mouth before she could think them through. 'I could cook up some pasta. What about spaghetti? Do they like that?'

'Uh — sure. But really, there's no need ... I mean, I can take them for a bite somewhere. There's no way I'd expect —'

'No, really, I'd be happy to do it. A way of thanking you for saving me last weekend.'

'Seriously, there's no need,—'

'Well, I'm insisting. Won't take me long to throw an easy meal together. And we can eat out on the terrace.' No kids inside was the subtext.

In the end Mark agreed, but there was a frown on his face as he switched off his phone.

As she made a quick dash to the supermarket, Tina wondered if she'd gone mad. Perhaps she had, when the company of four virtual strangers — three of them children — was better than spending her Sunday night utterly alone. For a split second, she felt as if she could cry at how pathetic it all was.

By six, when they arrived, she had everything ready. The four of them appeared at the back door, the children in togs carrying their towels, Mark with a bottle of wine and a couple of bottles of Coke. Digger brought up the rear, his tongue lolling in happiness. Maybe he was pleased to see the kids, Tina mused fancifully as she went out to greet them.

'Happy birthday, Chris.' She smiled at him. 'Did you all have a great day?'

'Fantastic!' David answered enthusiastically. 'The elephants were just the best!'

'Can we really have a swim?' Angie looked at her with big serious grey eyes.

'You certainly can. Just be careful.'

'They're all good swimmers,' Mark assured her. Then turning to his children he added, 'But no running around the edge or you'll be out of there quick smart. Okay, off you go.'

As the three of them headed for the water with the dog in tow, Tina accepted the bottle of wine from Mark's hand. 'Thanks. Very nice of you. Would you believe this is one of my favorites?'

He grinned at her. 'Well, let's put it this way — I use the same garbage bin too, you know. And I did think you might need some form of anesthetic, given the circumstances. I figured you don't have much to do with kids normally.'

'No, you're right. Unless you count some of those petulant businessmen I have to deal with sometimes.'

'No nieces? God kids?'

'No, I'm an only child. And no one ever asked me to be a godmother. Maybe they knew I'd be hopeless at it.' She decided to change the subject. 'I'm going to set the table outside.'

'Need a hand?'

'Well, if I give you these ...' She pulled out the cutlery and handed it to him.

'This is great!' David was on his third bowl of spaghetti. 'Better even than Mum's.'

Tina caught the look his sister threw him across the table. Instinctively, she knew what it meant. It was a look that warned him against being disloyal to their mother. How destructive divorce can be for children. Thank God she'd never had — the thought suddenly froze in her mind. Maybe she hadn't had any kids to screw up, but what if Dean had left his marriage as she'd so often hoped? Then it would have been his kids in the firing line. That was always the reason he had given her for sticking with Kathy.

It didn't make her present emotions any easier to bear but at least she knew she had done the right thing in walking away. Even if she had managed to convince Dean to leave, in the end they would have both felt equally guilty. It was better, she knew, the way things had happened.

As the five of them sat around the table, Tina watched the children enjoy the meal and realized this was the best she'd felt since things had ended with Dean. It was the company, she supposed. Where once she had enjoyed her solitude, it had taken on a different meaning after the split. Then there had been someone to miss.

For a moment, she let herself imagine how it might feel to have a family of her own. To sit around a dinner table every night with a husband she loved and the children they had brought into the world. It was almost impossible to transport herself into that space. She had always been a loner, responsible only for herself. Anyway, she had never bought the whole motherhood myth. Not every woman did these days, it seemed. Why take the risk of sacrificing identity, independence and career for the dubious pleasure of bringing children into a relationship that statistics promised had an almost fifty per cent chance of breaking up?

At least, she thought cynically, as she stood up to clear the plates, Kathy hadn't had to make too many sacrifices along those lines. She'd married young and relied on Dean for everything ever since. And, of course, Tina reminded herself, that was another good reason for Dean to stay. What would his dependent wife do without him?

'Want a hand?' Mark was on his feet as well.

'Okay, thanks.'

Leaving the children trying to teach Digger tricks on the lawn, they carried the dishes inside. As Tina rinsed them off, Mark began stacking the dishwasher.

'I hope it wasn't too much of a drag for you,' he said.

'Far from it. I don't know too many people who give me rave reviews for my cooking.'

'You never wanted kids of your own?'

'Not really.' She was filling the sink with hot soapy water to wash the pots.

'More women are thinking like that these days.' He was echoing her earlier thoughts. 'Probably a good thing too. Not everyone's suited to it. I always wanted a family, only it never occurred to me I'd end up divorced.'

'I suppose it rarely does when people get together.'

He gave a dry laugh. 'Yeah, but I considered myself a bit smarter than most. It wasn't going to happen to me.'

Tina knew she could change the subject now and keep their relationship at arm's length as it had been, or she could, as he so obviously wanted, let him talk.

'But it did.' Her non-committal comment left the choice to him.

He'd picked up a tea towel, was drying the things she'd placed on the draining rack. It should have felt awkward to have this almost-stranger in her kitchen, helping with the domestic tasks and starting to open up about his past. But it didn't.

'Yeah,' he went on. 'Our trouble was that Trish was dead keen on getting married, much more than I was at first. Wanted kids quickly too. Then, a few years later, she told me I'd "tied her down". When we finally split, she told me she was going to make up for all the time she'd lost by being married.'

'That must have hurt,' Tina replied. There had been no tinge of bitterness or anger in his tone.

'It did at the time. But it's been three years now. You get past it.'

Three years. Would it take her that long 'to get past it', she wondered. She couldn't bear the thought.

'You've never married?'

'No.' Her reply was curter than she had intended.

'I'm sorry.' He could sense he'd touched a raw nerve. 'I really didn't mean to pry.'

Tina shrugged. 'My personal life always took a back seat to my professional one.'

'Maybe it's safer that way.' He was hanging the damp tea towel on the rack.

'I'm sure it is,' she replied.

The children thanked her properly, then she stood at the front of the house watching them all walk up to the flat. When she stepped back indoors, she felt strangely unsettled and wasn't quite sure why. Was it because she'd allowed the conversation to get more personal than it should have with Mark? Or because she had enjoyed the evening much more than she could have anticipated and knew it wasn't likely to happen again?

Later, when his children were asleep, Mark Galloway sat with a cup of coffee and examined his own thoughts about the evening. A strange woman in some ways, Tina Christo, he mused. Ran a bit hot and cold. Clearly very protective of her personal space but pleasant enough when she relaxed. He'd thought she was in a relationship with the bloke he'd bumped into that time, but maybe not. He hadn't caught sight of him again. Not that that meant much, he supposed.

He didn't get the impression that his landlady was sending any vibes his way. Clearly, she was the sort of woman who'd got her life together, wasn't looking for a man to come along and rescue her. He'd seen enough of the other sort of female since he'd been divorced and he sure didn't need any more complications in his life.

Yawning widely, he decided it was time for bed.

Chapter 12

MARNIE NOW MADE REGULAR VISITS to her father in Melbourne. Usually she did it as a round trip, going down Saturday morning and returning in the late afternoon. Occasionally, she stayed overnight on a Friday with the Corkdales, because the house in Toorak had sold very quickly.

Anthony assured her that the monies realized by the sale had been prudently invested. 'There's no way of knowing just how long Charles might live and how much more specialist care he might need,' he had warned.

As time passed, Marnie saw a continuing decline in her father's mental and physical condition. He spoke less, was less mobile and his comprehension was more and more impaired. Often, he was deeply asleep when she entered his room. It might have been easy, then, to walk away, to tell herself how little point there was in making these visits, but instead she began to feel close to him, in a way she never had in her life before.

On those occasions when he was sleeping, she would sit beside the single bed in his private room and lose herself in thoughts of the past. She remembered the man he had been, so strong and capable; the husband her mother had loved so much. At other times, she would hold his bony hand and speak softly of all the feelings that often overcame her in his presence. They were emotions she felt unable to confront him with in his pitiful state, yet they overwhelmed her to the extent that she felt compelled to give them whispered expression.

Why, she asked softly, couldn't you have accepted me? Surely there could have been enough love in your heart for me as well as Mum? Was I so hard to love? Or was your love there perhaps, but you didn't know how to show it to me?

She wished so often that they could have resolved this gulf that had been so entrenched between them. Over the years she had simply locked her distress deep inside her, convinced herself that what had happened in her childhood wasn't an issue any longer. But now, in her father's presence, the sense of unfinished business welled up to choke her. And the fact that it was too late now to resolve things hurt even more than the pain of her memories.

Often, when she looked at his shrunken body beneath the sheets, she found it impossible to hold back her tears.

I'm here for you, Dad, she would whisper, *I always was. Because, deep down, I have to believe that you must have wanted to love me as much as I needed you to. I don't know what happened in your past to make you the way you were, but believe me when I say I no longer hold it against you ...*

Two weeks later, Anthony Corkdale rang to tell her that her father had suffered another, more serious stroke. It had left him paralyzed and without any apparent cognition.

It was then Marnie knew he was beyond her reach for ever.

Given the ongoing state of her father's health, Marnie twice postponed her proposed trip to Bali. She sent an email to an American friend who ran a well-known local restaurant in Ubud, not far from her house. Vivian would inform the Balinese couple who took care of the place for her about the most recent change in plan.

Much as she longed for a break, Marnie knew she couldn't leave right now.

On Friday afternoon, she had another session with her lawyers before catching a late flight to Melbourne. There was a glimmer of hope on the horizon regarding the battle over the controversial site. An independent expert, recruited by her legal team and grudgingly approved by the council, had completed his analysis of the contaminated soil. His report made it clear that the site could be made safe by following the recommended guidelines. That report would now be forwarded to council with another reminder about the urgency of the matter. Marnie felt quite certain that Rod Sawyer and his covert partners in the council chambers were going to find it almost impossible to jump over this one.

She had arranged to spend the Friday evening with the Corkdales. As a result of her regular visits, she found herself growing closer to them. In private talks with Anthony, she always brought the conversation around to her father, asking questions, wanting to know the man he had known, probing she knew, for clues that would pinpoint her father's reasons for treating her as he had.

'Charles was one of the most honest, principled men I've ever met,' Anthony had told her once. 'You don't meet too many like him in business. I was proud to be his friend as well as his lawyer.'

'Did he ever talk about me?' Marnie asked, nursing her brandy.

'He wasn't the sort of man to discuss his family life, my dear. Didn't say much about your mother either. He was an intensely private person that way.'

'I'm ... just trying to understand him. Trying to work out why he was so cruel to me.'

A silence hung between them. It was the first time she had ever spoken so openly of her father's treatment of her. It felt like a betrayal.

Anthony Corkdale sighed and shook his head. 'I'm sorry, my dear, I know it's important to you, but there's not much I can say to help you. There's only one thing I remember. Your mother told me once that he'd had a tough childhood. His own mother had died when he was very young, and his father was particularly hard on him. Making a man of him, it was probably called in those days. Losing his mother might explain why he was so dedicated to his wife above all else. He had already lost a woman he held dear, and perhaps Veronica filled that breach. Maybe it was only to her that he could show any real emotion.'

And perhaps, Marnie thought, grasping at this glimmer of an explanation that might somehow serve as expiation: her father couldn't stand anyone, not even his daughter, coming between him and the woman he had made the focus of his emotional need.

The following morning, Anthony dropped her at St Helen's on the way to his regular Saturday golf game. Afterwards, she would take a taxi back to the airport. He offered to go in with her, but she preferred to visit alone, and he understood her need for privacy.

'Don't let yourself get too upset, Marnie. Death is something that comes to us all, and your father's had a long and productive life.'

But what about happy, she found herself wondering as she walked away. How happy had his life really been, given his childhood and the loss of his wife so young? She would never be able to ask that question of him now.

Charles Ingram had been moved to the nursing home section and a staff member showed her to his new room. This wing, with its linoleum floors and hospital beds, lacked the comfortable, homey feel of the hostel. As she walked down the wide corridors, Marnie could hardly bear to glance into rooms where grey, wizened men and women lay in their beds clinging so tenuously to life.

Her father was in a room by himself. He looked peaceful enough, but his skin was the color of parchment and there was a feeding tube in his nose.

She felt her eyes fill with warm tears. Oh Dad ... Oh, my poor, poor dad. As she sat down beside the bed, her heart swelled with an overwhelming pity. Yet she felt another emotion too that was equally overpowering. Love. Unconditional love.

It filled her heart and left no room for grudges.

Eyes still blurred with tears, she literally bumped into him as she made her way back to the main entry.

'I'm sorry,' she muttered.

'That's okay.'

She looked up, instinctively reacting to a voice she vaguely recognized. It was the man she'd seen visiting his father a while ago. She couldn't remember his name.

'Steven,' he said, as if reading her mind. 'Steven Royce. We met some time back.'

She nodded, desperately trying to blink away her tears and wishing he would let her past.

'You're upset.' He looked at her with understanding. 'This place can do that to you.'

It was his sympathetic tone that undid her. She gave a gulping sob and the tears slid down her cheeks.

He laid a hand on her arm and said gently, 'Why don't I take you for a cup of coffee? There's a place quite near.'

She was beyond replying, simply nodded her head and felt his arm on her own as he led her out into the sunshine.

'I know exactly how you feel.'

Across the table, Steven Royce put down his empty cup. He'd taken her to a small coffee shop around the corner from St Helen's.

'I went through it with my mother and had to watch my father's anguish at it all happening as well.'

'I'm finding it so difficult.' Marnie was calmer now. Her tears had subsided and she'd been to the ladies' room to tidy her face. 'I just never gave a moment's thought to the fact that this might happen to my father. He was always so capable, so in control of his life.'

'None of us see it coming,' Steven Royce answered. 'It's the cruelest shock when it happens.'

'How ... long was your mother ...' Marnie's voice trailed off.

The man opposite knew what she was trying to ask. 'It's different for everyone. The decline took place over about three years. Started in her early seventies. She was dead at seventy-six.' He looked steadily at Marnie. 'It was a relief. I can honestly say that.'

She nodded. 'I think I understand.'

It was doing her good to be able to talk about it. After all, who could she discuss it with at home? It was easy with this stranger because he'd been through it too.

'How often do you visit your father?' she asked.

'I try to see him every couple of weeks, but sometimes work makes it difficult.'

He was an accountant, he explained, a partner in a large firm whose name Marnie recognized. 'We have offices in all capital cities,' he added. 'I get around a bit and that makes it hard to see Dad as regularly as I'd like.'

He was surprised when Marnie told him that she flew down from Sydney.

'Well, that makes it even tougher,' he replied.

She looked at her watch. 'I'm actually going to have to leave right this minute. My plane goes at noon.'

'How are you getting to the airport?'

'I'll call a taxi.'

'What about luggage?'

'All here.' Marnie patted her outsize satchel. 'I travel light. It's quicker.'

Steven Royce said evenly, 'Well, I'd be very happy to drop you at the airport, if you'd let me.'

The usual polite responses were ready to trip off Marnie's tongue. But all of a sudden, the idea of being in this man's calm, soothing company for a little while longer seemed just what she needed.

'Thank you. I'm sure you wouldn't offer if it were too much of a chore. So thanks, I'd be really grateful.'

On the way to Tullamarine, they exchanged a little more information and discovered, not surprisingly, that they had some mutual acquaintances.

'Melbourne's that sort of town, isn't it?' Marnie said. 'Go to the "right" school and there's always some connection you can find.'

For Steven, she learned, that school had been Melbourne Grammar. A typical choice for the son of a barrister.

'My father went there and his father too. They were both in the law. My brother as well. I was the one who broke the mold.'

In other ways, Marnie thought, Steven Royce quite fitted the mold of the men she had mixed with in her youth, those well-educated, conservative sons of equally conservative families. As a young girl, she had found them unbearably boring — trapped in their middle-class mindsets, staunch defenders of the status quo, driven primarily by self-interest. Yet, if on the surface Steven Royce seemed to embody those same attitudes and values, Marnie also got a sense of something beyond the predictable exterior. For one thing, as she'd already discovered, there was an emotional openness about him, a compassion and understanding that was hardly the norm in most men she'd met. Perhaps it had something to do with the trauma he'd faced with his parents. Maybe the impact of having to deal with their disintegration had had a salutary effect. Given her own experience these last few months, she knew how deep a mark that could leave.

She asked him if his brother shared any of the burden of caring for their father.

Keeping his eyes on the road, he considered a moment before answering. 'Phillip finds it ...' he searched for the right word '... difficult. Not only in the sense of trying to find the time, but also, I suspect, at being face to face with the reminder of his own mortality. He's more than happy to share any of the financial responsibility but he doesn't visit much. He'd always rather have second-hand reports from me.'

'Were you close to your father?'

It was a question Steven Royce might have considered too personal, but something told her otherwise.

He gave a slight shrug. 'As close as you can be to someone who worked eighty-hour weeks, I suppose. Our mother was always complaining. But he did make an effort to get to the important things — the speech nights, sporting finals, graduations and so on. Yet, in many ways it was, I suppose, like being brought up in a single-parent family. Without the financial constraints, of course.'

'And what about yourself? Do you have children?'

For the first time she felt something close off in him.

'No, my marriage broke up a few years ago. Luckily — or unluckily, depending how you look at it — we hadn't got around to having children.'

Marnie read the signs and left it at that.

At Tullamarine, they drew up at the departures gate and he opened the car door for her.

'Thank you.' Marnie put out her hand. 'For everything. It was good to talk to you. Probably exactly what I needed.'

His hand was cool against her own and, when he broke his hold, he reached inside his wallet and slipped out a card.

'If you ever feel like having a chat again, maybe I can offer you this.'

Marnie almost smiled at his strangely formal manner. This was not a guy who rushed his fences. Yet that said, she certainly hadn't been expecting any follow-up.

Good manners forced her to accept his card, but at the same time she attempted to step back from the implications. 'Just in case I need some help with my BAS?' she joked.

He held her gaze and his answer was uncommonly direct. 'No, I'm sure a smart lady like yourself has got her books under control. I was hoping you might have time for lunch with me next time you're in Melbourne.'

Marnie looked back into those assessing blue eyes. Jesus, a pick-up in the nursing home ...

Giving him a teasing smile, she responded with that well-used male line. 'Sure. I'll give you a call, okay?'

On the flight home, she found herself picking over their conversation. It was a change to meet a man who could discuss more than his work and the latest sports scores. Nor had he monopolized the talk with his own concerns.

Certainly an interesting one, she thought to herself, as the plane approached Sydney for landing. But not her type at all.

Furious, Marnie walked all around the SUV and swore out loud. She'd left the vehicle in the airport's short-term parking lot and now every tire was flat. Slamming her hand against the bodywork, she gave vent to her rage. Didn't they have security to prevent this sort of vandalism? How long was it going to take her to solve this bloody dilemma on a Saturday afternoon?

Her temper had improved little by the time she'd contacted roadside assistance, sorted out the mess and finally got home. By then, she was beginning to have second thoughts about who might be responsible for what had occurred. Maybe she was letting her paranoia get the better of her, but it was Rod Sawyer who came to mind. Was this another way of bugging her, of perhaps trying to frighten her off? Did the bastard really follow her every move? As much as she tried to tell herself she was letting her imagination work overtime, Marnie felt a sense of disquiet.

She tried to push her troubled thoughts to the back of her mind as she prepared for the evening ahead. She'd been invited to a dinner party at the home of Joanna and Hugh Dwyer. It was through her fund-raising activities that she had met the couple: Joanna sat on one of the committees and Hugh was one of the city's movers and shakers.

'There'll be eight of us,' Joanna had told her when she rang with the invitation. 'I'm sitting you next to Ian Raine. Runs his own multi-media set-up. Divorced — twice, I think — but good company.'

Why, Marnie mused, did married couples invariably feel the need to matchmake? Couldn't any of them believe that there were people who actually enjoyed being single? Still, she suppose she had to appreciate the fact that Joanna's intentions were well-meaning.

Taking a taxi, she arrived at the impressive Point Piper mansion just after seven thirty. Her hostess was one of those women with clearly nothing much to do except plan the various events in her life in fastidious detail — and that evening was no exception. It was Joanna's perfectionism, Marnie reminded herself that made her such an effective committee member.

Her dining companions were a barrister and his pediatrician wife, a well-known television presenter married to a high-flying advertising executive, and Ian Raine. Marnie judged him to be in his mid-forties, a tall, quite attractive man and more than able to hold his own in the highly competitive company. Yet, as the evening wore on, she began to realize that his conversation was almost entirely about the success of his business, his passion for skiing and the plans for his new yacht. The man was offensively self-satisfied and boring, she decided. For all that, when it was time to leave, she found her resistance low enough to accept his offer to drive her home. It would save her having to wait too long for a cab.

'I'm just at Woollahra, so it's not far out of my way,' he assured her.

'If you're quite certain it's no trouble.' As she made the polite noises, she caught the gleam in his eye that alerted her to what her dinner party companion might have in mind.

On the short drive to her apartment, Marnie tried to decide if she wanted to sleep with the man beside her or not. To be honest, with everything she'd had to cope with recently, she couldn't remember the last time she'd had sex. Weighing the balance, maybe she should take it while it was on offer.

'Would you like a quick drink?' she asked, when they pulled up outside her building.

He gave her an easy smile. 'I could manage that.'

Upstairs, she asked him to make himself comfortable in the living room while she poured them each a Drambuie. By the time she emerged from the kitchen, he was lolling back on the sofa, jacket thrown aside, tie eased from his collar. She handed him his glass and sat down beside him.

'There's only one way I can drink this,' he said and, tipping his head back, he downed the fiery liquid in one long swallow.

'Impressive. But I prefer the drawn-out approach myself.' .

'Oh, really?' He was looking at her with a suggestive smile. "Then I hope you realize it's only my Drambuie that I deal with so swiftly.' She felt his hand reach under her hair to stroke her neck. 'Everything else I like to take my time with.'

In that instant, Marnie realized that she didn't want anything to happen with this man. He was boring, self-centered and unbearably smug. No doubt his credentials as an eligible single male were all he thought he needed in this man-hungry city. But shit, she wasn't so desperate that she had to be grateful for the attentions of Ian "Success Story" Raine.

Pulling away from his touch, she rose to her feet. She saw his frown as he looked up at her.

'You know what, Ian, I've decided I'm probably out of touch with playing the prick tease these days. I'd hate to disappoint you a little later in the game, so why don't you and I just call it a night now. I'll get your jacket.'

At the front door, he looked at her with hard eyes. 'I must have been drunker than I thought. I broke my own hard and fast rule — no women over thirty.'

As he stepped out into the hall, Marnie said sweetly, 'You've got spinach stuck in your front teeth, Ian.' She waited a beat. 'It's been there all night.'

'If I told you I could be available for at least another six months, would you still be able to keep me on?'

It was a Tuesday evening. Veronique was closed and Lee and Anita were sitting in the nearby coffee shop.

'Are you kidding?' Anita's face lit up. 'I mean, would you really be available to stay on?'

Lee nodded. She was finally putting into words what she'd been wrestling with silently for so long.

'I've decided I want a break away from Brad.' Now that she had said the words out loud for the first time, she couldn't help feeling nervous.

Anita didn't seem surprised by her admission. 'I was beginning to get the impression you might be thinking like that.'

Lee lifted her shoulders in a shrug. 'It's just ... Well, you know, I feel like I've spent twenty odd years doing everything for the rest of them and absolutely nothing for myself. Now it's my turn. I want... I feel like I need to find out who I am at last. And I can only do that by having time on my own. The kids have their own lives now, and Brad ...' There was a sharpness to her tone. 'Well, as long as he's got a clean shirt and a meal on the table, I don't think it'd matter who provided them. Maybe he'll learn how to look after himself for a change.'

'Have you said anything to him yet?'

Lee shook her head. 'No. I wanted to speak to you first. If the work wasn't ongoing, then I'd have to look around for something else before bringing it up at home.'

Anita couldn't hide her delight. This was perfect timing. Her daughter was finally showing signs of recovery and wouldn't need her mother as constantly as she had the last few months. If Lee would stay on at Veronique, then Anita would be free to jump at an opportunity that had recently presented itself. While driving through the beachside suburb of Avalon, she had noted that a small, clearly unprofitable dress salon was closing down. Her business instincts had told her it would be the perfect location to open another lingerie outlet. Only the worry about finding responsible, capable staff had held her back. But if Lee could stay on at Chatswood, she'd be able to start the new place herself.

Face bright, she said to Lee, 'It could work out perfectly. Let me tell you why.'

That evening, Lee found it difficult to sleep. Now that she knew she had a job she could count on, there was nothing stopping her from taking the step of confronting Brad with her news. She couldn't pretend that the thought of it didn't make her nervous. There'd be a terrible scene, of that she was certain. And no matter how she tried to explain it, there'd be no way Brad would try to understand her feelings. Because it wasn't as if she wanted to walk out permanently on her marriage — that wasn't her plan at all. Her family were important to her; she and Brad had shared a lot and she had no intention of destroying their relationship. All she wanted was a bit of breathing space, some time on her own to establish her identity again. For all these years she'd been Brad's wife and her children's mother. Now there was a chance for her to be just Lee. To prove she could exist apart, achieve things on her own.

And to have this chance now, she told herself, would help make up for what had happened all those years ago. Then, everything had been truncated before she'd had a chance to really fly. What she wanted more than anything was to feel the heady sensation of complete freedom, to be answerable to no one and responsible only for herself.

The next morning, before she left for work, she had a call from Julie. Her daughter sounded upset and came straight to the point.

'Mum, I just wanted to tell you. I've split with Joel.'

'Oh, darling ... I'm sure that wasn't easy for you — either of you.' Lee hoped she'd found the right tone. She knew it would hurt and annoy Julie to read any relief in her mother's response.

'No, it wasn't. But ... well, the distance made it difficult. And Joel having to work on weekends didn't help. Plus I've got my work and so much on my plate at uni ...' Her voice trailed off and she sounded close to tears.

Lee realized that all her daughter wanted was her mother's comfort, and she did her best. 'He was a nice bloke, darling, but there'll be other nice men when the time is right. I really think you've done the best thing for yourself at the moment. Look,' she glanced at the time, 'I'm sorry I can't talk now or I'll be late for work. Would you like to meet for dinner this evening? We can talk things through then.'

'I — no, thanks, but I can't tonight. I'm working.'

'Well, what about tomorrow? It'll have to be after late closing though.'

'I've got lectures then. No, really, I — I'll ring you, Mum. I just wanted you to know. Just wanted to get it off my chest, I suppose.'

'That's totally natural, darling. So try not to worry about it and we'll see each other soon.'

As she hung up, Lee found herself with the uneasy impression that there had been something more Julie had wanted to tell her. When they caught up, she reassured herself, she'd get to the bottom of things.

That Friday evening, during the drive back to Newcastle, her stomach felt tight with nerves. She was dreading the confrontation with Brad, but nothing was going to make her change her mind.

Unwilling to spoil the entire weekend, she decided to delay bringing up the subject until Sunday morning. On Saturday night, they went to the club as usual and bumped into her sisters and their husbands and any number of mutual friends. Later, they all ended up having a meal together but Lee had little appetite, knowing how things were soon to change.

When they went to bed, Brad was keen to make love. But, given the circumstances, she found it very difficult to share his ardor. Even though there were few surprises or thrills left, their lovemaking had usually been satisfying enough, but tonight her sexual response was diminished by a gnawing sense of guilt and apprehension. Yet strangely, her other senses seemed more acutely alert than normal as she felt the weight of her husband's body on her own. It was as if she were storing away the memory of his taste and smell and feel for the time they would be apart.

Brad must have noted some difference in her because afterwards he asked, 'Anything the matter, love?'

She could still feel the heavy hammer of his heart against her ribs.

'Just a bit tired, I think.'

He kissed her cheek. 'You're working too hard. I'll be glad when it's all over and you're back home again.'

For a long time she lay in the darkness, listening to his steady breathing, her mind filled with her turbulent thoughts.

'*What* are you telling me?'

'Just for six months, Brad, that's all. I need to do this. Please, don't make it hard for me.'

They were in the kitchen. Danny was out and the two of them were facing each other across the table.

'Hard on you? How do you think it's been on me all this time?' His cheeks were flushed with anger. 'I never wanted you to go to Sydney, I told you that. And now you throw this crap at me!'

Steeling herself in the face of his temper, Lee stood her ground. She had known it was going to be like this.

'Just listen to yourself,' she retorted. 'I... I... I... It's always been what *you* want, Brad. Well, this time I'm doing something for *me*.'

She jumped as his fist slammed down on the pine table.

'Are you crazy? I absolutely forbid it! You are *not* moving to Sydney. What the hell are people going to think around here?'

'I couldn't care less what people think. I'm doing this for me! In a way, it'll help make up for everything I was forced to walk away from twenty odd years ago.'

'Oh, no ...' He rolled his eyes and shook his head in angry exaggeration. 'I don't believe it! You're still harping on all that? Grow up, Lee! We were both responsible and we've had to live with the consequences. So you didn't become a big star, didn't find bloody fame and fortune. So what? Is it that bad having a husband and kids who love you?'

She could feel the tears of self-pity gathering in her eyes. Why did she have to endure this onslaught? Why couldn't he just *see*?

'You don't understand! You'll never understand. Of course you're all important to me, but I want my chance to live too! To have a life before I'm too old. To remember what it was like to feel excited and happy and have something to look forward to.'

There was a long moment of silence. He stared at her, his expression tight and grim as he digested her words. When he spoke again, there was a harsh bitterness in his voice. 'Now I think I'm getting it. There's someone else, isn't there? That's what all this is about. I let you go to Sydney and you've bloody well met someone else!'

'No! You're absolutely wrong!' She spoke quickly, trying to reassure him. 'I promise you. That's not what I'm looking for. I'm not trying to end our marriage. I just —'

'I thought I knew you, Lee. I thought I could trust you.' His voice trembled with rage. 'Well, you bloody well do what you like. Maybe we're all better off without you if that's the case.'

Without waiting for her reply, he threw back his chair and strode out of the room.

She didn't try to stop him. It was obvious he wasn't going to listen to anything at the moment. Later, she'd make him understand that he had nothing to worry about on that score. She wasn't leaving home to look for affairs. That was the last thing on her mind.

Lee packed her things into the car and was ready to leave for Sydney not long afterwards. She looked for Brad to say goodbye, but he wasn't in the house or garden. Then she saw his pushbike was gone. Exercise had always been his way of dealing with stress. She had already written a note for Danny telling him as gently as possible what was happening and asking him to pass on the news to Troy. She explained she'd be in touch with them both and that they were welcome to visit her in Sydney any time. They had her mobile number and she also added the number at the shop.

Finally, she sat down and tried again and again to leave a message for Brad. That was a lot harder than a note for the boys. Nothing she wrote seemed right somehow. In the end, she merely put down that she'd call him and hoped that he too would keep in touch. *From time to time*, she had added. The whole point of the break, after all, was to give her time to be alone, to discover who she might still be when she was no longer suffocated by the roles of wife and mother.

On the drive to Sydney, Lee used her mobile to ring Julie. But her phone was switched off. She'd try later and hope she could talk to her before Brad did.

Now that she'd require longer-term accommodation, Anita had pulled a few strings and found another apartment in the same block which the owners were willing to lease on a six-monthly basis. Lee spent the afternoon shifting her bits and pieces between apartments and stocking up on groceries. In between times she tried Julie's number again, still without success.

Only after she had cooked a simple dinner for herself and sat down in front of the TV did she have a chance to reflect on how she felt about everything. It had been upsetting to see Brad's reaction. Of course, it had been a shock for him. But when he calmed down, she hoped he would try to understand why she needed to do this. Already, her 'aloneness' felt different now that she knew she wouldn't be going home every weekend. From now on she'd be dependent on her own inner resources, and the thought was exciting as well as a little scary. But, she reminded herself, it was a challenge she was looking forward to. She was going to make the most of this time by herself; it would help clear the air on her past so that when she finally returned to her home and marriage, she could do so without any further regrets.

Just before she went to bed, she tried Julie again. This time she finally reached her. As succinctly as possible, Lee told her what was happening.

'This is something I really need to do,' she ended. 'It's not easy for you, I know, love, but I really want you to try to understand.'

'But Mum, are you sure? Have you really thought about this? You know how Dad'll feel. He loves you. He won't be able to handle it. You can't do this to him.'

She heard the alarm in her daughter's voice.

'Darling, please don't judge me. I've got my life to live, just as you have yours. I need this time on my own. In the long run, it'll probably be better for our marriage.'

'But how can you say that?' Julie responded urgently. 'Six months apart is a long time. Anything can happen. Mum, please don't do this to him, or any of us.'

Lee tried her best to be soothing. 'Darling, I know you're a bit shocked by it all at the moment. That's only to be expected. I think you and I need to get together and have a really good talk about it. I want to explain things so you truly understand where I'm coming from on this.'

'But Mum —'

'Julie, please. Don't let me down, love. We're both in Sydney together now and I, for one, need you more than ever.'

By the time she hung up, Julie had agreed to join her for dinner the following evening and Lee assured herself she'd make her daughter understand.

But when they met in a small Indian restaurant, she found Julie withdrawn and reluctant to listen to her point of view.

'But why, Mum?' she asked plaintively. 'Haven't you got everything you want? A home, a husband who loves you, your family. What more can you be looking for?'

Frustrated by her daughter's lack of empathy, Lee did her best to explain. But how could she make a girl of Julie's age understand how stifled she felt, how trapped and claustrophobic? How could she open her eyes to the fact that life passed so much more quickly than you expected and she didn't want to waste a day of it any more? By the time they parted, she felt mentally exhausted by her efforts.

Outside on the footpath, she looked into her daughter's beautiful, yet strained face. 'Think about what I've told you tonight, Julie, and try not to judge me too harshly.'

She kissed her daughter fondly and gave her a warm hug. When they drew apart, she squeezed Julie's shoulder and said more lightly, 'I think we should eat together more often. You need to put some meat on those bones.'

Her daughter shrugged off her hold. 'I'm okay.'

With conflicting emotions, Lee watched her walk off. She didn't want to hurt her, or any of them. Why did they all have to make it so difficult? Why couldn't they just try to understand?

It had taken Tina almost ten minutes to find a spot in the crowded supermarket parking lot. Now, she thought grumpily as she headed for the entrance, there was the battle to face inside. These days it seemed that whatever time she stopped to pick up her groceries, there were always too many people, too few trolleys and never enough checkout operators.

Managing to snatch a trolley from under the nose of someone who gave her a filthy look, she steered it towards the turnstile. Twenty-five minutes later, she was finally back outside and heading towards her car.

'Hi!'

She turned to see Mark. He was carrying a couple of grocery bags. 'I see you've been looking for fun on Friday nights too,' he said.

'Sure.' She gave him a smile. 'The local supermarket, where it all happens. Now I have to go home and start cooking the damned stuff.'

He had fallen in step beside her as they headed for the parking lot.

'Not me. By Friday night I've had enough of my own cooking. I'm dropping this stuff at home and heading for North Sydney Leagues.'

'Lucky you.' It was an automatic response. The sort of reply you made even when you'd never stepped inside a Leagues Club in your life — which she certainly hadn't. But it seemed her flippant words had been taken at face value.

'Well, if you're not doing anything better, why not join me? I'd be happy to take you as my guest. A thank you for your invite to my kids.'

Caught unawares, Tina couldn't think of an excuse. 'Oh, really, I didn't mean —'

'Only if you'd like to come, of course. No pressure.'

Hell ... she was going to look pretty rude if she refused now.

'Well... okay. Thanks. I'll just put these away and get changed.'

'No rush. Give me a yell outside when you're ready.'

What did you wear to a football club, she wondered as she hurried upstairs after stashing away her groceries. Casual, she figured. Pants and a decent top. She wished she had five minutes for a shower; but then he might think she was taking the invite too seriously, spending too much time getting ready. Why, she wondered, as she peeled off her work clothes, wasn't anything simple any longer?

In the end, the evening turned out more pleasurable than she could have imagined. The place itself was a revelation. She'd read how much poker machines contributed to the facilities of these places, but still she was impressed. The restaurant meal was excellent too — both in value and standard. And on top of everything else, there was live music and entertainment.

They shared a bottle of wine with their meal and Tina felt herself relax. She realized she was actually enjoying herself. Mark was easy to be around. They talked about work, about his children, and he told her a little about his own childhood years in Armidale.

'I loved the country, it was the best place to grow up. Don't know if I could say the same now though.'

Almost without realizing it, Tina too opened up a little about her own background. She couldn't remember the last time she had spoken to anyone about her migrant parents or her tough upbringing, no matter how concisely. It certainly wasn't highlighted on her CV.

'So you're self-made, not a silver-spoon girl after all.'

She thought she heard genuine admiration in his voice.

'Absolutely,' she said firmly. 'I've worked hard for all I've got. Damned hard.'

He studied her a moment over the top of his glass. 'And would you say it's made you happy? Genuinely happy, I mean.'

The question, so unexpected, threw her.

Before she could answer, Mark spoke again. 'I only ask because when I owned a mortgage-free home, two cars, a boat and all the other bits and pieces, I thought I was real happy. It wasn't until I lost the lot in my divorce that I found I didn't need all those things in my life. They weren't what brought real happiness.'

Tina wasn't sure if she wanted to pursue this line of conversation. Still, she heard herself asking: 'What do you think does?'

He didn't have to consider his answer. 'People, friends, health, having healthy, happy kids. That's all that really matters.'

Even while she heard herself agreeing with him in principle, Tina knew that her home with all its comforts, her successful business and personal share portfolio, were always going to be equally vital to her idea of happiness.

Chapter 13

IT WAS SATURDAY MORNING. MARNIE was just about to leave for the airport when someone knocked on her apartment door.

She frowned. Why hadn't they used the intercom at the ground floor entrance? Her first thought was that it must be a neighbor, although occasionally, one of the residents didn't close the front security door properly. Someone was always sounding off about it at the body corporate meetings.

'Yes?' she called out, without opening up.

'It's Fran Morris, Marnie. D'you remember? You took me and my little girl in a while ago. Put us up until we had a place to go to.'

Marnie frowned again. What was the woman doing here? And just when she was ready to leave. Opening the door, she saw the large floral arrangement before she saw her unexpected visitor's smiling face.

'I'm sorry I couldn't ring,' Fran Morris apologized shyly. 'No one'd give me your number. But I just wanted to say a proper thank you from Shelley and me.' Her smile growing wider, she handed the flowers to Marnie.

'Oh, they're lovely. But, really, there was no need to spend your money on me. I was happy to help.' Marnie was touched by the gesture. 'I'm just about to leave for the airport, but come in a minute.'

'Thanks, but I won't keep you,' Fran responded. 'Just wanted you to know that everything's worked out. I got a job, cleaning in a motel. There might be the possibility of relieving the receptionist as well.'

'Yes, Judy told me. That's great news. And I have to say, you're looking so much better.' It was true: the haunted look had left Fran Morris's face.

The other woman smiled. 'Thanks. I'm feeling like I'm really on top of things now. And Shelley's doing a lot better at school now that things are quiet at home.'

'No more trouble from the ex?' Who probably wasn't yet the ex, Marnie realized.

'No. I took out the AVO but he's never found us. I feel safe now. Shelley too. It was her I used to feel so upset about.'

Marnie nodded. 'I can understand that. But you've done so well, getting this far. It's a real achievement, Fran. You should be proud of yourself.'

Fran Morris looked pleased at the compliment.

'Well, I know you're in a hurry,' she said. 'I won't hold you up any longer.'

Normally, Marnie would have insisted that she come in for a quick cup of coffee, but today that was impossible.

'I'm sorry I have to rush,' she apologized. 'But let me drop these inside and I'll grab my things and come downstairs with you.'

The flowers were in one of those little dishes of water and they'd be fine until that evening. She left them sitting on the dining room table.

As they took the lift to the foyer, Marnie asked Fran where she was living now.

'We've got a granny flat at Randwick. Judy helped us find it. It's not big, but it's all we need.'

'Did you drive over? Have you got a car?'

'No, not yet,' Fran replied. 'That's next on my list.'

'Would you like a lift then? It's on my way. I can drop you somewhere if you're going straight home. Then we can chat a bit in the car.'

The other woman was easily persuaded.

Back in Melbourne, Marnie found her thoughts returning to Steven Royce. Was there really any point in calling him? He was a nice enough guy but hardly the type she'd pick for a fling. Nor could she imagine that he'd consider her his type once he knew her a bit better. Some little lady in crushed linen and pearls, sitting demurely behind the wheel of her Merc, would be more in line for Mister Conservative.

No matter how many times she visited, it didn't get easier. Sitting on a chair by her father's bed, Marnie listened to his breathing. How many more breaths did he have left, she wondered. What date would she remember for the rest of her life as the day of his death? Her morbid thoughts engulfed her and took too long to shake off. Maybe she shouldn't come here as often; it made no difference to her father now. But it made a difference to her, she realized. There had been so few times in her life when she could be easy in her father's company. The bitter irony of the situation did not escape her that now she finally was. All her tormented memories were slowly vanishing, leaving only the intensity of her pity and love for this man, her father, who lay slowly dying among strangers.

When she walked away at last, her emotions were raw. How many more times would she have to see him like this? How much more could they both endure? She was choking on her grief and sorrow.

In the foyer, she rummaged through her bag to find her mobile. She had time to call in on the Corkdales before catching her flight back. And it would help her to talk.

It was then she thought again of Steven Royce. He had let her talk. He had understood, better than those who had never been faced with this trauma.

After a moment's hesitation, she found his card in her wallet and rang his number.

'If only you'd called earlier.' Even over his mobile, she heard the genuine regret in his voice. 'I'm just on my way back from Geelong. I've been seeing a client.'

'It doesn't matter. I just thought...'

Could she really say that she'd felt the need for his comfort? A near stranger? Yet one whose calm sympathy had helped her once before.

'Can you change your flight?' he asked, surprising her.

'No, not really.'

'Then what about next week? In Sydney. I'm planning to be up there on Thursday. In fact, I was going to try and find your number. Would you be free for dinner that evening?'

She didn't feel like playing games. She gave him her number and they made arrangements.

That week was as busy as any other. Council was stalling on the soil report and now her lawyers were talking about taking the matter to the Land and Environment Court.

'They're an alternative to council in a way,' her lawyer told her. 'It might be the pressure you need at this point. They're not going to be able to resist much after that.'

Still, the matter of costs continued to worry her: they were mounting up in a frightening way. But she'd gone too far to pull out now. Justice was on her side, she knew, but how often was that the deciding factor in a court of law?

On Wednesday, she was at the Blakehurst site when Mark Galloway walked by, following the other workers to the canteen truck on its lunchtime round.

'Hi,' she said. 'How're the lodgings working out?'

'Fine, no problem. Thanks again for your help.'

'Are you thinking of moving on? Back up the coast, I mean.' She hadn't really taken it on board before, but this was some hunky guy. And on the loose. Too bad Tina wouldn't give a simple tradesman the time of day — even one who looked like Mark Galloway.

Her employee shook his head. 'No. Nothing happening there. The work's in Sydney. And it's still near enough to see my kids.'

Oh, right. Now she remembered. Kids. Definitely not Miz Fastidious Christo's cup of tea, she thought with wry humor.

On Thursday evening, while she showered and got ready to meet Steven Royce at his inner city hotel, Marnie realized with a certain amusement that she really couldn't remember the last time she'd gone out with a man her own age. Maybe she was slipping. Or — she took a reality check — just maybe she was looking forward to spending an evening with someone she could talk to as well as ... Well, she wasn't quite sure of the sex bit here. Sure, it had been a while, but this bloke was turning out to be a friend, someone who was helping her through one of the toughest times of her life. And let's face it, she thought, she didn't know exactly what he might have in mind either.

It promised to be an interesting evening.

For convenience sake, they had decided to dine at the hotel. Marnie was almost there when her mobile rang. It was Judy and she sounded upset.

'I'm sorry to disturb your evening, Marnie, but I thought you ought to know. Remember Fran Morris?'

'Sure. She called at the apartment this week. Was silly enough to spend her hard-earned money on buying me flowers.'

'Oh, Jesus — so that's how ...'

'What's wrong? What's the problem.'

'She's in intensive care. He found her — the bastard husband. Broke into the flat and thumped the living daylights out of her then took off. Probably hoping she'd never pull through.'

Marnie swore quietly. 'What happened to the daughter?'

'She managed to get out, thank God, and ran to the neighbors. They called the cops, but by the time they arrived Kevin Morris was gone and Fran was in an ambulance on the way to hospital.'

'Je-sus. How the hell did he find her?' She had a sudden thought. 'Shit, you don't think it was the day she came to me? That he somehow picked up her trail that way?'

'Who would know? He's probably been trying to find her for weeks. But Marnie, I've got to warn you. Fran managed to tell us that he knew exactly who had helped her and — to quote her quoting him — he was going to "bash their effing brains in. Especially that rich effing bitch who breaks up effing marriages".'

There was a moment's silence and then Judy said seriously, 'I had no idea he knew where you lived. Maybe he was watching your place and saw Fran visit you.'

'Is she going to be all right?' Marnie ignored Judy's alarm.

'Yes, thank God. The doctor said she'll make it. Though who the hell knows what she'll look like after thirty odd stitches. I've got Shelley safely ensconced at one of our other places. She's totally traumatized as you could expect, but we're doing our best.' The social worker's voice tightened and revealed her personal concern. 'It's you I'm worried about now.'

'Well, don't be. Just tell those snail-paced bloody cops to pull their fingers out and get that nutter behind bars where he belongs. They've got plenty to hang on him now.'

'Sure,' Judy answered cynically, 'until some bleeding-heart public defender gets him off with ten Hail Marys and a smack on his hairy wrist.'

'Yeah. And don't forget, that's what we pay our taxes for.'

Marnie was still fuming over the incident when she walked into the foyer of the Sheraton on the Park.

Steven was watching for her and stood up to greet her, shunning the social kiss, she noticed, and giving her a smile instead.

He picked up her mood straightaway. 'You're upset about something.'

'I sure as hell am.'

'Let's go and sit down at our table and you can tell me about it, if you want to.'

It's crazy, Marnie thought, more than a little perplexed as they made their way towards the dining room. The minute this guy talks to me, all the adrenaline just drains away.

What was he? Some sort of guru?

While they waited for their meal, she told him all about it. How she'd met Fran Morris, how they'd done their best to spirit her away from the danger of her marriage, what had happened to her now.

It helped to get things off her chest.

Steven listened without interrupting. Now he asked, 'How long have you been involved with these halfway houses?'

Marnie told him, giving him a concise version of the history.

Steven stared at this attractive and unusual woman on the other side of the table with its shining silver and glassware. He'd known Marnie Ingram was different, but he hadn't known quite how different.

The evening seemed to be over almost before it had begun. They never ran out of things to talk about. It had been like a mutual confessional, Marnie thought: she disclosing how it had been with her father, the rejection, the pain, the lifelong gulf that had existed between them; and Steven gradually revealing what had happened in his marriage.

'We met at university. Caroline was very bright, topped every year, won the faculty medal and was immediately accepted into one of the biggest and most prestigious law firms. After we'd been married five years, I wanted to take a couple of months off and travel together. But she wouldn't hear of it. It would damage her career prospects, she said, to take such a lengthy break; there was no way she could think about leaving. By then too, she'd started studying for her MBA, so we agreed that we'd wait till she'd finished that and then fit in a trip to Europe.'

He shook his head. 'It just wasn't going to happen. As soon as she'd finished the MBA she was offered a posting in New York. Or I thought she was offered it. In fact, as I found out later, she'd applied for it. Even when she knew I wouldn't be able to leave my firm for the twelve months she would be away.'

He spread his hands in a gesture of futility. 'I knew then there was no future for us. Her ambition was always going to come first.'

'You were the one to bring up the question of divorce?'

'Yes.' He spoke quietly. 'Her response, I have to be honest, was clearly one of relief that I wasn't going to have to be factored into her future plans.'

'I guess that must have hurt.'

He nodded. 'It all did. I'd married for life I thought. I never dreamed it would be over in less than ten years.'

'So that's why no kids.'

He nodded again. 'She always put me off. After she did this, when she'd finished that ... And now it's probably too late.'

'Oh, I don't know.' Marnie let a small smile play around her lips. 'There's plenty of eager thirty-somethings with their biological clocks ticking like time bombs.'

He returned her smile with one of his own. 'Don't I know it. I've met too many of them.'

'And?' She left the question hanging. She was pushing the boundaries of politeness, she knew. But what the heck. Her curiosity was getting the better of her.

He answered lightly, not seeming to take offence. 'Let's just say I think I'd be swapping an ambitious career woman for an ambitious mother.'

'Meaning?' Now she was really pushing her luck, but for some reason she wanted to be very clear about where this guy was coming from. Or did she mean, where he'd been...?

'Meaning, I got the impression from a lot of them that it was having the child that mattered, and a husband was more or less incidental.'

Marnie shook her head with mock gravity. 'No wonder so many of you poor blokes are turning gay.'

He gave her a slight grin as he lifted his wine glass. 'Not me,' he said with quiet reassurance.

But even that wasn't enough to pitch them both into taking the next step. For the first time in a very long time, Marnie realized that the call wasn't hers alone. Steven Royce hadn't given any signal that he was desperate to bed her and she was still trying to figure out the authenticity of her own feelings on the matter. In the end, it didn't seem like a good idea to risk taking a step that might alter the balance of this very pleasant friendship.

They said goodbye at the elevators.

'I'm sorry I can't drive you safely home,' he said.

'No problem. I'm a big girl. This is my city now, remember?'

'When are you next coming south?'

She felt as if she had just let out her breath, as if she had been waiting to hear those words and now she could relax. And, at that moment, she chose not to analyze the reasons why.

'Maybe next weekend. It's crazy. He doesn't know me, hardly knows anything but I feel I have to be there. As if by sitting there I can remake the past. Pretend we had the relationship I always longed for.'

Shit, she was doing it again, spilling every bloody emotion she'd ever felt. What was it about this guy?

Steven Royce took her words on board with the same quiet equanimity he'd shown all evening.

'There's nothing that says we have to act rationally when our hearts are dictating quite the opposite. Sometimes you just have to go with your gut feeling.'

Marnie stared back into that calm, fine-featured face, trying to read what mightn't be there at all. Before she could think of a suitable response, he added, 'If maybe becomes a definite next weekend, would you let me know? Perhaps I can talk you into having dinner with me again.'

This time, when he said goodbye, he leaned over and gave her a kiss on the cheek. More than a peck but nothing that lingered.

Just enough to make her think about it the whole drive home.

It was Lee's second weekend in Sydney. She didn't feel like going straight back to the flat on Friday evening; not when the city was full of so many exciting places to go. Earlier in the week, she'd rung both Marnie and Tina, hoping to line something up. But Marnie was already doing something on the Friday evening, and on the Saturday was taking off again to Melbourne. It was clear there had been some fundamental change in her relationship with her father. Tina, meanwhile, had a full-on training seminar that would keep her tied up until the Sunday evening. It was hard for Lee to hide her disappointment especially as Julie too was busy, working both nights in the restaurant.

When she closed up the shop, she hoped she might receive another invitation from the girls in the adjoining shoe store. But while they waved and called out good night, they didn't ask her to join them again, and Lee found it impossible to invite herself. Of course, she could have gone to the bar alone in the hope of bumping into them. But what if they'd gone somewhere else? She'd never walked into a bar by herself in her life. She'd feel so self-conscious.

It was different for men, she thought enviously, they could go anywhere they liked alone. It only proved that she'd have to try to meet more people if she were to make the most of her time in Sydney. She was still sure that six months was all she'd need to get things out of her system. That would be long enough to really feel part of the tempo of the city; to satisfy the need inside her to find out who she was now, and what she was capable of.

She'd rung Brad only once since she'd left and that had been to sound out how he was taking things. The conversation hadn't lasted long. He'd still been angry and it had only made her angry too as she attempted yet again to make him understand why she needed to do this.

Nor would he accept that she wasn't having an affair.

'It's not about that, Brad,' she'd insisted again. 'I don't want you ever to think it is. Please believe me on that point at least.'

'I don't know what to believe any more, Lee. I thought I was giving you everything I was capable of. I thought we were happy — and look how bloody wrong I was. I never knew what was going on inside that head of yours.'

'You never knew, because you never took the time to ask me.' Her voice rose in pitch as she justified herself. 'You took me for granted every step of the way. When did you ever try to make me feel special? Did you ever buy me flowers? Ever take me anywhere besides the bloody club or the movies now and then? You spent more time coaching the damned football team than you spent with me.'

'And that's a reason to leave, is it?' he answered bitterly. 'Because I didn't buy you flowers? It doesn't matter that I fed and clothed you, paid every damned bill, and worked overtime whenever I could so we could have a decent retirement.'

Oh, Je-sus ... Her body heated with frustration. He would never understand. Of course those things were important, but she wanted more than that. She wanted the little things that told her he noticed her, that told her she hadn't disappeared into the background of his life where being Mrs Brad Kingsford was her only existence.

'Maybe it's better if we're not in touch for a while, Brad. It's not getting us anywhere having these sorts of conversations.'

'Suits me,' he said, and hung up on her.

Finally, on Monday evening, she met up with Julie. It was easier to eat out somewhere convenient for them both than for her daughter to come the distance to the apartment and then have to get home again. But it still amazed Lee how much it could cost to have a simple meal in this city. Not that Julie seemed to eat much despite all her coaxing.

'What's wrong?' Lee finally asked. 'Don't you like it?'

All Julie seemed to do was push the food around her plate. She'd been quiet all evening and it had been left to Lee to do the talking.

With a resolute gesture, Julie put down her fork and pushed the plate aside. 'I'm not hungry.'

Lee studied her daughter's gaunt, troubled face. 'Julie, something's the matter, darling. What is it? I want you to tell me.'

The girl looked back at her mother and the words came out in a rush. 'Mum, I just can't cope with this.'

'With what? Dad and me, you mean?'

Julie nodded. 'I can't.'

Lee looked at her daughter in concern. 'Darling, please don't let yourself get upset. I told you, this is between Dad and me. It —'

'No it's not! It's killing Dad. He calls me ... and I don't know what to say. I can't take sides in this, Mum. I just can't!'

The anguish in her voice alarmed Lee. She was angry at Brad for having brought it to this; it wasn't fair of him to dump it all on Julie.

'He has no right to upset you like this.' She kept her voice calm. 'I'll talk to him about it. He can't drag you into things that are between him and me.'

Julie looked back at her mother with tearful eyes. 'But I am dragged into it, Mum. We all are. It's the whole family that's having to bear this. The boys too. They don't say it in so many words, but I know they hate what's happening just as much as I do.'

'It's not for ever, darling.' Lee was fighting to tread the fine line between her sympathy and concern and trying to restate her case. Her voice softened. 'Listen, you don't understand all this at the moment and I don't expect you to. And maybe what I'm trying to do now, you'll never have to. It's a different generation. You expect your freedom. You'll never let yourselves be submerged as my generation of women did. You won't ever have to turn around twenty years later and try to prove that you still exist.'

But she could tell, looking into her daughter's eyes, that her words weren't making much sense.

On Thursday evening, Lee was finishing her usual quick meal in the coffee shop when someone came up beside her.

'Hi. Are you still talking to me?'

She looked up and recognized the man who had spilled the food on her. He was carrying a tray on this occasion too.

'Hello,' she said and added jokingly, 'I hope you're going to be careful with that thing.'

Graham Park grinned. 'Don't worry, I've learned my lesson.'

'Are you looking for a table? I'm just about to leave.'

'Thanks, they're busy tonight.' He put his tray down and pulled out the opposite chair. 'I'll have to time it better next time,' he said, smiling at her again. 'I hate eating alone.'

'I don't mind it. I guess I've spent too many nights at rowdy family meals.'

'This bachelor envies you then.'

'Not that I've had much of them lately,' she added, not quite sure why. Maybe it was just nice to talk to someone who was friendly and not a customer.

'Why's that?' He opened a sachet of sugar and emptied it into his cup.

'I'm temporarily in Sydney while the rest of them are at home in Newcastle.'

'Are you enjoying it?'

'Yes, love it. It's fantastic. Just a bit hard to meet people though.'

'Big cities always have that drawback,' he agreed. 'I'm from a small town myself, outside Wollongong. Took me a long while to feel at ease in this place. It's getting to know people that makes the difference.' He was buttering the slice of bread that went with his chicken casserole.

'I'm sure you're right,' Lee responded.

'Actually, taking classes or joining something where you have a common interest with people really helps.'

'Maybe that's what I should be looking at.' She was just making polite conversation now, wondering how to break away and get back to work.

Graham Park stuck his fork into his food. 'I'm a member of a local musical society. We're just about to start auditions for *42nd Street*. I've found that a great way to meet people.'

Suddenly Lee was interested. 'You mean they're after singers and dancers?'

'Yeah, but that's the easy part. It's finding the stage managers and choreographers that's more problematic.'

Lee felt her heart skip with excitement. What a perfect way to meet people and get into the swing of things. Not as a dancer or singer, of course, but she'd really enjoy the challenge of the choreography. She took a quick glance at her watch. Tracey wouldn't mind holding the fort a little while longer, she was sure.

'Tell me about this musical society, Graham. I've had a bit of experience with dance,' she said modestly. 'Maybe there's something I can do.'

Chapter 14

MARK WAS LISTENING TO MUSIC and relaxing with a beer. It was his weekend without his children and on this Saturday evening he'd rented a movie to fill in the time. He tried not to think how different his weekends might be if his marriage hadn't gone belly up. Then, there had never been time to "fill in"; there'd always been plenty to keep him busy around the house and he'd enjoyed doing all the little fix-up jobs. On Saturday afternoon he would take the kids to their various sports and hobbies, do a bit of gardening and book work, and in the evening they'd usually have a barbecue. He'd cook, and Trish would make the baked potatoes and salads. Then they'd sit outside on the patio until well past the children's usual bedtimes. Happy families, he had thought. As it had turned out, that wasn't the way Trish had seen it.

He frowned as he thought of his ex-wife. He'd sensed a restlessness in her the last few times he'd picked up the kids. She'd been going out with some bloke for a few months, but he'd heard through the grapevine that it had bitten the dust. Not that he cared, but word had also reached him that she'd been thinking about moving, that she wasn't happy any longer on the coast. And that worried him. He didn't want his kids disrupted any more than they had been; they'd been through enough already.

Did you ever understand women, he asked himself as he finished the last of his beer. How could you ever know what they really wanted? He sure as hell had no idea.

But he'd enjoyed his evening with Tina. An interesting woman, and one who had clearly known exactly what she wanted and gone out to get it. It was obvious that her background had been the catalyst to her drive and ambition. She certainly hadn't been waiting for some white knight to come to the rescue.

On the other hand, he mused, maybe these career women had to learn to bring a bit of balance into their lives. It was one thing to be successful, but there was nothing wrong with making a success of your personal life as well. Marriage was a great institution if you found the right person. Still, maybe that was the problem, he figured: finding the person who really fitted. You needed time for that, if nothing else. Not that he was a contender. As far as he was concerned, that race was over for him. And Tina Christo gave him the impression that she thought the same way. Not that he'd know, he reminded himself. His landlady played her cards close to her chest on that topic. But he certainly didn't get the feeling that she was out there looking.

Pushing himself out of the chair, he switched off the music and slipped the movie he'd rented into the machine. There was nothing on TV that appealed to him and he had to amuse himself somehow. But when he pressed the play button, nothing happened. With a frown, Mark went through the process again with a similar result. This is when you need your children, he told himself. David was a wizard with gadgetry. Was it the DVD or the player that was the problem? If it was the former, he'd have to make the trip back to the store and change it. But then it could be that his player had packed up on him.

He stood for a moment in indecision. Then, ejecting the DVD he looked out of the window. He could see lights on in the house: Tina was home. He picked up his mobile.

Even though she'd opened the windows and patio doors, the house still smelled of the salmon steak she'd cooked for dinner. It was an effort, but Tina tried her best to eat properly. It would be easy to make do with some sort of supermarket meal or takeaway when there was just herself to cater for. Those evenings when Dean had been able to get away, she'd enjoyed cooking for them both, had found real pleasure in setting the table properly, chilling a good bottle of wine and being creative in the kitchen. Now there seemed no point in bothering with all the frills.

She poured herself another glass of white and restlessly flicked through the offerings on TV. Nothing appealed to her and it was obscenely early to go to bed. It was at times like this, without much to distract her that her thoughts invariably turned to Dean.

She still missed him, even if the rawness of her emotions was beginning to fade. It didn't help to imagine him out somewhere tonight with Kathy, enjoying the company of friends, laughing and happy, his life going on as before while she sat alone with nothing to look forward to.

Was it better, she wondered without much originality, to have known happiness for those few short years or never to have met him at all and avoided enduring the loss? It was the sort of crazy, pointless question you asked yourself after three glasses of wine and with a lonely evening stretching in front of you.

The sudden ringing of the phone disturbed her reverie. Placing her glass down on the table by her elbow, she wondered who could be calling at seven-thirty on a Saturday night. She'd got over hoping that it might be Dean at the other end of the line.

It was Mark.

'Sorry to disturb your evening,' he said, 'but I saw your light on and was hoping I could ask a favor.'

Without giving her a chance to answer, he went on, 'Actually, I've got a confession to make.'

'You'd better tell me,' she replied cautiously.

'You're listening to the voice of a total numbskull when it comes to the mysteries of technology.' He told her what had happened and ended, 'I'm just wondering if you have a player and, if it's not too much trouble, if you'd mind letting me check this movie on it. It'd save me a pointless drive back to the shop.'

'No, of course not.' Tina answered. 'But I have to admit, I bought a new machine with the insurance payout and haven't had the time to connect it up yet.'

He gave a chuckle. 'Well, maybe between the two of us, we might be able to work it out.'

'Sorry about the fish smell,' she said as she opened the front door.

'Smells better than what I had. Frozen something that tasted like the cardboard box it came in.'

She led him into the sunroom at the back of the house and opened a cupboard. 'It's here. I haven't even had time to take it out of its wrapping.'

Mark lifted out the metal box and began to peel off the bubble wrap. 'It can't be that complicated, surely.'

The instruction booklet helped, and it didn't take him long to connect up the new machine and link it to the TV.

'Now, let's check this thing.' Squatting down in front of the player, he put the DVD into the slot. A wavy pattern appeared and then the first of the trailers burst noisily onto the screen.

'Well, it's not the movie.' Mark looked up at her. 'Must be a problem with my player.'

Tina's every instinct told her not to speak the words that hovered on her lips. The sensible, straightforward thing to do now would be to say good night and go to bed with a book. But her loneliness this evening felt so sharp it made her take the risk.

'Would you like to watch it here? I don't mind.' She did her best to sound casual.

She caught his quick glance. Was he wondering about her motives? Did he think her invitation was a come-on? Please, don't let him think that.

'I get sick of my own company sometimes,' she offered, in what she hoped was a disarming explanation. 'And there's absolutely nothing on the idiot box.'

Mark nodded. 'Yeah, I know what you mean — that's why I got this.' He held up the movie.

'Maybe I'd better ask what it is first.' She hoped the edge to her flippancy might prove she had no ulterior motive. Or at least, not the one he might be imagining.

'What about *The Big Chill*?' He held the box so she could see the cover.

Tina had seen it years ago. 'Great,' she said, 'I've always meant to get around to seeing it.'

'Look, you don't have to feel ... I mean… I don't want to interrupt your evening.'

Now she didn't know whether he was just being polite or trying to escape an unwelcome invitation.

'You're not, I promise. But you please yourself.'

'Okay.' He smiled.

The tactical dance was over.

'Did you enjoy it?'

Tina picked up their empty wine glasses. 'Loved it,' she replied. 'The music was great too.'

'Yeah, especially when you compare it to some of the stuff that's around these days. I used to love dancing when I was a kid.'

She was rinsing out the glasses under warm running water. Over her shoulder she said, 'Did you? Me too. Not that I had much chance of getting out, my mother was far too strict. Although I did manage to sneak out once to some sleazy local club where the music was totally wild.'

As he ejected the DVD and stored it in its case, he added, 'There's a band on some Fridays at the Leagues Club. They play pretty good dance stuff.'

Tina wasn't sure what was coming next. 'Do they?' she said carefully. 'That sounds like fun.'

There was a moment's silence and then he continued evenly, 'You know, if you're ever at a loose end any Friday evening, we could go up there again. Just a meal and a dance,' he added quickly. 'No strings attached — I think we're both on the same wavelength as far as that's concerned.'

Tina nodded slowly. 'You think right.'

'I'll leave it to you then. The Burn are a million per cent on any of that heavy metal, hip-hop stuff.'

Tina smiled. 'That might just tempt me.'

Later, after he had gone, she mused on the unexpected invitation. Was it as casual as it had seemed? Did men ever want just a platonic connection with a woman even when they stated exactly that? Yet there had been nothing in Mark's words that hinted at any personal interest in her. And why should there be? What did they have in common beyond the fact that they had each found themselves tipped out of their normal comfort zones and glad of a little company? Even if in her case, she thought sardonically, that meant dancing to some retro band at the local Leagues Club.

Marnie had rung Steven Royce on Thursday morning.

'If that dinner invite still stands,' she said, 'I'll definitely be in Melbourne this Saturday.'

'That's great. I'll book somewhere nice. Where will I be able to pick you up?'

She was about to give him the Corkdales' address then, in a split-second decision, she changed her mind. 'The Lindrum,' she said instead. It was a small boutique hotel on Flinders Street.

'I know it. Would seven-thirty suit you?'

'Fine,' she replied.

'How was your father today?'

They were sitting at their table, drinks in hand and the ordering out of the way. Marnie approved of the choice of restaurant. It wasn't one of those stark, noisy white-walled places that had been too long in vogue, but a quietly elegant, rather old-fashioned place just down from Toorak

Village. The carpets were thick, the tablecloths crisply white and the waiters were clearly long-term professionals.

She shrugged one shoulder in a hopeless gesture. 'I find it so difficult to see him that way. I keep remembering how he was and know how devastated he'd be to see himself reduced to this.'

Steven said sympathetically, 'The only comfort for you is that his unawareness is total. He'll never know.'

'I wish —' She stopped, and then began again. 'You know, I've always considered myself someone who can cope with anything. I just bite the bullet and get on with it. But this ... this is different. Nothing prepares you for it.' She gave a short, harsh laugh. 'Well, it's not like I'm telling you anything, is it?'

Steven shook his head. 'No. I felt exactly the same way when it happened to my mother. Dad's condition isn't as bad yet, but if he lives long enough, it will be. You feel powerless. There's nothing you can do. And when you're used to being proactive about things it's very difficult to cope with just standing by and watching nature take its devastating course.'

Marnie took another sip of wine, thinking how good it was to have this man to talk to. Somehow he made her feel comfortable enough to verbalize feelings and emotions that she'd kept buried for so long.

'It was so hard when I was a teenager,' she went on. 'The pain I felt in the relationship. Yet I never let myself be overwhelmed by his criticism and put downs. I fought back, I wouldn't let him destroy my self-confidence. In fact, if anything, his treatment actually made me stronger. I wasn't going to let him defeat me.' She looked across at Steven, her eyes bright with emotion. 'And now, somehow, in a way I can't really understand, I feel as if I've made my peace with him.'

He reached across the table and placed his hand over her own. 'Then that's what you've got to remember, Marnie. Now ... and when he's no longer with you.'

Over their meal they spoke of other things: Melbourne, travel, music, politics. Steven also asked more about her involvement with the halfway houses.

'I'm very impressed, I have to say. Altruism is not exactly a widespread virtue.'

'Well, I was lucky enough to have some money to start with and managed to turn it into more. In the end, there's just so much you need for yourself, isn't there?'

He gave her a dry smile. 'Not too many people share that view.'

Then, as they discussed the predicaments of some of the women Marnie helped, Steven asked, 'Aren't you worried that you might end up in the firing line of some of these violent men yourself?'

Marnie lifted a hand in a dismissive gesture. 'I can't worry about that. None of them have any idea where I live. The social workers are probably more at risk than I am.'

She didn't let herself dwell on the possibility that Fran Morris's husband may have discovered her address.

Outside, in the cool night air, they were walking to the car when she felt Steven's hand slip into her own. He had fine, slim fingers. They looked sideways at each other and Marnie gave him a teasing smile.

'I like you, you know. You're not too bad for a conservative Melbourne bloke.'

'And you're not too bad for someone from glitter city, if I can put it that way,' he countered.

She stopped in her tracks then and looked into his eyes. 'Don't ask me back for coffee, please. Promise me that.'

For a moment he appeared puzzled and she burst out laughing. 'It's such a waste of good time, isn't it?'

They spent the whole night together and, despite her attraction to Steven, Marnie was surprised by the depth of their passion. There was something very different about this relationship. Unlike most of the others in her life, it had begun with a different sort of intimacy. The two of them had been drawn together by the recognition of a common emotional bond, and Steven had seen her at her most vulnerable with her emotions exposed and raw. She had shown a side of herself to him that she'd never revealed to any other man. And, instead of feeling weakened by the exposure, she had found a sort of strength instead. For Steven's comfort and empathy had helped her as she was forced to confront many of the demons of her past.

And now, she thought, as she lay in his arms, listening to the early morning rain, their physical intimacy had brought her a different sort of comfort.

'Are you awake?' He whispered the words into her hair.

Slowly she rolled over to face him. 'More awake than I've felt for a long time.'

'Me too.'

Then he kissed her, and proved it.

Over the next few weeks, they saw each other as often as possible. Marnie would spend each weekend in Melbourne and Steven would take every opportunity to come to Sydney during the working week.

Sometimes she would chuckle aloud to herself as she drove to work, thinking how strange life could be. Whoever would have imagined she could be so passionately involved with a man like Steven Royce? Straight, conservative — her own age!

Maybe, just maybe, she told herself, she was ready for a little stability. It was novel, if nothing else. She couldn't remember how long it was since she'd seen any man for this length of time. Interestingly, with Steven there was none of the drama which she usually craved or manufactured in a relationship. Instead, she enjoyed the sense of calm she felt in his presence, admired his quiet confidence that didn't seem threatened by the demands of her own more impulsive personality. And that was without mentioning the sex.

How long would it last? She had no idea. It didn't take much to bore her but so far she wasn't bored by Mr Royce. Yet she wasn't going to fool herself. In her experience, all relationships had their use-by date and she didn't expect this one to be any different.

She was driving home from work when she got the call from Anthony.

'I'm very sorry to tell you, my dear, but the home rang and reported that your father died twenty minutes ago: It was as painless as possible.'

Marnie felt her heart lurch and her belly turn to water. Much as she had been preparing for this moment, it was still shattering when it finally happened. She and Anthony had already discussed the funeral arrangements and in the paperwork for St Helen's she had indicated that she wanted to see her father before his body was taken away.

'I'll get a flight as soon as possible,' she said, her voice shaky. 'I'll call you and let you know.'

To her frustration, all the flights were full. She was forced to take the last flight out of Sydney that evening. There was no point, she thought, in coming home and then flying down a day or two later for. the funeral, so she packed all that she would need. On the way to the airport, she put a call through to Steven. There was no answer and she left a message. It was short and to the point.

Anthony was waiting for her when she landed in Melbourne. They drove to the home in near silence, Marnie lost in her own emotionally charged thoughts.

Her father's body had been moved to the small palliative care room away from the main accommodation area. Outside, she steeled herself for what was to come. Anthony knew that she wanted, needed, to do this alone, no matter how distressing. He patted her arm. 'I'll be nearby, my dear. Take all the time you need.'

The room was softly lit. Fearfully, Marnie approached the bed. Charles Ingram lay dressed on top of the covers. His skin was waxy and white, his eyes closed. With her heart thudding painfully, she reached for his hand. It was as cold as marble. With tears running hotly down her cheeks, she looked at this complex man, who had given her life, but so little of the comfort and love she had yearned for. She thought of all the years that had been lost to them that they would never get back.

It would be so easy to let that painful notion overwhelm her but instead she forced herself to take Steven's advice: to remember that she had found the peace of forgiveness. And unconditional love.

'Goodbye, Daddy.' Unconsciously, she used the childhood term. 'I loved you, you know. I always loved you.'

And bending over her father's body, she kissed his cold lips, her tears falling onto his lifeless flesh.

Chapter 15

FEELING EXCITED, LEE FOUND A parking spot just around the corner from the community hall.

A day after talking with Graham Park, she'd received a call from the woman in charge of the new production. 'Graham tells me you might be interested in working on the choreography for *42nd Street*,' Emily Saunders said. 'I'd love to meet you and talk about it. Are you free sometime this week? We really can't afford any delays with this project.'

That very evening, Lee had turned up for their appointment in the community center meeting room. Emily Saunders was a slim, energetic-looking woman in her early forties, a music teacher who had been involved with amateur theatre and musical productions most of her adult life.

When Lee gave her a rundown on her background and experience, the producer's face had lit with delight. 'You sound just the sort of person we're looking for. What can we do to tempt you on board?'

And so tonight, Lee was attending her first meeting with the committee to formulate a schedule for auditions and rehearsals. She was looking forward to the challenge immensely.

There were six people sitting around the laminate-topped table. One of them was Graham and with a smile of welcome, he rose to greet her and introduce her to the others. 'This is our lucky day,' he beamed at them. 'This lovely lady has the talent and experience to really make our show special.'

For the next hour and a half the details were discussed, and afterwards Lee shared coffee and biscuits with her new friends. There were three men, including Graham, as well as Emily and two very pleasant young women in their thirties. They were all dynamic and focused and Lee knew she was going to love working with them.

This is exactly what I need, she told herself. A group of like-minded people who could make good use of her talents. The only thing she couldn't believe was that she hadn't thought of this outlet herself. It had taken the chance meeting with Graham to point her in the right direction.

When it was time to go, they locked up the hall and Graham walked her to her car.

'We're all delighted, Lee. I don't feel so bad about my little accident now. It was meant to be.'

She laughed. 'Maybe it was. I'm just so excited. I can't wait to get started.'

'Well, auditions get under way next week and then rehearsals are Monday and Wednesday evenings. So I'll see you then, eh?'

Lee smiled at him as she unlocked her car door. 'Without a doubt.'

The next day, she rang Julie to tell her the news.

'That's great, Mum. That should make you happy.'

'What's that supposed to mean?' There was an edge to Lee's voice.

'Nothing,' her daughter protested. 'Just exactly what I said.'

'Well, at least I'll be using the talents God gave me.'

The implication wasn't lost on Julie. 'Please, don't start, Mum. I don't need that on top of everything else.'

'What do you mean?' Lee's tone was sharp. 'Has your father been a problem again?'

'I don't want to talk about that. I told you.'

Lee took a deep breath. 'It seems to me, Julie, that there isn't much you want to talk about to your mother any more. When do you ever call me? Why is it always left to me to pick up the phone?'

'Look, Mum, just don't hassle me, okay?' Julie spoke tersely. 'I've got to go now anyway. I've got two assignments to finish before Friday.' She gave her mother a quick goodbye and hung up.

Lee felt concerned put down her phone. She didn't know what was wrong with Julie these days. It worried her that they didn't seem able to talk to each other. How many times had Lee done her best to explain what this time out meant to her? Even if Julie couldn't understand, was she going to let it create a permanent wedge between them?

As she started making her dinner, it occurred to her that maybe university might have something to do with the growing rift. Did Julie consider her mother too ignorant now? Too uneducated, compared to her new, clever friends? It was something that had never entered her mind before; Julie had never been a snob in any way. But who was to know how she was changing now that she was away from home and in such a different environment? Perhaps she really did think the rest of them were beneath her.

It was with that disturbing thought in mind that Lee ate her solitary dinner.

There was a new balance in her life. She'd always enjoyed her work at the shop and now had a social outlet that fulfilled her as well. Rehearsals for *42nd Street* had started and she looked forward eagerly to those Monday and Wednesday evenings.

The cast of the show came from all walks of life: there were teachers, green keepers, sales staff, students, even a lively female lawyer. All of them shared a love for the adrenaline rush of performing, for the discipline and fun, the nervousness and hype. It was an infectious atmosphere and Lee found a new energy and enthusiasm in herself as she set about playing her part in pulling the show together.

After most rehearsals, a group of about eight or ten of them would adjourn to a nearby late-night coffee shop. They were usually too wound up to want to go straight home and Lee enjoyed that part of the evening too. She knew she had found what was missing in her life. She needed this, reveled in being around people who were creative and expressive. The life she led now was so unlike the one she had lived with Brad: the boredom of suburbia and routine. She wondered sometimes how she had coped with it for so long.

And, for the first time, she admitted the worry that she wouldn't be able to go back.

She kept in touch with home through Danny, ringing when she knew Brad would be at work.

'How's it going, love? Are you doing your homework? Is Dad cooking you proper meals?'

'We eat takeaway at least three nights a week,' her son reported. 'On the weekend, Grandma or Aunty Cheryl take pity on us and ask us round.'

Lee could just imagine what Brad's sister had to say about her move to Sydney. But the familiar feeling of guilt washed over her as she listened to her son. He sounded miserable.

'Things can't be that bad, love. Dad can cook when he has to.'

'Yeah, well, you're a million per cent better.' He hesitated then added, 'You are coming home, aren't you, Mum? This isn't permanent or anything is it?'

'I told you, it's only for six months.' Lee tried to inject her voice with conviction. 'And more than a third of that has gone already.'

'How often do you ring Troy?'

'As often as I can. But he doesn't always answer.'

'Yeah, he's got a new girlfriend. But... he wishes you were back with Dad too.' There was a plaintive note in her son's voice. 'It's just not the same, Mum. For any of us.'

'Everything'll be fine, Danny. Just make sure you keep at your schoolwork and I'll be home before you know it.'

As she hung up, Lee felt torn by conflicting emotions. She loved her children. They were basically good kids and she was proud of each of them. The question she had to face was whether she loved them enough to bury herself alive for the rest of her days.

She had fallen into the routine of meeting regularly with Graham in the coffee shop on Thursday nights. It was always a quick meal but they still found time to chat, mainly about the production, but had eventually got around to exchanging more personal information as well. She explained her own situation as 'helping out a friend for six months or so.'

'You've got a very understanding husband.'

Lee merely nodded.

When she mentioned that her daughter had turned down an invitation to audition for NIDA for a university place instead, Graham had seemed to understand at once.

'It's a shame to see talent wasted,' he said. 'I'll bet you were pretty disappointed about that.'

Those few words of sympathy really struck a chord. If only Brad had offered her that much, she thought, instead of merely defending Julie's position, it might have made things a little easier to accept. But no, that had been beyond him. It had taken a stranger to understand how she felt.

Graham, she learned, had never been married.

'Too fussy, I guess,' he shrugged with a smile. 'Just never found the right one. But I haven't stopped looking.'

'I'm sure the right woman'll turn up one day,' Lee said reassuringly. 'Probably when you least expect it.'

'Yeah, in the meantime I'm enjoying my freedom. And look what that means.' He grinned. 'I can have dinner with a beautiful woman.'

'Oh, come on.' With a smile, Lee brushed aside the compliment, but it made her feel good.

Coming to Sydney had changed her in so many ways. She'd found a new confidence and strength in herself she would never have imagined possible. And that brought home to her how suppressed and shackled she had been. For too long, she had accepted that all she was good at was bringing up her kids and keeping house. These days, she felt as if she were flying. Not even the odd call from Brad could dampen her high spirits, even though they nearly always ended acrimoniously.

'I can't believe there's no one else, Lee. You're lying to me. At least tell me the bloody truth and stop making an idiot of me.'

'I told you a dozen times and I'll tell you again.' Lee spoke with heavy emphasis. 'There's no one! This isn't about looking for affairs. How many times do I have to say that? Don't you see how pathetic it makes me sound — as if I have to run from one man to another? This is about me taking charge of my own life and finding out who I am, Brad. Nothing more, nothing less.'

She hated the way his calls left her feeling.

On Wednesday evening a week later, she came back to the apartment shortly after eleven o'clock. The rehearsals were coming along well and everyone had been on a high. Afterwards, the usual crowd had called in at the coffee shop and it was late by the time they said good night.

As she drove into her parking bay, Lee didn't take any notice of the other cars lined up along the road. She was just turning the key in her front door when she heard someone coming quickly up the steps behind her.

Turning nervously, she saw who it was.

'Brad! Shit, you scared me. What in the world are you doing here?'

'I want to talk to you, Lee. I've been waiting outside for almost two hours.'

She could hardly refuse to let him in, but she was angry at his unexpected intrusion.

'Couldn't you have called me at least?' she said curtly as she snapped on the living room light.

'Maybe I didn't want to,' he replied.

She swung round on him. 'Oh, I get it. You're spying on me. Is that it? Is that what it's come to?'

They were standing awkwardly, facing each other.

'I came down to see Julie. Why shouldn't I call on my wife as well? Although I thought she might have been home before this hour of the night.' He fixed his gaze on her. 'Where have you been?'

'I don't think that's any of your business.'

'What's wrong with giving me an answer? Do you have something to hide? Because that's sure what it could look like.'

She could hear his heavy breathing, knew he was struggling not to lose his temper.

'If you must know, I was at rehearsals with a musical society I've joined. I'm doing the choreography for their next production.'

'Until this time of night?'

She rolled her eyes in exasperation. 'Some of us have coffee later, okay?'

'And how many men are in this musical society?'

She lost it then. 'Oh, for God's sake, Brad! Grow up! What do you want me to do, give you a resume on every bloody man I meet? I'm still married, you know. Despite what you so clearly think, I am not sleeping with anyone.'

Her outburst seemed to deflate his anger. He was silent for a moment and, when he spoke again, his manner was more conciliatory.

'Lee, we can't go on this way. I miss you so much. We all do. Please, tell me you'll come home. I'll do anything you want to make you happy.'

He moved towards her, his arms reaching out to embrace her. But she turned away.

'I told you six months, Brad. If you keep this up, you'll make me never want to come back.'

He was silent for so long that she was forced to turn and look at him.

'You know what, Lee?' His voice was cold, his face tight with suppressed emotion. 'Maybe I won't want to take you back by then.'

He turned and strode out of the apartment without bothering to close the door behind him.

Ever since her father's funeral two weeks previously, Marnie had found it difficult to shake off her despondency. When Lee had rung to try to get them all together for dinner, her first inclination had been to refuse. But on second thoughts, she had realized that it might be what she needed to brighten her mood. Especially as she had seen Steven only once in those two weeks. Work had taken him to Perth and he wasn't due back in Melbourne until the end of the week.

While he'd sent flowers, he hadn't attended the funeral and she'd been grateful for that. The day had been demanding as she'd gone through the motions: first the service, which had been attended by those who remained of her father's friends and colleagues, then the wake at the Corkdales' home, where Anne and Anthony had done everything possible to make the day easier for her.

It had been unbearably heart-rending to watch her father's coffin slowly lowered into the same plot where her mother was buried. Her regrets had been deep for all that she had missed from him. She'd done her best to convince herself that it didn't matter now, but deep inside her soul she knew it did, and always would.

Over dinner, she referred only briefly to her father's death and Tina and Lee respected her obvious wish not to dwell on the subject. They had both sent flowers to the funeral and called her with their sympathies and for that Marnie had been grateful, but she was still coming to terms with the complexity of her emotions. Instead, she told them a little about Steven Royce and how they'd met.

'An *accountant*?' Tina raised an incredulous eyebrow.

'And her own age,' added Lee. 'Wow, he must be something special.'

'Okay, so maybe I'm slowing down in my old age.' Marnie grinned at their reaction. 'But really,' she added seriously, 'he was a great help to me through all the trauma with Dad.'

'Then hang on to him,' Tina advised.

'I'm not the hanging on type, you know that. But I must admit, I was thinking of asking him to the house in Bali. I can probably get away now and I certainly feel as if I could do with the break.'

'What about the court case?' Lee asked as she dipped her spoon into her soup.

'Well, hallelujah, that finally seems to be getting somewhere. I'm just waiting for the decision from the Land and Environment Court. They have the last word, and my lawyers are very positive.'

'If Brad's not careful he'll be talking to lawyers soon too,' Lee said darkly. She told them about the unexpected recent confrontation and the fact that she was feeling more and more resistant about returning to Newcastle.

'Divorce is a big step, Lee.' It was Tina who sounded the warning note. 'Have things really gone that far downhill?'

Lee sighed. 'Oh, I don't know. I'm just enjoying myself so much. The show, my work, everything's fabulous. I dread the thought of having it all come to an end.'

'Well, don't get too carried away by this city,' Tina warned. 'It can also be hellish hard and lonely. Take it from one who knows.' She hesitated, then added, 'In fact, I admit I'm desperate enough these days to let my lodger take me dancing at the North Sydney Leagues Club.'

The others stared at her in silent amazement.

With a smile, Tina explained. 'Yep, you'd have loved seeing me dance to *Pretty Woman* last Friday night.'

'Well, well, well.' Marnie gave her an arch look. 'So you've succumbed to the charms of the hunk.'

'Oh, come off it, Marnie,' Tina responded quickly. 'Succumbed is hardly the word. He's sitting at home, so am I. It's just a very platonic arrangement where both parties are perfectly aware of the rules.'

'Men have a way of breaking those rules when it pleases them,' Marnie said provocatively.

'Not Mark Galloway,' Tina affirmed. 'He's in the once bitten twice shy category. And anyway, what would he and I have in common?'

Marnie and Lee looked at each other and answered simultaneously: 'Sex!'

Tina wished she had never brought up the subject. 'The day I need to bed my lodger,' she replied, 'I'll know I'm really in trouble.'

Marnie had enjoyed the evening; it had done her good. The three of them were so incredibly different, but that didn't seem to matter. It was the past that counted, having known each other so long, having a history. It gave you a sort of emotional shorthand where nothing needed to be explained or apologized for. They accepted each other as they were.

As she let herself into her apartment, her thoughts returned to the possibility of asking Steven to join her in Bali. Why not? Sun, sex and total relaxation — it was exactly what she needed. Tomorrow, first thing, she'd get in touch. If he could make it, he'd need time to arrange his work schedule.

She saw the light flashing on her answering machine as she walked down the hall. There were three messages. The first two were to do with work; the third stopped her in her tracks.

Marnie was sitting on the patio of Steven's South Yarra apartment. Sunshine in Melbourne was a precious commodity and you learned to make the most of it.

'Are you sure I can't help you in there?'

'Don't you trust me?' he called back to her from the kitchen where he was cooking their bacon and eggs.

'I never trust a man I sleep with,' she answered loudly, 'especially if he can cook.'

A couple of minutes later, Steven appeared beside her with a plate in either hand. 'Well, at least the neighbors know what you think of me,' he said with good humor as he placed their breakfast on the table. 'Okay, try that and tell me what you think.'

Marnie looked down at the perfectly poached egg, the crispy bacon and cooked tomato halves. 'Looks wonderful. Sex always gives me an appetite.'

Steven poured their coffee from the plunger pot. 'Then you should be as big as a house.'

Marnie laughed. 'Not with the workouts you give me.'

She had flown down late the previous evening. They'd had a light supper and gone straight to bed. She was still coming to terms with her reaction to Steven as a lover. With him, she'd found a deeper and stronger connection than she had ever thought possible. While she had always been turned on by sex, he had managed to touch another part of her that was rarely involved — her emotions. Foreplay with Steven was as much a mental seduction as a physical one. He talked to her and nurtured the feelings of intimacy which heightened the joy of lovemaking. Marnie had never experienced anything like it and wondered how long it would take to run out of steam.

'So, tell me your news of the week.' He broke into her thoughts.

She hesitated. Should she tell him about the phone message, the filthy language and threats no doubt inspired by Sawyer? She hadn't even bothered reporting it to the police. After all, what could they do? Instead, she told him about the recent developments in her fight with council. 'It's close to settlement. My lawyers are sure of it. And it can't happen soon enough as far as I'm concerned. After that, and the trauma of Dad, I'm ready for a good break.'

She told him then what she had in mind.

'I've had the house for about four years. It's in Ubud, up in the mountains. Lots of artists, craftsmen, Westerners included, live there. You can't own property of course, but I've got a long lease and I've made improvements to the place. I think you'd love it.'

Steven spread marmalade on a piece of toast. 'I guess the picture of Bali I've always had is of itinerant surfers and backpackers.'

Marnie shook her head. 'No, no, no! I've got to show you there's a whole different Bali than that. Despite those terrible events, I'll always see it as a place of culture and beauty and wonderful people.'

He smiled. 'Sounds like one of Margaret Mead's paradises on earth.'

'You're not far wrong. So ... what do you say? Have I talked you into it? Can you possibly get away sometime soon? I've only got a window period of about a week as far as my work goes.'

'Leave it with me. I'll see what juggling I can do and let you know. If it's as wonderful as you're describing, it sounds the perfect place for ardent lovers.'

He reached across the table and held her hand. 'And we're certainly that, aren't we darling?'

Marnie nodded. As long as she stayed in control of this, it was all going to be fine.

Two weeks later, they were landing at Denpasar. The air was like a thick warm fog of exotic and questionable scents: incense, flowers, fetid waste.

Their skin became clammy with sweat the moment they stepped out of the air-conditioned terminal.

'When I first came to Bali, the airport was nothing like this,' Marnie explained. 'Tourism's become big business.'

Her houseboy, Ketut, had come to meet them in his cousin's air-conditioned taxi. He was a slim, handsome man in his mid-twenties, dressed in loose-fitting pants and a cool short-sleeved shirt.

'Miz Marnie.' He smiled, showing perfect white teeth. 'Welcome back — and to your friend.'

Marnie made the introductions, and Ketut shook Steven's hand then placed their luggage in the boot.

'It's about an hour and a half, depending on the traffic,' Marnie told Steven, 'and wait until you see that.'

He realized what she meant as soon as they left the airport environs and entered the main road. Immediately, they were enveloped by swarms of small scooters. Some had pretty girls as side-saddle pillion passengers, others carried whole families, the baby sitting on the handlebars. In a few cases, another child was balanced on the wife's lap too.

'My God ...' Steven stared in amazement at the sea of vehicles. Drivers were weaving between each other, avoiding the rough edges of the road and occasional deep potholes yet no one seemed to get impatient or angry.

'How in the world don't they kill themselves?' he asked.

Marnie laughed at his reaction. 'They're experts. They drive the wrong way down one-way streets, cross in the path of oncoming traffic, break every driving rule known to man, yet somehow most of them manage to survive.'

'I'm going to need a stiff drink after this,' he murmured.

She patted his hand. 'I've got that under control. We've brought our own. Most things are cheap, but the price of alcohol in this place is mind-boggling.'

It was late afternoon when they arrived at the house. They had climbed up into the hills past streets lined with colorful home wares of every description: garden pots, intricately carved doors, handmade wooden bed frames, cane furniture, stoneware, woven baskets. The foliage was dense and as deeply green as only tropical downpours can produce, and the roads now thankfully thinned of traffic, wound higher and higher.

At last, they turned off into a short, rutted driveway. It led through the lush jungle to a clearing cut into a ridge that overlooked steep rice terraces and a deep river chasm.

'That's the river Oos,' Marnie told Steven as Ketut opened their car doors.

He was trying to take it all in. He'd been to Hong Kong and Singapore, but those urban Asian cities hadn't prepared him for this. The landscape was breathtaking. And then he looked at the house. It was built in what he recognized as traditional fashion: three linked pavilions with thatched roofs set around an interior courtyard. The doorways and lintels were sculpted from stone and the narrow arched entrance doors were intricately carved and painted in green, gold and red. Adding to the beauty of the place were the lush tropical gardens, pebbled paths and lotus-filled ponds.

He turned to Marnie, his expression evidence of his delight. 'I don't think I've ever seen such a beautiful place in all my life.'

Marnie was pleased. She had never asked a man to join her here. This was her sanctuary, a place to escape the usual turmoil of her life — both professional and personal. She would never have invited anyone here who might disturb what it offered her.

She smiled at him. 'And there's a pool in the walled garden out the back.'

He was still shaking his head as she took his hand and led him into the house.

Later, after they'd changed and had a swim, Rini, Ketut's wife, served them dinner on the patio. The scents of the jungle seemed more potent in the evening and the only sounds were the sawing of insects and the gentle murmur of water that ran down the sides of the weathered stone urns in the ponds. .

'This is idyllic,' Steven said, sitting back in his cushioned cane chair and taking in the scene. 'I can feel the stress oozing out of my pores.'

Marnie grinned and helped herself to more noodles. 'It does that to you, doesn't it? Now you know why I love coming here.'

'I can't believe it's taken me so long to discover the secret.'

'You just need to know the right people.'

Afterwards, they lay against each other on the carved wooden day bed with its array of colorful cushions. Rini had cleared the plates and left them to finish the wine. The Balinese couple lived in a small bungalow to the rear of the property and with their work done, they'd said good night and left Steven and Marnie alone.

'Do you think I'm too old to become a hippie?' Steven joked. 'I just love the smell of that incense.'

'It's sandalwood,' Marnie replied. 'The moment I smell it anywhere, it immediately conjures up Bali for me.' She was wearing a sarong woven from deep burgundies and gold, one of many she kept in the house. To combat the heat, she'd coiled her dark hair loosely on the top of her head.

Steven began to gently stroke her arm. 'What do you have in mind for tomorrow?' he asked.

Slowly, Marnie rolled over to face him. Her eyes looked back into his as she reached for the top button on his shirt. 'Probably much the same as I have in mind for tonight,' she said softly.

The next day, she took him into Ubud proper to explore the art galleries and craft shops. When they got hungry, they stopped for lunch at Casa Luna on the main street. It was an open-walled restaurant on two levels with old wooden benches for seating and friendly, willing staff.

'A very European name,' Steven commented.

'Lots of Westerners eat here,' Marnie told him. 'They even run a popular cooking school.'

Steven understood why when his meal arrived. He couldn't remember the last time he'd eaten chicken that tasted so good.

'Well, it's free range, isn't it?' Marnie smiled. 'You saw them by the side of the road. And not a growth hormone or antibiotic to worry about.'

'Makes you realize just what they've done to our food,' he observed.

'Bali makes you realize a lot of things.'

Later back at home, they took a nap and avoided the heat of the day. When they awoke, they refreshed themselves with a dip in the pool and padded on wet feet over the marble floors back into the bedroom.

The ceiling fan moved the sluggish humid air as Steven took her in his arms.

'Do you know how much it means to be here with you?' he said softly.

Marnie ran her hands down his spine to the swell of his buttocks. 'Show me,' she whispered.

In a moment they were on the bed, their mouths fused, their bodies heating against each other.

It's so good, was Marnie's last coherent thought.

So good it scared her.

Later, while she took a shower in the walled garden off the main bedroom, that thought came back to her. This guy was getting to her in a way nobody ever had before. And, for all her bliss, that was starting to make her fearful. All her life, she'd steered clear of attachment and now the danger signals were there and she didn't know what the hell to do.

That evening, while they were having a drink before dinner, Rini came up to Marnie and spoke quietly.

'You wish to invite him in?' she ended hesitantly.

'Of course!' Marnie replied. She turned to Steven as her housekeeper walked back into the house. 'We've got a visitor. Wayan Pinsa is the most brilliant landscape architect — he's planned the hotel gardens in some of Bali's most beautiful hotels. Because he has a house nearby, he did these for me here even though it was a much smaller job.'

A moment later, a handsome Balinese man in his early thirties walked across the marble floor out to the patio. He was taller than the average local and looked cool in his white linen shirt and cotton pants.

'Marnie! How good to see you again.' He took her hand in both his own. 'When I heard you were here I came, because I know you are still waiting for some advice on the lower garden.' There was a tinge of American in his accent. 'I hope I do not intrude,' he added, shooting an apologetic smile at Steven.

'Of course not.' She introduced the two men and they shook hands.

'Would you like a drink?'

'Maybe just a quick one. I didn't know you had company.'

Marnie hid a smile as she lifted the bottle of Australian chardonnay from the ice bucket. *Like hell you didn't, you wily bastard. The word would have been out the moment we arrived. You just wanted to do a little checking out for yourself.*

Steven asked their visitor about his work and discovered that Wayan had designed the gardens for major hotel chains throughout Asia as well as the British Ambassador's home in Jakarta.

'It is interesting to travel so much,' Wayan said. 'And to be paid for doing what I love is the best of all.'

'You're an artist, Wayan.' Marnie lifted her glass to him. 'You create magic.'

He bowed his head in acknowledgment of the compliment, then said with a smile, 'We are all capable of creating magic, I think.'

Their visitor left after finishing his glass of wine. 'Let me know when you are free to talk about the new garden,' he said to Marnie at the door. 'I'll be around for one week more, then I am back to Jakarta.'

Again they ate a simple yet delicious meal and afterwards strolled hand in hand in the garden. The night was brightly lit by the moon and they sat on a teak bench and listened to the gentle play of water in the nearby lotus pond.

'I don't think I ever want to go back to Melbourne,' Steven said, slipping his arm around her shoulder.

Marnie smiled. 'Perfectly understandable.'

'And I certainly hate the thought of going back without you.' His voice was suddenly very serious and Marnie felt herself stiffen.

Cupping her chin in his hand, he gently turned her face towards his own. 'You know I'm in love with you, don't you, Marnie? I want to be with you all the time. Every minute I'm away from you is a minute wasted.'

She tried to laugh off his intensity. 'I'd be a hard case to have around all the time. Take my word for that.'

He ignored her flippancy. 'I mean every word of it. And I hope I'm not wrong in thinking you feel the same.'

There was a pause as Marnie struggled to find the right words. She didn't want this, didn't need declarations. They were friends, lovers. Why couldn't he leave it at that?

Difficult as it was, she knew she couldn't leave him with his illusions. 'Steven ... look, we have a good time together. The sex is great and I'm really fond of you. But... I really don't want it to get any more serious than that. I'm sorry if you thought otherwise.'

She saw the change in his expression, but what else could she tell him except the truth?

'I have to be honest with you,' she added. 'Don't hold that against me. You were kind to me when I needed someone and we have a great time in bed, but—'

He interrupted her. 'That's the second time you've said that — about the sex. Is that all that mattered for you?' His tone revealed how deeply her words had stung him.

'Oh, please, Steven.' She had got to her feet, her back to him. 'Please don't spoil it like this. We're here on holiday, to have a good time. Why are we having this conversation?'

'Because I'm telling you I love you, Marnie. I didn't come here just because you were a good lay.'

'Oh, for God's sake!' She spun around to face him, guilt making her overreact. 'Don't be so bloody dramatic. A relationship, a long-term commitment — it's just not my style. I can't lie just to tell you what you want to hear.'

She made an effort and forced herself to speak more calmly. 'Let's forget this, Steven. Let's just enjoy the rest of our time together without all these unnecessary complications.'

He was on his feet now, this time the shadows of the trees hid his face.

'I'm sorry, Marnie. I made a mistake it seems. A big one. I guess we're not on the road I thought we were going down after all. I'll change my flight and leave in the morning.'

'What?' She stared at him in stunned surprise. 'Oh, come on, let's forget all this. It's crap! Why in the world do you want to leave?'

'Because,' he said quietly, 'in the circumstances I wouldn't feel comfortable about accepting your hospitality. I hope you'll understand that. I came here with you because I thought you wanted the same complete relationship as I do. Because I thought we had a future together. Now that you've proved me wrong, there's really no way I can stay.'

'That's crazy!' She grabbed his arm. 'Listen to me. Why spoil what we've got just because I can't throw myself in your arms and tell you I want you and only you for the rest of my life?'

He stared back at her for a long moment before replying.

'I hate to say this, Marnie, but do you think you'll ever stop punishing all men for the way your father treated you?'

His voice revealed his pain. But there was another emotion there that she only identified later. Pity.

They had slept in separate rooms: Steven in the guest suite in the adjoining pavilion, Marnie in the main bedroom though she'd hardly had an hour of decent sleep. She couldn't get out of her head the last words he'd spoken.

In the morning, the conversation was stilted and awkward as he discussed his arrangements to leave.

'I've rung Qantas,' he said. They were sitting at the breakfast table which Rini had set with fruit and cereals as if it were just another day. 'They can get me on a flight. I just need to organize a taxi to Denpasar.'

She looked at him, her features tense. 'I still don't think this is necessary.'

He held her gaze and she could tell he hadn't slept well either. 'Try to understand it from my point of view,' he said quietly. 'It'd be impossible for me to let you pick up the tab here after our conversation of last night.'

She saw he meant it. 'Alright.' She pushed back her chair. 'I'll organize transport.'

It was probably better this way, she told herself as she walked out of the room. The mood was broken. Nothing would be the same even if he stayed.

Ten minutes later, Ketut's cousin arrived in the same car that had met them. While his luggage was being loaded into the boot, Steven turned to her.

'I'm sorry, Marnie. I never thought it would come to this. I have only myself to blame. I guess I just didn't read the signs.'

She felt a tightening in her throat. Just go, she thought. Go, before ... But she resisted the formation of that thought.

'Take care, Steven. Thank you for everything. You helped me through one of the toughest times of my life. I'll always remember that.'

She turned back into the house as he got into the car.

After that, she couldn't settle to anything. Relaxing was out of the question. No book kept her attention. What else was there to do?

She was tempted to cut short her own holiday but saw the pointlessness of that. Would she feel any better at home? Probably not. Just stressed on all sides there.

She went into the village and sought company amongst some of the other Westerners who also had residences in the area. She had come to know a few of them quite well in the years since she'd had the house, but she was too distracted today to enjoy their company.

Steven's accusation about her father drummed incessantly at the back of her mind. Paying back men — how dare he say that to her! How dare he make such assumptions. Throwing his quack psychology theories around. As if anything were that simple ...

With little else to do, she called on some of the wholesale furniture suppliers she had contracts with and ran an eye over their ranges. It was something she'd have put off if Steven had been there, would have made do with the brochures they sent her. But now she needed to keep busy.

Which was why she also thought of Wayan.

When she called him, he told her he was free to look at the garden the next afternoon.

'Make it later when it's a bit cooler,' she said. 'I'm too old to go trudging up and down hills at midday.'

'Me too,' he chuckled.

They spent almost two hours deciding what to do with the lower terrace. It had originally been garden but the jungle had gradually reclaimed it. Now Marnie had finally found a time when she and Wayan were both free to inspect it and come up with a plan for its replanting.

'Time for a drink?' she asked when they returned to the house.

'Sure.' He raised an eyebrow. 'Where is your friend?'

Marnie made a dismissive gesture. 'Don't ask.'

Wayan grinned. 'So I was wrong.'

About to poke the corkscrew into the bottle of wine, she stopped and looked at him. 'What do you mean?'

'I thought he must be very special to be at the house with you.'

With a sharp movement, Marnie twisted the cork. 'Yeah, well, even Balinese geniuses can be wrong sometimes.'

Looking back, she knew she should never have asked Wayan to stay for dinner. But by then they'd finished the first bottle of white and were onto their second. Yet it certainly wasn't the first time she'd extended the invitation.

By the time they slipped naked into the pool, Marnie was more affected by the alcohol than normal. Usually, she could hold her drink without any problem, but today she'd drunk too fast, eaten too little, and maybe her emotional state had something to do with it as well.

'Still as beautiful.' Wayan swam up behind her and cupped her breasts in his hands. He spoke close to her ear. 'You know I have always loved these.'

The feel of that hard golden body turned her on. He was a beautiful man and a good lover. It had always been his habit to drop in on her whenever she was at the house; theirs was a casual, mutually satisfying affair. The sort I'm good at, Marnie reminded herself perversely, her head buzzing with the effects of the wine.

Turning, she held her body against his and slipped her arms around his neck. Their kiss was long and passionate.

The next minute Wayan was leading her out of the pool and through the house to the bedroom. Marnie clutched at his arm as she almost slipped on the marble floors. He laughed and she wondered if he was as drunk as she was.

In the bedroom, he laid her on the sheets and moved his mouth down the length of her body. At that moment, she had a sudden memory of herself and Steven on the same bed just two short days ago. Resolutely, she pushed the image away. She owed him no loyalty. He had left. It had been his choice.

Wayan's lips were on her nipples and she could feel his hardness against her thigh. She reached out a hand to the bedside table. Her head was spinning. 'In there ...'

He knew what she meant. They always used a condom.

She heard the drawer open, the sound of the packet being ripped open and then, a moment later, the feel of his shrouded penis inside her.

He started to move and suddenly Marnie felt like laughing aloud. If this was 'punishing men', then damn it, she'd picked the right way to go about it.

Chapter 16

TINA WAS BUSIER THAN EVER. The client base of Wealth for Women was growing all the time. But that didn't mean she could become complacent. Her competition had grown too as the market for the female client became more widely recognized. At their regular sales and marketing meetings, she always stressed to her staff that WFW had to ensure they were providing the best service possible to maintain their position in the industry.

As business grew, so did the pressures. She had always prided herself on handling her commitments without too much difficulty yet recently had begun to feel the strain of the growing demands. It occurred to her that no longer having Dean in her life had removed an important safety valve; the affair had been her major outlet from the burden of her professional commitments. By contrast, all she did these days was work.

At least today she was escaping the office for a little while. It was a working lunch but even that was a rare treat nowadays. She had arranged to meet her client at an up-market restaurant at Cockle Bay. The food was excellent and the place had the obligatory water view.

She entered the spacious, glass-walled room and gave her name to the welcoming attendant. 'You're the first of your party to arrive,' the young man said as he picked up menus and led the way to her table.

Then, as she crossed the room, Tina saw him. Dean. Sitting with three other men. Her footsteps faltered and her body flooded with a sudden warmth. He had his head down studying the menu but she could see they were going to pass right by his table. In that split second of realization, she faced the turbulence of indecision. Should she say hello? Or would it cause her less grief to pass unnoticed? Her heart hammered. Ahead, the waiter was waiting for her, a chair pulled out in readiness.

At that moment Dean lifted his head and saw her. His double take was obvious to Tina at least.

'Hello, Dean.' Somehow she forced her rigid lips into an approximation of a smile.

'Tina ...' He was pushing his chair back, rising to his feet, while his dining companions looked on.

He took her hand. 'How have you been?' The words were as loaded with meaning as the look he gave her.

Tina's throat felt dry. She was so intensely aware of his touch. She never wanted him to let go.

'I'm fine. And you?'

'Not too bad. Could be better sometimes of course.' His message was clear.

'I guess we all feel like that.'

Acutely aware of the others at the table, she said, 'Good to see you. Enjoy your lunch.'

'You too.'

Her legs barely carried her to her table.

After that, she found it almost impossible to concentrate on the conversation. Nor did she have any appetite for the food she'd ordered. As often as possible she let her gaze move surreptitiously to Dean. Perhaps he was doing the same, because more than once she caught his eye. But this time neither of them acknowledged the other.

It was the extent of her reaction that really affected her. She'd thought she had come to terms with the break-up but the sight of her lover had brought everything back: the wonderful times they'd had together, the joy of his friendship, their passion in bed. And the pain of the split. That felt as fresh and acute as if the months in between had never happened.

Thankfully he and his party finished and left before her own lunch wound up. Barely caring what her dining companion thought of her, she'd watched Dean walk towards the exit. It took all her self-control not to make some excuse and run after him.

Afterwards, on the return trip to her office, she sat in the back of the cab lost in her painful thoughts. When was she ever going to get over him? How long would it take for this terrible ache inside her to finally fade?

Maybe that was the catalyst for what happened next.

She came home earlier than usual that Friday afternoon. Her concentration at work had been affected by the chance lunchtime meeting and she decided to give herself the rare luxury of an early end to her day. Yet as she opened the front door, she wondered if she'd done the right thing. How was she going to face the evening alone after seeing Dean? It would be torment to sit and dwell on her thoughts. She could phone someone and arrange to go out, she supposed. Surely there was some other woman she knew who would be pleased to have some company. Or, she wondered harshly, did other single women cope more pragmatically than herself? Maybe she was the only one incapable of shrugging off the past.

As she walked through the house, she heard a noise from outside. Crossing to the kitchen window, she could see Mark slowly moving through the pool. Of course, he wouldn't have expected her home so early. Well, she wouldn't disturb him, she thought, turning away. At least someone was enjoying that damned pool.

Upstairs, she changed into pants and a T-shirt and, when she was dressed, glanced out of the window to see if he'd finished. She was just in time to see him haul himself out of the water. Walking over to where he'd dropped his towel, he began to rub himself dry. For a man of his age, his body was tanned and sleekly muscular. Physical work made the difference, she supposed. Somehow it seemed more genuine to achieve it that way than at some fancy overpriced gym. The silly thought at least made her smile.

While she waited for him to leave, she began to wonder if she should perhaps suggest they have a meal together that evening. After two visits, she was just about ready for a change from the Leagues Club. Yet even as it occurred to her, she rejected the idea. Much as she hated the thought of being on her own, she wasn't sure she had the mental energy to be good company for anyone else.

'Hi!'

Lost in thought, she hadn't realized that he'd looked up and caught sight of her.

'Hello.' She pushed the window wider so he could hear her. 'Did you enjoy that? I wasn't going to disturb you.'

'Just what I needed.' He slung the towel over his shoulder. 'Water's getting a bit chilly now, but it's invigorating.'

'Hang on a sec. I'll come down.' She felt impolite talking to him like that, and she was still playing mental ping-pong about whether to suggest a meal. A minute or two later, she opened the back door and walked outside.

'You're home early. Being good to yourself for a change?'

It was an odd comment, she thought, and her expression must have revealed her reaction.

'I've never known anyone work the hours you do,' he added in explanation. 'I'm glad to see you taking it a bit easy.'

In her already emotionally vulnerable state, his words had a real effect on her. Was this man the only person she knew who cared if she took it easy or not?

She nodded. 'It was one of those days,' was all she could trust herself to say.

He looked at her intently, as if picking up something of her mood. Then he asked, 'Feel like some company tonight? Or have you got something else planned?' His voice was deliberately casual.

She realized with a sudden flash of insight that it was probably every bit as difficult for him as it was for her to admit to the need for company. And to turn down his offer would be a form of rejection that he probably didn't need given the circumstances.

She made a speedy decision. 'Why don't I cook for a change? Something quick and easy. I've got a couple of porterhouses in the freezer.'

This time it was his expression that made her wonder if she'd said the wrong thing. Going out somewhere probably made it a lot less personal she realized, than an invitation to eat in her home. Now she'd made him feel uncomfortable. She was just about to offer the alternative when he answered. 'Sounds great to me, if it's not too much trouble for you.'

She shook her head. 'Not at all.'

'What about salad or vegetables? Do you need anything?'

'Hang on, let me see.'

She walked back into the kitchen and opened the fridge while he stood by the doorway.

'Hmm ...' She pulled out a plastic bag and looked inside it. 'I think this lettuce is history. But I've got tomatoes and a tin of beetroot.'

'I'll go and get some salad stuff then. The little place up the road'll have that — save me facing the supermarket.'

'You don't mind?'

'Not at all,' he answered. 'I'll have a quick shower and change. Give me about forty minutes. Is that okay?'

'Fine.'

At once, the knowledge that she was about to have company lightened her mood, even if it was only her lodger. Immediately, she admonished herself for the thought. There was nothing wrong with Mark Galloway. He was a good man. She should count herself lucky, she thought caustically, that he was there to save her from slashing her wrists.

By the time he returned, Tina had the steaks defrosted, a bottle of red wine opened to breathe and the table set in the sunroom.

'They had some homemade potato salad too.' he said, placing his purchases on the kitchen bench. 'You want me to wash this lettuce for you?'

'Great. There's a lettuce basket in the cupboard over there.'

He grinned. 'I always use a colander myself.'

But Tina was too busy thinking that she couldn't remember a single occasion when Dean had ever offered to help her in the kitchen. Maybe she had always accepted that he was there to relax, and she was happy to do everything herself.

She wondered if that was how Kathy treated him too.

'That was great. Perfectly cooked.' He poured the last of the red wine into their glasses.

'Glad you enjoyed it. Even I couldn't wreck a steak.'

He smiled at her. 'I think you're much more of an all-rounder than you let on.'

She raised an amused eyebrow. 'Thanks for the vote of confidence.' She pointed at the empty bottle. 'Like another? I've got a good Brie to go with it.'

He gave it a quick thought. 'Maybe not another bottle. But I've got a fairly decent port at my place.'

'Okay, then, d'you want to get it? I'll put the cheese and biscuits together.'

He pushed his chair away from the table. 'Give me a couple of minutes.'

While Tina stacked the dishwasher and prepared the cheese platter, she couldn't help thinking how much she had enjoyed the evening. It was the distraction she'd needed. Mark always surprised her with his wide knowledge of what was going on in the world; he obviously kept himself well-informed. She realized, even as she was thinking it, how patronizing her attitude was. Just because he built houses didn't mean he was brain dead. She'd met plenty of professional men in both her business and personal life who were so narrowly focused they had almost nothing else to talk about except their work and sport.

By the time they'd drunk their glasses of port and followed it with coffee, it was almost eleven o'clock. Mark helped her carry the bits and pieces through to the kitchen, but Tina refused his offer to help her clean up.

'Thanks, but everything can go in the dishwasher. I'll have it done in a couple of minutes.'

'Well, if you're sure. I'll say thanks then. It was good of you to invite me. I enjoyed it.'

She saw him to the front door.

'Digger'll be waiting for his last quick walk.'

She looked surprised. 'At this time of night?'

'A dog's gotta do what a dog's gotta do.'

'Oh, right.' She smiled. 'Lucky Digger, a moonlight walk. I should do the same after that meal.'

He looked at her. 'You're more than welcome to join us. I'm pretty sure Digger won't mind.'

She'd meant the words flippantly, but he had taken her seriously. Still, maybe a walk would do her good.

'Okay, then. Just give me a minute to change my shoes.'

'I'll meet you at the front gate.'

With the dog on his lead, they walked to the park at the end of the road. Most of the houses in the street were in darkness but there was enough light from the moon and the odd street lamp to see where they were going.

'Do you do this often?' she asked. The night was quite cool and she'd slipped on a sweater.

'Not usually as late as this. Don't forget I'm up early.'

'Well, at least you can sleep in tomorrow morning.'

'I'm not really a late sleeper,' he said. 'Used to getting up at the crack, I suppose.'

It was light, inconsequential chat that prepared neither of them for what happened when they arrived back at the house ten minutes later.

He walked her to the front door and thanked her again. 'I really enjoyed the evening, Tina.'

'Let's do it again sometime then.' Her response was spontaneous and direct. She saw no need for subterfuge. She meant it.

'I'd like that. Let me bring the wine at least next time.'

'Sure.'

They were looking at each other, and in that split second they both knew what was going to happen next. She felt one arm slip around her shoulders and the other press against the small of her back.

Without resistance, she let him draw her closer. Then she was tilting her face up to his and when his lips met her own, she was taken aback by the eagerness of her response. The desire that had lain dormant in her all this time suddenly sprang into life. Clinging to him, she kissed him over and over until her lips were sore and burning. Finally, breathlessly, they broke apart.

'We ... can't stand here like this.' Her voice was unsteady. She knew exactly where this would lead and had no idea if she really wanted to stop it.

'Is that an invitation?' he asked softly, stroking a fingertip over her cheek.

'I think so,' she breathed.

Their lovemaking was fierce and silent. She felt as if she could never have enough. It had been so long since she'd felt a man's body naked against her own, and this man felt good and smelled good and tasted good. She wanted to drain every last drop of him inside her and worry about the consequences later. Nothing mattered but what they were doing, what she was feeling. Head thrown back, legs locked around his body, she fed that part of herself which was so ravenously hungry.

When it was over, they lay breathless in each other's arms, sated yet aware that silence was no longer an option.

Mark was the first to speak. 'I didn't mean that to happen, you know.' He was stroking her back.

'Me either.'

'Do you think it's a one-off?'

'Did it feel like it should be?' She flipped the question back at him, silently taken aback at her own brashness. She felt as if she should be uptight and embarrassed, wanting him out of her bed, her home, as soon as possible. But she didn't want that at all.

'No,' he answered and kissed the top of her head.

'That's good,' she answered simply, a small smile playing around her lips in the darkness.

Sometime later, he slipped out of the bed. When she stirred, he kissed her cheek and said quietly, 'See you when it suits.'

She thought that a particularly nice gesture in the circumstances. He was even enough of a gentleman to dispose of the used condom.

The production was coming along well. Lee was tough on her team, but she knew they accepted it. There were only three weeks to go before opening night and they still had plenty of work to do to smooth the rough edges.

Graham was a great support. He had only a minor role himself and helped with everything else he could, especially the promotion. Through his efforts the show would be advertised on local community radio and in the local paper. As well, he had organized hundreds of flyers which would be dropped in to responsive local businesses. He was looking for volunteers to distribute them the following Saturday.

'I'll help,' Lee offered. They were rehearsing on Sunday afternoons now that opening night was drawing closer. It meant her whole weekend would be taken up with musical society activities but that didn't matter. Not when you loved the theatre as much as she did.

'Great.' Graham smiled at her. 'I'll pick you up if you like and we can cover a couple of areas together. That suit you?'

'Fine.'

She gave him her address and they arranged a time.

They divided the allocated streets between them, but it still took a lot longer than Lee had thought to accomplish their task. It was after five and getting dark by the time she and Graham met back at his car. Her feet were sore and she couldn't wait to kick off her shoes.

'I'm pooped.' She fell into the passenger seat.

'Would you like a drink?' he offered. 'We could find a pub.'

'You know what? I just want to get these shoes off. My feet are killing me.'

'Dancer's feet,' he said with a knowing smile.

'You're right.' She was impressed that he knew that about dancers. 'Ruined at an early age. Even with these flats on, I can't go the distance.'

'Then let me take you home.'

It was the first time, she realized, that she'd had a man in the apartment except for Brad on that one occasion. But she knew Graham and he wouldn't be staying long.

As she carried their coffees into the living room, she apologized that she didn't have anything to go with it.

'It'd be different at home,' she said. 'I was always prepared for drop-ins. With kids you have to be. To tell you the truth I haven't even got anything for dinner. I think it'll have to be Thai takeaway again. At least it's healthy.'

'If you've got a menu, I could go and get it for you, save you going out again,' he offered.

'Would you?' Her face brightened. 'That would be wonderful.'

Suddenly, she realized she had been backed into a corner of sorts. Not that it was any big deal.

'Would you like to share with me? Stay for dinner, I mean? Not a late night,' she added quickly. 'Tomorrow's going to be huge again for me.'

Graham looked pleased. 'Love to.'

While Graham went to pick up their order, Lee set the table.

When the buzzer sounded, she let him in.

'Here we are,' he said, carrying in the plastic bag with their takeaway.

'Smells good.'

'I picked up a bottle of wine too.' He set it down beside the food on the kitchen bench.

The last thing Lee felt like was a drink especially as she had to be on the ball tomorrow. But she'd have to have one glass to be polite.

As they sat at the table together, she couldn't help thinking about Brad. He'd go off his head if he could see her sitting here with another man, would definitely suspect the worst. Well, she knew she wasn't doing anything to be ashamed of, merely eating a meal with an acquaintance who shared a common interest. And as soon as they were finished, Graham would be out the door quick smart.

While they ate, they talked about the production, about the best ways to iron out some of the last remaining glitches.

'You've done a brilliant job with it, Lee. I'm so glad I found you. It was meant to happen.'

She smiled modestly. 'Well, you're only as good as the team you've got to work with. Everyone's put so much into this.'

They finished their meal and he started to pour her some more of the wine. 'Oh, no, really.' She put a hand over her glass in protest. 'I've had enough.'

Graham held up the bottle. 'You can't expect me to finish all this by myself.'

'Stick the cork in it then and take it home.'

'Well, only after I've helped you tidy up.' He stood up and began collecting the empty plastic cartons.

Lee rose too. 'Don't worry,' she said, as she picked up their plates, 'there's hardly anything to do. It won't take me a minute.'

He followed her into the kitchen and while she rinsed things under the tap, he found the cork and pushed it back into the bottle of wine.

The next moment she froze as she felt his arms encircle her from behind.

'Do you know how fond I am of you, Lee?' He murmured the words into her hair.

Oh, no…she hadn't expected this.

With an effort, she twisted around to face him, her arms bent stiffly against his chest. 'Graham, please. Don't do this. Don't spoil our friendship.'

He was smiling down at her, his arms still locked behind her back. 'I've always found the best relationships start with a friendship.'

'I'm married, Graham. You know that. And I'm not looking for a relationship.'

She could handle this, she told herself. Just keep things calm and make sure he understood she meant exactly what she said.

'Well, I can't help wondering how much a husband really cares to let a beautiful woman like you out of his sight.' He was trying to ease her closer to him.

For the first time, Lee became nervous. 'I don't think that's any concern of yours.' She kept her hands clamped against his chest, resisting his pressure to draw her against him.

But he took no notice. 'You don't know what you're missing, Lee. I've been hot for you from the moment we met.'

And. then she saw how defenseless she was against his superior strength as with one sharp movement, he managed to draw her into his embrace. His mouth was on hers, his tongue probing her lips, his breathing harsh against her cheek.

Lee could hardly believe this was happening. Surely he would listen to reason? Maybe all he wanted was a kiss and a cuddle...

With an effort, she twisted her mouth away from his. 'Graham, please.' Her voice was shaky. 'If you go now, we can pretend this never happened. Please.'

But his hold on her didn't ease. Ignoring her words, he was yanking up her skirt, at the same time forcing her back even harder against the edge of the sink.

'No!' Her voice was shrill with panic as she felt his hand on the bare flesh of her thigh. The next moment, with one abrupt action, he had ripped the side of her panties and was pushing them down her legs.

Breath shallow with fear, she did everything in her power to resist, but the harder she fought the more he forced her backwards. His chest squashed her face and the hard edge of the sink cut painfully into her back. A second later, she felt him ease away slightly and realized he was opening his trousers.

Totally panicked now, she began to cry, her sobs muffled by the pressure of his chest against her face. She knew she was at his mercy. He was going to do exactly what he wanted with her.

The next moment she gave a sharp cry of anguish as she felt the pressure between her thighs and the abrasive pain of his entry. With one quick movement, he hitched her up so she was perched on the sink edge and she heard his grunt of pleasure as he penetrated her more deeply.

Sobbing, she struggled feebly but knew it was no use. A few seconds later, he gasped, went rigid and she knew he was finished. As his hold on her began to relax, she grasped the opportunity. Pushing against him as hard as she could, she broke free and ran into the bathroom. With trembling fingers, she shot the door bolt behind her.

Gulping through her tears, her breath ragged, she leaned back against the door fearful that he might come after her. And he did. Her legs went to jelly as she heard his footsteps approaching.

'It didn't have to be like that, Lee.' He was speaking close to the door, his voice calm enough but a little breathless. 'We could both have enjoyed ourselves if you hadn't been so stupid.'

'*Get away!*' She screamed out the words. 'Get out of here! Get out and leave me alone!'

It seemed for ever until she heard his footsteps retreat and the sound of the front door closing. Only she couldn't be sure that it wasn't a trick, that he mightn't still be in the apartment waiting for her to emerge.

Crossing to the bathroom window, she stood on the edge of the toilet seat and peered out to get a view of the street. Her heart pounding furiously, she heard a car start up and then saw his car driving away.

Feeling the bile rise in her throat, she slid to the floor and vomited before she had a chance to open the toilet lid.

Chapter 17

MARNIE LET OUT A WHOOP of delight as she replaced the receiver. Her lawyer had just given her the brilliant news. She'd done it! She'd won her case! The development was cleared to go ahead and now neither the council nor Rod Sawyer would be able to cause her any more problems. Finally she could get the project up and running.

In her delight, she wanted to tell someone who would understand how much this meant to her. And immediately she thought of Steven. Even after more than two months, he still occupied her thoughts more than she liked to admit. Not that she had forgotten his comments, but she missed him. A lot. Yet she knew there was no point in trying to resume the relationship. Steven was looking for 'stability and permanency', he had made that clear. He wanted the whole commitment thing that would eventually lead to the ring, the ceremony, the happy-ever-after. Everything, in fact, that she had spent her life running away from. The idea of marriage and settling down stifled her, choked her. It always had. No matter how well they'd got on together, she wasn't the right woman for Steven. He needed to find himself some sweet, lonely little divorcee who was ready and willing to settle down. A suitably conservative match for a successful Melbourne accountant.

Instead it was Keith, her right-hand man, whom she rang with the good news. 'I'll get everything pinned down as soon as possible,' she told him. 'We need to get this all happening now without any more delays.'

After that, she put calls through to Tina and Lee.

'You've got to help me celebrate,' she announced, after telling them of her breakthrough. 'Let's go to Forty One. My shout!'

As she drove into the city to meet her friends, Tina realized it was the first Friday evening in over ten weeks that she hadn't spent in Mark's company. Except for every second weekend when he visited his children, they spent most of their spare time together.

There was nothing complicated about the relationship. They both knew where they stood. She felt reassured that Mark, like herself, had no expectations. Both viewed the relationship as a stepping stone to help them move on to the next stage in their lives. For Tina, it eased the loneliness she felt in the aftermath of her break-up with Dean. And for

Mark, it fulfilled the same need, she felt sure. It must have been difficult to move from family life back to being single and then come to Sydney where he had known no one.

Yet there were still days when she ached for Dean, remembered how good it had been and how much she had hoped for. But at least now she wasn't alone so often to brood on her loss. And sooner or later, she thought without much conviction, she might even start to forget him.

Lee drove into the city, anxiously watching out for the exit signs and street names that would take her to the nearest underground parking station to Forty One. Since that terrible episode with Graham Park, her confidence had disappeared. Where once Sydney had seemed so exciting and compelling, it now appeared a dangerous, sinister place where the most innocent situation could suddenly become threatening.

She found it difficult to sleep now, compulsively getting up and checking all the windows and doors half a dozen times a night. The smallest noise made her jumpy and fearful. At home, she remembered, she had slept with her windows open but with Brad beside her she had never felt afraid.

Traumatic as the incident had been with Graham Park, she had never once considered going to the police. For one thing, she'd read how difficult it was to convince the police of the validity of a rape claim, and for another, she knew she could never take the chance of Brad finding out. It would finish their marriage, of that she was certain. For how could she ever convince him that she hadn't led her rapist on? On the surface, the evidence was all against her: she'd been friends with him, they'd seen each other regularly and she'd invited him into her apartment. She knew she was innocent of any flirtation, but Brad would never believe her.

She'd been over that evening again and again in her mind, replaying the conversation, analyzing her behavior, wondering if in any unknowing way she might have given out the wrong signals. But she knew she hadn't. The impetus had come from Graham Park alone. If she was guilty of anything, it was that she had been a little too naive, too friendly. But nothing more.

What made it all so much worse was the fact that she'd had to face him over the following three weeks. There was no way she could have let down the rest of the cast at that late stage of rehearsals. And how could she ever have explained her reasons if she had? So as traumatic as it was, she'd been forced to walk into that hall and act as if she were the same Lee, had been forced to treat her violator as if nothing had happened when every nerve was screaming at her to run away from the sight of him.

It had taken every ounce of her courage. A couple of times he'd tried to corner her alone, wanting to 'talk', but on each occasion she had managed to avoid him, staying close to the others and making sure she left with the group. No longer did she go to the after-rehearsal coffee get-togethers, pleading tiredness from the demands of her role. But when she also avoided the party that marked the company's final performance, she knew she had raised eyebrows. Yet how could she risk letting Graham Park near her again, whether to plead his case or try once more to coerce her into a relationship? How could she be sure that he mightn't follow her when she walked to her car, maybe even shadow her as she drove home? There was no way she could chance that.

At the same time she also had to change where she ate dinner on Thursday evenings. She found another small cafe a couple of blocks away, yet was always apprehensive that he might come looking for her. She knew she was letting herself be intimidated but was too overwhelmed to respond in any other way.

Now all she wanted to do was go home. She had only a month or so to go with Anita and had let her know that she wouldn't be staying on.

'You've done me a wonderful favor, Lee,' her employer had said gratefully when they met for a coffee one evening after work. 'And I'm delighted to say I've got a girl working for me now who I think will be fine to take on Veronique. I've had a chance to train her properly and I'm sure it's going to work out.'

Lee was glad. She didn't want to leave Anita in the lurch, but she couldn't wait to go home. She knew she should ring Brad and tell him, but she kept putting it off. Fearful perhaps, that with the rape still fresh , in her mind, he might pick up that something was wrong. She'd leave it till the last moment she decided, then she'd call him with the news. And she knew Brad; he might be hard to bring round for the first week or so, but she had no doubt he'd be happy to have her home again.

Since the traumatic incident with Graham, she'd made contact with Julie a couple of times, yet was almost glad when her daughter wasn't keen on a meeting.

'Mum, I love you. I really do. But until you and Dad work this thing out between you, I just want to be left alone.'

She'd been tempted to tell her daughter then and there that she had made up her mind to go home. But again, she was deterred by her fear that in her still fragile state she was at risk of revealing more than she should. She would never want Julie to know what had happened. For then she too would be burdened with her mother's terrible secret.

As soon as Marnie saw Lee, she knew something was wrong.

'What's up? Have you been sick? You look terrible.'

The restaurant was the sort of place Lee had once dreamed of dining in. Well-dressed people, wonderful service, first-class food. It was everything that typified Sydney for her. But, at that moment, it meant nothing.

As she felt Tina's and Marnie's eyes on her, she desperately tried to keep her emotions under control.

'Darling, what's the matter?' Tina placed a hand on her arm.

Lee's face crumpled. Her eyes filled with tears and in a shaky voice she told them what had happened.

Marnie had taken her to the powder room to fix her face. Now they were all back at the table with the waiter hovering nearby, ready to take their order.

Lee's belly felt as if it were clamped tight. She didn't know how she was going to eat anything. But, without asking, Marnie ordered her an entree-size helping of scallops on the shell.

When their order was taken, Marnie turned to her.

'Why didn't you call us right away? Haven't we always been there for each other?'

Lee shrugged her shoulders. 'I... felt so ashamed. Even though it wasn't my fault.'

'Of course it wasn't your fault,' Marnie retorted. 'Don't play the victim. You weren't to blame.'

Lee gave a dry harsh laugh. 'I guess I got away with it all those years ago when Peter Holding tried it on. Only I wasn't as lucky this time.'

'Marnie's right,' Tina put in. 'You should have let us know. This was too much to carry on your own shoulders.'

'I know.' Lee nodded. 'I should have. And my biggest fear is that somehow Brad will find out. He knows me so well — I'm terrified he'll be able to tell something's wrong.' She explained then that she was ready to go home. 'This has tainted the whole experience for me. Maybe I was never going to fit into a city like Sydney anyway.' Again, she gave a tight laugh. 'Suddenly Brad and home don't seem so bad after all.'

Marnie put down her wine glass and picked her next words carefully.

'Listen, Lee, I don't want to scare you, but I think you should see a doctor.'

Lee looked at her and shook her head. 'Oh, no, at least that's not a worry, thank God. I had my tubes tied after Danny.'

Marnie knew this wasn't going to be easy. It was obvious that the thought had not occurred to her friend.

'I don't mean that exactly. What I'm getting at is you have to make sure the bastard hasn't given you anything.'

She saw the realization dawn in Lee's eyes.

'No, I don't mean HIV,' she went on quickly, 'the likelihood of that is very small. But there are other STDs, you know, things they can cure. Only you don't want to go back to Brad not having been tested. Just for your own peace of mind.'

'Marnie's right. You should see someone. I'll come with you if you like,' Tina offered.

For the next four days, Lee wrestled with her fear. The idea of having been exposed to the risk of a sexually transmitted disease had not occurred to her. Or if it had, she'd relegated the thought to the furthest corner of her consciousness. In her more irrational moments, she told herself that if she had picked up something serious from Graham Park, she just didn't want to know. For how could she live with that knowledge? It would drive her insane. Yet she also faced the fact that there was no way she could return home to Brad without doing what Marnie suggested. She would never forgive herself if she had caught something and then passed it on to Brad. Nor, she knew, would he forgive her. It was probably the worst thing a couple could do to each other.

The dilemma plagued her. There were many times when she berated herself that if she'd never left Brad, she'd never have found herself in the position she was in. But there was no point in torturing herself on that score. No point in painting herself as the wanton wife either. She had done what she'd felt driven to do; there was nothing to be gained by adding guilt to the burden she was already carrying.

Finally she made an appointment with a local female doctor. She didn't need Tina to come with her. She was a big girl now she told herself, as she braced herself for the most embarrassing conversation of her life.

In the end, she told the doctor exactly what had happened. The quietly spoken woman made no judgments, even when Lee explained why she hadn't gone to the police.

'It's never easy,' she said, 'but I understand your reasons.'

Lee lay on the examination table, swabs were taken and she was given a referral for a blood test.

'Try not to worry,' the doctor said. 'HIV is unlikely. And all the rest can be cured or managed.'

Lee knew she wasn't going to rest until she'd found out what Graham Park might have left her with. The pathology lab was nearby and she went there immediately. She just wanted to get the test over with and hear the results.

Two days later, as she listened to the doctor's unemotional tones, her body blazed with a sudden feverish heat. Yet, a split second later, she felt icy cold.

'Yes ... yes ...' She heard herself speaking but the voice sounded unlike her own. 'Yes ... I'll make another appointment.'

She hung up the receiver and sat down in the nearest chair. Her eyes saw nothing as she silently repeated the doctor's words. Herpes...genital herpes. That had been her everlasting memento from Graham Park.

'Once you have it, it's in your system for life,' the doctor had explained. 'But any outbreaks can be controlled with the appropriate medication. It usually lies dormant until something triggers off the characteristic blisters. That could be stress, your period or even having sex.'

Lee began to tremble. Her whole body shook as ferociously as if she were naked in an Arctic winter. Now she knew she would never be able to go back home. Because that would mean having to tell Brad. And she knew she could never, ever do that. Never.

Mark had tried so hard to avoid what was happening. He'd told himself repeatedly that there was no danger; they had both started the affair with their eyes open, their cards on the table. Sex and companionship — that was all they had been offering each other. If it had stayed like that, he wouldn't be feeling like he was feeling now.

Turning off Military Road towards the house, he told himself for the hundredth time how crazy he'd been to get into the relationship in the first place. It should never have happened. But he had been so certain that he could keep it under control, especially with a woman like Tina. Neither of them was looking for commitment. Each had known the unspoken rules.

But there were some things you couldn't control, he thought heavily, and emotions were at the top of the list. He'd never dreamed he would fall like this. And even if he had been in the market for a relationship, he would have never set his sights on a woman like Tina. She had more money than he did, more status, more everything in a material and professional sense. He couldn't kid himself that in normal circumstances, he would ever have dreamed of the possibility of falling for a woman like her. At the start, they'd been drawn together by a common need for companionship, with sex the obvious end-product of that. But as the weeks passed, it had gradually become more than that for him. He enjoyed the company of this smart, articulate woman, admired her determination and integrity, until in the end, he was as hooked emotionally as he was physically. And now he was thinking of her almost every waking minute, eagerly anticipating the next time they could be together.

Well, one thing was certain, he resolved, as he pulled into the driveway: he would never let her know what she was doing to him. And, as soon as he could find decent work back home, he'd be gone and his torture would be over.

The letter was the only one for him among Tina's mail. He dropped the lid on the letterbox and frowned as he recognized the writing. It was from his ex. Now what, he wondered grimly. More money probably. She was always crying poor, even though he was already handing over more than the courts demanded. There were always extras for the kids: school trips, dentists, sports fees. It was never-ending. Not that he ever jacked up, but sometimes he wondered if all the dough he passed over went on what it was supposed to.

Inside his tiny flat, he read the letter and saw that this was nothing to do with demands for money. Trish was writing, she said, *because it's easier to explain this way, instead of risking a fight on the phone.* His eyes flew over the preamble until he found the crux of the correspondence.

She wanted to move to Adelaide. As soon as possible. There was a chance to *start her life afresh away from family interference.* She'd been thinking of it for a while and needed him to agree to let her take the kids. *I hope you won't stand in my way, Mark. This is something very important to me.*

Expression tightening, he folded the sheet of paper. What he'd heard on the grapevine was true then, and he figured he could read between the lines as well. There was a guy — there had to be. She'd fallen for someone, and now she wanted to pack up the kids and drag them even further away. Mark swore silently. When was the woman ever going to grow up? Hadn't they all suffered enough for her selfishness and irresponsibility? Reading between the lines, he figured she must have had another bust-up with her mother and sisters and this time, with some poor sucker as a crutch, she was off.

Tossing the letter aside, he fought against blind emotion, trying instead to think the whole situation through more calmly. What could he do to stop her? Talk to her? The very fact that he was disagreeing with her would only harden her resolve. Of course he could go to a lawyer and try to fight it by legal means but that would cost far more than he could afford and he still mightn't win in the end.

Should he actually let himself consider her option? Follow her and the kids to Adelaide? He'd been so rootless since the divorce, what would another shift matter? And at least he would be near his children. For he knew that if he didn't have them he had nothing worth living for.

As his mind churned with the various alternatives, he realized there was another reason that might incline him to fall in with Trish's proposal. At least it would extricate him from the situation he'd allowed to develop with Tina.

Everything was going full steam ahead on the inner west project. Now that she was working on both fronts, with the Blakehurst construction as well, Marnie was busier than ever. After a long and demanding day, she was heading for home via Newtown's side streets in an effort to avoid the worst of the peak hour traffic. Suddenly from nowhere it seemed, an early model sedan roared up very close beside her. Startled, she swore under her breath and, glancing sideways, got a glimpse of a long-haired man at the wheel. What was the idiot trying to do? Overtake in a street made narrower by the lines of cars parked on either side? What the hell was he using for brains?

The next instant she felt a jarring jolt and heard the scraping sound of metal against metal. Swearing furiously, she hit the horn hard, but the driver made no attempt to drop back. Then, to her greater astonishment, it happened a second time. Marnie felt herself flung against her seat belt and realized that the crazy bastard was actually trying to run her off the road!

As she struggled to avoid hitting any of the parked cars, the sedan accelerated past her with a squeal of rubber. She did her best to catch sight of the number plate, but the old Holden pulled away at a dangerous speed, just missing another vehicle heading towards them. That made it impossible for Marnie to try to catch up; all she could do was wait until she found a place to pull over and inspect the damage. Shaken and furious, she stared at the long gouge across both passenger side doors. The paint was stripped off and both panels were buckled. Only her skill and quick reflexes had prevented her hitting anything else and now she could feel herself reacting physically to the shock.

'How much longer am I going to have to wait?'

Marnie didn't bother to hide her impatience as she confronted the duty sergeant behind the reception desk. A long moment passed before he lifted his head from the form he was explaining to the disheveled young couple in front of him.

'As long as it takes for me to attend to the people who were here before you,' he said curtly.

Marnie's mouth tightened in exasperation. She'd driven straight to the nearest police station to report the incident, but she'd been there almost an hour and not one other staff member had appeared to help attend to the half a dozen people still waiting in the reception area.

Fuming, she felt like asking if the cops were too busy arranging drug payoffs or attending Integrity Commission hearings these days to help the general public. Biting back her angry retort, she resumed her place on one of the uncomfortable chairs. Losing her cool wasn't going to get her anywhere. For insurance purposes, she had no option but to file an official report about what had happened.

It was another half an hour before she at last got to make a statement about what had occurred.

'It was a very early model sedan. Dark. Dark blue maybe, or maroon.'

'Any idea of model?' The cop was typing her statement with two fingers.

'I'm pretty sure it was an older Holden. I don't buy *Car World* too often.'

The cop gave her a long look and his typing suddenly grew slower. 'D'you think it could've been deliberate?'

'Of course it was!' Marnie snapped. 'Twice isn't an accident.'

'So, you got any enemies?' The man's expression suggested she might have a few to choose from.

Marnie was about to reply in the negative, when she suddenly caught herself. She might have beaten Rod Sawyer to the punch, but would he be revengeful enough to try on something like this? It made no sense. What would he have to gain by continuing to hound her?

Yet she could think of no one else with a grudge against her.

The next morning she awoke feeling unwell. Never ill, she put it down to the shock of the night before. She was still feeling off when she left her apartment for another appointment with her architect. On the way, she made a call to the insurance brokers and gave them a brief outline of what had happened.

'I'll fax you the statement later this morning,' she promised. 'As far as I could tell, there were no witnesses.'

Who needed this shit to start the day? she asked herself as she rang off.

It took her another two weeks of feeling off-color to finally check the dates in her diary.

Marnie turned pale. *Jesus.*

The next morning, she stared at the result of the pregnancy test.

Positive.

How could it have happened? She was almost forty-five, her chances of falling pregnant were minimal. It didn't make sense. Any of it. Less than three months ago, she'd been in Bali with Steven. Right from the start of their relationship, they'd always used condoms. She used them with everyone. And they'd been very careful. So how could she possibly have fallen pregnant?

Then, as the incredible notion occurred to her, she felt the blood drain from her face. *Oh no.* Surely not. Not Wayan.

Marnie kept trying to remember the details of that evening with Wayan. She knew they'd both had a lot to drink yet she could have sworn they'd used a condom. It was something she was obsessive about. So what had happened next? Had she only imagined the sound of the packet ripping open? Had Wayan been too affected by all they'd drunk to follow their usual practice? She didn't remember finding the used condom anywhere the next morning, but no doubt he would have disposed of the evidence himself.

It was then that another possibility occurred to her. What if the condom had burst? It happened, she knew. And if that were the case, where did that leave her? Every bit as exposed as Lee had been.

So what the hell was she going to do? Ring Wayan and ask him if he remembered the gory details better than she did? Marnie cursed out loud. Why the hell was all this crap happening to her?

Over the next couple of days she could think of nothing else but her dilemma. There was no way she would consider having a child. She'd never wanted children so certainly had no intention of becoming a candidate for motherhood at this late stage. In one of her more irrational moments, she tried to imagine the reaction among her parents' friends and her former school friends if she produced a late-life, coffee-colored baby. Now *that*, she thought with a tight smile, would certainly cause a stir among Melbourne's matrons. Because she was as certain as she could possibly be that the child could not be Steven's. They had been too careful; he was every bit as cautious as she was. After all — she tried to find some humor in the situation — he was an accountant. Risk-taking wasn't high on the agenda.

Even now, she realized, she couldn't get him out of her mind.

She made an appointment with her doctor. The pregnancy was confirmed and tests done for STDs.

'So, Marnie, you're going to buck the trend again?' Dr Ingrid Pryor raised a challenging eyebrow. She had known her patient for a long time.

'What do you mean?'

'Well, late-life babies are all the go with career women. Are you sure you wouldn't reconsider? You can certainly afford it.' It was the nearest she felt she could go to framing the options.

'Oh, please, Ingrid, don't try the guilt trip on me. What poor kid needs me as a mother?'

The other woman ignored the flippant reply. 'It's a serious decision at any age, Marnie. I just want you to be sure you've considered all the options.'

Marnie stood up to leave. 'I appreciate what you're saying, but I'm having an abortion. As soon as possible.'

She got to the door, turned and added defiantly, 'You can see this as some form of pathetic justification if you like, but I wouldn't want to take the chance of scarring a child the way I was scarred.'

Yet, for all that, she found it much harder than she'd envisaged to face the psychological hurdles of her decision. After a lifetime of affairs, this was the first time she'd ever had to face the reality of an abortion.

The night before she was due to attend the clinic, she found herself bombarded with turbulent emotions. Every platitude, every truism now held a personal resonance: she was carrying a life force inside her, something with the potential to become a human being, a cluster of cells that, if they went to full term, she would later call her son or daughter.

The thought affected her more than she could have imagined. Perhaps it was because this unlikely event had presented her with what was probably her last chance to have a child. Her attitude would have been much less ponderous in her twenties, she felt certain. She recalled her recent joking remark to Tina and Lee about having a daughter to look after her in her dotage; now that flippancy carried a poignant irony.

While nothing was going to make her change her mind, she was keenly aware of the finality of the step she was taking.

Her appointment was at 9 a.m. and she caught a taxi to the clinic. At least it was legal these days, Marnie thought, recalling the time when Lee had found herself in the same predicament. She could have asked Lee or Tina to pick her up afterwards, but there seemed little point in putting them to the trouble of rearranging their working hours. This was something she would face alone. And the less she spoke about it, she convinced herself, the easier it would be to put it behind her.

It was Friday evening and Tina was preparing a meal for herself and Mark. Usually she found little pleasure in cooking, but it made a difference when you had someone to share with. Certainly Mark was always appreciative of her efforts. A smile played around her lips as she checked the curry for seasoning. Of course, he might just be easy to please.

She looked forward to weekends now. The more time she spent with Mark, the fonder she became of him. Everything was so easy when there was no other party involved. If only it could have been like this with Dean, she thought. No lies, no deceit, just total freedom to be together. But she clamped down on such musings. There was no point in dwelling on fantasies.

She was setting the table when her phone rang.

'Tina speaking.'

'Tina ... it's Dean.'

Her heart lurched and for a moment she was too taken aback to reply. It was as if her thoughts had suddenly conjured him up.

'Dean ...' She finally found her voice. 'How are you?' The polite inquiry was purely instinctive.

'I'm really not in a good way, Tina.'

Her heart leaped again. Was he ill? Was he going to tell her some terrible news?

'What do you mean? What's wrong?'

She heard the tremor in her voice, and the sudden rush of fear inside her proved how much she still cared for him. All the months apart hadn't changed that, no matter how hard she'd tried.

'You're probably going to slam down the phone on me and, in all truth, I couldn't blame you. But I hope you'll hear me out.'

She felt as if she were holding her breath. She didn't dare speculate on what she was going to hear.

'It's been hell for me,' he went on. 'Every single day since we said goodbye has been hell. I kept telling myself I was doing the right thing — by everyone. That I had no real option. But then I saw you that day at lunch and I've hardly been able to cope since. I ... I made a mistake, darling. A huge mistake. I need to see you, I need to talk to you. I need to know if you still feel anything for me.' His voice faltered. 'I don't think I can go on living without you. It's you I want to be with. Only you. And I'm prepared to sacrifice everything for that.'

Afterwards, all she needed was to be alone, to remember again the words Dean had spoken and try to come to terms with the fact that he was offering to leave Kathy. If Tina still wanted him, he said, nothing else mattered. His children would adapt. But he couldn't keep existing as if he were only half-alive.

'I can't expect you to give me an answer straightaway. But please, let me see you. Just give me the opportunity to tell you exactly how I feel. I need you, darling. I can't live without you.'

Her hands had felt as if they were soldered to the phone. The shock of his words rendered her almost speechless. There was a part of her that could barely contain her joy, it bubbled up like a gas, desperate for release. Yet another part warned her to be cautious, not to open her heart for fear it would be sucked dry once again.

'Please, Tina ...' She could hear the desperate longing in his voice.

Dry-mouthed, she had asked him where and when he wanted to meet.

And now, she was sitting at the table trying to get through the evening with Mark. They were finishing their dessert and she realized she had barely taken in a word he'd said. Her thoughts were light years away.

'What?' She realized he'd asked her a question and was looking at her, waiting for an answer. 'I'm sorry. I didn't ...'

'Is there something wrong?' His brows drew together in concern. 'I've felt all night as if you were somewhere else.'

With an effort, she pulled herself together. 'I'm sorry,' she apologized. 'To tell you the truth, I think I'm getting a migraine.'

It wasn't that much of a lie. The tension generated by Dean's phone call and his change of heart was making her head thump.

'You should have said, Tina! We're good enough friends by now, aren't we? I can still manage to spend a night with Digger now and then, you know. Come on ...' He stood up and picked up their plates. 'Let me clean this up and you go off to bed.'

Yet she found it almost impossible to get any rest that night. A war of indecision raged inside her. Had she done the right thing in agreeing to meet Dean? Or was she setting herself up for another emotional roller-coaster ride that would end the same way? Was he really as determined to leave his wife and family as he'd sounded on the phone? The last thing she needed was to put herself through the anguish of a break-up all over again.

For all her confusion, his call had made her face the fact that her feelings for him were still very much alive. And that made her vulnerable, because she couldn't bear to repeat the grief of her loss. But surely he wouldn't have contacted her if his mind weren't made up one hundred per cent about leaving his marriage. He must realize how much she had suffered.

Finally, among all her agitation, Tina realized that she faced another complication: her relationship with Mark. Not that either of them had any claim on the other; but if she allowed Dean back into her life, it would be far too awkward to have Mark still living on the premises. Somehow, as tactfully as possible, she would have to find a way around that one if it came to it.

Everything hinged on her meeting with Dean. On whether he could convince her that he was really ready to leave his marriage.

They met on neutral ground, in a quiet suburban restaurant. As soon as she felt his lips on her cheek, Tina knew she was lost.

'I've missed you so much,' he whispered, gripping her hand tightly.

She nodded, not trusting herself to speak. Pure happiness at being with him again overrode all her apprehension.

Their meals went uneaten as they talked and held each other's hands across the table.

'I've made up my mind, Tina, I promise you that. All I'm asking is your patience until my girls finish the school term. I hope you'll understand that. It'll give me time to find an apartment and get the rest of my life organized.'

She felt as if she had woken to one of the dozens of dreams she'd had in the time since they'd split. The dreams in which Dean walked back into her life and told her he would be there for ever. Now she had to convince herself that this was reality.

'Just knowing we'll be together,' she answered, 'that's all that matters.'

Afterwards, as they walked hand in hand to her car, Dean said light-heartedly, 'I guess I should feel lucky you weren't snapped up by anyone else. That would have been unbearable.'

Tina thought of Mark. She had no reason to feel guilty about their affair; she'd been a free agent. She was very fond of Mark; his companionship had been invaluable to her during the last few difficult months. But now she would have to extricate herself from the relationship. And the only way she could do that, fairly and honestly, was by telling him the truth.

Two evenings later she invited him to the house for a drink. As she walked down the hall to open the front door, Tina felt a nervous flutter in her belly. It was never going to be easy. Not only was she stepping back from their friendship, she was asking him to find another home as well.

'Hi.' He stood smiling at her on the doorstep. His hair was still damp from his shower and he smelled of some lemony aftershave. In his hand he carried a paper bag. 'Vine-ripened tomatoes,' he said as he handed them to her. 'Bought them up the coast last weekend. Nothing like those red bullets from the supermarket.'

Tina peeked at the fruit. 'They look lovely. Thanks.'

He was always generous, rarely joined her for dinner without contributing something.

In the sunroom, she put out the glasses while he opened the bottle of wine. She did her best to sound normal as they chatted.

'Cheers,' he said, touching his glass to hers.

'And to you,' she responded.

They sipped at their wine and he started to talk about his children.

'Angela won a swimming competition last week. She was disappointed I wasn't there to see her, poor kid. Happens too often the way things are now.'

Tina grabbed at the opener she'd been searching for.

'You wouldn't think of moving closer to them again?'

He shrugged and shook his head. 'Work's the problem. It's just not there.'

Putting her glass down, she took a deep breath. 'Mark, I've asked you here this evening because something's come up for me. Something I never expected to happen.'

The intensity of her tone focused his attention and he listened without interrupting as she told him, briefly and for the first time, about Dean, the break- up and the reason for it.

'I thought it was over,' she explained. 'I did my best to put it all behind me. And I thought I had. But now everything's changed. He's prepared to leave his wife. He wants it to work with me and he's promised it will.'

For a long moment there was silence. Tina was watching Mark's face but it was difficult to read his expression. Maybe it was a relief for him too, she thought. Maybe he felt the affair had run its course and this would give him an excuse to extricate himself without hurt on either side.

He took a long swallow of his wine and put the empty glass on the table.

'That was the bloke I saw here that night?'

'Yes.'

'You've been carrying a torch for him all this time?'

Tina frowned. She hadn't expected a cross examination. 'Not really. Or I didn't think so. As I said, I thought it was over. Completely. But things are different now.'

'Does he have kids?'

She wondered where the conversation was heading. 'Yes, he has. Two girls. What about it?'

'I guess it always seems so much worse when there are children involved.'

She stood up then and said coldly, 'I hope I'm not going to get a lecture on morality, Mark.'

He too pushed himself up from his chair. 'No, you're right. It's none of my business.' He hesitated. 'I wish you luck then. I hope it all works out. Obviously, I'll move out as soon as possible.'

Guilty, she retreated. 'No, really ... I mean there's no great rush. He wants to wait until his children finish the school term. That's about a month away.'

She went over to him and put her hand on his arm. 'Look, I'm handling this very badly, I know. I don't want you to think for one moment I was using you, Mark. What we had together was what we both needed. It was good for us and I hope we can still be friends.'

She could see the tension in his expression as he looked for the right words to reply.

'I shouldn't be saying this,' he said at last. 'Especially now. But since it's a day for being upfront... I... stopped being friends with you quite a while ago, Tina. I guess I really couldn't help what was happening to me. Maybe this way at least, it takes the problem out of my hands.' He shrugged his broad shoulders and forced himself to smile. 'I guess I always knew I didn't have a chance with a woman like you.'

She stared back at him. There had never been any sign. She had always thought...

'Oh, Mark, I'm sorry. I never realized.' She stopped, wary of sounding patronizing or coy and hurting him further.

'Well, it doesn't matter any more, does it? As it happens, I was probably going to be moving on myself pretty soon.' He wasn't sure why he was telling her this. To save face? But it was too late for that.

'Moving? Where to?'

'My ex wants to shift to Adelaide. I'm invited, too.' He gave a short, humorless laugh. 'She knows it'd be the only way I wouldn't fight her over the kids.

'Not,' he added tightly, 'that I can afford that. So I'm almost letting myself be convinced.'

Tina took his hand in her own and held it tightly as she looked steadily into his eyes. 'You were very, very good to me, Mark. I can only wish you every happiness and thank you again for all you did for me. You made me happy when I thought I was never going to feel that way again.'

She was about to reach up and kiss him, when, with an abrupt movement, he pulled away.

'Good night, Tina.' The hurt in his voice was unmistakable. He strode out of the room and she heard the front door close behind him.

Chapter 18

PERSISTENCE AND PATIENCE HAD PAID off in the end.

The man felt the gratification of having his diligence confirmed. He had persevered and now there would be no more delays in bringing the situation to a close.

As he followed the flow of traffic onto the Harbour Bridge, he reached for his mobile and put a call through to the number he now knew so well.

It was surely time to take the next step.

Now that the option of returning to her marriage no longer existed, Lee began to panic about her future. What was she going to do? Surely, with the six months almost up, Brad would issue an ultimatum: come home at once or forget about their relationship entirely. Even though she now longed to return to Newcastle and all that was familiar, she would be forced to tell him that was no longer a possibility. Yet she could never explain why. The truth was too shameful. And for the same reason, she would have to lie to her own family.

As the deadline neared for the end of her time with Anita, Lee felt her panic grow. She was going to have to find other employment but she knew how difficult that could be for a woman of her age. Tina and Marnie had promised to put out feelers and do whatever they could to help but Lee knew she was going to have to pursue every avenue possible. Each day she scoured the employment options but the few advertisements she'd replied to had led to nothing. It crossed her mind to ask Anita for help, then she dismissed the idea. That would have necessitated further lies and deception and she really didn't feel able to cope with that.

On another front she knew she would have to tell Julie that she wasn't returning home — and she wanted to do that face to face. But whenever she rang her daughter's number, there was never any reply and the messages she left elicited no response. Lee wondered if the course Julie was doing might involve some off-campus work. Or had she really meant what she'd said the last time they'd spoken — that she wanted to be left alone until her parents had worked things out?

Well, that was never going to happen now. And somehow Lee had to face her sensitive daughter and make her understand that.

The thought of the mess she'd made of things was never far from her mind. Stress had robbed her of her appetite and she had trouble sleeping. One Saturday afternoon, feeling totally overwhelmed, she rang her sister desperate for a connection to the familiar. But her tentative questions about Brad and the boys didn't meet with the comforting response she'd expected.

'We never see Brad but the kids drop around now and then — usually at tea time.' Joy's retort was sharp, she saw no reason to beat around the bush. 'When are you going to stop playing games, Lee? Hasn't this gone on long enough? How long are you going to pretend you're still a kid?'

'You don't understand, Joy.' Lee's voice was plaintive.

'Like hell I don't! We all have our disappointments you know. The difference is the rest of us aren't destroying our families trying to escape into some fantasy past. We just get on with it!'

By the time she rang off, Lee was close to tears. Yet how could she blame her sister? In many ways, Joy's words were true. It had all been a fantasy. A crazy search for what she felt she'd been denied all those years ago.

And now the fantasy had turned into a nightmare.

Stress was a factor the doctor had told her. It made you more susceptible and the initial outbreaks were usually the worst.

'Gradually, over time, the sores become less painful,' she'd explained. 'It's best if you get onto the medication the moment you feel the first tingles.'

The morning after her call to Joy, Lee had awoken with a burning feeling in her genital area. By later that day, the sensation had become more intense and, stomach churning, she had been forced to inspect herself with a small hand mirror. The sight of the reddening blister had overwhelmed her with shame and disgust. Oh God, why had this terrible thing happened to her? How was she going to live with it for the rest of her life? She was so ashamed she couldn't even tell Tina and Marnie.

It occurred to her then with shattering clarity that if sometime in the future she found herself in the unlikely position of beginning a new relationship, she would be faced with having to admit her terrible secret. It was a notion that totally overwhelmed her.

As she stood waiting for her prescription to be filled, Lee felt certain the eyes of the pharmacist were upon her. Aware of her dirty secret. Assuming she was promiscuous. And the same paranoia filled her when the young shop assistant handed her the script to sign. No doubt the girl was thinking the same thing. With cheeks blazing, she grabbed her medication in the paper bag and hurried away from those accusatory eyes.

Marnie had spent the afternoon in a meeting with her selling agents. Most of the sales on her last project had been finalized and she was cashed-up to embark on the first stage of the inner west site. Yet, as good as that news was, she'd found it hard to concentrate on the detail.

Earlier that day she'd had a call from the police. To her surprise, they'd turned up a witness to the incident involving her vehicle. A woman weeding her small front garden had seen what had happened; she'd even managed to catch some of the license plate belonging to the sedan. The Good Samaritan had made contact with the police and as a result, the car had been traced to a Kevin Morris. They hadn't managed to pick him up yet, the policeman explained, but did that name ring a bell?

Fran Morris's estranged husband — somehow he had managed to track her down. Perhaps, as Judy had suggested, it was the day Fran had come to her house with the flowers. Maybe he'd been following his wife even then, biding his time until he could hit back at all those who had assisted her escape.

Marnie told the policeman what she knew. 'Do you think he's likely to threaten me again?' she asked.

'Hopefully, it's a one-off. Just trying to scare you. Don't worry about it too much, we'll pick him up soon.'

Now, as she drove home, Marnie found herself checking too often in the rear-view mirror. It wasn't like her to get rattled. She could handle the upfront battles, it was the unpredictable that made her uneasy.

At home, she picked up her mail in the foyer and glanced through it as the elevator carried her upstairs. One envelope was clearly personal mail, but she didn't recognize the writing. Turning it over, her heart skipped a beat when she saw the sticker with Steven's name and home address. Why, after all these weeks, had he written to her now?

Entering her apartment, she dropped her big carryall and the rest of the mail on the nearest chair and tore open the envelope. As she read the brief note, a surge of conflicting emotions ran through her. He had written to tell her that his father had passed away the week before.

... respiratory failure, and a relief in a way. I dreaded facing the same ordeal again. At least the end was quick and dignified.

He ended with: *I still think of you often, Marnie, but I've always been a realist — as you are too. As always, I wish you the best with everything.*

For the rest of the evening, she could think of little else but Steven and that note. Why had he written to her? Because he'd needed to express his feelings to someone who would understand? Because he'd helped her to face her own grief and maybe now needed comfort himself? As she let herself ponder his feelings and motivations, she found herself beginning to examine her own more closely.

She still missed him. She wondered now if the reason the relationship had ended went deeper than her mere resistance to a commitment. She realized that Steven was the only man she had ever allowed to see her vulnerability. And that had frightened her, because she remembered what vulnerability had felt like when she was a child. The ache for her father's love had eaten her insides raw until eventually, she had convinced herself that it didn't matter. She had promised herself that she would never allow any man to have a hold over her again. She would be the one in control.

But Steven's note had reminded her that he hadn't been afraid to expose his own vulnerabilities. He was that rare sort of man who was willing to open his heart and express his feelings on the things that really mattered. And she remembered how she had scoffed at those emotions.

Finally, that evening, she admitted to herself that there might be more than a grain of truth in the accusation Steven had thrown at her. Perhaps she *was* punishing all men for the way her father had treated her. And that forced her to confront the most penetrating question of all: where Steven was concerned, had she ended up punishing herself as well?

It was more than three weeks since Mark had left. Tina had come home to find a note slipped under her door, asking her to hold any mail until he could give her a forwarding address. A strange sense of loss had engulfed her. Crazy as it was in the circumstances, she knew there was a lot she was going to miss now that Mark was gone. The easy friendship, the conversations over a bottle of wine, the evening walks they'd taken with the dog. Simple things, but they'd meant a lot when she'd been at her lowest.

The next day before leaving for work, she'd let herself into the flat. As she'd looked around, she realized it had probably been left tidier and cleaner than when he'd moved in. The bed was stripped and the mattress left on its side against the wall to air. Even the garbage bin had been scrubbed clean. Not a trace remained of either Mark or his dog. It was as if they had never existed.

Dean now dropped in whenever possible. A couple of times he managed to stay for dinner and inevitably they ended up in bed.

Disconcertingly, Tina found she had to get used to his body again, to the ways they had pleased each other sexually. Occasionally, when she closed her eyes, she would suddenly find herself remembering Mark, and her heart would leap with guilt as she drove such thoughts from her mind.

Yet while she fell back into the relationship with Dean, the sense of deja vu was never far away. So little seemed to have changed. The quick dressing afterwards, the sound of his car door slamming as he went back to spend the rest of the night with the woman who was still his wife.

'I wish I could spend more time with you, darling, but at this stage I've got to be careful.' His excuses, she noted, were as valid as ever.

Then one evening he spoke about his daughters and the guilt he felt at what he was about to do. 'It's the hardest step of all,' he said despondently. 'I couldn't bear to have my girls turn against me.'

Tina could find little to say in comfort.

The new pool man came on Saturday mornings when she was at home. While she watched him at his task, she found her thoughts returning to Mark. She remembered how slowly everything had happened between them, what comfort she had found in his company, how uncomplicated the relationship had been. As she continued to ponder, she arrived at a simple but penetrating insight. Mark had touched her life for a while and then moved on. Dean wanted her now, but was still fighting his own demons. The more she thought about it, the more she knew he would never be able to relinquish his guilt. And, sooner or later, she began to realize, she would come to personify that guilt.

The woman who had cost him his children.

It was the weekend Dean was to have moved out. He'd found a flat for himself, a small serviced apartment in North Sydney that would serve as his home address while the divorce proceedings got under way. Only now he was asking her to wait another week.

'It's Belinda's speech night next Thursday. She's won a prize and I really don't want to spoil that for her, darling. Can I please ask you to be patient for just a few more days?'

The bargaining was familiar too.

It was after seven when Marnie let herself into the apartment. She was glad to be home. The day had started off badly with the engineer missing their on-site appointment, and had got gradually worse. It seemed that everyone she dealt with was an asshole, a moron or both. Maybe she was getting too old for all this stress. But what the hell would she do instead?

In the kitchen, she poured herself a glass of wine and checked the fridge. Eggs, a block of cheese and a couple of oranges. Well, she was too tired to go out again. An omelet would have to do and damn the cholesterol. But first she'd take a shower or maybe even a bath. It would help her relax.

She saw it the moment she snapped on the bathroom light, and the wine glass almost fell from her fingers.

The words were scrawled across the mirror. Written in red Texta.

You're not safe bitch.

Then she saw the red liquid in the washbasin, and the razor blade stuck into the cake of soap.

An obscenity burst from her lips. Turning, she hurried to find her phone.

After the police left she waited anxiously for the locksmith to arrive. Whoever it was had gained access by the front door. Stupidly, she often didn't bother with the deadlock. The police had dusted for fingerprints and warned her to get the locks changed.

'I'm sure it's that bastard Kevin Morris.' She'd relayed the story again about Fran Morris and her estranged husband, told the police about the recent incident on the road.

'Well, I don't want to scare you,' the young policeman said, 'but if he's still on the loose, you'd better make sure you get a locksmith tonight. I can give you a number. And maybe you should think of having someone to stay with you for a couple of days.'

The tradesman showed up a short time later and while he completed his task, Marnie made a call to Tina and told her what had happened.

'I have to admit it's freaking me out. Until they catch this bastard, I'm never going to feel safe. I was hoping you could put me up for a night or two maybe? Tomorrow I'll start looking for another apartment and security will be the priority.'

Tina's voice expressed her concern. 'Of course you can stay — as long as you like, you know that. Come over straightaway. Have you eaten yet?'

'No, but I think I've lost my appetite.'

'I'll make you something light.'

Marnie felt a sense of relief as she switched off her phone. Things seemed to be getting on top of her lately. She couldn't cope like she used to. Maybe the abortion had something to do with it, screwing up her hormones. Thank God she had her two true friends.

Tina made her a toasted sandwich and they sat together in the sunroom.

'Surely the police have enough to go on now?' Tina protested. 'Can't they pin this creep down?'

'No fixed address, it seems. Stays with friends, acquaintances, and moves on.'

'What about work? Can't they trace him through that? Or the welfare lot?'

'Marnie shook her head. 'I guess they're trying. I just wish to hell it would happen before he dreams up something else to rattle me.'

'Well, you know you're welcome to stay here for as long as you like. Certainly all this weekend. I'm speaking at a seminar up the Coast so you'll have the place to yourself.'

She told Marnie then about Dean coming back into her life.

'This time he says he's leaving for sure.' She gave a brittle laugh. 'Except that the date keeps changing.'

Marnie gave her a sharp look. 'You don't sound very happy.'

With a heavy sigh, Tina leaned back against the sofa. 'I just don't know if it's going to work. Leaving his wife is one thing, leaving his children quite another.' She paused, and then put into words what she'd barely wanted to admit to herself. 'And you know the really weird part about it?' She looked up and held Marnie's gaze. 'I'm really not sure if I feel the same way about him any longer.'

Marnie gave her a speculative look. 'It's changed? Why?'

'You're going to think I'm crazy if I tell you.'

'Try me.'

And so she told Marnie about the affair with Mark, the thoughts and feelings she was unable to dismiss. If Marnie was surprised, she made a good job of not showing it. Tina and the hunky tradesman — who would have believed it?

'I'm just totally confused,' Tina went on. 'I keep going round in circles thinking about it. All I know is, until I can work myself out, I don't think I can let Dean go ahead and break up his family.'

Marnie saw her point. 'I guess you're right on that score. Not,' she added, 'that Auntie Marnie is the right person to be giving advice to the lovelorn, darling. I'm enough of a screwed up mess myself.'

Then it was her turn to explain about Steven, about the kiss-off scene in Bali and the note she'd received just recently.

'The guy's got under my skin. A bloody, straight-as-a-die accountant from Melbourne! Can you believe it? He said things to me that really pissed me off, but since I've had time to think about them, maybe he's got me worked out.' She laughed. 'That's the worrying part.'

'Are you going to make contact again?'

Marnie shook her head. 'I think I blew it. I told him to find some undemanding little divorcee who was in desperate need of home, hearth and husband.'

'But he's written you a note instead?'

Marnie met her gaze. 'Yeah.'

With every day that passed, Lee became more and more desperate. She hadn't managed to find a job and the lease was up on her apartment in less than two weeks. Avoiding the details, she had finally sounded out Anita on the possibility of staying on at Veronique. But of course everything had been set up for the new manager to start and the shop couldn't afford to pay the wages of two seniors.

Anita had been both upset and confused. 'I really hate to let you down, Lee, after you've been so good to me, but you were quite adamant you were going home. Otherwise I'd never have gone ahead with this new girl. What changed your mind?'

'Oh, a rethink.' Lee kept her tone light. 'Thought I'd made too hasty a decision. But don't worry, I'll find something I'm sure. I've got lots of feelers out there.'

It wasn't quite a lie. She'd had a long discussion with Marnie and Tina the last time they'd all met for a meal and both had promised to ask around and see if they could come up with anything. Lee knew she could count on them to do their best. The trouble was she had so little experience in anything. Marnie had promised to chat with people she knew in retail while Tina, bless her, had offered the use of her flat above the garage — rent free — until Lee had sorted things out.

Otherwise, the few interviews she'd managed to land had been stymied she felt sure, because of her age. There was nothing any anti-discrimination legislation could do when attractive twenty-somethings were lined up against a woman in her mid-forties. It was all so demoralizing and defeating.

If after all her attempts, she didn't manage to find a job, what could she do next? Face the ignominy of social security? Stand in line for some government handout? She didn't even know if she'd be eligible when she told them she was still married and had a home of her own. She had no idea how the system worked. The thought of the humiliation of having to tell some indifferent stranger the details of her life was unbearable. Yet in the end it might be her only alternative.

She was home that evening, beginning to pack up the apartment she could no longer afford, when the phone rang. Lee frowned. It was almost ten. Who could be calling her at this hour?

She picked up the receiver. It was Brad and she knew at once that something was wrong. Her heart kicked wildly against her ribs as he quickly told her what had occurred.

'I'm coming,' she said sharply. 'I'm leaving straightaway.'

As she snatched up her bag and keys, she was already saying a silent prayer.

Chapter 19

MARNIE WAS ALONE IN THE house. Tina had left that morning for the seminar up the Coast and wouldn't be home until Sunday afternoon.

'I'll think about things while I'm away,' she told Marnie while they had coffee together in the kitchen. 'But my gut feeling's still there. It isn't fair to let this drag on if there isn't going to be a future.'

'Follow your heart,' Marnie replied. 'That's the only cliché I can offer.'

Tina sighed heavily as she rinsed her mug and turned it upside down to drain. 'Sometimes I think I'm losing the plot entirely. Mark's in Adelaide, he's tied to his kids. How can I possibly fit in with that scenario?'

'To offer another cliché,' Marnie said, 'if it's meant to be, you'll find a way.'

'Well, one thing's for sure — I'm not leaving Sydney. My career's here, my home, my business network. There's no way I'm walking away from all that.' She shook her head in exasperation. 'It's all too hard. Maybe when I've chewed it over, I'll find I don't want to be with either of them.'

Marnie grinned at her over the top of her coffee mug. 'D'you reckon it's too late for us to turn gay?'

At least she'd managed to bring a smile to Tina's face.

Left alone, Marnie looked through various accommodation options and rang half a dozen letting agencies to inquire about places that sounded appealing. Half-heartedly, she forced herself to go and take a closer look at some of the advertised apartments. They turned out to be okay, but nothing special. Perhaps a serviced place would be the way to go, she mused, as she drove home. Then, as soon as she knew Kevin Morris was safely put away, she could return to her own home and skip all the expense and bother.

Back in the house by mid afternoon, she found it difficult to settle to anything. There was nothing on TV that caught her interest so she flipped through some of Tina's business and fashion magazines until that too bored her. It frustrated her to think of all the paperwork she could have been doing at home.

Alone with her thoughts, she found her mind wandering back to that threatening scene of the night before. Her fear was slowly turning to anger at being driven out of her own home. Surely the police would nail that bastard soon? Until they did, she was never going to feel safe. If the new project hadn't been up and running, she might have gone away somewhere for a while. Not Bali — the thought of her house there didn't appeal, not after everything that had happened. First with Steven, and then the aftermath with Wayan.

She realized then that she had never really stood still long enough since the abortion to dwell on her reaction to it. Her decision had been pragmatic but there had certainly been a sense of sadness and pity too. Could she have managed a child this late in her life? Would it have brought her something she didn't even know she was missing? Clearly she would never know.

The same way she would never know what might have happened if she'd been able to offer Steven what he had wanted: a love that was fully committed, a relationship that might have brought her real happiness as she entered the final third of her life.

Well, she told herself, standing up from the sofa, it wasn't going to do her any good dwelling on all that. The past was over, and she was too jaded and cynical to believe there were any second chances in life.

While she was out she'd bought a ready-cooked curry and now heated it in the microwave for dinner. After she'd eaten, she watched TV for a while and finally decided that bed seemed the preferable option. A good night's sleep was probably what she needed.

There were two main bedrooms in Tina's home, both larger than normal and each with its own ensuite. She'd forgotten what it was like to have all this space. You could get lost in a place this size. She cleaned her teeth and then tried to read for a while before switching off the light. As she drifted into sleep, she felt the security of knowing she was safe. No one, certainly not Kevin Bloody Morris, had any idea where she was.

At the Central Coast resort, Tina too was getting ready for bed. Her session that afternoon had been well received and she was due to speak again the following morning. It would do her good to have an early night. But she found it difficult to get to sleep, her thoughts preoccupied with her personal dilemma.

On the surface it might appear that nothing had altered between herself and Dean but her heart was telling her otherwise. She hadn't realized it at the time, but she had changed in the months since they'd broken up. It had taken their reunion to prove that. In Dean's absence, she had found a different sort of happiness, an easier connection with a man who was so much his opposite. Mark Galloway wasn't sophisticated but she had learned that wasn't necessarily a fault. He was a bright, articulate human being who had helped her to grow in a way that Dean never had. In some gentle, unbidden way he had taught her more about herself than she could have thought possible: how to be open, how to find pleasure in simple things, what was of real value. Yet at the same time she couldn't help wondering if she was being foolishly sentimental. Her emotions had been raw when Mark came into her life. Had that colored her attitudes, blurred her judgment? She was so used to thinking of herself as decisive and definite that her current indecision was all the more unbearable.

She remembered what Marnie had said about following her heart. It had been obvious to her then that her friend was facing her own regrets. Clearly the man she'd met in Melbourne had been Marnie's catalyst — and she had let him go.

Tina didn't want to make the same mistake.

There wasn't much traffic at that time of night. Lee drove as fast as she dared, willing every kilometer to pass so she could get to her daughter's side.

Brad had told her on the phone that it was Joel that Julie had turned to, and that knowledge cut deep. In her daughter's time of need, it wasn't her mother she had reached out for. Nor even her father.

Lee's heart squeezed in anguish as a dozen questions ran through her head. Had she caused so much damage that it had come to this? Was it her own selfishness that had brought things to such a crisis point? Had she been so caught up in her own troubles and fears that she hadn't had the perception to see what was happening to her daughter?

Brad had told her nothing beyond the bare details on the phone. Julie had had 'some sort of breakdown'.

She'd taken the train back to Newcastle and begged Joel to let her stay at his place. But by the second evening, she'd apparently got herself in such a state that Joel had been forced to call Brad and tell him what was happening.

'You'll see for yourself, Lee.' Brad's voice had sounded tight and strained. 'She's in a bad way. I've got her at home now and she's on some sort of sedative. But it hasn't stopped the crying.'

Lee had been too shocked to listen for any accusation in his tone. Now as she travelled the dark road towards the only place she thought of as home, she felt choked with guilt. Whatever Brad threw at her, she knew she probably deserved it. Not that it mattered. Julie was all she cared about at this moment.

He heard her pull into the driveway and came outside to greet her. They both stood awkwardly for a second not sure how to react to each other.

Brad put his hand out for her bag. 'She's inside. In her room.'

'What's the matter?' Lee asked quietly as they headed into the house. 'Does Joel know what this is all about?'

'He's in the living room. You can ask him yourself.' His tone was neutral, she noted, as if he were disciplining himself not to inflame the situation.

'I will, but I want to see Julie first.'

The bedroom was softly lit by the old lamp that stood on the desk where Julie had once done her schoolwork. There was just enough light for Lee to see, with shock, how much weight her daughter had lost. She was lying in bed, her face gaunt, her arms frighteningly thin over the covers.

'Darling ... I'm here ...' Perching on the painted wooden chair beside the bed, she stroked a tender hand over her daughter's brow.

Slowly, Julie turned her head, as if she were shifting some great weight. She looked at her mother through red and swollen eyes.

'Julie, my pet.' Lee unconsciously used the childhood endearment as she took her daughter's hand in her own. 'It's going to be all right. I'm here. Dad's here. We're all here for you now.' She took a deep breath and her grip tightened. 'And we're never going away from each other again.'

Lee felt as if her heart would break when she saw the tears fill her daughter's eyes.

She sat in the living room, the cup of tea Brad had made her warming her hands. Joel, looking tired and drawn, sat in the armchair opposite. It was past one in the morning, but Lee couldn't let him go until she found out what he knew.

'Please, Joel, tell me everything. I have to know exactly what happened if I'm going to do my best to help her.' She threw a quick glance at Brad. 'We both need to know.'

Joel sat hunched, hands hanging between his knees. 'She's been ringing me every now and then, even though we'd officially broken up. I ... I think she wanted someone to talk to. She said she was finding it difficult to adapt to uni, it was so different from school. And there was so much to do in so little time.'

'You mean assignments?' Lee asked.

Joel nodded. 'Yeah, and work too.'

Lee frowned. 'I know she was doing quite a few hours in that restaurant. That worried me.'

'Lack of time was the main reason we broke up.' Joel's voice was plaintive. 'I think she thought it wasn't fair on me when she was so flat out.'

'You feel she was under a lot of pressure then?' It was Brad who asked the question.

'Absolutely. She felt guilty as hell at turning down the chance at NIDA and then she found herself struggling with what she'd chosen to do at uni. I think she was totally confused and didn't know whom to talk to about it.' He kept his eyes on the floor, avoiding the gaze of the two other people in the room. 'She felt as if she were letting everybody down, including herself.'

'I tried to talk to her,' Lee put in. 'I rang her, but she wouldn't discuss anything with me.'

Joel looked uncomfortable. 'She was angry with you — for leaving, she said. She wanted everything to be like it was.' He lifted his head then and met Lee's gaze. 'Julie's very family-oriented, you know. She just hated letting any of you down. And from what she told me, that's what she feels she's done.'

After Joel left, Lee and Brad faced each other in the silent house. Lee steeled herself for the recriminations, but Brad said nothing. Slumped in his chair, he looked tired and uncomprehending.

She knew there were things that had to be said, no matter how late the hour.

'Brad, we've both got to help Julie through this. No matter what the problems are between us, I'm sure you'll agree she has to be our first priority.'

He raised his eyes to hers and shook his head. 'I still can't believe it's come to this. Why couldn't she have just come home if things were so bad?'

'Joel gave us some of the reasons. But what matters now is that she is home and we're all going to have to help her.'

He looked at her a long moment. 'Does that mean you're back to stay?' A wary edge had crept into his voice.

Lee's mouth was dry. She dreaded what she had to say next, but she knew she had no choice.

'Brad ...' Her heart was racing. 'There's something I have to tell you. I want you to know it's the absolute truth. Exactly as it happened. You can believe me or not, that's up to you. But it's the reason I was never going to come home.'

While she told him about Graham, the rape, the health problem he'd left her with, she didn't have the courage to meet her husband's eyes. Her cheeks burned with humiliation as she explained exactly what they faced. 'Herpes is infectious and it can't be cured, only controlled with medication. I could never expose you to that. If this hadn't happened with Julie, I'd probably have made up some other reason why I wasn't coming back.'

Finally, she lifted her eyes to his. His face was pale and tight.

'Why should I think you're not lying now?' he asked gruffly. 'How do I know you haven't had a dozen affairs?'

'You don't, Brad. I can understand how you're thinking but believe me, I've told you the truth. In retrospect, I should never have done what I did. It was selfish and totally irresponsible. But I promise you, I didn't go to Sydney looking for flings with other men.'

'We had a good marriage, Lee. At least, I thought so.'

'It wasn't the marriage I was running away from, Brad.' Her sister's words echoed in her mind. 'I was trying to recreate what I thought I'd missed out on all those years ago. Pretending I was a kid again, running away from my responsibilities.' Her voice shook. 'I guess ... I had to learn the hard way how to grow up.'

Brad took a deep breath, his agitation clear. 'I don't know, Lee ... I just don't know how I feel any more.'

She forced herself to meet his gaze. 'I've done terrible damage to everyone. And I can't expect you to forgive me for what's happened. But I have to be here for Julie; she needs both of us now. I know how difficult it must be for you but no matter what you think of me, we're both going to have to pretend — for our daughter's sake. At least until she's better.'

That night, for the first time in months, she slept in her own familiar bed. When Brad said he'd go to Troy's room, she was relieved. In the circumstances, it would have been impossible to lie next to her husband and not feel uncomfortable and awkward.

Yet despite everything, she felt a sense of overwhelming comfort at being back in her own home. Among familiar things and the human beings with whom her life had always been so intimately entwined.

Her first priority as she had told Brad, was to get Julie well again. Everything else was in the hands of the gods.

It was after 2 a.m. and the house was in darkness.

By the light of the half moon, the man hoisted himself lightly over the front wall. He knew the occupant of the garage was gone — and, more importantly, the dog as well. That would certainly have made things far more difficult.

Now that he was safely out of sight of the neighboring residences, he switched on his torch and carefully made his way down the steps to the house. Security systems didn't worry him: they were easy to disarm when you'd worked with them as long as he had.

He smiled in the darkness. All he had to do next was cut the glass on a downstairs window and release the lock. Child's play.

He quickly figured out that the bedrooms were on the upper level. The thick carpet absorbed any noise as he made his way upstairs. On the landing he swung the narrow beam of his torch into the nearest room and saw a desk and bookshelves. Quite clearly a study. The other two rooms were at the end of the hallway; the main bedroom had to be one of those.

Moving lightly, he came to a standstill in front of the door on the right. It was closed. The other, across the passageway, was ajar and he felt certain she would be in the former. With careful, deliberate movements, he turned the handle and shone his torch quickly into the room. The sight of the made- up bed with its assortment of cushions took him aback momentarily. He'd guessed wrong.

Leaving that door open, he turned towards the other. Cautiously reaching out, he pushed it slowly wider and let out his breath.

She was there. He could hear the soft sibilance of her breathing and see her sleeping form beneath the covers.

The man's fingers gripped more securely around his heavy torch.

Chapter 20

Tina had made up her mind. Now it seemed imperative that she talk to Dean as soon as possible. What was the point in delaying when there was the potential for causing even more pain for everyone concerned? She knew it was essential she spoke to him before he broke the news to Kathy. Perhaps he might still leave his marriage, but it wouldn't be because of her.

As she neared the city, she called his mobile number. When he answered, she could hear the buzz of conversation in the background.

'Darling!' She heard the pleasure in his voice. 'Where are you? At home yet?' He'd known she was going to be working for most of the weekend.

'Almost. Half an hour or so away. I ... I was hoping you might be able to meet me somewhere. Not at my place,' she added quickly, 'maybe a coffee shop somewhere. Can you get away?'

'I'm at the yacht club. Just having a drink with the guys. I'll leave a bit earlier and meet you, say, at The Oaks? Out in the garden?'

A noisy beer garden wasn't exactly what Tina had in mind, but maybe it wouldn't matter. In fact, on second thoughts, it might be better than some too quiet coffee shop or wine bar.

'Okay,' she agreed. 'See you in about half an hour.'

'Look forward to it. And darling,' his voice softened, 'soon we'll have every weekend together for the rest of our lives.'

She murmured something and ended the call.

He was waiting for her, a bottle of wine in an ice bucket, two glasses on the table he'd managed to commandeer from the Sunday-afternoon crowd. It was a measure of his commitment, she realized, that he had chosen so public a meeting place.

Smiling, he stood up and kissed her. His blue eyes looked even more intense against his tanned skin and Tina caught the quick admiring glances of other women, those sitting at tables without men. For a moment, she couldn't help wondering if that was how she was going to end up: single, well past her prime, throwing cagey, envious glances at other women's men. Resolutely she pushed the thought away. Whatever happened to her in the future, it was over with Dean.

Five minutes later, with the small talk out of the way, she told him exactly that. Even under the tan, she could see the paling of his complexion.

'Why are you telling me this now? When we're making our plans?' His voice was tight and his fingers gripped the stem of his glass.

'Because I know it isn't going to work, Dean. For a while I tried to pretend it would but now I'm sure. I've changed. Things are different now. And I don't want you walking out on your marriage for the wrong reasons.'

She was blunt in her honesty she knew, but as she spoke she felt flooded with relief. She was doing the right thing. No matter what the future held for her, she would never be happy in this relationship.

'Is there someone else? Is that it?'

Her first reaction was to deny the accusation, then she realized that her honesty would have to extend to his questions as well.

'Maybe... I don't know.' It was a crazy response and he rightly challenged it.

'What sort of shit answer is that? Aren't I owed the truth at least?'

She tried not to flinch from his gaze. 'I... did meet someone. Whether it'll work or not, I have no idea. But,' she hurried on, 'that's not really the point. I had to face the fact that it wasn't happening for me with you any longer, whether there was someone else on the scene or not.'

He stared at her, his face set and hard.

'I can't believe you're doing this to me. Do you know what I was prepared to give up for you?'

She looked back into his angry eyes and knew she'd have been told often enough as the years passed.

She said quietly, 'I'm sorry, Dean. I'm really sorry.'

Without another word, he pushed back his chair and strode off through the noisy drinkers.

She had just walked back to where she'd parked her car when her mobile rang. Her heart twisted as she felt for it in her bag. But it wasn't Dean. It was a Detective Sergeant Dunthorpe.

The policeman was waiting for her when she arrived at the hospital. Assuring her she could speak to the medical staff in a moment, he took her into a small conference room and quickly told her what had occurred.

'An ambulance was called just before three this morning. It appears the victim came to long enough to dial emergency. Of course, when she was brought in, it was assumed she was you. Officers called to the scene spoke with the neighbors and there was no reason to think anything else. It was only later when we checked the registration of the SUV in the garage that we realized there could be a question over the victim's identity.'

He pulled a notebook out of his pocket. 'I'll get a more detailed statement from you later, but for now I want to establish a few basic facts.'

Tina answered his queries as best she could. 'No, there's no immediate family. I don't know about uncles, aunts or cousins.' There was a family solicitor, she recalled. Marnie had mentioned him a few times when she'd been dealing with her father's decline. But the man's name eluded her.

She went on to explain about the break-in and the threatening message left at Marnie's apartment. 'I'm sure this must be the same bloke — Morris was his name, Ken or Kevin, I think. It'll be on the record. He'd had a go at running her off the road a couple of months ago. She reported the incident, I know that.'

'So you don't believe this was a random break-in and assault?'

'No.' Tina was emphatic. 'Absolutely not. This psycho was after her. She came to me to be safe. And I can't believe he found her there. I just can't believe it.' Her voice was shaky.

'We'll pursue that line of course, but we can't assume anything until Ms Ingram's capable of being interviewed.' The sergeant paused, and watching her carefully, he added, 'It was in your home the attack took place, Ms Christo. I don't want to alarm you, but I have to look at all the possibilities. Is there any chance that the intruder could have been targeting you?'

Tina stared at him, her eyes widening in shock. The idea had never occurred to her.

'No!' And then suddenly she remembered. 'I mean ... I was broken into quite a few months ago, twice in fact, but I wasn't in the house at the time.' Emphatically, she shook her head. 'No, I'm sure this isn't connected. It has to be that woman's husband. It's the only possible explanation.'

Finally, after agreeing to go to the station the next morning to sign a formal statement Tina was free to seek out the nursing staff in charge of Marnie's admission. The news from the tired-looking nurse was not comforting.

'From what the ambos reported she appears to have hit her head on the bedside table during the struggle. There's a deep gash and severe bruising plus the possibility of internal cranial bleeding. At present, she's sedated. It'll be a matter of monitoring her closely for the next twenty-four hours or so.'

Tina was reluctant to return home. She wanted to be there just in case. Not that she let herself consider what she really meant by that. It crossed her mind to ring Lee but she decided against it. There was nothing Lee could do and she had enough problems of her own at the moment. Best to call her when the news was better.

Most of the next few hours, Tina sat with a coffee in the hospital cafeteria but every so often one of the nursing staff allowed her to spend a few minutes by Marnie's bedside. Looking at her friend's still form and ashen face, she was struck by the injustice of it all. Marnie could have lived the vacuous, easy life of a rich woman; instead she had put her money to a useful and compassionate purpose. Now she was paying the price for her altruism.

Tina's eyes pooled with tears. For all Marnie's kindness and concern for others, she realized for the first time how truly alone her friend was. Apart from herself and Lee, there was no one else. No parents, no husband, no child. It suddenly seemed a sad and lonely existence.

With a sharp poignancy, Tina realized that the same could be said for herself. And as happened so often these days, that led her thoughts to Mark. The contentment he had brought her had been followed by a growing sense of loss after he had gone. Yet hadn't that been her lesson? For losing Mark had made her look more closely at her relationship with Dean and realize she was making a mistake – one that would rebound on everyone concerned. At least that had been resolved now. Though whether she had any chance of a future with Mark she was still unsure.

She decided it was too late at night and she was too emotionally drained to pursue that particular line of thought. After spending another five minutes by Marnie's side, she walked wearily down the brightly-lit corridors towards the elevators.

Back at the house, Tina looked nervously into the bedroom where the attack had taken place. Fingerprint powder was everywhere and the sheets had been removed, no doubt in the hope of finding DNA evidence. The detective had told her that their analysis of the scene was complete and she was free to clean up but at the moment the task was beyond her. In just a few short hours she'd endured both the confrontation with Dean and the shock of the attack on Marnie.

After a quick shower, she swallowed two sleeping pills and went to bed.

The next morning she rang the hospital and was told there was little change in Marnie's condition. More worried than ever she brought up the White Pages on her PC and searched the Melbourne listings. Maybe she would recognize the solicitor's name if she saw it.

And she did. Anthony Corkdale… That was it. She put a call through to the office number right away.

When the solicitor came on the line, Tina introduced herself and explained what had happened. 'The police wanted to know about next of kin and I really couldn't help them.'

'There's only her father's sister, an elderly lady.' The man spoke with calm deliberation. 'She doesn't need to know about this just yet.'

Tina understood what he meant. Only if Marnie didn't pull through would it be necessary to inform the elderly relative. She gave him the hospital details and hung up.

Only then did it occur to her that perhaps Steven Royce should be put in the picture too. According to Marnie, the relationship was over. But she thought back to the conversation they'd had just three short nights ago. It had been clear to her then that Marnie still cared for the guy — and that maybe he too hadn't quite accepted that it was finished. Should she let him know what had happened?

It was the thought of Marnie lying in that hospital bed so alone that finally convinced her. In the end, Tina wanted to believe that there would be someone else who cared.

Steven was just leaving for lunch with a client when he took Tina's call. His secretary informed him that there was 'a friend of Marnie Ingram on the line'.

With a frown, he picked up the receiver. A moment later, as he was given the shattering news, he felt his stomach clench in shock. 'Thank you for letting me know.' His tone was formal. 'I appreciate it. Marnie was very special to me. I'll keep in touch with the hospital and hope for the best outcome.'

He put down the receiver, trying to come to grips with what he'd been told. It took him only a second or two to realize that he had to be with her.

It was another twelve hours before Marnie's eyes finally fluttered open. For a moment she thought she was dreaming. Someone who looked exactly like Steven was smiling down at her.

'Marnie ... darling ... I'm here. You're going to be fine.'

The voice too sounded like Steven's and she was gradually aware of a hand holding her own.

'Steven?' She stared at him until recognition finally dawned. It really was him. A slow tear ran down her cheek. 'Don't leave me, Steven,' she whispered. 'Please don't leave me.'

He leaned closer and gripped her hand more tightly. 'I won't be leaving, my darling. I promise you that.'

Later Marnie was able to tell the police exactly what had happened. She had woken with a start to feel a crushing weight against her chest and a pillow over her face. Then a man's harsh voice: 'Keep away from him, okay? This time it's just a warning. Leave lover boy alone. Or next time I come back, that pretty face won't be tempting any man again.'

Disoriented, with no idea what her assailant was talking about, she had reacted instinctively. With one sharp movement she thrust back as hard as she could and the soft gasp told her she'd found the intruder's belly. Quick to take her momentary advantage, she'd thrown off the pillow and tried to roll off the bed.

But the intruder was too quick for her. Catching his breath, he swore furiously and hit her across the face. The blow knocked her backwards over the edge of the bed and as she fell, she flailed wildly to save herself. It was her attacker she gripped, feeling something give in her hands as he struggled to break free. The next moment, her head connected with the sharp edge of the bedside table and she gave a wild cry of pain. It was the last thing she remembered.

The police had shown her mug shots and even though her assailant had been masked, she had the impression of a well-built, youngish man. Certainly nothing like the thin and wiry Kevin Morris whose photo she was also shown. Given the added impetus of this most recent attack, the police had made a concerted effort and Fran Morris's estranged husband had finally been apprehended and was now in custody. But his fingerprints, while matching those found in Marnie's apartment, were not those taken from inside Tina's house. In the struggle to stop herself from falling, Marnie had managed to pull off one of her intruder's gloves and the police had found a clear set of prints where the man had exited the house.

Also of great interest to the detectives was Marnie's report of her assailant's verbal threats. Since talking again to Tina, they had changed the focus of their investigation and it hadn't taken long to track down their culprit.

Over the next few days, the police checked their records and were eventually able to match the fingerprints taken at the scene. They belonged to Gary Osborne who did the kind of 'security' jobs that had brought him to the attention of the law on a number of occasions. Taken in for questioning, a blustering Osborne did his best to deny any involvement but given the physical evidence and the detectives' persistence, he eventually came out with the truth.

At first Tina found it hard to believe. The news that Kathy Ashley had employed some thug to report back on the details of her husband's affair left her shaken. She realized that the day she'd met Dean's wife at the business lunch, the woman might already have had Osborne on the job. She was equally sure that the lunch meeting had been anything but a coincidence. Kathy Ashley's unwavering niceness, her friendliness, had all been part of the strategy to make Tina rethink her relationship with Dean. And it had worked. Yet even when they'd broken up, Dean's wife had kept up the surveillance, wary of the affair resuming. When it did, she was so desperate to hold on to her marriage that she instructed Osborne to take the step of frightening Tina off.

Confronted with the evidence of Osborne's admission, Kathy Ashley had admitted everything. According to her statement, the break-in and confrontation were never meant to be anything more than a warning. She'd been horrified when the irrational plan had misfired. Not only had Osborne ended up threatening the wrong woman, his actions had also caused what could have been a serious injury.

Under further questioning, Osborne emphatically denied responsibility for the earlier break-ins at Tina's home. At that stage he hadn't even met Kathy Ashley, he stated; and without any evidence linking him to those crimes, there was nothing the police could do to press their claim. Perhaps, after all, they told Tina later, the break-ins had been totally unrelated.

It was a couple of weeks later that she received the letter from Dean. She had no idea what to expect as she slit open the envelope and took out the single sheet of paper.

...I know I treated you badly that Sunday afternoon. I can only apologize for my behavior and hope you'll forgive me. Because you made the right decision, I know that now. There is no way I will ever be able to leave Kathy — even if my reasons for staying in the relationship are questionable. It goes without saying I had no idea she would take such extreme measures to keep our marriage intact and in the end, I can only be grateful that your friend was understanding enough not to press charges and bring the whole messy business into the public arena.

That said, I have to thank you sincerely for all the love and joy you brought me during our time together, Tina. You are a very special human being and deserve every happiness life can offer. I wish you all the very best...

Refolding the letter, Tina felt her heart at rest.

They had left in plenty of time. Saturday was always busy on the roads and they didn't want to be late.

Lee glanced sideways at Brad and thought again how attractive he looked in his suit and tie. They didn't often get the chance to dress up but they'd excelled themselves today, she thought with a half smile. He'd been full of compliments too about her new dress.

It was four months now since she'd come home. So much seemed to have happened in that short time. Julie had been her first concern and, thanks to their many open and forthright talks, they had managed to sort things out between them.

Lee had found it difficult to forgive herself for the pressure she'd placed on her daughter. She had faced the fact that she'd been trying to live her life again through Julie and both of them had paid the price for that. Crushed with guilt, she had listened to Julie explain how she'd blamed herself for not doing what her mother had so clearly wanted her to. That had been one of the main reasons she'd found it difficult to make the transition to university. And when things had really got on top of her, she hadn't known where to turn. At the time when she had most needed her, Lee was the last person Julie felt able to talk to.

But, with honesty and forgiveness on both sides, they had managed to get beyond what had happened. Now Julie was looking forward to resuming her studies in the new semester, reassured by the knowledge that her mother was totally supportive of her decision, and happy that her family was together again.

And they were. While she and Brad had started off making an effort for Julie's sake, the tension between them had gradually lessened. Lee was fully aware how lucky she was. Brad loved her enough not to judge her and it hadn't taken long before he'd made it clear that he believed wholeheartedly what she had told him that night.

'It doesn't have to make a difference between us if we don't let it, Lee. None of it does. If we love each other, we can cope with anything.'

Her eyes had filled with tears at his conciliatory words and when his arms went around her, she knew she had been given a second chance. It was more than she could ever have hoped for. She had learned a hard lesson about how truly precious her marriage and family were.

'Who did you find to take over this morning's class?' Brad's question broke into her thoughts.

'Coral didn't mind doing it. I'll take one of hers next week.'

That had been another bonus about coming home. The chance to take over Coral's dance school business had been offered to her a month ago.

'I've been at it almost twenty years, Lee.' The older woman had brought up the subject late one afternoon when they were locking up the hall. 'I've got to ease up a bit, but I don't want to close down the place entirely. Thought it might be right up your alley.'

It was an idea Lee found irresistible. She would never have considered starting her own place and stepping on Coral's toes, but taking over the existing school was a perfect solution.

When she'd discussed the offer with Brad, he'd been equally enthusiastic. 'I think you should go for it, love. You'll be in your element. No one could do it better.'

Now, as they headed down the highway to Sydney, Lee felt a contentment that had long been missing in her life. With a smile, she reached out and laid a hand on her husband's knee.

'Life's okay, isn't it?' she said.

Taking his eyes off the road for a moment, Brad smiled at her and nodded.

Everything was going to plan. The garden looked perfect and the caterers were already setting up in the kitchen.

Upstairs Tina was slipping into her dress. As she pulled up the zip, she glanced out of the window and couldn't help smiling. How often had she looked down on Mark from here? Today, dressed in his suit and wearing the red silk tie she'd bought him, he was wielding the secateurs, making some last-minute adjustments to the gardenia bushes.

Tina hadn't dreamed she could ever feel this happy. When she had first split from Dean she'd prepared herself for a future alone, certain that at her age she would never establish another relationship. But then Mark had come into her life and slowly and cautiously, they had both discovered a magic neither had expected to find again.

He still lived in Adelaide where he saw his children regularly, but they took turns to visit each other a couple of times a month. At the moment, it was an arrangement that suited them both. It gave them their own space, and Tina knew it was important for Mark not to feel torn between her and his kids. She saw the three of them occasionally on her visits to Adelaide. They were a little wary but that was understandable. She had always known it would be a gradual process getting them to accept her as part of their father's life.

As for the future — well, who could plan that? His ex-wife might end up back near her family again or the children might choose to study in Sydney when they had finished school and that would bring Mark back too.

In the meantime Tina intended getting on with her life. She had learned the futility of trying to manipulate fate. There was an old song that had been one of her mother's favorites: *Que sera, sera ... whatever will be, will be.* That summed things up pretty well, she figured.

The buzz of the front gate jolted her out of her reverie. 'I'll get it!' she called out to Mark as she hurried down the stairs.

It was Steven. As she released the gate to let him in, she looked at her watch: he was early.

'She kicked me out!' he said in mock dismay when Tina welcomed him into the house. 'For a woman who never wanted to get married, she's suddenly gone all traditional on me.' He raised an amused eyebrow. 'Not allowed to see the dress I was told, in no uncertain terms.'

Tina laughed as she shut the door behind him. 'But she still wouldn't let us play, *Here Comes the Bride.*'

'Oh no, on that she was absolutely firm. Said everyone she knew would need oxygen if they had to watch her waltz in to that.'

Tina liked the man Marnie was marrying. There was a calm and quiet self-assurance about him that formed a perfect balance to her friend's more intense and impetuous personality. Since he'd moved to Sydney they'd met a few times and she had been able to observe the relationship at close hand. It didn't take her long to recognize that the same qualities existed between Marnie and Steven as between Mark and herself: love based on mutual respect and equality, on kindness, understanding and trust. And like herself, Marnie had had to wait almost half a lifetime to find what she hadn't even known she'd been looking for.

'Mark's outside cutting back bushes so the bride doesn't trip,' she said as she led Steven out to the garden.

'God forbid,' he smiled.

It was an intimate gathering of a dozen or so people. Chairs draped in white and decorated with white blossom had been set out on the lawn. Among the guests were Anthony and Anne Corkdale, happy to share the happiness of the woman they had come to know so well through one of the toughest times of her life.

The celebrant was an ex-Anglican priest, a choice that Marnie had found suitably ambiguous.

'No way I'm having my nuptials celebrated by one of those women with their too-tight perms who keep checking their watches to rush off to the next happy coupling,' she'd declared resolutely to Tina and Lee when they'd discussed the details. 'The guy I've picked has almost no hair and just enough of a whiff of Canterbury left on him to make me feel officially married.'

And now Marnie stood waiting to walk between the seated guests and join the man who had brought so much joy to her life. She knew without a doubt she was doing the right thing. Steven was the first man who had ever looked inside her soul, and the thought that she had almost lost him made her appreciate him all the more.

As the music began to play, she saw Lee and Tina's smiling faces turned towards her. How far they had all travelled together, she thought. And how precious was the love they had all found.

To the strains of *Ode to Joy* she stepped out into the sunshine.